Naked Revenants
and Other Fables of Old and New England

NAKED REVENANTS
and Other Fables of Old and New England

Jonathan Thomas

Hippocampus Press

New York

First Edition
1 3 5 7 9 8 6 4 2

ISBN13: 978-1-61498-199-2

Contents

Plenty of Irem

The beginning of the end for Kingsport was its junior college. And by "Kingsport" I mean that grand jumble of seventeenth- and eighteenth-century structures on perennial last legs, on the rickety brink but never quite collapsing into crooked cobblestone lanes, or teetering over the waterfront as if yearning to drown lemming-like in Massachusetts Bay. Duncan Hines guides of the 1930s sang Kingsport's praises for the more intrepid antiquarian sightseer, but lamented the absence of decent eateries. A Beaux Arts hospital and neoclassical courthouse little detracted from the overall "scenic decay" described in the '40s by landscape painter Eric Sloane.

The postwar college campus, on the inland edge of town, also took no bite out of the historic core, but set the tone for "modernization" and "urban renewal." By the Nixon era, Kingsport as ramshackle time capsule had been gutted for glazed brick and reinforced concrete office blocks, commercial rows, and "affordable housing," while Eisenhower-era optimism and subsidies had ebbed away, especially from the junior college, leaving it fiscally high and dry, subject to decades of neglect, the statewide butt of snarky jokes.

Here's where I belatedly came in, a lifer in this region, though neither I nor anybody I'd met growing up had ever been to Kingsport. Some places just emit that uninviting vibe, which was definitely the case there, whether as colonial slum or postmodern dump.

Still and all, my North Shore roots and attendant local sympathies, bona fide or not, won me the position of capital campaign manager and PR troubleshooter at Kingsport Community College, commonly abbreviated KCC. That in itself underscored the public-image problem, an acronym that called fast-food chains to mind, a portent of graduates' tragically plausible career outlooks. Imagine my double-take on discovering the original name had been, in gratitude to its principal `backers, Kingsport Freemasons' College, presumably before southern fried chicken had made northern inroads.

To identify and promote Kingsport's residual cultural assets, fostering native pride and attracting outside interest, struck me as beneficial to both town and campus. Besides, high time I made up for my unblemished record of ignorance about the place. The lack of historical society, tourism bureau, or chamber of commerce wasn't helpful. But Monday would be my first day at KCC, so how better to combine vocation and leisure than with a data-collecting ramble the Saturday before?

From the Puritans' hilltop burial ground on the outskirts, I could see clear across the valley to the patently less bucolic cinderblock sprawl of the college. Even from this distance it projected ennui, inadequacy. Look elsewhere while the choice remained!

Amiable June breezes dispelled the pall of solemnity up here. I could have been moseying through an air-conditioned Soho gallery as I admired gravestones' carven slate hourglasses, skulls, and cherub heads, all sporting wings. Someone had come around lately with a lawnmower.

Then on the lee hillside, away from sun and civilization, I descended among markers of brown basalt, shaped like stiletto scabbards. They tilted every which way in scruffy grass as if apathy weighed on them, and were more weathered than their hilltop counterparts as if considerably older, too old for inscriptions to survive. But how could that be, when hilltop epitaphs from the 1650s lauded Kingsport's founders? A malaise of confusion chafed me harder every minute I lingered, till I climbed back into the sunshine.

Between burial hill and main drag were dowdy neighborhoods the wrecking ball had spared, but that persisted cringeworthy in their own right. To tell how old these houses were, or in what style, was impossible thanks to vinyl siding that expunged any ornament, personality, or integrity, a scourge of architectural lobotomies in effect.

To cheer up I had to invade another graveyard, this one belonging to a monumental Episcopal church with square belfry, hipped roof, and Gothic windows. Unfortunately, the antiquity on the hill spoiled me for these tombstones, adorned with nothing earlier than Victorian willows-and-urns and suns ambiguously rising or setting on straight-line horizons. More intriguing to me was the decision to construct the massive Beaux Arts hospital on the other side of cemetery fieldstone wall, as if no thought had gone into the demoralizing influence of death en masse out the windows of morbidly ill patients.

The inner village was on egregiously hummocky ground, compelling a street plan of curves and switchbacks to avoid steep slopes, as if the settlers had singlemindedly built upon acres of prehistoric tumuli. Hence "old Kingsport" dictated the traffic flow of "new, improved Kingsport," structuring it like new flesh under old bones; the prohibitive Plan B would have entailed flattening the topography. I, however, began to despair of finding Kingsport's architectural old flesh. It inspired a pang to picture bygone appearances of streets like Frog, Mechanic, and Gingerbread.

Naturally nothing green, not the meanest crabgrass, was extant on Green Lane. But between an HMO "wellness center" with a façade like stale Triscuits and a "professional building" elegant as freshman foamcore models was crammed a miracle of preservation, easy to dismiss as a mirage of wishful thinking. Its massive proportions reminded me of a barn more than a home, as did its broad gambrel roof, in head-on outline like a longbow. A second, narrower gambrel protruded at right angle from the first, and fronted on the street.

This frontage, with paint flaking scabrously from brown clapboards and red trim, led me to wonder how archaic the house was; its upper stories overhung the sidewalk by a good six inches, like an Elizabethan vestige. And from the overhang swung a strake with woodburning-kit gilt lettering, "Mugford Museum of Quaint Kingsport." A flagstone path, fringed by stockade fence to rebuff the neighboring HMO, led from the street, alongside the broader gambrel-end wall, to a simple peaked portico.

In a blink I was at the door, a warping assemblage of vertical planks with a latch instead of a knob. Extremely promising! I loved small-town museums, the tackier the better. Unlike too many nonprofits whose management profited royally, they tended to be bottomless money pits, ever one slippery step from receivership; a first opportunity to visit might prove the last. These seat-of-the-pants sideshows would have had to be astronomically slicker, more "respectable," to generate the faintest blip on the radars of funding agencies. Maybe I loved them because they'd never exasperate me in a professional capacity.

I pressed on the latch, and entered a period restoration, with no display cases in evidence. A hulking blanket-chest flouted domestic naturalism by blocking the staircase in the front hall. On the chest's lid was a cracked tureen and a sign entreating ten-dollar donations. Initially I balked, but hell, I might have been that day's sole income. Between the museum's rabbit hole of a location and its dearth of wherewithal to attract anyone beyond rare passersby, the owners were laboring under a double whammy. I forked over a twenty.

Where was everyone? Customers to disturb the sepulchral hush I hadn't expected, and docents or rent-a-cops would have been reckless luxuries, but the curator surely hadn't left both makeshift cashbox and premises at the mercy of the honor system. I hadn't broken in, and I'd given generously, so why was I padding around like a trespasser, as if I were casing the parlor? Not my fault if the proprietor was shirking his post!

These homey surroundings were textbook authentic, yes, but banal like a paint-by-numbers copy of an Old Master, and past due for Swiffers and air freshener. The obligatory features were accounted for: diamond-paned windows, ponderous corner and ceiling beams, a kettle hung on a crane in gaping fireplace, a wax effigy in bonnet, apron, and gown at a spinning wheel, two other mannequins in doublets and knee-breeches on a high-backed bench by the hearth, and against one wall, a pendulum clock flanked by two ladderback chairs. No ticking was audible, as seemed apropos, since time purportedly stood still here.

One mannequin, though, hadn't stayed put, and I staggered back, my heart bucked, and I cast up my hands palm-outward in feckless self-defense. A smile opened like a fissure in the waxy complexion of pilgrim impersonator. If his sallow skin were real, then so, I gathered, was the stringy shoulder-length gray hair; no self-respecting wig shoppe would stock such crappy merchandise. He'd sprung from the bench and crossed half the floorspace to me in the instant I took verifying the clock had stopped.

"Oh, did I make you jump?" He bowed almost fulsomely and introduced himself as "Eldred Mugford, at your service." Jesus, was this his customary joke on the walk-in trade? Repeat business was probably a moot point anyway, and word-of-mouth too. The rest of the waxworks abided, for the duration of my nervous once-over, quiescent.

Mugford, who must have exercised eagle eyes from his hearthside perch, tendered effusive gratitude for my "liberality." Yankee sonority contained a raspy, buzzing undertone, as if cancer surgery had implanted a mechanical larynx, but the throat above broad linen collar showed no scars.

Whereas Kingsport's sourpuss pedestrians had studiously ignored me, Mugford overdid the lively solicitude, importuning my name, livelihood, mother's and grandmothers' maiden names. Every answer rated an approving nod. Finally he strode to an oval table with spindly rococo legs and procured, as first impression had it, a church-offerings plate replete with silver dollars. Was he hitting me up for more cash?

"Here's a taste of tradition for an esteemed guest," he announced and, with an exuberance that brooked no refusal, thrust under my nose the plate of coins, which close-up became a dozen mini-pancakes, white as communion wafers, on a pewter salver, its pocks and seams black with embedded soot. "They're journey cakes, or johnnycakes, a delicacy among those who predated the English forefathers."

I warily chose a specimen atop a couple of others, free of contact with the grungy pewter. Mugford didn't withdraw the salver till I was chewing. As treats went, warm, fresh, less pasty and gritty would have been better. It tasted most like cornbread or hominy.

"I'll take these along to munch on," Mugford beamed, hefting the tray. "Much to see." Was he a well-meaning eccentric or a cunning, upbeat passive-aggressive?

He was trotting toward the front hall and, I presumed, the stairs. "Can I help you push that chest aside?" I called after him.

He stopped and eyed me quizzically before catching my drift. "We're not going up. Nothing that way." Really? All that space, that seventeenth-century layout, wasted? "We're going down." He loped over to the paneling that enclosed the area beneath the stairs and unbolted a door therein. Its upper edge reiterated the stairs' incline and made me think of expressionist movie decor. Tray of johnnycakes in one hand, he threw a switch behind the doorframe and beckoned me into dank, unappetizing cellar updraft. Hardly archival environs for heirlooms!

Split, worn treaders instilled no confidence as they corkscrewed interminably below, but my guide traipsed away carefree, often out of sight around the next bend. He paused once and turned, and I awaited some breezy remark to encourage me along, but instead he sang out, "You'd be amazed at how long this property has been in my family!" Then he soldiered on without sharing any specifics.

Not till I'd passed a third electric Christmas candle did I observe how its niche, and this stairwell, had been chiseled from steely blue granite. What sane Puritan or Yankee descendant would have tackled such quixotic labor? Bewilderment increased an order of magnitude on the bottom step, where I wavered like an astronaut surveying alien planet from an open airlock.

"A bit winded?" sympathized Mugford from halfway across an antechamber hacked, like the stairwell, out of onerous bedrock. "How about a couple more johnnycakes? For quick energy?" I resolutely shook my head, seeing myself choke on a dry, doughy mouthful; my throat was already constricting in the dustbin air. What's more, Mugford's delicacies were now direly unpalatable in the fish-belly fluorescence of tube lamps overhead. I advanced tentatively into the sallow glow, but without further understanding of where I was.

Here was the mere forecourt of multiple spaces bereft of structural rhyme or reason, lacking even the consistency to qualify as something sui generis, perhaps most like drunken doodling by M. C. Escher. These spaces, and still more beyond them, I could observe through three apertures set evidently at random in this anteroom, which was shaped like the inside of a collapsing pumpkin. And no less arbitrary were the frames of these apertures, a hexagon, a semicircular arch, a pair of squat columns to support ribbed vaulting that petered out shy of the ceiling's midpoint.

These spaces singly and in aggregate came across as too deformed, too inchoate to tell whether suite or catacombs or arcade had been the idea. The one certainty was of man-hours by the thousands squandered excavating. Did the results signify blindness or disdain toward basic virtues of coherence and harmony?

Meanwhile, Mugford reluctantly retracted his arm with the salver and waved with free hand to either side of me. "Well, feel free to browse through our gift selections as you collect yourself." Behind me, flanking the well of spiral stairs, were twin alcoves, crowded with rickety, backless shelves more suitable for cobwebbed homemade preserves. The shelves were rife with "gifts" that might have emerged from nineteenth-century trash pits, unwashed patent-medicine bottles, rusty horseshoes and stirrups, chipped, chintzy porcelain statuettes and saucers. Interspersed among the detritus were vintage, hand-tinted postcards of Kingsport's colonial-holdover streets and wharves and market squares, depicted woefully past their prime.

"Maybe I could concentrate better on the merchandise after we make the rounds," I feebly professed. I then discerned a shadowy mass in the cavity behind the shelves. Before I could make out any details, its raggedy, limp contours explained why Mugford had concealed it. Even by his patchy standards it was overly skeevy, unfit for public view. Too bad, for what rinky-dink exhibition was complete without a ride, coin-operated or not, for the kiddies?

This one had never likely scored much kid-appeal. Diffuse illumination seeping past the shelves cast misshapen, dim strips, as of busted Venetian blinds, upon pitted, filmy brown sculptor's wax, the same hue as ear pickings. At best guess, the effigy was of a harpy, arms in mantis position shielding crumpled breasts, mildewy leather saddle between drooping, tattered batwings. Behind the saddle were murky intimations of a feathered serpent's coils, or was it a bee's bristly, striped hindquarters? I envisaged this monstrosity as mockup for a fanciful merry-go-round, rejected even in pristine state as too nasty, too aberrant.

Mugford discreetly went "Ahem," and with a borderline patronizing flourish urged me along. Here at last were typical display cases, lined up scant inches apart along the walls like coffins in a busy mortuary. But before he'd uttered a sound, I blurted, "Whoever could have quarried all this rock?"

He shrugged as if I begged the obvious. "Our heroic ancestors, who else? Allow me to share their most precious bequeathals from our homeland, and some treasures from their voyages." He bent over the nearest case to blow off a veneer of dust, and motioned me over. I briefly grimaced at the johnnycakes amidst a flurry of airborne particles, a fine new mineral gloss on sticky surfaces.

His fingertip clinked three times upon the glass. Directly below was a bowl the diameter of a cantaloupe, with ornament suggesting a rudder and a stubby prow, in silver prismatic and black with tarnish. "Here's a miniature of the unmanned boat that fetched Saint Petroc to his holy island, across the Great Ocean River east of Jerusalem. They churned these out as souvenir junk for pilgrims, yes, but now this is a priceless rarity." Great Ocean River? Where on any reality-based map was that? I had no chance to wonder because the spiel pushed on into dottier terrain.

Sidling deliberately to the next case, he pouted at the miscellany under glass till he blew off more dust and jabbed decisive finger at a swatch of mangy black fur with sinuous gilt edging and a gold clasp at each end. "Ah, here's the formal sable tiara for the grandmaster of the furrier's guild in Norumbega, not many latitudes to our north. The country's Romance language is unfortunately extinct, except for a few bills of lading. Did you know they worshipped an Abenaki solar god?"

I could scarcely mouth "No." The struggle to wrap my head around Mugford's alternative history, to accommodate it with all else in my corpus of knowledge, had me tongue-tied, topsy-turvy, woozy. My brow was hot and a knot throbbed in my stomach, but might these be the fault of tainted cornmeal? And there was Mugford at the next case, beckoning me forward.

He was indicating a soapstone artifact, at first impression an oil lamp, with nozzle fashioned equivocally into a camel, or hippo, or capybara head. "Now this was an offering bowl to fill with corn and bury under a stable, to curry divine blessings for the livestock. It's from Paititi, the stronghold in Peruvian jungle the Incan hero Inkarri legendarily built single-handed as a refuge from the Spaniards. But that's ridiculous, of course. He couldn't have built city walls by himself. He simply used the ones abandoned in 10,000 B.C. by the People of the Other Sun when they migrated to the Underworld."

I followed hapless like a balloon on a string as Mugford shuffled sidelong. Overlapping my befuddlement was angst over the risk of insufficiently humoring him, ideally situated as I was to disappear forever into the same void as mermaids or Jimmy Hoffa. Nobody knew where I was, and my car was out by the town line. The knot in my stomach was tightening.

The sheer volume of curios must have been weighing on Mugford, for he began giving them short shrift, barely hesitating to toss off thumbnail descriptions. "This lump of amber came from the Gothic island of Baltia, off the Karelian coast. It contains a crab claw, which is fairly unusual. And this processional brass bell was fished out of the lake-bottom cathedral of Kitezh in Mongol-era Russia." I'd meanwhile been brooding unduly on the non-issue of what relics were supposedly from Mugford's homeland, and what were travel mementoes.

He wheeled on me then and thrust the salver a hairsbreadth from my cramping stomach. "You're flagging a bit, I fear. How about a few more of these?" The proximity of oily biscuits decked with cellar crud almost made me ask if he was joking, but I dared not set him off and only shook my diffident head.

Or had my instincts nailed the correct question? Mugford's manner consistently verged on the theatrical; maybe he actually was joking, maybe this museum was an extravagant put-on and he had nothing better to do than pull the legs of infrequent rubes. Yes, that accounted for the bulk of the daftness here, brought this whole experience down to earth, freed me from the sensation of penetrating deeper with every display case into a phantasmal world. Mugford, anyway, was nobody to accept at face value.

"Now isn't this incredible?" he enthused, recapturing my attention. How could any one item be more deserving of that understatement than any other? Yet he wasn't wrong. A petit LED spotlight starkly accented the intricacies of an orca's or T-rex tooth obsessively scrimshawed into translucent basketry, like baroque china, with a silver cap enclosing the root. I obligingly mumbled it was incredible, but Mugford was referring partly if at all to the artistry per se.

"The Tibetan monk who whittled it swore it was a demon's baby tooth from the Himalayan caves descending to the ghost-infested citadel of Agartha. He had to drill latticework throughout the enamel to drain the pulp of brimstone, which would have disintegrated the tooth eventually." Perhaps it was my disordered wits talking, but I had to admire Mugford's steamroller conviction and bonhomie. He'd have made a topnotch fundraiser, an MVP of telethon phone banks, given his prowess at gab and arrant bullshit. If I took his psychometric profile, though, would he come up a card or a psychotic?

"Ah, the jewel in the crown!" he exclaimed, on the move again, ducking through the hexagon to the next lopsided cell. What to do save bob along with wobbly-balloon passivity? He swiveled toward me as if I had yet to prove worthy of looking into the case. "Where are you from?"

"Down the road a piece in Ipswich," I volunteered, "but my job's in Kingsport."

He nodded thoughtfully. "Did you know there's also a Kingsport in Massachusetts?"

My jaw gaped for an instant like an unmanned puppet's, and I came dangerously close to countering, "Where the hell do you think we are?" Instead I shut my mouth with a noncommittal grunt. Either he was pranking me, and I'd be fueling his amusement at my expense, or he wasn't, and I'd be challenging delusions in a soundproof de facto death chamber. And damn his power of suggestion, his blatantly addled remark that nonetheless compounded my sense of displacement into a strange world.

He scuffed back as if ceding me the benefit of some abstruse doubt, his open palm hovered over the glass, and he exhorted, "Behold!" A single object rated an entire case, like giant full-stop punctuation, as if it were its own emblem of primacy in the collection. It upped my malaise at first blink by bringing to mind a monstrous, ossified Ur-species of johnnycake. "This is too extraordinary a relic to show just anyone," he confided, "but seeing as we're related, why not?"

"Related? How?" Each time my stupefaction at one transgression against normality started wearing off, Mugford hit me with another from utmost left field. I had to affirm my host's genius, deranged or not, sinister or not, for keeping me off-balance, whatever his endgame.

He raised puckish eyebrows. "Everyone whose family's been around here long enough is related. Join me?" So saying he popped a johnnycake into his mouth and extended the salver again.

"Really, no," I demurred, training my gaze on the "extraordinary relic," figuring he'd desist with the snacks by and by.

I concluded his relic was a truncated section of ancient column from a palace or temple portico, even as he expounded, "You must appreciate the rarity, the privilege, of contemplating as much as this of resplendent Irem, City of Pillars, sunk by divine envy to the bottom of Arabia's ocean of sand, and for eons beforehand, invisible to human eyes. None of us can fully appreciate the perils to body and soul of seizing, smuggling, and enshrining it, with infernal pursuers on its scent."

Listening to Mugford's earnest rant magnified my wrenching cramps, my throbbing congestion, driving me to focus for diversion

on the stonework. The dark basalt made it hard to distinguish its re-
peating motif, beyond basic V-outline. To block out ongoing drivel
about "numinous pillars," I studied a single V more minutely till its
nadir resolved into a goat cranium, slit-pupil eyes peeking over the bottom edge, and horns stylized into helices that coiled up past the top
edge. And from a groove in the horns there burst, thick as peas in a
tortuous pod, the heads and forequarters of myriad tiny goats.

On some visceral level, this spectacle of rampant parthenogenesis
was obscene, repellent. But since it was nowise salacious, I couldn't
justify, let alone articulate, my disgust. "I can tell you're profoundly
touched," Mugford empathized, "as are we all. No need to be self-
conscious. You're among friends. What a unique trace of obliterated
majesty!"

Not only had he grossly misread my expression; I might also have
accused him of imperfect candor. Recently I'd come across rock of
that same brown, and ransacking the day's memories gave me ample
cause to doubt Mugford's chunk of Irem was unique. But catching him
in a lie, if that's what it was, only backfired, for it tipped me toward
lending more credence to phantom city's reality.

Whether from Irem or wherever, plenty of that basalt languished by
the town line, on the lee slope below the gravesite of Kingsport's Anglo
founders. In hindsight, eroded, blunt fingers of stone readily passed for
sad splinters of once-mighty columns. Centuries of storms and frost
would have eradicated any carvings. What the hell had Anglo founders
made of that hillside littered with cenotaphs, scoured blank already or
not, and of the people responsible for them? And most puzzling, who
were those people, those johnnycake fanciers, if not Native Americans?

Their absence from Puritan records may have argued against their
actuality, reducing the hillside to an ignoble potter's field, or may have
designated them too odious for written mention. I was steeling myself
to ask who Mugford's people allegedly were, but he was sighing, "Alas
for the rootbound glory that can nevermore sprout and flourish upon
the earth!" His lament was palpably heartfelt, which hardly lessened its
ring of pathologic litany. All his bric-a-brac and rubbish now amounted to sacred fetishes in a cult of one.

Between the lines I glimpsed a possible insight into Mugford's
psyche, a mundane interpretation of this farcical museum. Mad as he

decidedly was, that madness may have functioned as a happier alternative for a fragile, devoted antiquarian, a sanctuary from the wasteland his beloved, venerable hometown had become. I was sorry for him even as I took increased care to pussyfoot around him.

Then his drone of gloom and despair exploded into elation, which perversely intensified my cramps and giddiness, as he trumpeted, "But be of good cheer! Revelation is ours!" His grating mechanical undertone grew harsher and more prominent with each syllable, as if slipping from his control. And at that unguarded juncture, my forearm was suddenly in his unnaturally cool, dry grip as he tried tugging me toward a portal, impeccably round as a punchcard hole, committing me to yet another remove from the right-side-up world.

Frowning uncertainly at my alarm, he relented, though without letting go, merely to proffer the tray again. "I recommend you have some more of these, to enhance the experience."

I shook my head and pressed my lips together as if he weren't above forcing johnnycakes past them.

"No? As you wish," he conceded, disapproval writ plain across chalky complexion. For once he sounded like an everyday professional guide as he reluctantly unhanded me to duck through the portal, high-step over its inch of threshold, and fan me toward him, intoning, "Mind your feet, mind your head."

I gambled that indulging him was still the safer course. Let's get this "revelation," this well-entombed *pièce de resistance,* out of the way, after which he'd have no further excuse to detain me, right? He'd emerged a sympathetic character after all, a victim of the crass modernity that had rendered quality of life impossible for him in Kingsport, as it had for uncounted others of his disposition elsewhere, if not everywhere.

In accord with the unreason I'd come to expect down here, this most cramped, low-ceilinged cell so far, this putative hindmost recess, felt more like a foyer than the foyer itself. It was also the brightest, and its entire rear wall was a dazzling, milky screen of incandescence. I averted my overwhelmed pupils and reeled at a fresh renewal of that shock I'd weathered when Mugford had revealed he wasn't a mannequin.

For two of her to exist, when one was too many, beggared belief, but it absolutely couldn't be the same retired chimera from behind "gift shop" shelves; this had to be another moldering wax harpy. Bathing her in ivory light failed to soften scarred, leprous surfaces or help me identify component species. And worse, in these confines the festering leather of shabby saddle was within sniffing range, spurring my upset stomach toward conniptions. Nor was this a simple assault. At my next breath, a whiff of rancid cornmeal, fermented sewage, slimy mushrooms infiltrated the bouquet, threatening to bowl me over.

I coughed and gasped and realized the infiltration was taking over, displacing the rotten leather funk and proceeding not from the sculpture, but from the wall of radiance behind me. I turned involuntarily toward Mugford, puffy-sleeved arms outspread as if to hug the wall as he exulted, "When we can sever earthly tethers, when the other side is clear and unwavering, we can soar home again! Paradise regained!"

Yes, the brilliant haze had thinned to impart a shimmering vista, but how could Mugford see what I was seeing and act so jubilant about it? The foreign world to which he'd slyly escorted me, and ballyhooed like a promised land, fit no human idea of paradise. Or was my distorted vision the problem? At the very least my sense of scale, of perspective, was out of whack, for the rippling glare, the background murk left me guessing whether I surveyed a canyon or a cavern. Or was it a microcosm enlarged, the innards of a capacious geode or a modest sinkhole that teemed with fleshy worms?

But if this was an empire of ordinary worms, squirming orgiastic around fingerling stalagmites, basking around oily puddles that receded toward clouded horizon, how to explain the hundreds of human carcasses half-sunk among them and of equal or lesser length? Whatever occult window or projection screen or hypnotic talent Mugford had, hadn't he just implied I could, under proper conditions, physically transition into his "paradise"?

It was a permeable enough membrane, anyway, for sickening miasma to leach in, along with a sibilant drone as of surf, or chanting, or mastication, indefinable but as sickening as the odor, and most unnerving, of the same raspy pitch as Mugford's. And to judge by toxic atmosphere, and by the human remains, nothing but death would receive me over there, and who or what was he to expect otherwise?

I'd peripherally noted that courteous Mugford and his johnnycakes had retreated, ceding me space in which to gawk appropriately awestruck. Still, I wasn't comfortable leaving him to his own devices, and strove to bring him slowly, casually into view. He was leaning over the harpy, cupped hand to his mouth, whispering, I didn't care what; the bare fact of talking to her demonstrated how much more unhinged he was than I'd already inferred, how much more potentially volatile. I shifted from foot to foot, scarcely reining in my urge to bolt.

And though I conjectured right away the flickering glow may have fostered the illusion, that didn't stop me from racing headlong when I witnessed pocky wax head cocking an ear to hear Mugford better. In my panic I forgot his warning about the low doorway, smacked into it at hairline level, and crumpled like a poleaxed heifer. The back of my skull hit the stone floor.

I clung to semi-consciousness, in hypnogogic stupor, phasing in and out of clock face time. Clumsy mitts fumbled at my collar, undoing buttons past the breastbone. An instant or maybe minutes later, Mugford was apologizing, "My mistake! This should never have happened. His behavior should have tipped me off. Imagine turning up his nose at journey cakes! Any of us would know damn well you can't look beyond without a bellyful! Not with a jot of clarity! That pedigree of his was so misleading." He heaved a weary sigh. "Optimism played me for a fool."

Squinting through the blurry, pulsing keyhole of my awareness, I was thankful to ascertain Mugford wasn't conferring with a wax chimera. But this conferee was scant improvement, studying me from under a bonnet that blotted out her face so thoroughly I entertained doubts there was a face; when last I'd seen this bonnet, it was on a mannequin upstairs.

A knuckle was thumping my chest. "Feel that? It's solid. No vent. You can actually hear a heart beating inside."

The voice from under the bonnet buzzed more harshly than Mugford's, past the frontiers of comprehension.

"I'll handle it," he pledged. Then a spark of indignation no sooner flared up in me than it guttered. Mugford, damn him, had covered my eyes with johnnycakes like dead man's pennies, and whether they or emotional overload were to blame, I short-circuited into oblivion.

I had no luck blinking away the merciless sunshine or pressing against uncompliant backrest into shady refuge. I accepted with euphoric post-blackout grace my revival seated among the tilted brown basalt markers, as if I'd never decamped from the hillside. But at the realization one of those obelisks was propping me up, my skin crawled and I staggered to my feet.

Mugford's nightmarish museum, details of which were recurring to me in kaleidoscopic onslaught, had positively been no dream. His parting johnnycakes were nowhere on the nearby ground, though what else could explain the viscous, grainy rings around my eyes? More damnably, my hair and heels and shirttails and trousers from butt to cuffs were caked in sticky mud, and I smarted all over, as if a hasty or unskillful party had dragged me through earthen tunnels. As for crosstown wormhole's trapdoor exit, through which, I was inflexibly convinced, I'd arrived here, searching for it, even dwelling on it, would have wasted time better spent fleeing to my car.

On Monday, of course, I reported to KCC and took over as chief fundraiser. I needed the gig; a no-brainer, that. So was my aversion to venturing farther into town than the campus, from whose drab, soulless cinderblocks and treeless paved courtyards I derived comfort and serenity. I never reflect on how my sentiments about loutish modernity have changed. I function, I'm solvent, and any deviation from smooth sailing would be stupid.

I did once deviate and learned my lesson. A shortcut to the cafeteria brought me to an organic garden behind the biosciences lab. The smell of freshly turned loam gave me vertigo, and that of frisky, clumping worms disinterred by the rototiller was, I swear, even more unbearable, like cornbread spoiling in the rain. It was all I could do to shamble along and fight the urge to ask the kids sowing seeds whether they too could hear the worms chorusing, in the same buzzy register as Mugford's, how they envied me my peek into their realm beyond.

Ritual Damage

Grubbing about his back garden, in the literal shadow of the abbey ruins, Gareth brooded on a marital perturbation like an eyelash in the soup, hardly there but impossible to ignore. His musings flourished best in the medium of disturbed topsoil, as did Anne's in the kitchen, where she, to presume on their habitual rapport, would be grappling with the same enigma.

They'd been in wholehearted agreement down the line: swap their empty London nest for a B&B in the more spacious north (in Cumbria, as it panned out), improve the acreage with free-roaming chickens and sheep and organic horticulture, exploit a seller's market to screen for guests worthiest of Anne's farm-fresh cuisine. And in a couple of miraculous years, they'd checked off their whole list; foreseeable prospects were rosy.

They were the beneficiaries of wish fulfillment, they were succeeding, outwardly they were in perfect tune with each other and the world they'd adopted. Yet a paradoxical note of dissatisfaction, of tension, hinted at a subliminal state between togetherness and discord, or like both at once, an emotional tide stuck at slack water. He'd been reading it in her flinchy eyes and was discomfited to grasp she was reacting to whatever was in his. Projecting it, however, didn't make him conscious of what it was.

Having troweled out a row of miniature mineshafts for the daffodil bulbs, he dragged over the plastic tray from Tesco's and snorted peevishly. He'd have to expand his excavations or cram the bulbs in and mangle their roots. He jabbed his trowel into the leftmost hole and swizzled it around impatiently, only to bump into something to one side. Damn! On its molehill scale, here was Pelion on Ossa, another frustrating hitch in a dead-simple chore. And lest the obstruction disfigure the bulb as it grew, dig he must, deforming his neat circlet into an ever sloppier trench. Damn and damn!

He'd hit his irritant at an outthrust angle, whence it retreated left and right like the less perishable corner of an otherwise corroded strongbox. It was still an unseen quantity when he surmised he'd removed enough surrounding clay to wedge the trowel's point beneath the angle and pry it free. Not till cruddy prize was in hand did he grimace to recollect *Daily Mail* headlines about unexploded Jerry ordnance.

Ordnance it wasn't, but a weapon it was. Picking off its earthen jacket, he identified his V-shaped artifact as a dagger, albeit bent more like a safety pin. Might it clean up okay, or was it solid oxidation? Depended on its age, Gareth supposed; it used to be nice, based on the convex line of spirals along the hilt, cast into starker relief by accreted rust. But whether prehistoric or merely Victorian, legality dictated he fork it over to the English Heritage staff next door.

He dourly peered beyond his garden palings at the looming section of medieval wall, replete with three Gothic arches and two buttresses like butcher's blocks. Sod him if "British soil" wasn't one big archaeological site, with the government commandeering more scenic countryside and its precious contents daily. Who'd miss one unreported hunk of scrap? What possible loss to science was at stake? He'd earned it with the sweat of his brow, on his own sacrosanct property, not on "scheduled monument" grounds.

Possession was nine-tenths, after all, and to clinch making this detritus his, he'd perform the proprietary service of straightening it out. Like planting bulbs, though, the job was unfairly freighted: gripping an end in each hand, his efforts increased from gingerly to no-nonsense. But instead of conceding a millimeter, the dagger broke at the bend with a startling clap. As he knelt there blinking, he harbored no gloom of foreboding, despite an intuition he'd hark back to this moment as significant, a tipping point somehow.

*   *   *

The knife disliked being broken, if such animistic terms applied to numinous relics weathering trauma. And on those terms, it supplicated its owner, who'd gone to dormant seed with the extinction of his worshippers. The dagger had become his by deformation, by its ritual death, before its immersion in the shallows, when the land was floodplain, a liminal zone, most often submerged, never altogether dry, except atop the pagan tumulus. On this artificial plateau above the water-line, native deity's log stockade was supplanted by a Roman-era temple to Janus, demolished for a Late-Antiquity chapel, evolving into the Norman abbey. Sanctity's aura may always have enveloped the locale like dirt on the sundered dagger, but nothing since the Iron Age had energized its *genius loci*, not till Gareth arrogated votive offering to himself by compounding its damage.

*   *   *

Cleaving to nonchalance, Gareth exited the shed beside the hen-house, conducting furtive reconnaissance to confirm his sole witnesses were stupid poultry. How'd that chestnut go—nobody here but us chickens? The dagger's halves he'd stashed under the cantilevered tray in the tackle box on a bottom shelf patrolled by spiders; Anne detested spiders. If he just exuded business-as-usual, she'd never suspect him of secrecy, such had been their mutual trust from day one. For now, certainly, best to keep his find on the QT, as she could be a stickler, quite likely to harp on his marginally scofflaw attitude till he caved.

Traversing the lawn, he avoided eye contact with the moody black rooster and in the kitchen sink washed his hands, careful not to add soapsuds to the beets and carrots soaking in the casserole dish. Short-term memory must have been shortchanging him, for planting daffodils summed up his day's accomplishments, while Anne had replaced guestroom bedclothes, hired roofers to redo the lead flashing, weeded the lettuce, and organized the menu for tomorrow's full house. But for now, the deceptively taxing onus was on him to stay out of Anne's zig-zag way as she cooked supper.

She was handsome, he observed from his neutral corner by the breadbox, sturdy, scarcely the grossest case of middle-age spread on a given day, and his *sine qua non* in making dreams come true, as he hoped he was hers. His dreams, naturally, had been different before they'd met. On rebounding from the utopian zeitgeist of the '70s, reconciling with his truer bedrock self, he'd aspired to become a prep-school headmaster. But then, everyone's beset by conflicting desires; and the promise of love, of long-term stability with Anne, sidelined his admittedly farfetched ambition, what with her career track tethering them to Greater London.

Still, he couldn't complain, he'd settled on a livelihood that amounted to an inglorious slog, but on the bright side, no regrets about early retirement! "No regrets"—what a motto. Yet didn't the Abbey View, in its fashion, reward his Thatcher-generation hankering to run a tight ship, wield plenary sway over an august institution? Never mind that the premises dated to the mid-1800s, barely ankle-deep in the gulf of history.

Really, he had no pretext for the malaise he felt she echoed in her keyed-up bustling over dinner for the two of them. There was no fuss or rush tonight involving boarders. She came to a rolling stop, antsy feet in motion again before she finished exhorting, "If you're simply going to stand around, why don't you uncork the wine so it can breathe?" Yes, obviously for it to breathe; her emphasis on "breathing" led him to mull the insinuation his mere presence was stifling.

They dined in the terseness he deemed typical of silver-anniversary couples, roiled mainly by her request, "If you've room on your agenda, first thing in the morning could you despatch Charlotte or Emily for the evening table?" He chose not to treat this as a dig at his underachieving afternoon. Bleak news, though, for one of the Brontë sisters, happy-go-lucky innocents who'd never offended him, unlike other feathered denizens, but who'd committed the deadly sin of outlasting their laying prime.

Come the dawn he was up, resolved to mete out summary judgment, briefly stalling in the shed to contemplate his secret artifact, his broken badge of initiative and selfhood on the bottom shelf, before unswaddling the cleaver on the top shelf. He'd have to decapitate and, while he was at it, dress his prey, beyond wringing her neck. The flaccid head flopping about made Anne squeamish.

*   *   *

That awful man, the brazen reiver, was back to gloat, to lord it over the votive gift he had desecrated. What a fool, to linger where the aggrieved knife could show its master how the touch of defilement on corroded surface matched the soul of the perpetrator; and that master, all the more baleful for being groggy, disoriented, starved for worship lo these many centuries, would exact retribution not on the man directly, but through him, the better to assuage its elemental appetite, to multiply the afflictions due the transgressor.

*   *   *

My God, was she steamed! Once she'd identified the plucked and headless anatomy on the cutting board, she bridled, "I distinctly told you to cull one of the old hens. Not the rooster, for heaven's sake." Because they were impeccably attuned to each other's moods, Gareth alone would be privy to Anne's volcanic ire smoldering behind jerky body language, bulging peepers, a waxy mask of composure; she abstained from emotional displays when guests might totter in anytime. Self-control was essential in riding herd on a two-person operation, no denying that.

Nor any denying they'd have it out later, and Gareth would have to be unflappable, conciliatory without shouldering blame, ready with a rationale. What added luster to a day like the certainty of a showdown at bedtime? The fucking rooster was notorious for staging kamikaze charges at Gareth as if it owned the place, so pleading self-defense was an option; though honestly, chanticleer's downfall was dim like ancient history, receding into the welter of myriad farmyard slaughters, a gruesome routine whose details he preferred blurry.

Would that he could remember, though, getting the drop on the damn rooster before it drew first blood. Where had that once-in-a-lifetime scintilla of triumph gone? An actual synaptic pothole would be scary, and worse than futile in deflecting Anne's displeasure, as it would absolutely alarm her, if she bought it, into strong-arming him through an intolerable gauntlet of exams and scans and tests. Anyhow, neurological issues were moot while there was spiffing-up to do for impending wayfarers who'd be anything but spiffy themselves.

To count his blessings, mid-October meant mowing was finished, and the withered grass afforded less of a hindrance in his unglamorous chore of searching, particularly along the gravel path to the portico, for critter shit to shovel into a wheelbarrow. Accusing Anne of male stereotyping in saddling him with this role would merit a wry titter at most. The current cleanup was especially gratuitous, as the roofers had shown up ungodly early to erect a grand eyesore of scaffolding beside the entrance. Who'd ever notice a few turds?

A cancellation had shoehorned several idle days into the tradesmen's schedule; Anne had leapt at their sudden availability. Otherwise that leak around the chimney might have gone unremedied till next spring, with resultant water-stained wallpaper and rotten wood. And they could erect the staging and get a jump on the repairs at daybreak without disturbing guests.

Anne had probably reviewed the paperwork on who was coming and from where. And from where in the world hadn't they come, hikers overwhelmingly? Far-flung points of origin were less notable to Gareth than the marvel of maximum occupancy in the dead of autumn, when guidebooks discouraged treks into fickle conditions, gales, cold rain, hail, flurries. Come October, many innkeepers locked their shutters till May. A dearth of choices might explain the hardy or foolhardy six descending on the View.

During the season, the sun never set on an empty house, vindicating the gamble that a classy, historic location would be enticing in its own right, despite lying a mile or three off every waymarked trail. If the guys on the roof had it in them to admire the landscape amid their many breathers, the squiggly River Eden was in the mid-ground, and eagle-eyes could trace the Hadrian's Wall, North West, Pennine, and of course Eden paths. They might take the measure of tonight's footsore pilgrims an hour before Gareth's first opportunity.

After scraping his load of dung into a gully behind the outbuildings, fatalistically fuming as always that officialdom would someday declare his compost dump a protected Bronze Age ditch, he parked the wheelbarrow in the shed. Sunlight through the dusty window shone warmly on the tackle box, coaxing him to contemplate the relic within. What a pity his bid at fixing it had backfired. Why not seize an interval where he was safe from supervision, unpack his soldering kit on the workbench, and rejoin the riven blade, maybe braze it straight again?

Impromptu project insulated him from the ticking of his watch, the sun fading in the window, till he ogled his unspectacular results as if waking from a trance. The blade was back together, but along an axis that brought to mind a severely herniated disc. Waning daylight admonished him to go pull his weight on the home front.

The brawny galoots were still on the roof. Hurray, he couldn't have been AWOL terribly long. In fact, they seemed to occupy the same positions in which he'd last surveyed them. Maybe they overindulged in stoppages to avoid careless mistakes born of fatigue, calling dibs on comfy spots to leeward and sticking with them. Nonetheless, they must have made substantial progress. Too bad Gareth couldn't tell at a glance.

He never did trust strapping specimens, however skilled and affable: he lacked the knowhow to verify they weren't getting away with murder. He'd learned in tender boyhood that challenging bullies didn't pay, whereas Anne could talk as she liked to bruisers whose macho code forbade hitting women, in public anyhow. One bruiser waved at him, and he awkwardly returned the gesture without pausing, not that he'd have understood half of their gobbledygook. No, that was unfair. Initially, laborers had had to repeat themselves past the limits of their patience. Nowadays it was the rare Northerner who gabbled incomprehensibly.

Damn the luck, four pairs of boots were lined up along the wall past the front door. Anne was already hip-deep in hospitality. The roofers on their eyesore scaffolding had indeed subbed as default welcoming committee. And leaving Anne in the lurch was doubtless one more failing to hash out in bed.

*   *   *

The Maydays from the crooked dagger grew shrill as mortal hubris mounted. To burst from dormancy at being split in two and separated from sacred immanence had been acutely degrading. But to be fused ineptly together again, a shocking demotion from divine to fleshly ownership, was vastly worse.

The reunited knife cried out for death, for immediate redress, but its rightful master shrugged off these stimuli, overrode them with a stolid insistence on sating millennial hunger. Yes, the blasphemer deserved the cruelest punishment, which supplied a pretext to prolong his suffering as a conduit of sacrifice, nourishing the supernal maw to the utmost, seasoning that nourishment with the offender's own damnation, blacker after every killing.

As for the victims, whom otherworldly prescience had earmarked before their executioner had, the sapient among them couldn't go unawares to their dooms. Efficacy demanded they be cognizant of advancing the greater good, willingly or not, in a transaction promoting grace and balance between mortal and sacred realms. Proud godhood, in

serving its next victim nocturnal notice, drew no facile distinction between harmonizing the universe and reducing its monumental hunger.

$*$ $*$ $*$

Of the first four guests, only their boots remained. They were already in their quarters resting up, or else had slipped into espadrilles to
poke about the abbey. Gareth was in the veritable nick, alas, to eaves-
drop from the library door as the reservations for the Stanwix Room
clumped in and disabused him of ever expecting to screen out 100%
of the riffraff. Anne was framing house policy as nicely as possible,
and ensured compliance by bodily blocking the hallway. "Your feet will
feel so much better after trudging around if you set your shoes there
beside the others."

Anyone of decent upbringing would have respected this injunction
against tracking mud across immaculate floors, besmirching potpourri
atmosphere with boot funk. But the newcomers were balking, and one
brassily opined their footwear was clean after several miles of sun-
baked trail, and traveling light as they did, they'd packed no spares.
Anne let frowning impassivity convey how their lack of foresight was
not her problem, that a standoff would get them nowhere. Shortly they
tugged off their Keens without unlacing them. They acquitted themselves as if resigned to humoring her, and Gareth wasn't the least
thunderstruck to detect Yank accents.

The tonic note right now was of Anne's indomitability, never in
doubt really. Why not tackle some last-minute tidying in the library?
He'd scarcely unpocketed a dustrag, though, than Anne hallooed him
to the kitchen. She wasn't forgoing the customary cake and coffee for
weary newcomers, despite inauspicious first impressions. That was
Anne, hospitable to a fault. She charged Gareth with toting the tray
out the backdoor, traversing the gravel apron and lawn to the picnic
table, where the Yanks sat opposite one another, with each one's
stocking feet up on the other's bench. Unnerved expressions lingered
from their shoeless lope through knobbly pebbles and stiff grass.

"Enjoy," he bid them, and added a caveat about chicken dung lurking
in the turf. One fowl had shat on the table in an illustrative capacity.

The welcoming repast was typical of Anne's genteel touches, and
talking her out of it was always a waste of breath. Today in particular,

best not to tweak her subcutaneous tension after his slipup with the rooster and his dagger-welding sojourn. To convene in the library for pre-dinner ice-breaking, meanwhile, had been his brainchild. In a re-fined but homier ambience for small talk than the more formal dining room, fellowship could burgeon among instinctively standoffish strangers. The mature Yorkshire couple gamely entered into the socia-ble spirit, as did the plain-spoken Geordie and the casual Chelsea pro-fessional.

The Yanks, on finally slouching into the library, were the holdouts, eyes darting toward every face except Gareth's as if seeking clues to what was going on, as if getting acquainted had no value per se and Gareth was wantonly remiss in withholding sherry or aperitifs. Typical bloody-minded Americans, always keenest on what was in it for them! Their desultory mumblings marred his pleasure at presiding over the pleasantries, and he sighed relief when the mantel clock chimed seven.

At the communal table, the tall, weedy American continued taci-turn, a canary-eating grin on his pinched-in features, behavior that proved, in the event, preferable. His average-height compatriot, with the bland sheen of a Ken doll, designer active wear, and supercilious demeanor, conquered his reticence and bared his personality, to gen-eral embarrassment. As a rule Gareth was, to be candid, a smooth fa-cilitator, poised by the sideboard throughout dinner to wade in and abet the flow, the art, of conversation, anyway when Anne didn't wheel in the next course and loom there describing every blessed in-gredient of each dish.

This minimally posh procedure clearly flummoxed the Americans, unequal to chiming in with even the glibbest compliments. Worse, while everyone else burbled at uniformly indoor volume, the Ken-made-flesh was seemingly striving for audibility above a squall, every pronouncement a catapulted boulder muddying the verbal stream. And true to stereotype, he kept reprising the Yankee know-it-all, coopting British history as if it were his, even averring six paltry years had gone into building Hadrian's Wall. Nobody was tactless enough to belabor how primitive Romans couldn't have spent less than twenty years stacking 83 miles of masonry. But however accurate his assertions, what a berk!

Or perhaps something was wrong with his ears, or his brain. For

Gareth's money, nobody's dialect was too thick, so what was the Yank playing at? The Geordie, in the starkest instance, aphorized that it sometimes paid to get away from home to appreciate it. The Yank professed amazement that yams were such a British staple that people undertook cross-country rambles to escape them. Everyone, especially the poor Geordie, was dumbfounded, puzzling whether the Yank was having them on or mentally impaired. After further gaffes, always delivered with a maddening, steadfast confidence, Gareth could only be grateful the other American held his tongue behind a simper.

Some evenings, Gareth was sorry no other dining choices existed for miles around. He had captive patrons, but they had a captive host. And the Americans, damn his wife, were staying two nights, when her vaunted character judgment should have read their inelegance between the lines of their email enquiries. On the theory a good offense was the best defense, he rehearsed his preemptive salvo for the impending bedroom tiff while they slogged through kitchen cleanup and overall battening down amid the standard mute fatigue.

Borrowing a page from her book of indirection, he gargled and then repined from their en-suite bathroom doorway, "Shameful how those Americans abused our hospitality, pearls before swine really, nary a mention of your culinary brilliance, never mind their rudeness to you from the get-go. What's more galling, they're staying tomorrow night too, aren't they?"

"Maybe they're planning an extended tour of the abbey or that Roman rubble on the Brampton road you crow about in the brochure." In pyjamas already, she was leaning toward the vanity mirror and addressing his reflection, a quirk as off-putting tonight as ever. "In fairness to them, though, nobody else was raving about dinner."

Oh no, she wouldn't sidetrack him so easily. "I'm surprised, actually, you didn't suss out anything uncouth in their inquiries and simply inform them we had no vacancies. Would have saved us some uncomfortable pauses. Hope this doesn't lead to bad reviews."

She'd quit the mirror to peel away her bed's coverlet. "Rather close in here," she remarked. "I'd open the window if the heat wouldn't come on later when it gets chilly. But yes, I hope we don't see complaints about the food. The mains would have been tenderer had it been a hen instead of that rooster in the pot. It would also have been better if I'd been able to spend longer at the stove without having to get all the guests settled in this afternoon."

Outflanked again! Before locking the bathroom door to use the toilet, he scrambled to regain ground, with no guarantee she'd hear him past the rustling of her sheets, by wishing those steeplejacks she'd hired would shake a leg because all that ruckus and scaffolding was as bad for their image as any marginally tough chicken.

Her riposte had just the lilt to penetrate the door. "Tell them yourself if you must, dear." With that, damn her, he had to picture the upshot of criticizing brutes in jumpsuits, which mushroomed into reviling them for being, albeit fortuitously, on Anne's side. When he flicked the bathroom light switch, his sight had to adjust to the bedroom's hermetic darkness.

*   *   *

If the dagger had jabbed cracks into the innkeepers' domestic foundations, supernatural agency infiltrated those cracks like water, dilated them into fissures. In the fissures were grudges and discontent to aggravate, fertile soil where baleful seeds germinated and fructified. Nor were countervailing powers afoot to temper destructive influence, but if they were, the names by which mortals could appeal to them were forever lost. Numinous vengeance could proliferate like an untamable weed, feed like a ravenous pox on those from whom the ages had stripped any tokens of resistance or shamanic remedies.

*   *   *

The damn roofers woke Gareth, and by inference everyone else, before cockcrow, smacking a ladder against the wall and clattering it into position to access an oriel or some such excrescence unreachable from the scaffolding. "Here's your golden chance to tell the workmen off," Anne croaked, exhibiting no other sign of life beneath crown-to-toe sheet. Oho, so her bedtime sarcasm had evolved overnight into a clarion to manly duty?

As he flung wide the bedroom door, a puff of draft blew by, ruffling shin hairs below the hem of his flannel robe, while from Anne's bed wafted the Delphic afterthought, "Be gentle, love." What? Was she consciously entreating him, or God-knew-who in dreamland?

Whether he was bound for shame or glory would be a wash in one respect, as nobody was up yet to witness the fracas for which he braced himself by refusing to think ahead. Or more strictly speaking, he bumped into nobody all the way to the portico. From its shadow like a pocket of night, he gandered leftward at the scaffolding, placid as a theatre set between shows, and rightward at the ladder, shaking slightly with the screak of prying and arrhythmic thudding of a claw hammer, at an elevation obstructed by the portico ceiling.

He was suddenly up to his eyes in a rising gorge of indignation at this crass imbecility: spoiling the lodgers' rest, alienating them, negatively impacting Gareth's livelihood, maybe irreparably. Stop that racket, stop it this instant!

When his wits were back about him, he was favoring the slippered foot whose arches hurt. The ladder he'd kicked with that foot lay flat, half on gravel, half on grass. The roofer was prostrate and motionless, head twisted too far into profile, eyes agape. Gareth was goggling down at him: yep, dead all right. Could a gap as pertained to remembrance of toppling the ladder signal a worrisome "senior moment" at his unripe age?

Asking himself this jump-started his higher-functioning cognition again. Flight response kicked in, and only the competing survival reflex of scanning around for onlookers curbed his sprint for cover. He was about to vent a pent-up breath when his vision meandered above the staging, under the eaves, to the open window of the Stanwix and the formerly loudmouth American. Had he been gawking all along, or had the tumbling laborer shouted and alerted him to a fait accompli, too late to catch Gareth red-handed? Damn his Swiss-cheese memory!

"Call 999!" he bellowed petulantly at the Yank, but several seconds elapsed before the demand punctured his catatonic daze. Not that an American necessarily had a mobile that could connect with local emergency services. The casualty's coworker was still on the far side of the gable peak, hollering, "Kyle? Kyle? Answer me, for fuck's sake!"

Gareth dashed inside lest he present an incriminating tableau to the coworker or anyone else. Anne was prepping in the kitchen, bleary and blowzy as on any pre-coffee morning. "There's been an accident!" he barked at her.

He broached neither his instructions to the Yank nor, obviously, his unremembered felling of the ladder. Proactive Anne dried her hands and dialed 999. For the police record, he could honestly declare that none of the English lodgers soon rubbernecking the "accident scene" had been astir till ambulance siren had rousted them. The Yanks were no-shows, and once the eczematous constable had corroborated Gareth's blanket statement about the bystanders, he wheezed upstairs with Gareth to the Stanwix Room and knocked. Both Americans, though fully dressed, acted like muddled sleepyheads and denied they'd seen anything the others hadn't.

Their dopey protestations of ignorance weren't supremely convincing to Gareth, but what should they do, denounce him as the murderer? He and the constable stumped back down to the foyer, where the surviving roofer had accepted Anne's offer of a blanket-chest seat and a therapeutic brandy. The rangy geezer hoisted empty tulip glass toward Anne for a refill, then beckoned over the landlord and the lawman with it.

He gulped liquid breakfast and rasped, "The fuck of it is, Kyle had an awful nightmare the middle of the night, summat about getting pushed off a sea cliff into a floating coffin, couldn't sleep anymore so he rang me at bloody four A.M., insisted we get this job done like it was life-or-death, guess what you'd call a self-fulfilling prophecy? And he's the one always told me, don't muck around up ladders and such unless you're well-rested and easy in your mind." Charitable Anne poured more therapy into his upraised glass.

To preclude further mishap, the constable packed logy artisan into police-car passenger seat; he, like any native, knew where everyone lived. And nothing contradicted the verdict of accidental death. With the body's removal to the county morgue, horizontal ladder afforded sole physical trace of the incident. Gareth was off the hook, though fretful at his "senior moment's" erasure of the lethal instant.

But the highest priority now was to reinstate normalcy, prevent tragedy from stamping the overriding, indelible impression on his clientele. When word-of-mouth included "death," it could tarnish the most sterling reputation. Breakfast was already egregiously late, and for the sake of the Abbey View, of something bigger than himself, the show had to go on.

The British guests, eyes downcast, stunned, funereal, were filtering into the dining room. Their need for a dose of coffee, stat, was dire;

where the hell was Anne? More vexingly, where were the Yanks? Any problem keeping tabs on them triggered twinges of anxiety. He paced the ground-floor hall and—aha!—espied them sitting in the library. They regarded him quizzically, and the taller, weedy specimen overcame his coyness to prate how they'd inferred from dinner that guests were supposed to assemble come mealtimes in the library.

"Breakfast is in the dining room!" Gareth huffed. Were they kidding, or had he misheard the smarmy low-talker? Where else would someone in his right mind go for breakfast? Whatever it was about these two that continually stoked his hostility, it hinged—didn't it?—on how that hostility called into question his self-image as a good person, quite apart from the potential repercussions of their window-gazing.

Adding the Yanks did nothing to sweeten the table's gloomy mood. Gareth could only exacerbate things by referring to topical reality. He had to rise to the occasion, revive lighthearted vibes, a more idyllic air. As most often befell, he resorted to the centerpiece on the mantel for inspiration, a stuffed badger in a child's deerstalker. The taxidermist had posed his subject on hindquarters, arms outspread like a fisherman exaggerating the one that got away.

"I'm sure you've noticed Sherlock the Brock," Gareth expounded, "and noting the claws, I must remind you not to approach these normally retiring omnivores should you meet any on the trail. In October they can be most temperamental because they're under pressure to bulk up on every available calorie, to survive the winter."

"Wild kingdom!" whispered the mouthier American to his countryman.

"What's that?" challenged Gareth as if bearded in his den, a headmaster sorting out rebellious pupils.

"Nothing, really," the Yank parried, "just a flashback to a TV show when we were kids. This guy Marlin something-or-other used to lecture about wildlife and always segue somehow into a sales pitch for insurance. Pretty ingenious, actually."

Well, when the explanation for nonsense is more nonsense, what reply should dignify that? Gareth proceeded as if the Yank had said nothing. "The deerstalker is more than a whimsical affectation. I'm courting a publisher for my series of children's novels, in which forest animals solve crimes together: poaching, biohazard dumping, vandalism. The animals enjoy natural advantages of superior instincts and senses; and the badger, for one, on being tasked with a mystery, has all winter to sleep on it. I'm going for a mélange of Kenneth Grahame and Graham Greene. I may adopt the pseudonym Kenneth Greene Graham."

True to form, Anne wheeled in the squealing cart of breakfast platters and pots of coffee precisely when Gareth's writerly morale was hanging on some kindness from strangers. "Sorry we've been delayed," she lilted. "I hope this morning's dreadful circumstances haven't spoiled your appetites completely." Damn her, she was barging right into the minefield he'd scrupulously tiptoed around, and worse, was managing it in terms that made him seem oafish for doing otherwise. On top of which, her long-suffering pout while she doled out dishes indicated her trenchant awareness of what he'd been selfishly touting in her absence.

Nor could he cut his losses and retreat discreetly without her intercepting hand on his arm. "And please shift that ladder from the yard. Put it in the roofers' van. Let's not have a constant reminder out there of what's happened."

Declining to answer, he slunk onward and ventured a backward glance to establish if her bossiness had carried within ear of the breakfasters. She stopped him cold, though, with her pensive inspection of his ill-concealed limp, and then he discerned the Yanks following suit, for which he unequivocally blamed her, and was the Yorkshire hausfrau staring too? Anne had seldom misread which behavioral blips of his were telltales of bigger problems; despite that rapport of theirs honing her perceptions, he did have to wonder at junctures like this, whose side was she on?

If the Americans had witnessed his kicking the ladder, how was it in their interests not to report him? And if an intuitive brainstorm made Anne the wiser, would she shield or betray him, would kneejerk morality trump loyalty? Gareth was sickly with angst but not guilt. Since that crucial interval was a mental blank, he couldn't conclusively rule out the killer was someone else. His conscience, heavily invested in his noble self-image, concurred.

*   *   *

Disinterred, deprived of earthen sealant, the knife was ill-qualified to apprehend its numinous charge was dissipating: maybe that was why a single death sufficed for its appeasement, why it aspired merely to abide in divine communing. Its owner, meanwhile, chafed at how one victim had scarcely whetted his appetite, how his reborn hunger for nourishment via panic and fatality was a great many victims away from satiation, how the procurer of that nourishment was shaping up as ever more incompetent at honoring protocol, at wringing the most from each sacrifice. He'd attend to his importunate possessions when they'd best serve him, and never the other way around!

$*$ $*$ $*$

Anne foisted the passkey at him with a flintiness he could interpret without recourse to their fabled rapport. She hadn't forgotten how he'd left her in the lurch yesterday. He, however, had to wrack his hippocampus for what had waylaid him, his hobbyist patch-up of that rusty dagger, a gewgaw reduced by "circumstances" to vagueness, irrelevance. Hers was the doleful concern of a creditor for a debtor in perilous arrears. The Londoner and the Yorkies had decamped, the Geordie and the Yanks had not, do up the rooms accordingly: a gesture spanning paltry inches was pregnant with subtext galore.

He attached little importance to the shoelessness of the hall by the door. Opting to get the Stanwix over with first, he'd hardly lifted a finger when the want of backpacks, comb, toothbrush, any belongings hit him. Anne was in the kitchen, loading the dishwasher. He practically pounced at her, jarring her into dropping a saucer. "Those Americans!" he blustered, apparently oblivious to his own ferment. "When did you see them last?"

"Twenty minutes ago, half an hour maybe." She'd bent a fraction of the way toward retrieving busted crockery, but refrained as if he were flubbing a nonverbal cue to clarify why he was so agitated.

"Did they say where they were headed?"

She repressed a wince at the harshness that smacked of interrogation. "Not right then, but earlier they had an ordnance map out and were circling the castle ruins off the Military Road." And during any interrogation, wasn't it a given that forthright answers presaged harm to others, whereas evasion presaged harm to oneself? Wary body language intimated she was humoring him, that she was always afraid he'd come to this.

Gareth, in turn, balked at her fraught stance, her agate stare. Why the devil wasn't she cleaning up those jagged shards, why totter there addled when figurative bells were clanging for all hands on deck?

"They've taken off with their backpacks!" he blared and careened away. Let her draw her own conclusions! Resentment ignited as he read aspersions on his clarity in her cagey reserve. Fucking hell, he had reasons to be upset, and Anne should be bloody grateful she wasn't privy to most of them. Too bad if he'd spooked her, but he wasn't the enemy; no thanks to her deficient vigilance, the enemy had absconded, and unless the Yanks were orienteering through fields and forest, they were stuck with the tortuous Brampton road for a good three miles.

The ratchety vintage Escort started right up, which shouldn't have imposed cognitive dissonance but did, because on the heels of reflexively venting "Thank God," he overheard himself musing, What god, specifically? No names leapt to the fore, nor any rationale for that peculiar rumination. Then with a screech of rubber and spray of gravel, the driveway was behind him, the hunt was on.

Anne was welcome to believe he was overwrought about a couple of deadbeats skipping out. Scurvy weasels they may have been who routinely flouted honor systems, though Gareth alone had insight into why they expected to bilk the Abbey View with impunity. If they did have what he did not, his homicidal footwork enshrined in memory, how implausibly petty of them to squander that as a deterrent against pursuit for the sake of two hundred-odd pounds, as if any truncated life had no greater value as a bargaining chip.

The range of stronger likelihoods incensed him to step on the gas, to hell with the throbbing in that foot, the hairpin curves putting the horizon a furlong away, the meager margin of error between vehicles on this nominally dual carriageway, the estate walls and towering hedges on both sides amounting to a chute where drivers had nowhere to swerve or pedestrians to vault. And Gareth was no less hemmed in by an endgame unamenable to forethought or second thoughts, just as he had been when hammering had awakened him.

Gareth couldn't imagine his nemeses effecting any agenda that didn't presuppose their knowledge of his guilt, even if that only entailed a safe distance from him. But once they were out of his clutches, he'd be, somehow or other, in theirs. If their ambitions transcended welshing on a hotel bill, they might be plotting blackmail. Or far ghastlier, they might be seeking a pub, a shop, anywhere to phone the constabulary, without risking Gareth's retribution at the B&B or the abbey's tourist center, where they might worry he had allies.

Thus far, anyway, his luck had held. He'd had no traffic to pass or dodge. A crossroad was imminent, where a few shabby houses mimicked a hamlet, but before it popped into view, around a bend, hurray, he was almost on top of those two craven weasels, trudging doltishly side by side. They were just turning around as Gareth revved the engine, which deafened him to his inner bookkeeper's lament, Drat, we'll never see those two hundred-odd pounds now.

* * *

Mortal ineptitude, in setting after victims yet to receive oneiric warning, had pushed divine tolerance to the limit. Then to liquidate them a prodigious arrow's-flight away, on an arid surface utterly insulated from the sacred precinct and its liminal conditions, was inexcusable. The *genius loci* got scant good of them, absorbed nothing save the most insipid flavor. Frustrated, unmollified though he was, he had none of his desecrated knife's thirst for punishment and revenge, not when hunger rankled. Instead, dissatisfied with one means to his cardinal end, he pragmatically endeavored to eliminate that means, survey his options.

* * *

He caught up with her making the Geordie's bed. He was bracing for sarcasm, as she'd evidently equated his quest for the delinquent Yanks with shirking his agreed tasks. Therefore he dithered over her superficially straightforward inquiry, "Should I change the sheets in the Stanwix?"

"What?"

"Will we ever see their boots again? Have they skipped, as you presumed, or did they obey some eccentric urge to bring their backpacks on a day-trip?"

"They've gone to ground, I'm afraid." Hah! His own snappy wit, like a kind of grace under fire, floored him at times, but lest cleverness obscured his lucidity, he added, "I'll go change their bedding."

"Or perhaps they'll be back? Just because you couldn't flush them out . . ." Was she testing him, angling him into verifying he knew damn well they weren't ever returning?

"I won't bother then," he shrugged. "You're right. We've no one else booking that room till the weekend. Best leave it for now." In retrospect, an hour later in the shed, it clicked that her frown branded him a goldbrick for palming off on her the tidying slated for the Stanwix whether or not the Yanks reappeared. In self-defense, though, his helpful intent had been quite sincere for its duration.

Still, congratulations were in order: he'd been conversational, hell, he was relatively composed. This functionality he attributed to the mental blank where the instant of vehicular impact should have been, similar to the incident with the ladder: he retained nothing to inflict guilt, nothing to cover for, as if someone else must have committed murder because he, to the best of his remembrance, hadn't. The pity was, his aura of innocence, or impunity rather, guttered when he went to deal with the ladder and boggled down the driveway at the Escort's crushed bumper, cracked headlamp, and parallel, monstrous scratches halfway up the bonnet to the windscreen.

He wasn't scurrying to the shed to huddle timorously, heavens no, though that had been his destination well before he conceived of marshaling resources there for automotive makeover. Ironic, wasn't it, how a few cosmetic dings obliged him to proceed as if remorseful, despite his unladen conscience? Along the workbench he'd arrayed a ballpeen hammer to smooth crumpled bumper from the inside out, a sander to buff away the "harrowed" area, a crowbar to jimmy open the van in case the roofers had better tools; while mulling further requisites, his eyes lit on the tackle box.

It unsteadied him with a wave of nostalgia for that halcyon era, a measly two days but personal eons ago, before his situation became, frankly, untenable. The tackle box joined the implements on the workbench, and Gareth reverently retracted the lid and the upper tray, as if delving into a treasure chest or a reliquary, to peer upon that emblem, by default, of what was previously an unencumbered life. Funny how an archaic knife, like every exciting find from beachcombing, jumbles,

Oxfam shops, was promptly relegated to triviality, forgetfulness, by intervening distractions.

Yes indeed, exhuming the dagger had coincided with the tipping point between his orderly existence and chaos, as if its rust-blunted business end were a symbolic fulcrum. And as symbols went, the dagger didn't exactly redound to anyone's glory: its original owner had obviously discarded it as rubbish, and cheap it must have been to have bent so deplorably.

Gareth couldn't, of course, condemn any metalcraft as inferior to his slipshod welding job, a poor recompense for the ham-handed damage he'd wrought. But wait, had the rust been flaking away in the fresh air? In which case, why wasn't the blade nestled on dun specks and dust, since rust couldn't vaporize, could it? The longer he stared, the more he had to marvel and credit the testimony of his vision. The rust was receding with the deliberation of time-lapse footage in reverse, except with the sundering, the soldering, even the venerable bend edited out.

Seventy-two hours ago, to predict he was on the cusp of complicity in murder would have been ludicrous, and yes, complicity was the word, to evoke that "other" who must have administered the coup de grâce while he'd blacked out twice for as few seconds. Ludicrous, too, that he'd ever be guilty of more than the petty deceits conducive to marital stability, but there he was, a red-handed fugitive in his own shed, so why dismiss as ludicrous a dagger molting rust, resuming edges and contours, trading a uniform, sooty gray for a silvery blade, for white and carmine chips in the row of spirals enclosing studs along the hilt?

The wherefore of this transformation, its potential basis in delusion, in optical trickery, put too much food for thought on his plate, one dilemma too many to process. He was already saddled with the effacement of damning blemishes on his car, the PR nightmare of three deaths in one day involving the B&B, daunting prospects of convincing Anne he was above suspicion, of keeping her loyally on board, of what to do if he couldn't. What a joke, he brooded mirthlessly, that she was miffed with his goldbrick attitude, when in actuality he'd been criminally busy.

"Gareth!" Speak of the devil, Anne was in the doorway, goggle eyes and tense frown as the usual tells of turmoil behind quiescent features. Pathetic, the bother he'd expended to shroud a rusty artifact in secrecy, fretting she'd dispute the truism that possession was nine-tenths of the law! God only knew what she'd make of that artifact transmogrified, and how trifling the knife in any condition had become, what with triple manslaughter to shroud in secrecy.

Her lips uncoupled as if syllables were exerting pressure to emerge, but none did, as her line of sight bypassed Gareth and latched, with a likely semblance of his own mystification, onto the contents of the tackle box. Probably she was spellbound by the same mirage as he; this she didn't, or couldn't, verbalize, and he dared not coach her in case he were wrong about their common vision.

After a blank interim, of a piece with his prior lacunae, he heard her intone, "A pair of officers outside would like a word with you. They're interested in what happened to the car." She might as well have glared down at him from a judgment seat for all the love and sympathy she'd withdrawn from circulation. The rapport so seminal to their solidarity was extinguished, and at this earnest of desertion his self-restraint broke and he charged past her and across the threshold and into the truncheons and handcuffs of two goons-in-uniform who'd anticipated a runner.

His kaleidoscopic vortex of resentment, fright, and frustration, mostly centered on Anne, was too confusing for him to grasp they'd read him his rights twice. He'd no idea what he finally gibbered through his bleeding mouth to stop them shaking him by the shoulder after their third repetition. The dullards, he noted, had been unheedful of anything tantalizing on the workbench.

Anne had no desire to watch constables bundle her husband into a patrol car and speed off. Enough to listen in on sounds of an inexorable outcome, and recognize in them the echoes of a murky dream, although she'd never experienced ESP before. Technically, Cumbria's finest shouldn't have hightailed it without checking in on her, not that she begrudged them a clean getaway from the raving, hysterical housewife she might have been.

His arrest, she had to admit, had lifted a burden, unearthed the home truth that she'd never achieved much rapport with Gareth, had borne with him twenty years because of the kids, and had bought into the View as last-ditch conjugal CPR. Oh well, she smiled ruefully, that patient hadn't survived the surgery. Was she callous? Could be she was in shock, but then she had the wherewithal to contrive a silver lining: in jail with nothing else to do, perhaps poor Gareth might get somewhere on that silly whodunit about badgers.

If self-assessment were trustworthy, though, she was in awe as opposed to shock. Above the pristine, shining blade, which she'd never seen in any other state, hovered fleeting swatches of iridescence, then brilliant dapplings like sunshine on rippling water, but minus the water. They elicited a resonance from somewhere deeper than her gut, a hard-wired response to sublimity, and why shouldn't sublimity emanate from a garden shed, was a burning bush in a grubby desert any more apropos? The coruscations rewarded her enraptured gaze by coalescing into a billowy nimbus, which, ipso facto, had to surround divine lineaments.

Those lineaments partook of no fixed definition, at least none that Anne's human optics could embrace. But she was positive they were nowise akin to Gareth's beloved Kenneth Grahame hogwash, no "Piper at the Gates of Dawn." Her only certitude was of ecstatic attendance upon the amorphous splendor in the halogen effulgence until it either immolated her retinas or blessed her with instructions.

*   *   *

How exhilarating to be rid of that churlish servitor! Moreover, the act of rejection had yielded that pivotal iota of sustenance, empowering him to diffuse partway into the world on which he fed, where the innkeepers who'd basked in preeminent exposure to him were thereby privileged to see his knife as he did, were most receptive to his voracious will. How gratifying as well to apprehend the knife at its happiest, its most numinous, since undergoing ritual damage.

On reflection, he longed for the savory ministrations of a priestess and behold how she cradled the knife, not as rust-and-solder dross, but as the holiest, loveliest prize under the sun. Her piety struck a chord, sonorous with his more profound longings for the devotion of a cult, and he averted her eyes from his gibbous effulgence before she went blind, and he taught her to grip the dagger properly by the haft.

Meanwhile, this was the first she'd thought of the kids in ages. She'd have to summon them to break the news, about their dad, and then? She'd never outright asked for offspring, couldn't swear under oath she'd liked having them around, or even altogether liked them. But seeing as they'd soon be underfoot again, it was down to a coin toss, wasn't it? What need was more pressing, for acolytes or sacrifices?

Whatever a coin was, the *genius loci* could sympathize, without troubling overmuch about a future so many intermediate events away. Hunger would decide what was needful when the time came.

Old Graveyard in the Woods

There's a skull with wings, and an hourglass too,
And a cherub who sings that our days are few,
And to weeping willows cling lichens green and blue
In that old, old graveyard in the woods.

Down that road seldom taken, there's nobody around
Where once they had the makings of a flourishing town.
Now the aspens are quaking where the walls all tumbled down
Except around the graveyard in the woods.

And there's a little of that place in you, my friend,
Where what used to mean so much gets lost in the end,
And where once we were together, there's nobody allowed,
And nothing mortal stirring in there now.

No flowers ever grow inside those mossy walls,
Whatever seeds you sow come up crooked and small,
Maybe someone long ago laced the ground with salt,
In that godforsaken graveyard in the woods.

Beside the cemetery, once a chapel stood
Where people came to marry or to pray that life be good,
And now they all lie buried deep within the woods,
In that old unhallowed graveyard in the woods.

Foolish men once came around in the dead of night,
Just to drink and carouse and do what harm they might,
But they heard some kind of sound, now they'll never be quite right,
Best avoid that old, old graveyard in the woods.

Gone to Doggerland

Nobody much liked Grandma Fiona toward the end. Among themselves and to our faces, social workers, nurses, housecleaners, therapists labeled her pigheaded, dotty, combative. Millie and I let it slide. For months, out of general earshot, we'd been calling her worse. And most others had better cause for acrimony. Rather than tackle the messy, unhygienic side of eldercare, we lived rent-free in return for shopping, cooking, keeping up with bills and dividend checks, providing 24-7 company and a semblance of continuity.

Given our wretched job outlook during chronic recession, we were grateful of course for no-cost shelter, and would it have killed her to reciprocate, to express some gratitude for unstinting efforts on her behalf? Instead we, her last worldly vestige of family and well-wishers, rated the same paranoid accusations of theft and shiftlessness as other helpmeets. Too bad we were only human, as apt as anyone to repay negativity in kind, and I at least regretted how soon we stooped to name-calling, in effect objectifying, dehumanizing ninety-odd years of Yankee character. But really, so little personhood shone through prickly disposition and arid patina.

I always imagined she'd die more or less *compos mentis* in her sleep, like my paternal grandparents, and with morbid confidence and somber resignation steeled myself each dawn for the expected shock; yet she celebrated one birthday, and another, till Millie and I started considering the house ours as much as Fiona's, and why not? To whom else would it go?

Not that we'd be reluctant heirs, any more than Fiona had been on entering middle-aged widowhood. In the meantime, dwelling under the same roof would have been unbearable if not for buffer zone of empty rooms between her and us, the precious illusion of separate quarters. Her saltbox cottage was among the eccentric few to qualify as "sprawling." Generations of owners, dissatisfied with the extra space of traditional lean-to spanning rear wall, had added ells to the sides and back and then ells to the ells, for a floor-plan resembling Lego dendrites, with a mansion's worth of elbowroom.

At the terminus of several ells, Millie and I took refuge in former carriage house, converted to a tourist rental in the 1920s. It afforded the property's best view of stark, alluvial Heron Beach, and was in fact doubly secluded because Fiona's in-laws had wielded the clout to preserve their homestead when neighboring premises too near the dunes were demolished for a conservation area. Based on the vista from any window, ours could have been the only house in the world.

Independent to a fault, Fiona disdained intrusive video monitors or intercoms, declaring she'd summon us during an emergency via medic alert necklace and have switchboard operator, maybe thousands of miles away, phone us six rooms over. For months she bickered about the expense of unused lifeline, somehow dragging herself from bed each day and inching the walker ahead of her into the breakfast nook. We never suspected how perniciously far she'd declined till the incident that would have justified whole galling outlay for lifeline system, had she actually been wearing it.

Her oatmeal and coffee were on the table at ironclad 7:30 A.M. and untouched at 7:40. Uh-oh! Millie and I trooped through front hall and parlor to no-show Fiona's bedroom, where the shock in store wasn't the one we'd expected. She was on the floor, hoarsely moaning and cussing. She'd taken the plunge into dementia by rolling out of bed.

Millie sprinted to nightstand landline and dialed 911. I kind of fluttered around Fiona, afraid to move her, afraid not to, exclaiming her name and waving frantically to penetrate her cloud of muttering incoherence. She was scrunched up on her side, cotton nightgown like a full-length caul, fixated on jabbing gristly thumb at carmine disk within white-gold medallion, on gold chain around crinkly throat.

Emergency pendant was nowhere in evidence, and the neckwear she'd somehow swapped for it was like nothing I'd previously seen on her, or anywhere. It captured the supple power of a moray eel, flexing into a circle to catch fleshy tail in bolt-cutter jaws. Stippled skin and jagged teeth were impeccably realistic, whereas overall lines and features, like its Mohawk of a dorsal fin, suggested the unearthly vigor, the wanton mysticism, of art nouveau, Maori tattoos, Mayan frescoes; sundry appraisers have remarked on these similarities, but none can pinpoint age or provenance.

On that pivotal morning, though, Fiona finally glared up at me and squalled, "Why'd you ignore me when I was down here buzzing and buzzing for you all night?"

Where to begin addressing that? I was flustered speechless, while more decisive Millie knelt beside Fiona and coaxed her into sitting up, resting her back against the bedframe. Naturally, Grandma was spitting mad when rescue workers rang. After they'd examined her, picked her up, dusted her off, she carped, "You had no right letting in strangers to manhandle me! I wasn't even dressed!"

Yes, physically she was none the worse, with hearty appetite for reheated oatmeal. Health aide and massage therapist reported no "senior moments" to us, but during a supper of Welsh rarebit and canned asparagus, her deterioration became obvious. "Where was the smoke damage?" she demanded.

What smoke damage? She'd never suffered dunces gladly. Jesus Christmas, she railed, wasn't I there when those firemen rousted her out of bed? Weren't they the nervous Norrises? Nothing was even singed! Was it grease in a skillet? Lit match in the wastebasket? The worry on Millie's face mirrored mine. Whether memory, cognitive, or language impairment was shaping this outburst, it was a signpost writ large of scary slope ahead.

"I see you have your emergency necklace again," I noted, thankful for that, for excuse to change the subject. "Where had it got off to, when you had that other jewelry on?"

"What do you mean?" she snapped. "I always wear this damn whoozis. I pay too much not to."

Conversations ever after with Fiona tended toward such no-win dead ends. The ongoing round of suits and uniforms assisting her took non-sequiturs in stride, outwardly deaf to them, probably accustomed to loopier. They seemingly thought no less of her than when she was merely crotchety.

Genuine communication occurred more and more rarely, on her emergence from stream of fragmentary consciousness, that isolated realm where she'd first landed upon tumbling from bed. By and large she'd slipped the moorings of circadian rhythm, floating adrift through her life story. She threatened to spank me for busting in before dawn when I woke her from La-Z-Boy nap at suppertime. Or she'd denounce me as an impostor, since everyone knew I was stationed in Italy! It eventually clicked that she'd conflated me with wartime casualty husband.

No, Fiona was by no measure competent and belonged in long-term facility, however strident her denials. Unfortunately, the law was on her side. We had no power of attorney, and obtaining it, warned our health-industry professionals, was complicated, costly, and protracted. As next of kin, we were entitled at best to approve procedures ad hoc, such as treatment for Fiona's fast-spreading, sudden-onset psoriasis and slow-healing lesions sustained in bedroom mishap.

Hence two or three new specialists joined Fiona's daily carousel of caregivers, the more the merrier for Millie and me. How fortuitous that we had more time to ourselves even as Fiona became more unmanageable—and to clear our heads, where better than the beach? But this wasn't the enchanting seascape of my boyhood, despite abiding features of tidal flats, dunes, and breakwaters, any more than Fiona was the same charming hostess.

Rather, to gaze seaward always put Fiona foremost in mind, only reinforced how stuck with her we were. Out there was a surface that might be placid or agitated or foggy, with no indications of what went on underneath, just as Fiona's past was hidden by changeable surface and always had been, except in broadest strokes. She'd married my late mother's father and had always lived by the ocean. Impossible to picture her anywhere landlocked, even one town inland. Of where she grew up, of her people I knew nothing, except they weren't from spousal stomping grounds of Ipswich and Gloucester.

Ironic, wasn't it, Millie proposed, that here was our gilt-edged chance to really get acquainted with Fiona, when she was about as forthcoming as an oyster. Surreal utterances aside, Fiona had severed contact with this world, none the wiser if we invested idle hours exploring, organizing, purging nine decades of biographic clutter, like spelunking from storeroom to storeroom in this chambered nautilus of a cottage encasing her soul. Who could say it was too soon to locate the will, the deed to that cottage, the title to classic Eldorado?

We'd hardly lifted a naive finger before the magnitude of crushing labor hit us. To archive photos alone involved rummaging for albums on shelves behind dusty sofas, through drawers of framed portraits in guestroom captain's bed, in kitchen cupboards with Fotomat packets accordioned between bookends of chipped mugs, or in slots meant for 78s beneath the turntable of archaic clawfoot Victrola. Further hundreds languished even more obscurely. I had to revise my opinion that ours was the most overdocumented era thanks to smartphones, Facebook, CCTV, the NSA. Nope, cheap cameras had opened the informational floodgates by 1900.

Here were snapshot annals of forebears from cradle to coffin, literally in some cases. Citizens of Gilded Age, Roaring Twenties, New Deal, Greatest Generation wore boaters or cloche hats, lace collars or celluloid, pince-nez or aviator shades, ball gowns or bomber jackets, in regal stances or equally stagey horseplay, against backdrops of picnic grounds, picket fences, snowdrifts, carny midways, yachting marinas. Too late to learn who and where these people had been; that was all forever sealed away in the skull of sole surviving informant.

In her sprightly prime Fiona had cut a modish figure, sporting mid-length black sheepskin coat on autumn holiday in a squalid, decrepit townscape. Where the devil was she, and why did she seem okay about it? Her smile partook of Mona Lisa ambiguity, shading toward tolerant in more guarded poses, mischievous as if putting one over on somebody, or conspiratorial, in cahoots with the shutterbug or others out of frame.

She stood with hands in pockets or arm draped along rusty wrought-iron fence, in classy counterpoint to façades of shabby Georgian mansions with rags stuffed in broken fanlight panes, of former Masonic Lodge according to gray silhouette of extirpated square-and-compasses emblem, or of rickety gingerbread hotel where only "Gilm" remained of gilt letters above the portico.

In one shot, Fiona, with her most reserved smile, accompanied presumptive native in front of a dingy lunchroom window peppered with flyspecks. No brain-teaser to see why she'd be leery; his sentiments were unreadable. His eyes goggled, blubbery lips gaped open, hairless, tumid head was like territory disputed between cyanotic complexion and scabrous patches resembling those of modern-day Fiona. Whatever his connection with her, I had to hope this slump-shouldered, bloated specimen in baggy overalls wasn't typical of his hardscrabble environs, was maybe a destitute victim of the Depression or chromosomal defects.

Humoring our optimism, we liberated these photos from copper-clad firewood box for Fiona to comment upon. She was nodding the afternoon away like a hothouse orchid in the solarium, where a health aide jotted down vital signs. "She's doing great!" was the professional assessment. Heaven help anyone doing poorly! Grandma, conveniently for us, was in high-functioning fettle, berating departed nurse's bossy attitude. I promised with the usual bad faith to discuss it with the agency, and Millie had her leaf through the pictures, wincing as Grandma plastered fingerprints all over them.

She was seemingly on autopilot, unmindful of the images she pawed at; and after she'd stared vacantly past the last, Millie, a conservator at heart, snatched them off the fleece blanket on Fiona's lap. Fiona prolonged her unblinking hundred-mile stare, but may have been responding to visual input when she recited apparent oldfangled aphorism, "The frog's plug-ugly to the tadpole, and they're both plug-ugly to the devilfish!"

The oracle had spoken, and favored us with no more. Back to the geriatric deeps! However, photo tour of New England bidonville must have registered on some psychic level because her erratic behavior immediately escalated. When she demanded her "rightful tiara" at dinner, Millie cleverly prevented a scene by plucking silver cardboard coronet from around a candlestick holder on the buffet. Party Store trinket had "Birthday Babe" emblazoned across it and had sat there since Fiona's eightieth. It did the trick, thank God, and henceforth adorned Fiona's wondrously luxurious hair, morning till night.

The amateur shrink in me diagnosed ensuing quirks as reversion to childhood, and squinting between the lines, I gathered she'd spent that childhood in the derelict setting of those Kodak moments. From out of the blue she channeled preteen trauma, histrionic adolescence. Won't Grandpa ever come out of the water again? I don't wanna go to school, they're mean on the bus to Rowley! Those goddamned G-men, I hate 'em, they burnt down Uncle Eb's cannery! Daddy, will Grandpa be okay? They said they're gonna torpedo the reef! Jesus, I grimaced, were these flashbacks to a real and ghastly upbringing, or to highlights of radio dramas?

Either way, plain English was rare amidst pure gabbling. She often regressed to baby talk, or a facsimile thereof, except that she repeated nonsense syllables with increasing vexation, till she clamped her dentures together and glared in disgust at our stupid lack of comprehension. Or during cheerier spells the gibberish better resembled uncouth language because it supplied the lyrics to quavery, keyless songs.

Once, in the kitchen, a girl from social services removed Fiona's coronet to brush her hair, then recrowned her and held up a mirror for Fiona's approval. She promptly broke into a sort of jaunty revival-tent hymn in articulate English, which made it no more intelligible. Offhand I recall the couplet, "We'll all wear the gold tiara by and by, / In the kingdom hidden from the sky." The helper found this performance "cute." I refrained from disagreeing, as I had no handier term for it.

I also had to admit my poor grasp of the aging process. Physical and cognitive signs had been advancing in tandem, but were bulging eyes, hoarse mouth-breathing, and wattles spreading from under her chin to encompass her carotids "normal," no big deal? Spot check by an RN ruled out circulatory, ocular, or respiratory degeneration, though I'd say she was a tad glib dismissing my concerns as nothing that couldn't wait till regular office visit.

Supposing Fiona were technically "fine," she could linger indefinitely, a strong heartbeat in a soulless vessel. And supposing she outlasted her trust fund? House and assets would be forfeit, she'd vegetate in "assisted living," and we'd be out on our ears. The lesser evil, our best option, boiled down to strengthening joint bank account with Fiona, via family friend Mr. Crocker, an antiques dealer who'd been after Fiona's heirlooms for decades. A stopgap measure, but an extra month or two of solvency might prove key in deciding where Fiona died, in whether we'd be homeless or not.

Granted, in selling Fiona's valuables we'd be going over her unsound head, and it was in Mr. Crocker's interests not to question she was in no condition to receive guests. He let us sell him Civil War swords, Bakelite radios, and first editions of Washington Irving and William Cullen Bryant from rooms off Fiona's beaten path, and then the tic possessed him, as it did at fraught moments, of flexing Adam's apple as if his turtleneck collar constricted it.

"You know, I was just curious," he hemmed, "about your grandmother's jewelry, specifically some artifacts in white gold, with designs of marine animals. I saw a necklace, a brooch, and a bracelet once upon a time, but she never wanted to discuss them again." The corners of his mouth flicked up and down, as if smiling might be inappropriate.

I, meanwhile, could scarcely mask my amazement at his want-list duplicating ours, singling out moray pendant among countless items. It was the jackpot whenever Millie and I went ferreting, but had evaded us in Fiona's bedroom bureau, nightstand, and vanity, every logical nook where she might have switched it with lifeline necklace. Ergo it had to be somewhere illogical, and our search widened till nowhere indoors was too far-fetched. Except now, our singular treasure had become part of a trove.

"You can see what it's like here," Millie leapt in. "We've no idea where to hunt for anything." She shot me a cautionary glance, and I scowled right back. As if I'd blab about the pendant before he volunteered why it was so special! "We'll be on the lookout, though I'm not sure we have enough to go on," she hinted.

"Well, if any of it comes to light, I'd be interested," parried Mr. Crocker, who perhaps had no more to say on the subject simply because we wanted him to say more. Subtle old hustler would have been delighted at steering us into redoubling our search efforts. Amidst mounting frustration, I entertained possibilities rejected as harebrained days ago, such as inspecting musty stacks of books and magazines in a corner of Fiona's bedroom for cavities carved out of pages.

Not halfway through Edwardian bodice-rippers and flaking *Harper's Bazaars,* the cover of a quarto-sized scrapbook was repulsively tacky, but within its frame of tooled-leather cherubs and garlands a square of cardboard had been pasted, containing in graceful calligraphy "My Cape Ann Atlantis." The yellow clippings on black cardstock paper were from Newburyport, Gloucester, and Salem dailies of the 1930s, and surrounded Fiona with a wealth of context, as priceless in its own right, and as baffling, as her elusive jewelry.

Above the first articles, a heading in glittery silver ink was cribbed from racially insensitive lyrics, revealing not only that Fiona was a child of less enlightened era, but that she no longer dwelt "Way Down on de Manuxet Ribber, Far, Far Away." Had teenage Fiona been collating news to remind her why, or make her grateful, the folks had pulled up stakes from native turf? A recent Highway Department map of Massachusetts confirmed my lifelong perception of no towns whatsoever on the Manuxet, which we crossed on drives between Ipswich and Gloucester.

Nonetheless, area journalists used to situate benighted Innsmouth on the river's estuary, and Fiona's snapshots of Swamp Yankee slum fit verbal descriptions to a T. An undertone of bluenose disapproval united all the reportage, along with mention of a 1927 bootlegging raid by the Feds implicating virtually every resident. The stories, to me, smacked of kicking the populace while it was down, all but gloating at labor-law violations, gold smuggling, "miscegenation," vice-squad raids, and barbaric occultism among a skid-row minority who hadn't joined the exodus with Fiona's people.

The last block of column inches, followed by a slew of blank sheets, explained Fiona's reference to Atlantis and the town's absence from modern records. The severest mayhem from the infamous Hurricane of '38 rated only tardy, indifferent shrift, almost as an afterthought, buried next to the funnies, as slapdash scissoring attested. Just up the coast from Gloucester, which had withstood an unprecedented 50-foot wave, corrupt, fading Innsmouth had been annihilated, swallowed whole by storm surge, muck and shallows in its stead. The authorities, busy in more respectable locales, hadn't noticed, or chosen to notice, for weeks.

In the same silver penmanship, the remark "Alas!" below the write-up may or may not have been ironic. Regardless, it was plausibly the most sympathy Innsmouth ever garnered. Fiona must have disavowed unsavory roots successfully enough to marry into Brahmins, yet kept tabs on former co-citizens. She'd also retained black-and-white proof of at least one excursion to ancestral seat, albeit filed among kindling. To whatever purpose, Fiona had done her bit, ambivalent as it was, to commemorate Innsmouth, when everyone else was gleefully consigning it to oblivion.

As if merely pronouncing "Innsmouth" in Fiona's house had worked grotesque magic, come suppertime she bore unnerving new resemblance to her companion in the photo. Beyond the scaly inflammation and bug eyes they already shared, her lips mimicked the rubbery swelling of excess Botox, and she acted unused to them, making us cringe at half-chewed calf's liver and Brussels sprouts that plopped from clumsy mouth. And the Innsmouth yokel's bloat was manifest in Fiona's cheeks and hands, rendering her ham-fisted with the cutlery. Millie discerned hypoxic blue finger above gold wedding band, screeched, and ran for the hacksaw.

For once, inspiration blossomed in timely fashion, versus hours later. I fetched hand mirror and held it for Fiona to admire herself, while Millie pinned down flaccid wrist and with gliding, precise strokes notched the ring deep enough to snap off with pliers. Fiona's reflection distracted her throughout the procedure, and in rhythm with the saw teeth she warbled, "Fare thee well to the tadpole tail, / Soon you'll change your skin for scales."

The tune would have been more at home in a log cabin than a saltbox, and the lyrics more at home with Moondog than Grandma. Then, predictably, the notes went minor-key haywire, and folksy vernacular lapsed into drivel. The performance continued as long as mirror confronted her, and she was blithely unaware of severed ring snatched from finger, of finger sluggishly reverting to normal pallor.

Afterward, she'd cuss out whoever had just been around for stealing unwearable ring, till we risked making it one more object to confuse with emergency pendant by attaching it to a chain around her neck. There it was in plain view and constant contact, but not even that curbed the accusations.

For all our piecemeal insights into Fiona's ill-starred birthplace and its obliteration, we had yet to get a cogent handle on the reality of Innsmouth. Metamorphosis and marine allusions figured in its arcane creed, conceivably grounded in genetic disorder bequeathing froglike features, as extrapolated from a single snapshot. And into what overall vision could we connect these few dots? As young Fiona might have sighed, Alas! Potential revelations about my family, about this region, maybe about mermaids and mythic seaside ilk sank as irretrievably in AD 1938 as they would have in 1,000,000 BC.

At best we can deduce and speculate and grasp at straws spewed from grudging fathoms, at taunting glimpses of submerged eons. What vexing gaps in human evolution, in cultural milestones might be bridged if ocean bed that had been coastlands in the past two million years were accessible? Before my stint as librarian was defunded, examples to this effect in *Scientific American* captivated me for no explicit reason.

I daydreamed of touring Doggerland, prime real estate between England and Denmark for millennia after the Ice Age, till insidiously rising oceans put it under 400 feet of North Sea. A few flint tools and butchered soup bones caught in trawler nets couldn't begin to flesh out the societies, the technologies, the bloodlines extinct now or flowing in extant Europeans, on what its occupants would've believed had always been and would be *terra firma*. And cruelly, sixty-odd fathoms blot out any credit Doggerland deserves for paving the way toward civilization.

Even more fascinating for its novel perspective on human origins was the infamous "aquatic ape theory," which posited a water-dwelling phase among our precursors to account for otherwise pointless adaptations in *Homo sapiens,* such as distribution of body hair, a layer of buoyant fat, the ability of newborns to swim. Anthropologists were content to ignore rather than confute the theory, partly because lowly amateurs had propounded it, partly because it lacked fossil proof. And this in a discipline with the caveat, "Absence of evidence is not evidence of absence!"

That evidence might well be entombed off East Africa, India, China. Of course, science stands better chance of discovering archaic germs on Mars than of ever unlocking secrets in offshore silt. But to play out schismatic implications, how profoundly could aquatic apes have acclimated to high seas? Could some have swum out past tidal zone, never to return except in legendary encounters with earthbound cousins? And to brainstorm recklessly, could recessive genes from prehuman epochs still regroup in especially inbred backwaters like Innsmouth?

Not that mapping the genes behind ostensible Innsmouth syndrome would help identify artisans of marine-themed jewelry, or Fiona's hidey-hole for it. And the pressure was on, as her voluble phase of senility was already proving a false bottom. Despite spillage from uncooperative lips, that supper of calf's liver had been the last she'd attacked with robust appetite. Every meal thereafter, however much we harangued or enticed her with surefire favorites, met with a few half-hearted bites, and she pushed the rest around with indifferent fork.

What's more, no matter the menu, the dining room or anywhere she occupied for a minute smelled of acrid fish, killing our appetites too. Chalk it up to undermanaged hygiene or progressive disease or the increasingly protean face of "normal aging," the reek served as miserable reminder of how ill-equipped we were for dealing with, bluntly expressed, a basket case, maybe for a week, maybe months. Who could tell, when we hadn't a clue why she'd survived this long?

Up to now we only thought we'd felt trapped and desperate, and going forward, our meager plan amounted to begging social services for more expert, full-time reinforcements. True to bureaucratic stereotype, they hedged and stalled, but at least we'd made such conscientious noises they couldn't charge us outright with elder neglect, could they? Meanwhile, the party unlikeliest to denounce us was Fiona, who spoke more seldom than she ate.

Her guttering self had turned yet further inward, circling the eleventh-hour wagons, as if showing mortality her disdainful back. Hers, for all I knew, was an enviably rich and happy dream state, wishes fulfilled, absent friends resurrected. Or recalling the daftness she'd been wont to spout, was she a crazed Alice confined to a looking-glass realm of distorted, harrowing memories? None of it was readable in slack jaw, lolling neck, palsied shuffle.

Millie I spied at odd intervals gaping into nowhere, or into a boundless gulf of more intimate caregiving than she'd signed on for, potentially a marital deal-breaker, or so I parsed from nonstop petulance, one-word answers to my attempts at reaching out. I resented Fiona no less on musing that, with my luck, she'd die the same day Millie procured a divorce decree.

I guess neither of us could clamp a lid forever on seething resentment by badmouthing Fiona in the privacy of carriage house. And I don't fault Millie for her role in the greater good, really, of hastening the inevitable. She'd been lobbying to cut down on one expense anyway by canceling the lifeline contract, since Fiona, we agreed, no longer realized she had the pendant. It's only that if Millie had maybe set a less imperious tone, I'd have behaved differently too.

Fiona had performed daily miracle of inching walker into breakfast nook, and went through autopilot motions of downing a spoonful of oatmeal, a sip of coffee. I was thoroughly convinced Fiona's hands and wattled neck on starvation diet were contrarily fatter and not just swollen, though Millie was incredulous. She can be so blinkered by preconceptions, and worse, harbors no faith that seeing is believing.

Fiona had already subsided into morose, wilting stupor, and the contrast with her vibrant girlhood, with everyone's halcyon mood, feigned or not, in olden photos, sent a pang through my heart, a lump to my throat. Could none of that sunny outlook withstand the decades, nary a mote of happiness once in a blue moon to leaven the bitterness, the lethargy? Today's Fiona was like a betrayal, an affront to the game youth in black sheepskin, a morbid shadow of doubt marring my confidence in aging gracefully.

My anger at her, I'll freely admit, was misguided, as was Millie's impromptu bid to achieve our cost-saving measure. She loomed over unblinking matriarch and went to grab necklace chain, announcing, "Grandma Fiona, I think you're right. That whoozis isn't doing you any good. Let's not waste money on it."

Fiona came to alarming life, clutching at plastic pendant with animal ferocity. "This is my birthright!" she bawled, glaring white heat at us, the most engaged with anybody she'd been all summer. "This goes home with me!"

"What the hell are you talking about?" I exploded, as if at a willfully oppositional child. Millie lurched back from the both of us, unprepared for the fireworks she'd sparked. "Yes or no, are you really out of it or would you be able to use your damn whoozis if you had to?"

"You're not one of us! You're not entitled! Get out of my purview, you and your lousy groundling wife!" Huh? To what exactly, besides my vitriol, was Fiona responding? What words had she hallucinated issuing from my mouth?

"Come on," groundling wife urged me. "If Fiona wants quiet time, we can accommodate her." Millie reached out to take my arm till something in my face stopped her. I was pissed off, yes, but I don't remember feeling as formidable as all that. And I did oblige her.

"Ugly little tadpoles!" Fiona snarled at us. "Begone!" Those few steps to the doorway lowered my blood pressure appreciably, and I sighed in resignation at Fiona sitting up straight, supercharged with indignation, a queenly degree of resolve suffusing ruddy countenance. How sad that derangement alone had power to revitalize her.

At noon she hadn't budged, marble-statue focus intact, ignoring cold oatmeal and coffee and me. Incredibly, the pathetic tiara designating Fiona "Birthday Babe" didn't undercut her regality. After lunch, from the study where I wrote checks for utilities, I overheard arrivals of a nurse's aide and lesion-care specialist. They didn't seek me out, so Millie must have fielded their complaints about Fiona's noncompliance. The wife, in any event, was hurling fed-up invective, muffled by intervening walls, at 1:40 P.M.; Grandma made no audible reply.

Midafternoon, Millie barged into walk-in closet where I was stuffing Fiona's more mildewy vintage gowns into garbage bags, and history repeated itself: the shock in store wasn't the one we'd expected. Fiona hadn't simply died at table while sticking to her inscrutable guns, no, she'd disappeared from the house altogether.

How literal a disappearance was this? Walker was still beside breakfast-nook chair. Emergency necklace was bunched up on the walker's plastic shelf. The tiara she'd kept. For her to surrender fiercely defended "birthright" was perplexing; clinging to chintzy cardboard headgear was poignant. I was also more heartsick about her than anticipated, considering our decayed relations, but not heartsick enough to stall the wheels spinning between my ears, buzzing that if Fiona wasn't indoors, she had to be outside, absurd but true.

I lit out back and toward the ocean as if no other direction existed, Millie at my heels. I overlooked her insolence in shouting, "What makes you so sure she went this way?" Nor did I ponder why that was insolent, or why my certainty grew at beholding daytime full moon, low above the seaward horizon, whitish gold like a medallion. Both of us had plainly suspended disbelief in Fiona covering this much distance, whether on shank's mare or all fours.

We scrambled across hard-packed sand rootbound by coarse, shin-high grass, down zigzag path among compact dunes, and onto broad pungent flats, soon after ebbtide. Millie wisely forbore harping on the absence of evidence Fiona had preceded us. Maybe geriatric husk was airborne on westerly gusts? Ahead, the berm became piebald with smooth, flat outcrops of bluish stone. A tidal pool in one of these was minutes from inundation by advancing wavelets.

At first I presumed its surface mirrored the 14-karat moon, but no, genuine gold shone below, entangled by clump of ultrafine seaweed, which was actually grey bouffant. And embedded within, sodden shiny cardboard established Fiona had indeed been here, and had sported a hefty wig, night and day, for years. "What the hell," muttered Millie, gawking into the pool. I'd bet she too was mystified we'd never caught the scent of unwashed hairpiece. Or had Fiona shed a portion of her tadpole phase, in favor of new flesh incompatible with scalp?

I was of two minds about this notion, which struck me equally as fair interpretation and obtrusive lunacy. No inner conflict arose, though, about withholding flight of arrant whimsy from the wife. She, the diehard pragmatist, was kneeling at poolside and gingerly teasing submerged gold from sopping hair with one stalwart finger. To nobody's astonishment, she sprang up with moray pendant on gleaming chain, wagging it dry between thumb and forefinger, in her grin an unflattering cross of triumph and avarice. Fiona, in confusion, haste, or excitement, must have accidentally forsaken necklace along with coiffure that had ingeniously concealed it.

I was glad to have the artifact safe, but more compelling was the jumble of Fiona's flannel housedress and sweatpants and fuzzy slippers, some yards farther out, where the tide had risen so that each incoming ripple floated them for a second. The sea, from which she'd never ever strayed beyond earshot, had beckoned irresistibly, might well have dissolved her save for these non-bodily vestiges. Perhaps it had, given that stripping down to naked cranium fell outside textbook specs on senile wandering.

I soaked my loafers sloshing over for a closer look, though I shied from touching her clothes, even with my foot. "Jesus," Millie murmured, slipping her free hand in mine, "Fiona wanted to die pretty badly, didn't she?" Her other hand, I noted, was in blouse pocket, firmly gripping necklace.

These grasping petty groundlings, I found myself brooding, and then no less enigmatically I blurted, "Or she wanted so badly to live, and she's gone to be rejuvenated."

Millie had the gall to lean in and sniff my breath. I couldn't decide if she were joking, and maybe she couldn't either. I did know I was almost irritated enough to say something regrettable. Often nowadays, I can only stare askance at her and debate whether she and I aren't breeds apart.

Just as well our cellphones were in the house. To babble at 911 while contemplating the earthly last of Fiona would have felt irreverent, disrespectful. Millie trotted off to summon the authorities and left me on guard duty. They pulled in a minute after I dragged the garments to the lip of tidal pool to prevent them washing away. They formed a dam protecting the wig, which I still refused to handle.

Luckily for Millie and me, an exercise therapist had parked by the saltbox at the right moment to witness us dashing toward the beach, supporting our story of Fiona's incredible "death march," helping to eliminate us as "persons of interest." The cops could have been nicer searching the property for signs of foul play; Fiona's body remains MIA.

Brooch and bracelet remain missing too, and we've offered Mr. Crocker first-refusal privileges on them, via voicemail invitations to come ransack the place. We suspect the ambiguity of her parting spooks him out of returning our calls.

The everyday side of me is sorry for poor, batty Fiona, expending superhuman effort to drown herself. That side of me is reconciled to a marriage probably as good as any, and waits with patient optimism for probate court to award us house and assets. That side is despondent solely because it looked forward to a glorious head of nonagenarian hair, but Fiona's wig bodes otherwise.

Another nascent side of me relishes pernicious fantasies that Fiona waded to freedom and transformation, envies whatever she's become, has coined the trope she's gone to Doggerland. More fools we to dream of knowing Fiona better when there seemed less of her to know, as if photos and ephemera could reconstruct her total self. And what might it portend, when that nascent side of me can't go bald soon enough? House and assets may prove the least of my inheritance.

The Poor in Spirit

The wall was hulking, monumental, some might say Cyclopean, and because I'd plodded alongside it to and from work for years, invisible. On Islington Avenue, anyway, the ground was of greater concern, a half-mile-long grassy ribbon, instead of sidewalk, between wall and curb, bisected by a weaving dirt path, under the spotty shade of scattered sycamores. The unwary pedestrian risked tripping over roots and bumpy terrain or, thanks to negligent dog walkers, skidding in shit. Otherwise, welcome to a green respite from the genteel monotony of immaculate sidewalks, spiffy homes, prissy yards across the street and all over Elmcrest Hill.

The wall, in fact, only reentered visibility that November morning when it suddenly presented less to see. Slippery leaf litter covering the path and any Fido dung should have made me extra mindful of my footing, but a cavity, the width of a hatbox and right at eye level, was arresting, startling like a nineteen-gun salute. Its interior was black as an eye socket, too deep to gauge, with no clues handy to blame it on frost heaves, say, or vandalism. Conclusions I had none, or nothing beyond the bromide that no wall, however staunch, was really impervious to time, was it?

Likewise, however solid a history someone builds of his town through years of amassing data, so much goes unsuspected. Profound holes suddenly gape in the securest of understandings. Some robber-baron alum, I'd always presumed, hadn't scrupled at surrounding university athletic field with masonry that could wear down a battering ram; as an educated guess, it sounded legit. Deep pockets, in any event, had bought a rugged drywall masterpiece, from boulder foundations to gently tapering eight-foot height of fieldstones to shale-slab coping, smooth enough to bike upon.

These observations recurred as if by mental reflex as I grimaced at the hole each morning. And each morning the hole felt a little more atrocious, more grisly, like an untreated wound. Afterward a cloud of gloom followed me for seven workplace hours, reinforcing chronic discontent at wasting my potential as a lowly clerk at campus bookstore.

I'd have been more philosophic had this been a real bookstore at least; but no, half its shelf space had been sacrificed for a Starbucks knockoff, and a hunk more for an expansion of university-logo sweatshirts, mugs, teddy-bears, and worse. I might well kill a shift as barista or kitsch-monger, which hardly cushioned the irony of resorting to employment here only after prospects of mountainous debt forced me to drop out as a 3.5-average sophomore. Fortunately, trudging home I picked up no booster dose of gloom because it was already too dark for the cavity to show.

Not that morning downer ever wore off completely. Straddling a line between subliminal and bothersome, like a cold that wouldn't go away, it dragged on till I lost count of the days. Then finally the university, if only because campus eyesores ill-suited its august image, stepped in, though with results acutely more perturbing to me.

One sunny Monday the hole was plugged with rubble and mortar like a poultice, no surprise at this quickest of fixes, but obscuring the plug was a wreath, or anyway plastic lilies, roses, and carnations stapled to a Styrofoam ring, draped over a no-frills white cross, a.k.a. the top 18 inches of a fencepost for an upright, and another foot or so as crossbeam. A roadside memorial of this ilk wouldn't have rated a second glance next to crumpled guardrails or on phone poles at dangerous intersections, but on sedate Islington it was invasive, jarring, a colorful, déclassé sore thumb.

I couldn't picture a fatal crash in this placid neighborhood or detect any trace thereof unless the former hole qualified, which realistically it didn't. Nor could I see stuffy homeowners honoring traffic fatalities with painted fenceposts and plastic roses. But how else to account for this fetish of sorrow? No signage named the casualty.

A quarter-mile ahead, where Islington ended at right angle to busier Devoll Street, the grinding of a V-twin engine set my teeth on edge. From around a clump of bushes at the corner swerved a sit-down mower, marring pristine 8 A.M., and had I been two minutes earlier, I might have become collateral damage of lawn care. In the bucket seat, lo and behold a fortyish classic hippie, ponytail and Van Dyke and shiny ear stud, hurtling toward us. And funny how I used "us," as if the plastered hole and I comprised two personalities.

I was keen on neither Woodstock affectations nor fumy noise pollution, ditto reckless endangerment by yard-crew clowns. But who would likelier be in the know about the wall's recent alterations? I put on my perkiest hypocritical smile and flagged him down.

He didn't visibly mind canning the racket for an unscheduled break. I told him my name was Stan, and gestured at the rough patch with an affable "So what happened here?"

He introduced himself as Bernie, blinked twice as if an inner sparkplug had misfired, and switched topical lanes. "Hey, you work at the bookstore, right? For like several years?"

"That's where I'm going now, yeah."

"Shame what they did with it! I hate setting foot in there anymore."

"Me too." Egad. Somehow this had come down to small talk, ungodly early as it was for personal interactions. Still and all, what a mood enhancer, meeting a kindred spirit where I'd expected a landscaper cowboy. "You live around here?"

"Ever since I was a student. The apple sure hasn't rolled far from the alma mater."

"Huh. What'd you major in then?"

He said something like "relly stew." I had to rifle mental drawers before that clicked as studentese for "religious studies." "Yep, that BA was great prep for manual labor."

Yikes, the manual laborer was better schooled than I was! Even his aggressive mowing became more understandable. Had different positions been open during our post-collegiate job-hunts, my malcontent self might well have filled the bucket seat, bearing down on him. "Reli stu," through youthful lens anyhow, may have seemed a rational choice, but to ask where he'd planned it to lead was scarcely sporting at this juncture.

Again he blanked out an instant, as if the record needle of his awareness had skipped a groove. "But you were curious about the wall? Bet you'd never guess it wasn't even university property till not so long ago."

He had me there, and as he swung out of the seat and planted boots on the grass, I worried he was nowhere near done with me. To cut him off right now, though, and fuss about punching in late would be pretty rude. I wished in vain for magic words to assert my interest in the hole, and the overlying memorial, and no more.

"Where we're standing was on the edge of town, cow country practically, when this wall went up. In fact, Andrew Jackson was president then. A local philanthropist, Rhett Eleazar Barron, made his fortune in the China trade and the first textile mills, and in his will donated some acreage to the city for a poor farm. And that was a big deal a hundred years before welfare and disability and Social Security; it was the whole safety net.

"Building this wall according to his specs was a condition of the will, for which he never gave a reason, maybe to allow the inmates more privacy, maybe to spare respectable people the sight of them. Those are the standard theories. Personally, I think he wanted a humongous wall to keep the farm in one piece, to discourage selling any of it to developers. And it worked, even after the last pauper died off in the 1950s, which made the farm a going proposition from Jackson's era till Sputnik went up."

We don't have paupers any more, do we? I mused. The homeless, panhandlers, outpatients, yes, but this last poor-farm "pauper" must have been a walking relic long before Elvis recorded "Jailhouse Rock."

"Ever since the city deeded this place to the university," Bernie rambled on, "it's remained intact, and it's still called Barron Field in a nod to the original owner."

Okay, that was enlightening. I'd never realized Barron Field was the official designation, buying into the received wisdom it was a punning critique of the loser jocks who trained there.

"Well, can't fall behind," he announced, boosting himself back into the saddle. "Back to the grind!"

"Yeah, me too." Did my tone insinuate he'd been the one making me late? Not that I cared if it did. I'd never seen him before, and why assume I would again? But then in this airtight terrarium of a town, I've never met someone once and once only. Them's the rules.

Thereafter I continued scraping by, as did Bernie I supposed, at the low range of incomes in this zip code, strapped for discretionary funds after paying rent on attic studio apartment off posh Smithy Square. Absurdly, it was the best deal I could find in hoofing distance from the bookstore. A car's no more affordable than a diploma. Dreams of saving enough to finish my degree, to acquire the scholastic credentials of slightly older guys in yard crews, had become the stuff of despair rather than deferment.

By the refined standards of this culture, this century, I was poor, and small consolation came of comparing what "poor" meant else-where or in Great-Grandpa's generation. Yet upward mobility, oppor-tunities for advancement, limited as they were for me, must have been microscopically rare for Barron Field occupants, in upshot serving out life sentences. Where to go outside their virtual prison except from bad to worse?

As armchair fatalist, of course, I operated purely on conjecture, and every slog along Islington conjured a bleaker unconfirmed image of poor-farm oppression. The mystery marker triggered the morbid question of whether the indigent dead received dignified burial, hasty potter's field consignment, or ignoble disposal in an intramural mass grave. Bernie, I bet, could have set me straight, were he only around, which he wasn't till autumn passed that tipping point when overnight winds stripped trees of last leaves and buffeted the painted cross askew but couldn't dislodge its nail from the mortar.

The season had turned to show its ugly side. This, however, scarcely camouflaged eyesores from administrative view, and a tacky shrine couldn't hope to fare better than a hole in a wall. Bernie, if any-one, should have been inured to the fate of anything out of decorous place around campus, since expunging it might be his job.

Yet the Bernie I approached through murky drizzle was patently no realist, for he was kneeling in wet, brown grass below the wall's cement blemish, newly bereft of flowery tribute, which had melted away like the ice-cream cake it resembled. His knuckles pounded the dirt, and with sharp hiccups he choked off racking sobs, hoarsely in-haling to hurl invective in perplexingly Irish cadences at the cement. Out of the torrent I distinguished, "Can the bloody bastards let us have nothing?" Jesus, it's not as if he'd put up the memorial himself, was it?

I wasn't about to ask, opting to give him wide berth before im-pinging on his radar. Too late! His look darted toward me, angst-laden as if he'd been caught red-handed. Then he hopped to his feet with an instant cancellation of affect, as outwardly easy as switching TV channels, oblivious to the tears in his beard. I tried for an empathetic smile.

The immediate past was cancelled out, or was he his "old self" again? "How you doing?" he greeted me. I didn't mind relaunching this encounter from scratch. And amazingly, my burning question for him sprang to mind.

"Bernie, hi. I've been meaning to ask, when you refer to a 'poorfarm,' is that just an expression, or did actual farming happen?" Workplace punctuality paled in importance next to satisfying myself Bernie wouldn't relapse into hysterics and run amok.

"They called it that because that's what it was," he clarified, brushing flecks of leaf off jumpsuit shins with an air of cluelessness as to how they'd gotten there. "Unlike urban farming nowadays, it wasn't for eco-friendly liberals, but it was progressive for the time, and it could accommodate two hundred down-and-outers. The sale of milk and eggs and vegetables helped pay operating costs, and sometimes it earned a profit." His head twisted aside, toward the mortar patch, and bookish objectivity gave way to bitter editorializing. "And for all that, the grub year-in, year-out was bread and gristle!"

"Gristle? Really?" Seemed a baldly visceral detail to glean from official records.

Another tic of the neck, and he was facing me again. "I wonder how closely they'd identify with the underprivileged of today." The flare-up over food, like his conniptions over the cross, was no sooner done than forgotten. My urge to clock in ASAP was gathering steam.

Nor had he raised an issue that could bear contemplation without growing thornier by the second. For starters, how to define "underprivileged"? Did we include pensioners choosing between food and meds, the "working poor," the long-term ex-employed, ourselves? I shrugged resignedly and opined, "Guess it's not ours to know." Bernie's piercing stare may have accounted for the feeling I'd uttered famous last words. I couldn't explain it otherwise and tossed off parting niceties, first to insinuate today who was putting whom behind.

I did and didn't ever want our paths to cross again. No doubt I'd hardly skimmed his wealth of knowledge about Barron Field, and his fascination with it was contagious. On the other hand, my prior impression of Bernie as lawn-mowing maven on local lore wasn't the whole story either, and I couldn't ditch a wrongheaded notion that whatever troubled the waters of his psyche might also prove contagious.

Maybe his remark about identifying with the inmates wasn't altogether casual. He, like me, may have pondered whether we qualified, or soon would, as poor. And like me, was he also uncomfortable fancying himself in the same ballpark as grossly more downtrodden forebears? Yes or no, outside this marginal common ground, he remained a 99% unknown quantity. Proceed with caution!

What's more, I suspected his sympathies with the bygone destitute extended to channeling them, or their undeparted souls, in response to hopelessly recondite cues. He'd exhibited two separate personalities in as many minutes, right? Given the context of nineteenth-century poverty, an Irish accent fit the bill. I further suspected his alter ego could only get scarier, the better his grounding in Early American hardship.

I wouldn't put it past me to pretend I'd formed these suspicions before Bernie went into harrowing tailspin, to frame myself as smarter, more intuitive than I am. I did definitely try retracing his mental steps to the conclusion that his nine-to-five was haunted, that his mortal shell served as ghostly guesthouse. I had only to surmise he believed in ghosts and in their residency at Barron Field, and since I could well believe the same, these weren't quantum leaps of faith, were they?

How could some residue of abject spirits not cling to the acreage, a haven for six generations of abject bodies by the hundreds? Poor-farm structures had been flattened pre-JFK, but perimeter walls had not, and may have demoralized would-be runaways during miserable lives and afterlives alike. Besides, within the walls, mightn't defunct occupants continue inhabiting architecture as defunct as they? I wish I'd thought to ask Bernie for any anecdotes of raggedy spooks terrorizing students on the running tracks or hockey rink. And heck, why not ectoplasmic cows and chickens?

But regrettably, my last civil exchange with Bernie was behind me. The Tuesday before Thanksgiving dawned Arctic clear, and sounds carried extra far in the bone-dry air. On Islington, dull, dogged thudding was audible several blocks away, and no mystery who the responsible party must have been while he was yet a grainy, agitated speck. His wheezing imprecations were soon audible, and then I discerned him bashing a grenade-shaped rock against the mortar plug. Now that he was wielding a blunt weapon, I was especially leery of announcing myself.

Craven of me to cross the street, but I preferred repenting at healthy leisure over tempting physical harm to no good purpose. In the shadows of houses, skulking from tree to tree, I practically tiptoed even after grasping I'd need a bullhorn to win Bernie's attention. When he was directly opposite, I paused to listen, leaning back against a high boxwood hedge as if I had chameleon powers to blend in. Amidst the garbled invective, Bernie, whose brogue imparted he "wasn't himself" once more, bawled, "My pals can't get out! My girl can't get out!" He'd pummeled out a soupbowl-sized pocket and slaved away as if rescuing trapped miners.

We must have been comparably absorbed, he in his exertions and I in watching them; for we were both startled when three guys in jumpsuits like Bernie's, though manifestly his higher-ups, swooped in from apparent nowhere. They had to yell and wave their arms before he whipped around, with a full-body shudder as if he'd stepped on a live wire. They berated him into dropping the hammerstone, and his sunken shoulders bespoke an escapee nabbed by guards.

To read anything uncanny into this tableau would be ridiculous. And thank God he hadn't answered brickbats with a cobble! Bernie had cracked under pressure economic or existential, plain as that, however complex the precipitating factors. Still, I arbitrarily saw him as I felt he saw himself, a postmortem deadbeat, and from there, no big strain to see ranking coworkers as postmortem warders. After all, if phantom denizens dwelt in phantom housing, fair enough to posit phantom orderlies abiding to bully them.

As they led him away, he cast about for one last eyeful of the outside world. He homed in on me and crammed a bonfire's worth of glaring into a heartbeat. Did he reckon I'd betrayed him or simply resent my freedom of movement? The impact of his rancor turned my legs to clay a minute, and when I did begin trailing his tight-lipped group, my knees were unsteady as if I waded through their choppy wake.

I weathered more unsteadiness at realizing Bernie's mere ten words had made my case, had certified he was, or considered himself, possessed. What else to infer from uproar about pals, about his girl, bound by an enclosure breached on two sides decades ago for driveways and parking, a woefully dysfunctional barrier unless Bernie's were a vision mired in the past? The chintzy cross had to be his, or his alter ego's, to commemorate inmates who'd died anonymous and unmourned; he, like me, had evidently brooded on the quality of their final arrangements.

And that temporary hole, to lend unquiet ectoplasm an escape hatch, or even enter otherworldly awareness, must have come of actions divorced from modernity, no bulldozers or jackhammers. Otherwise, Barron Field's deceased would have stampeded as soon as any square foot of wall was dismantled, whereas I had it from the defunct horse's mouth that friends and girlfriend still languished in posthumous custody.

As Bernie and the orderlies hung a left onto Moses Avenue, hypothetically en route to whatever service entrance used to be the asylum gate, I couldn't tell if a forlorn last-second glance at me were Bernie's or his passenger's. More jarring, I only now apprehended how contagious his brainwaves were, how much I'd built from them, treating them like valid facts, granting I'd correctly second-guessed his delusions.

I did correctly guess we'd never meet again on Islington. I wish I could have verified he was posing as a ghost that knew it was a ghost, as implied by nonextant persona mounting a memorial to nonextant peers. But wherever Bernie was, Thanksgiving traditionally guaranteed I wouldn't be going anywhere to see anyone. And if, miraculously, he hadn't gotten the axe, I'd be none the wiser because my jaunts to work were off till Monday. Among the bookstore's few virtues was its disregard for Black Friday, its unceremonious shutdown for the four days campus was deserted.

I, on the other hand, was effectively housebound, no one to spend the holiday with, and loath to overspend at a restaurant on a depressing table for one. Thanksgiving was always my least favorite holiday anyhow, nothing more to me than sanctified gluttony, and what the hell was I feeling thankful about? Okay, I wasn't locked up on a poor farm, I wasn't out of a job or out of my mind like Bernie, not that these were blessings so much as happy rolls of the dice.

All the same, despite holing up in my fuggy closet of an apartment, I did celebrate along more authentic lines than most of America, in substance if not in sentiment. Against a background of holiday-themed sitcoms, *Bewitched, Beverly Hillbillies, Bob Newhart* on the "classic" digital channels, I tackled a four-pack of high-test brew, an imperial stout, pumpkin-infused yet. The first Thanksgiving feast would have been a total bust without kegs galore. The pilgrims had beer for breakfast, fergodsakes, women and children too, unless they could afford brandy. And indeed, one bottle down, my kindred feelings toward Plymouth forefathers warmed significantly.

I was picking up the church key, congratulating myself on an especially tasty remedy for annual bummer, when pounding at the door wrought instant buzzkill, accompanied by hysterical bellowing. "Stan! They're after me! I'm in need of a hideyhole!" Speak of the devil! Gonzo Bernie, in full-blown Gaelic bluster, had sniffed me out, a feat that in itself argued for supernatural guidance, since he'd tracked me down without knowledge of my surname or my bona fide forename.

"Are you deaf, man? Open up!" Then again, to my layman's ears, it was transparently bogus "stage Irish" he was spouting, a travesty of natural usage. Bottom line, regardless: like hell was I going to open up or be at home to him, whether or not spectral X-ray vision had me dead to rights. I'd padded up to the door, paltry inches from raving meltdown, ineptly trying to gauge how much of *Newhart* would carry into the hall, oblivious to holding my breath behind slack lips till I drew a strangled gasp.

"By damn, but I hear voices in there! Am I not getting through to you? Can I not? You with your soft life in a shop and a roof over your head and a bed of your own! Too good for the likes of me, are ye?" Baiting me to let him in struck me as the tactic of a treacherous disposition; sorry, Bernie, anyone with a Bachelors, even in Reli Stu, should have seen that one backfiring. How much education, though, could a penniless Gael have enjoyed?

"You've no clue how it is! We have a jail, did ye know that, boyo? Our own jail, a jail within a jail if you follow me, and a regular pesthouse it is, but a palace beside the maniac cells. That's where the screws put you, in with the loonies, if you stand up for yourself. That's where they tried putting me, and it was me or them, but I got the drop on 'em, on three of them, and out the gate like a shot, but now it's the gallows sure if you don't help me!"

The boastful vein amid the desperation was almost as unnerving as Bernie's implicit confession, without even touching on jailbreak as pure figment versus a basis in pathologically distorted reality, including a body count. Flabbergasted, I nearly gave the game away by shouting, "You mean to say you killed somebody?" I caught the first syllable while it was still a glottal stop in my throat, and had to wonder if I should award Bernie's inner fugitive higher marks for manipulation.

"Are ye lily-livered, begad? Or just in your cups, is it, too soused to grovel up to the doorknob?" Yeah, I could go along with that, an easy enough out, and saints preserve me, I had to stifle myself once more, on the brink of blundering, "Yes, that's it!" He had me more flustered than I cared to admit.

"Is that music in there? Do I mistake the swellings of an orchestra? The laughter of a merry gathering? Is it a party you're throwing, with food and drink, and you pretending not to hear me, and me parched and famished?" Damn those blaring canned laughs and music cues! Now I was the one getting hot under the collar. How the hell long could he yammer, galling the other tenants, before my non-verbal message of non-engagement sank in?

A bated hiatus misled me into hoping for the best, before a last-ditch spate of pounding shook the door. "They're coming! This is on your head, ye cowardly shite!" Were "they" another illusory symptom of paranoia, schizophrenia, whatever? My ears registered nothing of "them," unless my kettle-drum pulse and the *Newhart* end theme conspired to drown "them" out.

Exasperation had sustained me through our stalemate, and then it ebbed away and I deflated into frailty as Doc Martens footfalls stomped down the stairs, leavened with ranting profanities. Front door slammed with a vengeance and brought home how close a shave I'd had, how much grief I'd have courted welcoming him in: at best, obstruction charges for harboring a wanted man; at worst, death or a mauling, should I have dared try to eject or otherwise cross him. Rooted to the spot, I swayed like a tree about to topple, aquiver like PTSD in aspic.

Revulsion at an '80s *Garfield* cartoon spurred me into action. Grab the remote! Better to zone out at this week's hundredth airing of *Miracle on 34th Street,* though I couldn't focus on the screen for all that reeled across my mind's eye. Flashing back to when our sights previously locked, I appreciated my shave had been way closer than first estimated. If I'd read his expression aright, he had me pegged as an informer, under whatever pretext, so yes, he'd beseeched me for protection, but I'd have been at his mercy once he was inside, and he with a score to settle.

But if his heated look contained room for interpretation, plainspoken contempt at my "soft life" did not, as if labeling myself poor were an affront, and I a fraudster just because being poor now didn't involve being as poor as being poor then. And reflecting how a 150-year-old Irishman was really a guise for Bernie's maladjustment, he had some nerve venting spleen at me, since his wages were very likely higher than mine, or at least had been till getting fired lent him even keener empathy with yesteryear's insolvents.

Whether poor-farm persona hated me for alleged betrayal, or Bernie resented me watching him hauled off in disgrace, he'd been at leisure ever after to tail me from the bookstore or learn my address by happenstance. No paranormal intervention required! This dismal Thanksgiving, he too may have been "in his cups," and pissed off that I was on a payroll and he wasn't. The most esoteric details about Barron Field didn't prove him possessed. Maybe there had been "maniac cells," and claiming he'd been condemned to them maybe amounted to an indirect admission of psychosis.

I retrieved the church key and was soon toasting my success at downgrading Bernie to a "loony" for good and all, certainly not a vessel of spirit anguish. But come Black Friday, the news at noon that should have cemented this verdict only convinced me I'd oversimplified him as a phenomenon, done him a profound disservice. He handily upstaged the typical headlines of annual retail-sector carnage, of have-nots fighting tooth-and-nail to have a deep-discount thing or three more, at what price dignity? I was also hard-pressed to stave off self-reproach at my defects as "brother's keeper."

In boilerplate TV parlance, police responded to complaints Thursday evening from residents in the capital city's Elmcrest section, where a bearded white male was attacking a stone wall with a pickaxe while yelling hysterically. The man disobeyed police orders to drop his weapon and shouted at them in a foreign language, which one officer, with family in Galway, maintained was Gaelic. The visuals consisted of murky, mute dashcam footage of Bernie, obliquely lit by headlights, shaky, frantic.

I had to say, he'd been delving mightily, like someone who'd been around to dig the Erie Canal, and he'd already reinstated the cavity's hatbox diameter. And if I alone took note of his handiwork, I alone would have noted the optical quirk it encircled, the fault of random vibration grazing the dashcam, perhaps, or electrical-system glitch in the headlights. It came across as a wobbling silhouette in the cavity, like a bubble in a syringe or a ball riding the chute in a daily-numbers drawing, except this I'd have missed had I blinked.

Vagrant impression of the silhouette behaving furtively distracted me till Bernie hefted his pickaxe in a display I parsed as saber-rattling, and the police opened fire. The picture at this instant switched to a buff, slick reporter in rayon finery, prating by broad daylight against the background of asylum wall. He confirmed the man was pronounced DOA at Mount Hope Hospital. Authorities released the name of the deceased as Bernhard Hesselhof. His motives remained a mystery. The officers' names were not disclosed, pending a review.

Damn, a rare excuse to be smug, insofar as who else was wise to Bernie's motives? But I had no stomach for it. On the flip side, to shoulder blame for Bernie's demise, to repent of shutting him out would have been gutless of me. The cops, and not I, had shot him, yet another case of exerting deadly force against the mentally infirm, against scary "otherness." Had cops from the benighted age of "maniac cells" been as quick to waive sympathy for the expressly deranged, to execute them before exhausting sublethal measures?

Conversely, as a noncombatant John Doe, I'd had to err on the side of caution around someone committed to a "maniac cell," or under a delusion to that effect. No telling how far I'd have accidentally pushed him, and me unarmed, unversed in self-defense. He didn't belong in my parlor, no debate there, unlike my indecision over who, exactly, had come knocking. Bernhard Hesselhof didn't sound like someone from a household that would lapse into Gaelic under stress.

And dicier as a cornerstone of belief, but weighing ever more heavily as a nagging enigma, was that brief shift of darkness in the hole, like a will-o'-the-wisp in eclipse. At each recollection I humanized it slightly further, both sorry for and queasy at the wretched skulking, as I saw it, of a soul toward freedom, lifespans after that freedom could fulfill any corporeal purpose. Whether I theorized dead Irishman's pal or paramour emerging was unimportant; to personify a trick of shadows per se signaled Bernie had won, had inveigled me into accepting a ghost had recruited unwitting flesh to smuggle comrades out of death-defying confinement.

From here it followed logically, if logic were involved, to ask where stray revenant or revenants were now. And with logic ever-waning I linked them to the changes out my window this drowsy Saturday after Black Friday. At curbside was a blue plank, sticking out of a fresh cap of asphalt that replaced a slab of sidewalk. The plank was twice the height of the hydrant on the other side of my building's driveway and, together with the bulging asphalt, reminded me of a marker over a grave mound.

I was too busy pondering why occult agencies had planted a cenotaph out front to entertain its more sensible origins in sewer connections or phone cables. Bernie had led those agencies to my address, and what did they mean showing me this somber display, what was I supposed to do? Would I appease them by adorning it with wreaths of plastic flowers, a memorial to asylum shut-ins, to Bernie?

Or were they staking a claim on me, as they had on him? Would I remember being possessed, which begged the questions of whether I heretofore had been, of whether possession could be differentiated, by me or anybody, from a fugue state? How else to explain the Glock on my nightstand? These were, as Bernie had demonstrated, not saintly underdogs who reciprocated our kindliness toward them. Rather, styling ourselves their latterday counterparts stirred their vitriol, as if we were aligned with their oppressors by the simple virtue of being alive.

I could argue, uselessly, how our playing field differs from theirs, our current prospects bleaker than Dad's or Gramps's, how I'd love contributing to charities, working for good causes, donating cans to food drives, were I not always so damn strapped. Jack up my rent again and I might wind up homeless, or definitely renting in a shittier neighborhood. But victims of old-school destitution aren't having any, deaf to nuanced positions on the relativism of poverty. Or worse, is their cognizance of me limited to my utility as a vessel? Begad!

Fists more imperious than Bernie's beat on the door, rouse me from Sunday afternoon nap, make me grateful for whatever circumstances put a semiautomatic on my nightstand. I stride from my pillbox of a bedroom and unceremoniously fling the door wide. Three strangers loom boldly as if blind to the gun I'm pointing. Their groundskeeper jumpsuits are dirty and rumpled as if from days of on-going wear. The foremost man, externally Hispanic, quips with a swagger unbefitting a groundskeeper, "Proud of the chase you've led us since Tuesday, I'll warrant, my bully Mick! Now come along peaceably; you've had your lark."

I could say, "Gentlemen, there's some mistake," or "Too late, I sent him packing," but their gravity warns they wouldn't buy it. Careless of me to forget about poor-farm screws pursuing fugitives! Right here I have to question if I am myself, for I'd never mow down three fellow creatures in cold blood. And Christ, what a mule kick for a little pistol, what a racket! Despite which, nobody drops, or even grimaces at multi-gunshot tinnitus. Judgmental frowns, in fact, only sour toward irritation or disappointment, though point-blank abdominal perforations bleed copiously.

I may be facing down seasoned veterans of Civil or Mexican-American War. With soldierly élan they've leveled handguns at my chest, and their spokesman scolds, "No more shenanigans! Drop your piece and step lively, or else!"

I comply, of course, and dagger-eyes testify I'm tempting fate by pausing to pull the door locked behind me. If any neighbors are home, nobody's peeking out to investigate the small-caliber ruckus. I hear myself mutter, "Cowardly shites!" Ah yes, Bernie's parting shot at me, and why did bullets snuff him out and not my escorts?

I mull the likelihood, as we trudge in tight formation with a steel muzzle to my spine, that the "bully Mick" is a Machiavelli among beggars, embroiling me in a scheme to substitute a mortal for himself, wherein Bernie's death was integral or just a minor setback. As we near the corner of asylum wall at Islington and Moses, I can't feel too bad about wracking my brains with nary an insight into his putative scheme, since he's spent a century and then some in conniving.

Our cozy group continues down Moses along the everlasting wall, with the Quaker prep school same as always across the street. But what the hell is that fortress gate doing where athletic-field driveway should be? A spasm of nerves makes me stammer, "Hey, you've been tricked—I'm not the Irishman!" The guards have a good laugh.

Fancy iron key solidifies in a custodial hand as if from up jumpsuit sleeve. In a trice we're in, and day is night, and always is, I suspect. An ungentle palm thumps as much as pushes my shoulder to abort a glimpse at the world behind me, where it may or may not still be day.

The stars above are superabundant and cast a glow brighter than ever I've seen in a modern town, helping me distinguish the mansard roof and sheer ells of a hulking institution where the hockey rink should be. It's oppressive even in dim outline, but we're not going there, no, we're headed someplace worse, a flat-roofed, one-story row of bays, like a slapdash remodeling of stables with steel bars instead of stall doors. Our footfalls crunch on gravel and rouse a light sleeper in one stall who commences screeching hoarsely, in long and short bursts like messages in that newfangled Morse code.

Another iron key, in the grip of another gaoler, twists squeaking in a lock plate the size of a Bible, barred door groans open, and smelly of piss and swill as it is from outside, it's tenfold smellier once I'm shoved in and the door clangs shut.

Hey, if I'm crazy enough to pump bullets into guests on my welcome mat, I'm crazy enough to hallucinate all this, or better yet, dream it in my relatively posh bed. But intuition heckles I could pinch myself till doomsday without waking up, as if I only think I'm the man I called Stan. I whip around in my squalid "maniac cell" to find my captors have withdrawn. I'm alone in the stink and the starlight, apart from the screamer one cell over.

Whatever had I done in my underfunded, underachieving life to merit this? Is it a judgment on me, and whose, and by what right? Faith and begorra, I should have stayed in the old country, famine be damned. I never had to put up with the likes of such abuse there.

The Dark at the Top of the Stairs

Wait and see who dares
The dark at the top of the stairs.
All we know is something's wrong;
This house has stood empty so long.

The longer it's waited for someone to care,
The more people say that it's haunted in there.
But who used to live here and why they moved out
Are questions we don't know the first thing about.

Pause a while at the door,
Look out for the boards that were pried off the floor.
No more treasure to be found.
Do owls and wind make that sad midnight sound?

The longer it needs someone giving it love,
The more that its darkness will scare people off.
On the innermost soul, no one stops to reflect,
Is it wholesome or all eaten up with neglect?

Be careful as you go,
A step may give way to disaster below.
From above comes a sound.
Someone or something is moving around.

The longer you wait before going ahead,
The more that your feet seem as heavy as lead.
It feels just like déjà vu after a while.
Was this your worst nightmare when you were a child?

In the dark, start to see,
Something is waiting for you and for me,
Closing in as we draw near,
With an expression inspiring fear.

It does what we do when we stop or we go
As if we are mocked by a devil we know
That turns out to be a reflection in glass,
While a voice in your head says you've come home at last.

Naked Revenants

Real magic, far from the vocation of ragged crones in filthy hovels, was a pastime of wealth and privilege, or leastwise was in the cabal where Vargo sought entrée. Though magic did indeed steep him in rot and defilement, this was scant deterrent to him who in his first fifty years had amassed a fortune on slave ships, on plantations, in the proverbial "dark satanic mills."

Results were everything, and real magic was measurably effective, regardless of participants' skepticism, as Vargo came to appreciate during his ordeal of initiation. To be sure, his robust skepticism would not die quietly. Five Archimages, all of disconcertingly younger appearance than he, escorted him in manacles to the moor where they partly dismantled a cairn, fastidiously, cobble by cobble, to reveal a slab-lined compartment. They swathed him in bandages infused with pungent herbs, flipped him like a raw trout into a black pine casket, ceremoniously nailed down the lid, slid the casket into the cist, and rebuilt the cairn as carefully as they'd disassembled it.

Vargo pacified his dread of premature burial by reviewing the safeguards on his resources against treachery; the cabal would profit only by exhuming him hale and intact. He sank into a salutary night's sleep, or so he presumed on waking to the scraping and clatter of stones, the jostle of his coffin inch by squeaking inch from its recess, the laborious groans of nails pried away, his unswaddling into sunny glare, before the Archimages insisted he'd been in the cairn not overnight but a month, pointing out their beards on chins clean-shaven when he'd last beheld them. Vargo's own chin was smooth.

To quarrel, to tug on those implicitly false beards would have been impolitick, of course. Still, he was loath to concede that magic, like fluid in the womb, had sustained him, till he looked in on his leviathan business to bridle at weeks of mismanagement, assets in disarray, bookkeeping in arrears, and a purge incumbent of subalterns who'd bungled or exploited the rudderless situation.

Thus, however, was he validated in his choice of cabalists, convinced they shared in his purpose, were qualified to fulfill his profoundest yearning. After expending half a century in the accrual of luxury and opulence, to have at least that long to bask in them, and as much longer as he could hoard, seemed only fair. Shouldn't the victor flourish to enjoy his spoils, impossible within a lifespan's proverbial threescore-and-ten?

The baby-soft skin and fleecy beards of his seniors in the cult clinched them as kindred spirits, fellow pilgrims into the virgin country of longevity. Whatever of his wealth they demanded was worthwhile; elsewise aging and death would rob him of his delectation and then everything.

The first levy upon Vargo during his novitiate, amply reinforcing why magic was not for the poor, benefited the extortionate black market in very particular corpses. These were delivered to the lodge where Vargo was the greenest among those who had yet to pass the first test of their worth. The lodge was wedged between two equally narrow, dilapidated façades in a verminous neighborhood, and its interior was scarcely less squalid, certainly unfit for genteel residency. Languorous upon the stained and mildewy divans and settees throughout the house reposed naked, ravishing women of diverse complexions and features, little more motile than the furniture, aloof to the chilly drafts.

When Vargo answered his first summons to the lodge, he observed several novices shut doors behind them to one room or another containing a listless beauty, and then the house dean accosted him with some palaver about being "one short" because Vargo was there, and to genuflect before entering the "enlivening room."

This chamber was especially spacious, its air especially fetid, perhaps in keeping with its look of an Augean kitchen stripped of its appointments, empty save for a pallet overstuffed with straw bristling through crudely stitched rips. Supine on the pallet was the desiccated, worm-eaten corpse of a willowy young woman, going by the length of remnant tresses. This is what had cost Vargo so dear?

A leather-clad duet launching into a discordant chant and a brazier puffing forth bitter herbal smoke had materialized while Vargo blinked

agape. The rubicund dean barked Vargo's name and waved perfunctorily toward the pallet. "Fuck her." Vargo's countenance did its best to
convey incredulity without defiance. "You have to fuck her," the dean
brusquely elaborated. "You can fuck her from behind. I recommend
that. One initiate did it from the front, 'missionary style' if you will, to
watch her become beautiful again. The instant her eyes re-formed and
brightened, she bit through his jugular. You should also doff the cravat."

The dean anticipated Vargo's doubts about the feasibility of coitus
by declaring the mummy "properly anointed." And despite further
concerns his weight would pulverize the body like a clump of brown
leaves, its gauzy integrity held, and penetration, courtesy of the lubri-
cant oils perhaps, conferred a euphoria, a disregard for the putrescent
funk. He lost himself in plugging away.

His wits rallied to the clangor of gongs all around and the exertions of many gloved hands to pry him off the thrashing flesh to which
he clung as if she were salvation itself, the while she screeched for his
blood. "I'm not done!" he blurted pathetically, as expert attendants
tackled and bound his would-be killer.

Resurrecting a wench bestowed no proprietary stake in her, which
suited Vargo nicely even after his had exhausted her frothing agitation
in a padded cell and joined the docile harem, not that he'd necessarily
have recognized her whom he'd never met head-on. In that glut of
pulchritude, what normal man would prolong his attachment to any
one specimen? By the same token, Vargo may have had her on multiple occasions in that lodge where novices were free to come and tarry
and go, with no explanation why this privilege fell to them, or how it
prepared them to progress through cult ranks.

Likewise, the education they gleaned about their undead consorts
possessed no foreseeable value beyond or even in the lodge. Who
cared that when the wicks of revenant will, so explosive at first, soon
burnt low, revenant minds persisted intact, but void of initiative? If a
concubine could perform calculus premortem, she could again, upon
command—which only begged the question, who would want her for
any such function? More pertinent was the admonition that the wom-
en wouldn't eat or drink or bathe or use the commode, starvation, in-
fection, or worse resulting, except under timely orders.

Vargo should have chafed at the dearth of guidance in the house toward further learning, at this shameless detour from his path to immortality where only those deceased beforehand cheated death, and what help was that to him? Apart from the laconic dean, none but novices were present, and they content to wallow in fornication larded with indolence and alcohol. Vargo, like his fellows, never pondered why he deserved endless regalement, why the cult left them to their profligate devices. They were there, according to unspoken consensus, to accept their lot pending new instructions; what did they have to quibble about?

Though Vargo esteemed himself more important, ambitious, and ingenious than his compatriots, he was for some time on a par with them in his susceptibility to women absolutely submissive, malleable, uncritical of the most demeaning urges. As a rule, these women received all the partiality of cruel masters for exotic pets. Meanwhile, an insolence, an inflated worldliness, a sarcastic sparring characterized the disposition of the men toward each other, in which Vargo could have read that the others thought as little of him as he of them, had their outlooks been of interest.

All the loftier became his estimation of himself as the awareness dawned that he, unlike his fellows, was growing jaded with unstinting carnal gratification. He missed the banter, the bargaining, the backtalk of an ordinary whore, and ultimately her surrender and mortification. Such was his habituation to the lodge, however, that seeking a harlot outside its neighborhood, or bringing her anywhere but there, never occurred to him. To none of Vargo's brothers-in-depravity, in fact, did it occur that advancing to the cabal's next level might simply entail eschewing the lodge, outgrowing it, forsaking abject hedonism.

From benighted archway to awning to portico, Vargo followed his criteria of intact teeth, unpitted skin, a relatively healthy odor, a modicum of fight when he grabbed a wanton wrist by way of invitation. And superficially it was a feisty, stout-hearted tart he herded into sordid front parlor, till she panicked caterwauling at the novices fondling naked revenants, yanked free of him, and reeled out, still wailing.

Vargo styled himself a discerning observer and noted how the men and not their consorts had incited her hysterics, which escalated as a debauchee shambled in from upstairs, to peak uncontrollably when her eyes met Vargo's again. Till then, though, he hadn't observed the faint blemish in one man's cheek, the slightly drooping eyelid of another, the vaguely dragging foot of a third, and, in a vanity mirror, his own cracked and puffy lips. The resurrected women, meanwhile, continued in prime condition, and if anything, glowed more rosily than ever.

Once those first inklings of wastage sank in, Vargo found them more and more grossly widespread and soon hard to ignore, forcing him to wonder at his blindness to them for so long, at everyone else's ongoing blindness. The corruption leaching from subcutaneous depths was lending the men a cadaverous blueness, a hamstrung gait, the rancid breath of lepers. The dean was an exception, in whose piercing expression Vargo read a prescience of every affliction and more. Vargo, the newest initiate, was showing the mildest signs, but they boded decidedly ill for his aspirations toward immortality.

The dean intercepted Vargo roaming the premises, casting dissatisfied grimaces at every revenant, and ushered him into the chilly fug of the latrine to demand, "What vexes you?"

Disgruntled Vargo vented his desire to postpone senescence indefinitely—and did the dean bite back a smirk before evidently changing the subject? "The novices' decline is palpable to those who enter the lodge unmoved by its temptations. The same magic likewise masks its toll from common vision outside these walls, and from those in here on whom it battens. That magic acts to right a balance, to make up a deficit where vitality has been imperfectly restored from those who undertook the restoration. And even if recourse to a prostitute shows you're not altogether of this house, you're compelled to linger in it." The dean wryly studied Vargo. "But immortality's your holy grail?"

"As I just said," Vargo riposted, slipping into wonted arrogance.

"You've led a tempestuous life," the dean expounded, skirting Vargo's impertinence. "And now you covet decades to savor your rewards. But you pose a contradiction, don't you? Listen to yourself: do you sound like someone ready to mellow, to cease from avarice and aggression?"

Quite against his will and better judgment, Vargo was lapsing into torpor, jaw too heavy to mount arguments, swaying as if the dean's harangue were swig after swig of aquavit.

"You put us in a most extraordinary position," the dean droned on. "You resist the enticements of this house, yet cannot transcend your attachment to the house. Therefore you cannot proceed beyond it."

With bleary, stinging eyes Vargo gawped at the dean, groggily rubbed his grizzled chin with elderly, scaly knuckles, shifted his weight on bowing knees and numb feet, and could not begin to hazard the number of hours or days since he'd ventured outside the lodge.

"As you should already have gathered, magic is an instrument for promoting balance, compromise between conflicting forces. If you'd merit the gift of centuries, if you would wear that mantle, yours must be a more seemly deportment, more serene, detached from volatile passions."

Vargo never heard the dean's concluding phrases; he was slumbering in fetal crouch upon the lavatory flagstones, insensible to their cold, to their embedded, sticky miasma.

He awoke both beclouded and refreshed, untroubled at the incongruity of pairing these two states, as he would henceforth be untroubled by most things. His groping mind first surmised he'd been reburied in the cairn by dint of the stifling darkness pressing upon him, wherein a hemisphere of light shone somewhere ahead, like the mouth of a tunnel. He stretched his neck toward the light, instinctively, and was amazed at how it bore him out of the dark and into the lamplit front parlor of the lodge.

To him was the issue moot of whether his spirit had been transferred, or his body transformed, into a colander-sized variety of tortoise. Within the constraints of an intellect housed in a reptilian brain, he was passively content to embark upon a lifetime thrice the human allotment, compassed by the viburnum withies of his cage in the corner. The dean assigned an acolyte to clean and provision his domain and punish any who mistreated him. Magic had also secured the cabal access to those funds of Vargo's needful for his upkeep and liberally more.

And while he munched on cactus meat and melon, he watched with ebbing cognizance his former peers succumb within hours of each other to the pernicious magic that externalized their moral putrefaction, their cankered tenacity. All had been too far gone to question, and the majority to acknowledge, the sudden appearance of a tortoise pen among already outré surroundings. They moreover never perceived, much less understood, the repercussions of their own sorceries, thinning their blood to ichor, rupturing viscera, dissolving cartilage and tendons, ulcerating skin, even as they essayed final copulations with those revenants into whose pores their vitality flowed.

With the literal dissolution of their would-be masters, the women shuddered and gasped, overwhelmed by their regenerate wills and capacities, agog at their nakedness amidst a charnel house awash in mushy body parts, confounded at their patent complicity in necrophilia. Their memories were fragmentary and disordered, but a black spark igniting in their eyes burned away their disorientation.

And so Vargo, chomping on a delightfully rotten carrot, looked on dimly as the dean and his assistants bagged up the grisly mess and scrubbed down the floors with the harshest lye, to ready the lodge for its next initiates. They toiled with the indifference of consummate evil to the gore, and with myopic indifference to the women who ransacked every cranny for clothing and valuables and then hastened outside, some alone and some in one another's company, to resume their premortem places in the world or not, to act in any case upon the world according to whatever magic had made them.

Sand Bar

On that lonely stretch of beach at dawn,
The gulls are crying and fog comes on.
There's decay in the air as the tide gets low
And a sand bar like bone begins to show.

You can travel so far when the tide ebbs away
As if on a road halfway into the bay,
And clues come to light as the fog closes in
Why they say that the sand hides uncountable sins.

Sometimes you and I are exposed that way,
Strange discoveries under the everyday.
But spend too much time out upon that limb,
You may well be drowned when the tide rushes in.

Who can tell if disaster had taken a hand
In those things that you find all but buried in sand?
An overturned rowboat or some clothing in shreds,
What might be an arm, but it's driftwood instead.

Then you feel the tide rising and turn back at last,
Where the water around you seems deep as the past.
Keep your feet on the path or you'll be out of luck,
Things with stingers and claws come awake in the muck.

Vade Mecum

He wasn't out to fall down some damn rabbit hole. All the same, he had poison-tipped glowers to outdistance. England had been good to him for a whole 45 minutes so far. Few waiting areas at Heathrow had TV screens, and those were tuned to the BBC. He hopped an express train to Paddington station, where no New York papers were evident at newsstands. Still, London was too damn big. He'd be lost therein, but someone uncongenial was bound to find him.

At the info counter, he requested an out-of-the-way haven that wouldn't be total dullsville. Doughy attendant was right at home, Ratliff observed. For a national rail hub it was kind of a dump. Hadn't been remodeled since Queen Victoria probably, and that skeevy sheet plastic to mask the ceiling's disrepair looked like a mainsail off the *Flying Dutchman.*

The flack wasted no time thinking. As if itching to get Ratliff out of his salt-and-pepper comb-over, he spouted, "Bath is considered very nice."

Bath? Ratliff had never heard of it, and maybe that worked in its favor. Maybe Bath had never heard of him, as opposed to Manhattan, where everyone down to his own super was giving him the stinkeye. By what right did the fucking hoi-polloi pass sentence on him?

"It's out of the way, but plenty to do. Museums, beautiful architecture, cultural events, a wealth of history." *Okay, muzzle the propaganda,* Ratliff almost griped, but were veiny geezer eyes straining to peg him from news footage or tabloids?

"Sounds great!" he tossed off, already slouching toward the ticket windows. He covered the fare with his Sapphire card, and so what if that made his whereabouts a less-than-airtight secret? He wasn't on the lam, for Chrissakes.

On the train, he was philosophic about his situation when picturesque Tudor villages or green hills like colossal muffin tops rolled by, and dour at bleak office-block towns or acres of school-bus parking. God help that shabby flack in Paddington if Bath was really some crappy industrial park! Oh, the grievous injustice of exile in dicey terrain, or enjoying "well-earned R&R" as the boss put it. Bullshit! This "vacation" amounted to taking one for the team till the harebrained media spotlight shifted and he was no longer a liability.

The defendant, meanwhile, was off tenterhooks, back in the saddle of luxury, thanks very much to Ratliff's coaching despite cocky sales resistance. Ratliff didn't even like flashing on the defendant's name, as if it would draw fresh broadsides of post-trial juju upon him. Inured as he was to white-collar callousness, this guy was hardcore swinish. Droves of bilked clients were homeless, penniless, minus the fragile several opting for hari-kari. A tough sell to any "jury of his peers," excluding robber barons.

Out Ratliff's window, giant gouts of steam curdled above the cooling towers of a power plant, and he reminded himself, Don't go soft; every American's entitled to the best legal defense he can afford. Far be it from him to play judge, maybe timid souls should abstain from investing; to paraphrase more than one hardball mentor, Wash a pigeon in ten pints of a bleeding heart, he's still a pigeon.

Gleaming white sheep moped around a waterhole like sewer-pipe leakage and he brooded, So I prevailed on the swine that the courtroom wasn't a boardroom, and don't showboat as if the bailiff's there to fetch you a latte, and act hurt at how rank-and-filers betrayed your trust, and deeply regret how your brutal schedule precluded monitoring their every keystroke.

And when rank-and-filers took the stand they smelled Sing Sing on the prosecutor's breath and CNN would tout their downfalls as justice triumphant and they'd appease plebeian hunger for corporate heads to roll, lesser heads, fine, just so they rolled. But one of them fingered Ratliff in the gallery as the "flunky" overpaid to school alpha dogs in "bamboozling" jurors, and now Ratliff, and by extension his firm, were pariahs in the dock of public opinion, and he a scoundrel at large, though no charges stuck to the swine.

He stewed in life's unfairness, blind to the world, till canned announcement of arrival in Bath jarred him back to reality. He squinched

at a landscape like a punchbowl encrusted with mineral scales or crinkly meringue. Then he put on his glasses and the vista resolved into
scores of stone houses on terraces, the white of dusty bone china, lining the slopes of an encircling vale. Quaint or oppressive? He couldn't
decide.

Indecision persisted like the squeals of the wheeled Samsonite he
towed while scouting for a halfway presentable hotel. Narrow slate
sidewalks were sparsely peopled in broad May daylight; this must have
been the off-season. Brownstone and brick he was used to, and the vinyl siding of his native Long Island, but the sallow masonry that en-
sconced the Labor Party HQ, a Baptist church, the constabulary,
everything, made England deceptively foreign. And wasn't that coun-
terintuitive, since his language, name, favorite TV whodunits were
across-the-board English?

To compound the creeping alienation, ancient Romans must, like
him, have fetched up here somehow and left enough behind, including
a bathhouse apparently, for the locals to get a complex about it. He
encountered a Roman Baths Kitchen, Museum, Gift Shop, a Roman
Guesthouse, Foodhouse, and Spa, they even called their sore thumb of
a stonework mall the Forum. He was losing his grip on what the English meant by England.

Thank God he discovered a Krispy Kreme, one refuge of familiarity to curb nagging hunger, though its intrusion here was mirage-like,
bemusing. Figuring the counter girl, if she had an opinion, wouldn't be
mired in the cronyism of a tourist bureau, he asked about decent ho-
tels. Another Yank, cornfed inflections a dead giveaway, stopped labo-
riously counting his change to chime in about somewhere on Parade
with Park in the name. The girl scurried off for Ratliff's Original
Glazed.

"Not a dive?" If the question bordered on impolitic, so what? This
shorts-and-bucket-hat informant, already chomping on a Chocolate
Custard, wasn't exactly a bastion of refined taste, and to court friendships here, least of all with Yanks, would be asinine. The informant,
fuzzy cheeks bulging as he masticated, shook his head without visible
umbrage, gulped, and reeled off directions. Ratliff paid for his doughnut with the Chase card and did his countryman the solid of pointing
at madras shirtfront. "Big spot of goo there." To the tune of squeaky

wheels, Ratliff vamoosed, smug at slipping anonymous past his first American.

The hotel, a literal minute away, was actually okay, hands-down more quaint than oppressive. Yes, he had to book a suite for a modicum of elbow room, but the view out front of tidy park and licorice-black river was idyllic. A remorseful twinge accosted him for not being more personable with his fellow doughnut-fancier, but what the hell? Ratliff might not even recognize him in different clothes. The Original Glazed, lingering as sticky fingertips, had made a more lasting imprint.

In fact, the heft of it in his stomach coerced him to sit and then recline on his nearest of three beds. Maybe he should have softened up that sinker with coffee. He'd pulled an all-nighter flying over, hadn't he? His manners might well have been milder had he not been bucking jetlag. That comforting premise he nestled under as a blanket; a little nap, and his nicer true self, its theoretical existence a cherished article of faith, would rise and shine, why not?

That exemplary self had atomized like a dream when next he blinked in mellow afternoon light, more disoriented than ever, positive it was morning. The vileness in his mouth, his crusty eyes, his crying need for the bathroom reinforced this error. His normal acerbity was soon up to speed, unflinchingly self-directed, on ransacking luggage in vain for toothpaste. Stupid of him!

He filled his cheeks with tap water till they distended like a chipmunk's, swished loose the bacterial film, spat dissatisfied into the toilet, and sallied out. Gad, he still tasted like shit, and his vision bounced around, seizing on nothing. Maybe he'd overlooked a dozen pharmacies in as many minutes. Concentrate! Okay, there was a Yankee Candle, and a Subway, and an "American Nails," whatever the fuck that was; why not a CVS? From some turgid reservoir of trivia, he cottoned that a green neon cross above an entrance meant drugs.

Great! Now he made out three such crosses in bunting range, even minus his glasses. The sign in the window of the closest boasted expertise in shingles, erectile "disfunction," and antimalarial treatments, so dental hygiene was probably in their skill-set. The open door squarely framed the druggist's oak-and-glass desk at the end of a spacious aisle.

His vision continued in disarray, though, debasing the merchandise into a semi-legible welter of tubes, boxes, oblongs, frustrating him into a lunge at what should have been Aquafresh. But obviously he wasn't seeing straight yet, because he confronted the monobrow pharmacist with a package, as best he could ad lib, of "Vaid Meekum." Ratliff bluntly challenged him, "Is this toothpaste?"

To behold a rise of monobrow was an unsolicited first, followed by the snotty rejoinder, "'Voddy May Come' is indeed a venerable brand of toothpaste, sir." Ratliff subdued a grin at hoity-toity diction from the service sector. Monobrow prissily added, "Latin, you know. For 'Go with me.'" Ratliff paid with credit card and clamped down on his shaky composure. Christ almighty, did everything right down to the toothpaste have to get in on the Roman act?

A wave of self-congratulation floated him along at readily accessing the fact that Romans spoke Latin. He wasn't like some overeducated, silver-spoon lawyer with dead-language legalese at his fingertips. He barreled forward happy-go-lucky and too late fathomed how many tortuous streets fit in this fiendishly compact downtown. His hotel could have been at the center of a corn maze. The Vade Mecum in its flimsy bag was locked in his overwrought clutches like an underperforming talisman. Well, something beyond wrong-way intuition had to guide him out of urban-planning snafu, and the toothpaste had gotten him into it.

He trod major avenues that promised to connect with helpful landmarks; when none did, he went contrarian and tried seamy, stunted lanes. Swallow Street, belying any association with pretty songbirds, was the worst, a grungy conduit between sunny boulevards, lined with plastic dumpsters and trashcans up against sooty walls with featureless steel fire exits and stout pipes emerging from upper stories to embed themselves like vertical entrails in the grimy tarmac. Squat orange traffic cones across the tarmac might have discouraged meeker sightseers than Ratliff.

A jerry-built pavilion of bedraggled plastic sheets like those in Paddington half blocked the street beyond the cones and protruded from a formerly classy wall with a triangular outcrop of masonry, as on Greek temples, surmounted by a carved lion and bear propping up a shield. No one told him not to ignore the orange cones or forbade him from brushing past the tent flap to see what was inside. Bath was a tourist resort, he was a tourist, didn't that award him carte blanche unless civil authority intervened? If citizens expected strangers to honor a certain etiquette, the onus was on them to clarify that.

This must be what caverns are like, he speculated. *Way bigger than you'd guess from the entrance.* The weather-sheeting walls rustled in back-and-forth stereo, thanks to faint updraft, and had the support of slapdash scaffolding; this anteroom for scrap lumber, jumbled rock, and mud-spattered pumps and shovels gave onto a gaping hole in the Greek-temple wall. Wooden post-and-lintel beams held open this snaggly mouth of stone, softly exhaling rotten-egg corruption via the gullet of a ramp with nonskid industrial flooring.

The gullet led fathoms deeper than a normal cellar, had an undulating roof of the ever-popular plastic sheets, and was lustrous with basket lights fixed to posts left and right. Since no one stopped him, he exercised tacit permission to tromp into this bewildering mélange of sulfur mine and construction site. He chose to be a good sport about the sewer air. Honestly, it was tame compared with the Meadowlands by Secaucus.

The tunnel bottomed out in a modest rotunda, no Mammoth Cave, but panoramic after small-town congestion. And to the ambience of mineshaft and foundation pit he had to add public restroom, à la Port Authority, between harsh arc lighting and harsher funk. Hell, the streaky tile floor could have been lifted wholesale from bus-station squalor. A forest of wooden beams supported a dim brick vault like the inside of a barrel.

In the forest, androgynous personnel in jumpsuits and hardhats futzed around on folding tables with strainers, basins, clipboards, balled-up cheesecloth, toiling incomprehensibly like peasants in that Monty Python movie about King Arthur. One sixtyish fogy without hardhat on his spray of frizzy silver hair had rows and piles of dull metal flecks on his table, as if he were sorting a mess of fish scales. He hastily donned hardhat at Ratliff's approach. In the center of the rotunda, toward which a flight of nubby steps slanted like a continuation of the ramp, was a rectangular, skanky, rust-brown pool.

Silver Frizz seemed undecided whether to treat him as a trespasser who should have known better or as an unscheduled functionary from a funding agency. Ratliff's gamesman reflexes kicked in. Stance was everything: project a domineering front and it scarcely mattered what he said. Plus, he wore the silk pinstripes of officialdom. In low-grade managerial eyes he deftly read the conflict between ejecting Ratliff outright versus forgoing an ugly scene. The course of less resistance won, of course. No sooner was Frizzy committed to a mannerly smile than cocksure Ratliff spread uncouth hands. "What is this place?"

To let slip accidentally-on-purpose how he didn't belong here was just his under-the-skin way of rubbing in that he'd put one over on the prof, who was also at a disadvantage as Ratliff had caught him flouting rules about protective headgear. More egregious yet, a spare hardhat doubled as a cooler full of half-melted ice and a half-liter of lager. Presumably this was the helmet scofflaw Frizzy should have offered his guest.

"It's a well, isn't it? Or more strictly, a wishing well." Was the prof a mite snippy because he hated being imposed upon, conned into dialogue with a boorish Yank, or because he found the question stupid? In either case, fuck him. "There've been articles in the *Times*. You've heard nothing about this?" Ratliff shook his provocatively blank-faced head. Which *Times*? The *New York Times*? He glanced at the *Wall Street Journal* when he had the leisure for more than CNN.

"A girl was killed when the wall partly collapsed," the prof related testily, as if Ratliff's ignorance automatically made him callous. Ratliff maintained wide-eyed dummy mask, relishing egghead chagrin. "The water table, the humidity level, were on the rise for decades; they seeped into the oak timbers, the rock and mortar. The rising damp was taking its toll, but nobody suspected, or had any notion of what was below, till after the fact."

A few of his crew paused in their obscure tasks to give Ratliff the once-over and shrug him off as someone else's problem.

"Tragically incurious eighteenth-century builders had installed a cellar drain for a scullery without investigating the void where the water drained, and they inadvertently provided a means for more to enter as dank exhalations than flowed out, in the long term. We had to pump a lake of stagnant muck before we could dig down to the Roman level and isolate the source," he explained, waving toward the pool, "which had been paved over, forgotten since the Saxon period.

"Luckily for us this area hasn't refilled immediately. We had a dry April, and the original inflow from the runoff of the Roman baths had

been choked with rubble for over a millennium." Evidently this disclo-
sure rated a double-take, for Frizzy expounded *con brio*, "That's right,
this sacred well was supplied from the channel for second-hand bath-
water that emptied into the Avon, to our south. But people would
never have dreamt of taking a drink or swimming here. Instead of the
state-sanctioned priesthood, some cult or private landowner kept this
backstreet operation solely for the deposit of *defixiones*."

If the egghead had to lob ten-dollar words, it behooved Ratliff to
play extra dumb, shake his head vacuously, and breathe through slack
mouth.

"Curses!" At crotchety translation, Ratliff, and the jumpier hardhat
drones, had to stop and process that he wasn't the bull's-eye of an outburst. "Curse plaques, petitioning the gods to punish wrongdoers, they
were dropped into springs and wells across the Classical world, in-
scribed on lead so they'd sink to the bottom, that much closer to the
underworld." *Yeah*, Ratliff drily noted, *what kind of idiot wouldn't know that?*

"The cistern in the ancient temple site, over by the present-day abbey, yielded hundreds of *defixiones* to Sulis, the local goddess, who also
received gifts of coins and jewelry. Our catchment, meanwhile, has
produced thousands of *defixiones* and practically nothing else. And
they're addressed to a shortlist of Celtic gods with nasty reputations,
Abandinus for whom captives were drowned, Balor whose look could
kill, Ogmios with chains from his tongue to shackle dead souls. Not
gods you'd care to meet in a dark alley."

He seemed to have warmed to his subject, if not to Ratliff. Striding
to the heap of metal, he plucked one at random, its top and bottom
edges curly, and creased with ripples like a starchy scroll unfurled or a
jumbo gray potato chip. "Here," he dithered, stretching and retracting
his arm to finesse the optimal reading distance, "this one says, 'To
Him Who Binds and Scourges'—which could describe several infernal
deities, so maybe the customer's hedging his bets—'Afflict Hortensia
the whore with burning sores on her pudenda for afflicting me with
crabs.' All right, well, this one's unusually salacious."

Jubilant whooping, no stiff upper lip about it, turned heads toward
a crewman who'd been gently hosing down something inside a punch-
bowl-sized colander. "Just as I predicted!" he rejoiced. "I win, yeah?"
Silver Frizz joined the nerd stampede. Ratliff didn't and sneered at the

excessive ruckus as if the glop had coughed up a Fabergé egg. Then he sidled to the table, checking and rechecking that everyone was engrossed in their huddle, like hens around a night-crawler. His dainty forefinger and thumb extracted a plaque off the top, while he clenched his teeth against the remote possibility of the whole heap collapsing like in a round of Jenga.

He set a jaundiced eye on the chumps, as if unaware of his own hand sliding sneakthief trophy into paper bag with the toothpaste. They'd never miss one lousy little scrap, and it'd make a great souvenir, framed on his office wall. Pilferage like this, he reasoned, was their own damn fault for posting no security down here. Serves 'em right! As vacationers went, he doubtless wasn't unique in vacationing full-on, right down to impulse control.

He padded over for a tiptoe squint between shoulders aquiver at this phenomenal find, and damned if it wasn't a dirty, beat-up hand mirror. His brow crinkled in disdain at giddy fuss about some design on its hindside, marred by crusty patches, that hinted from different angles at scattered pinwheels or an owl head or a scarecrow's grimace. The prof spun blithely out of the gaggle and toward the table, the makeshift ice bucket, and Ratliff, and he began to enthuse, "A prize brilliantly earned, Mr. Barry! I hereby award . . ."

Academic eyes popped a little at uninvited guest, as if already forgotten amidst the excitement; he paused in midstep.

"I don't see the fuss," Ratliff cut in, "about a mirror someone threw away."

"Not thrown away," the prof amended. "Consecrated, rather. A mirror was a big-ticket item, which only the aristocracy could afford, so this represents a serious token of supplication or gratitude to a god here, the equivalent of sacrificing a BMW. And it tells us this site appealed to society high and low."

Sleep deficit, Ratliff reckoned, meant never having to say he was sorry for the yawn he tardily covered. His above-average gulp of cesspit funk made him ogle the lager and wonder how anyone could imbibe pleasurably in such an atmosphere. They must have really liked their alcohol. Silver Frizz followed Ratliff's line of sight and sidestepped to block tabletop view, and he huffed, "I'm afraid you can't stay any longer without protective headwear. Health and safety, you know."

Ratliff could have busted him on that off-label use of an otherwise free hardhat under both their noses, but why bother? He wanted out as badly as the prof wanted him out, however dissimilar their motives. With deadpan guise of innocence, he scanned the chumps once more, smirking inwardly at how many gawked at noticing him for the first time. "Enjoy your beer," he saluted the drone with the mirror, "if you can enjoy anything in this pit."

As Ratliff trudged up the ramp, someone in a higher pitch than the prizewinner's and, palpably uncertain how to counter a backhanded toast, piped after him, "Cheers!"

Swatting aside the plastic tent flap, Ratliff drew cleansing lungfuls of Swallow Street's relatively sweet air and rambled on. The little mousy scrape of metal tidbit against toothpaste box in paper bag brought an irony, equally droll and irksome, to mind: he'd vowed to steer clear of rabbit holes, but what the hell had he just exited? And what a crazy rabbit hole, with unisex lackeys at damnfool chores, a Mad Hatter egghead babbling about gods and whores and gobbledygook history, and everyone getting panties in a bind about some cruddy mirror.

Were his zigzags up and down Bath thoroughfares developing a furtive, unhinged edge? The rising after-hours foot traffic often stared at him askance, or were people staring back because he'd been unconsciously staring at them? They all couldn't have caught wind at once of who he was, and they hardly had X-ray vision to glom onto the thievery in his bag.

He had no guilty aura to detect subliminally, no guilt on any score. His clothes were likelier to exude sulfurous whiffs than his conscience to project telltale body language. Why permit conscience any say among strangers, among foreigners, during R&R, if it rated none professionally, where its input would amount to dividing his loyalties, compromising job performance? His conscience was welcome to propose charities, liberal causes, noble writeoffs under his accountant's supervision; to ungag it otherwise was foolhardy.

With renewed grip on himself, the world, like magic, also set itself to rights. There at his elbow was the Krispy Kreme; he was out of the woods through no ingenuity of his own, like jiggling a key endlessly in an uncooperative lock until the tumblers inexplicably drop, the door opens.

No matter, he was back at basecamp, his toothpaste on the wash-stand, his ill-gotten memento on the bureau. He was ready to enjoy enforced leisure—but what a drag for the sink to drain so sluggishly of foamy toothpaste water, likewise the bathtub of shower suds, pulsing like sickly respiration. And rear-window view was so bleak with its frilly medieval steeple and boring backsides of apartment buildings, tacky kitchens and dens framed in stone discolored by black mold or moss.

Come to think of it, he'd eaten nothing today but that lousy doughnut. Low blood sugar, an empty stomach, overexertion could all take the rap for his downer mood. He ventured into happy-hour twilight and prudently memorized street names and landmarks on his quest for supper. And how apropos, how inevitable to end up at the Roman Baths Kitchen, which sounded more appetizing than the Pump Room across the square.

He was both relieved and disenchanted that a Roman Baths burger was a dead ringer for a US burger, and that the signature cocktail was a standard Long Island iced tea. At least they hadn't screwed up his native beverage. Amidst this further existential crisis over how foreign a country Britain was, his laggardly bowels finally demanded action. He followed signs to a "Gents" down staircases to sub-subcellar wishing-well level, or was one paltry drink distorting his depth perception?

He'd have rejoiced at normal digestion restored, but to his embarrassment had to flush lame-ass toilet twice. The sink, like the hotel fixtures, had poky drainage. Hadn't the prof said something about a rising water table, underground flooding? On top of which, the pipes under the floor clattered as if BBs and not human waste were flowing away, and kept pace with his footfalls as if his heels contained magnets. Pathetic, wasn't it, when the plumbing, such a basic component of infrastructure, was in citywide distress?

That, or something else outside of him, yes, and intrinsic to this town, was tilting the balance from quaint toward oppressive. Whatever it was, it didn't justify brooding uselessly, losing another night's sleep. Two Ambiens guaranteed his internal clock would reboot after eight oblivious hours. Still, his spirits next morning were subpar as he joined shuffling seniors, scruffy backpackers, and rumpled businesspeople for the breakfast buffet. At his table for one, neither postcard riverside view nor three salami-and-toast sandwiches dispelled arbitrary blahs. A thick-waisted waitress with a phlegmy Slavic accent swore he wasn't drinking decaf.

The Yank from Krispy Kreme would have been happy here, cheeks bulging with processed cheese wedgelets. Ratliff didn't recognize him among the chowhounds making their rapacious most of a complimentary meal. The majority were in mini-conferences over maps, guidebooks, pamphlets; and godawful frumpy as they were, they had one thing he didn't, and there was his problem. They all had something to do, places to go, whereas enforced leisure, idleness, didn't agree with his Type A dynamism.

Up in his suite, contriving some about-town activity threatened to become the activity in itself unless he went bonkers first. He mistrusted the quality of whatever was touted in brochures, attractive to pensioners. Then a dull gleam from the overhead bulb on his leaden morsel curtailed his restless pacing. Shit yeah! Showing off a curse plaque on office wall would be doubly impressive if he could reel off its message, and in fact would kinda fall flat otherwise. And that required he exploit the learning of the very party he'd ripped off, while sidestepping how he'd obtained the Latin to translate.

This ought to be no big deal. His forte was sussing people out, which he'd done with these beer-chugging, bookish galoots in the proverbial Manhattan minute. First, though, he had to copy the inscription onto hotel stationery in generic block print, avoiding imitation of archaic penmanship lest its resemblance to that in the mother lode cast suspicions. Simple task soon devolved into a tough slog, with graven words rubbed smooth or corroded into illegibility, besides the obstacle of letters that must have been borrowed from some other alphabet.

Patience was his least favorite virtue, but he doggedly recopied the mumbo-jumbo till it formed straight lines of equal length and height, clean of second thoughts and cross-outs, and indistinct at a glance from a note for the doorman. Each faulty draft he crumpled upon rejection and flung into the wastebasket; gurgling stomach and eyestrain he ignored.

Even more laudably, he resisted testing the Latin acumen of honchos at the much-hyped museum and the C-of-E cathedral, and not just on the general principle that those institutions were a bore. He had to scout an optimal locale for tonight's operation. And once he'd done that and withdrew the max at an ATM on the street, he frittered away midafternoon over an alcohol-free lunch at an unduly snooty brasserie ill-schooled in nuking beef stroganoff, then stationed himself catty-corner from the weather-sheeting pavilion on Swallow Street, feeling every macho inch the lion in wait.

Yesterday's chicken-or-egg dilemma came back to haunt Ratliff when he spaced out, blinked, and debated anew whether passersby were staring at him or returning his unmindful stare. He was just standing around, fergodsakes: why single him out unless this was a gay pickup spot or something? In any event, becoming an object of scrutiny implied he deserved scrutiny, imposed unacceptable guilt on him, precisely what he was here to escape. He alone knew he was returning to the scene of his crime.

He glared at the tent flap, shutting out all else, and with iron restraint counted to three and then gave chase when the first drudge emerged in denim and tweed. A distasteful ensemble, but never mind. This drudge was an interchangeable part, as were they all, suitable patsies in his audaciously basic plan. Sometimes the obvious worked best; true smarts meant appreciating that.

While his mark plodded up the left side of Swallow, Ratliff sprinted ahead on the right, keeping a shallow stream of pedestrians between them, tracking sienna jacket with snide backward glimpses. The surrounding inner town was a commercial promenade, and at the Abbeygate terminus of Swallow he darted among stronger currents of shoppers to a doorframe vantage for watching which way his quarry went. Hurray, the Tweed Geek hung a right, putting Ratliff a dozen yards ahead, well-situated to waltz out and pretend they came from opposite directions.

Smiling Ratliff blocked the frump's path and glad-handed him: "Hey, this is fantastic! You were one of those guys at that excavation yesterday when the mirror turned up, right after I wandered in off the street. Maybe I brought you luck!"

Tweed geek stopped with a full-body twitch like a sleepwalker hitting a wall and foundered in confusion, manifestly failing to place Ratliff. Or had he never been aware of on-site visitor? Ratliff let go his callused mitt upon the owner's goggling acknowledgment someone was shaking it. "Yeah, thanks for that," mumbled absentminded savant.

"I was absolutely fascinated by everything," Ratliff gushed, "and I want to learn all about it. We don't have anything half as ancient in the States."

Blindsided savant frowned through residual daze as if sweeping statement had incurred skepticism or dissent. Ratliff fancied his case would have been more convincing had he been a beautiful blonde, or at least had one at his disposal, and hastily added, "Drinks are on me for as long as you feel like chatting, and you happen to be heading toward a great little place."

Ratliff hadn't physically set foot in said place, but how was that germane? The weedy specimen did indeed perk up, as any of his colleagues doubtless would at prospects of free booze, and mumbled again, more sociably. As they strolled, Ratliff broke the ice with the usual twenty questions re where the guy had grown up, higher education, was he married with children, et cetera, and promptly forgot each answer.

Self-congratulatory pride welled up, as if he'd beaten the insubordinate street plan, on sighting the relevant lane. It had cobblestone paving and its entranceway, a substantial arch, doubled as an enclosed bridge between the buildings on opposite sides, all quaint as hell, even for Bath, except the inverted U-shape of the arch was too similar to the ceiling above the skanky Roman well.

But cheer up, there was his destination with its several bays of multiple windowpanes in black frames, set into the obligatory off-white stone façade. Out front were black hitching posts like lightning rods, and if anyone was too myopic to scan "Gin Bar" on black-and-scarlet signs overhanging the flagstone sidewalk, one pane at eye level in the central bay candidly proclaimed "GIN."

"Ever been here?" Ratliff asked his guest, who demurely shook his head.

Through the door, the bar confronted them, op-art retro and spanning the length of narrow anteroom. Ratliff glimpsed a side lounge with round tables flanked by ice-cream chairs and window benches. He ushered his guest to an inner-sanctum seat with the air of treading familiar ground.

The barkeep was affable enough for a hipster with wool vest and watch fob, though the baffling menu of gins tried Ratliff's patience. Floral? Fruity? The PC option of "buying local" offered the easiest out; after a careless perusal he ordered a Bathtub Gin-and-tonic for himself and a martini, nice and strong, for his "depressed friend who needs to vent."

"All right, Bath Gin for you," the barkeep emended with a bonhomie that concealed any irritation. "You might want to try our martini bar upstairs, though. We're gin and tonics down here, obviously."

To nip these argumentative stirrings in the bud, Ratliff smacked a ten-pound note on the oaken surface between them. "Do they tip in this country? This is for you on top of the tab for the first round, and you can count on several more." The barkeep nodded coolly as he slid the tenner off his edge of the bar and started reaching for bottles. Ratliff was unclear on how pounds translated into dollars, and wasn't overly concerned. It still looked like play money to him; what harm in throwing it around?

He also curbed his disdain as the weak-chinned philistine dipped beaky schnozz like a thirsty bird toward his brimming martini on the table, slurped down a quarter-inch to prevent spillage before toasting Ratliff, and confessed, "I'm pretty much a shovel bum, you realize. Clive's in charge, he's the real fount of knowledge, but I can provide as good a boots-on-the-ground rundown as anybody, I daresay."

Ratliff shrugged like a decent sport. "I'm just a member of the lay public. The great unwashed. All the technical stuff is wasted on me." Whatever a "shovel bum" was, he crossed his fingers it didn't rule out basic Latin. "Anyhoo, I gather something's extra special about your particular wishing well."

Ratliff had to concede Shovel Bum points for talking an authoritative game and for mounting enthusiasm as empty glasses proliferated, till they outnumbered Ratliff's three to one. The well was fascinating primarily because of its insights into the sordid underbelly of ancient Bath society. Elsewhere, coins in a body of water dated its popularity as a religious site. "Here, though, coins went into managerial coffers, so establishing a timeline was dependent on handwriting styles instead, which was better really, since few coins circulated during the well's later history, when the priests would have had to make do with payment in kind, or in kine, if you'll pardon the pun." *Huh? What a fucking fruit loop,* bewildered Ratliff chafed.

From second-century AD beginnings, Shovel Bum recounted, the submersion of pagan tablets persisted after Christianity became the Empire's sole religion, and for decades after Rome abandoned Britain, into the mid-500s, past King Arthur's era. In brief, backstreet temple flourished illegally for 200 years, its baneful services in ongoing demand. So why, Ratliff puzzled, did the racket of underfoot plumbing in hotel and restaurant bother him then, and why did he have to ask, "Nobody's reported anything weird, have they, no hoodoo down there, not after all this time?"

Laughing Ratliff off would have been more reassuring than Shovel Bum's coy, loopy grin. "Not yet, but that's another extraordinary aspect of our creepy old waterhole. Unlike sacred springs and ponds and bogs in general, this cesspit's been hermetically sealed, festering, left to its own devices for about fifteen centuries." He hiccupped without missing a beat. "Bad vibes, ill-wishes by the thousands have been trapped, fermenting with nowhere to dissipate, compacting under psychic pressure like a fossilizing sponge. Practically inconceivable, all the numinosity that must have accumulated!"

What? Whatever numinosity was, his willingness to babble about it aptly demonstrated why this New Age dipshit would never, ever enjoy executive responsibility. Meanwhile, time was a-wasting. Ratliff fished around suit-jacket pocket for folded-up hotel stationery, snapped it flat with a whiplash gesture. "Yeah, along those lines, I'm intrigued by the curse plaques. I've Googled whole websites devoted to 'em." Hey, why shouldn't such websites exist, in which case he wasn't making them up? And it's not like Shovel Bum had the wherewithal to expose white lies about Internet research.

"Long story short, one inscription mentioned a god that was worshipped here according to your boss." Dipshit eyebrows rose quizzically at that. "Unfortunately, some websites copy out the words but don't translate 'em." Ratliff thrust his paper over the row of martini glasses. "So maybe I could test your language skills, just for fun?"

"Well, four years of schoolboy Latin have come in handy on the job." Shovel Bum punctuated these credentials with another hiccup. He dragged the transcript within inches of his chin, his flighty eyebrows waggled, and his lower lip sagged, making Ratliff afraid his drinking partner was about to drool. But as eyes penetrated text, the worm turned into an intellectual snob. He clucked in disapproval, sat up headmaster-straight, and archly mouthed several passages, leading Ratliff to conclude that lack of opportunity alone prevented academe's bottom-feeders from behaving as arrogantly as their superiors.

"I must say, either this is gutter Latin or the copyist was a dunce," Shovel Bum huffed. "Barring sheer guesswork, I can't make head or tail of half these words. Plus the usual slew of abbreviations."

And a poor carpenter blames his tools, Ratliff stewed defensively, stung after his painstaking efforts to print in big, neat letters. "But what does it say, roughly?" he pursued, with Cross pen poised above the blank backside of doughnut receipt from a different jacket pocket. Sadly, Shovel Bum couldn't jot the English version on hotel stationery because he'd plunked it among the overlapping rings of condensation from three martini glasses. It was soggy, as good as fused with the tabletop's glossy black paint.

Ratliff scribbled diligently as pie-eyed interpreter sighed bleakly and recited, with the *de rigueur* pomp of a Monty Python centurion, "I, Segomarus Vitellus, beseech supremely cunning Ogmios . . . silver conveyed to you through your priests . . . never to relent . . . scourge Claudius Antoninus for committing perjury . . . my lands forfeit, an exile in Britannia . . . let him not escape punishment . . ." Shovel Bum bit his upper lip, pondered "gutter Latin" less haughtily even as its ink diffused into blotches, and remarked, "Amazing how much your text sounds like it's from Bath! Really, it wasn't from something online about the *defixiones* dredged up here in 1980?"

No, Ratliff truthfully hedged, it wasn't. Allusions to perjury, exile, and punishment, though scarcely a perfect match with his circumstances, were like icy needles striking a nerve. Heroic willpower alone dissuaded him from lurching to the bar for a booster dose of composure.

"Something wrong?" importuned Shovel Bum. "Someone step on your grave?"

Ratliff rallied, shook his head vigorously. It wasn't strictly fibbing to parry, "I'm fine, just that the wallpaper's creeping me out a little." Shovel Bum peered at the wall behind Ratliff and nodded compassionately. The pattern was, putting it mildly, eccentric, a mob of vermilion corpuscles against a black background. To the fore, on each square of paper, cowering from the stampeding cells was a man, bloodless white, and not merely nude but anatomically bared, like the ghastly preserved corpses in that Chinese traveling exhibit.

"Fair enough," Shovel Bum opined. In pace with the dilution of block letters into a fuzzy-edged Rorschach blot, he'd reverted from stern highbrow to a big fuzzy-edged drip, who was, to go by sheepish body language, wringing figurative hat in hand. The weak are so transparent, reflected Ratliff, who with mission accomplished was anxious to ditch this wimp, as if his weakness might be contagious. "Much obliged for the bevvies," Shovel Bum slurred, "but if it's all the same, I should be shoving off. Long day. Okay if we split a cab?"

Ratliff knew damn well that splitting a cab with anyone in Shovel Bum's state, or demographic for that matter, meant springing for a cab. Buying drinks, that paid for information, but flushing money, even play money, down the toilet was reprehensible. The gall of this parasite! "You'll be fine!" promised Ratliff as he scraped back his chair and motioned logy parasite to his feet.

On the other hand, the parting gift of ten more pounds for the barkeep as Ratliff steadied Shovel Bum through the door was no idle liberality. Well-practiced winning smile and chummy "Good night" were further investments in thwarting nosy questions about Shovel Bum's best interests. Outside, tipsy informant appeared content to stand forever on leaden feet till someone else's strength of personality overcame the inertia leavening goofball features. Ratliff conquered his repugnance at earthtone tweed to brush lint off it like a pal, pulling away when Shovel Bum hiccupped again.

Mercifully, the proposal to share a cab must have slipped Shovel Bum's porous mind. "Okay, let's point you in the right direction!" chimed Ratliff with skin-deep camaraderie. Shovel Bum's domicile was clearly in walking distance; where else would he have been going when Ratliff ambushed him? And this couldn't have been his first-ever night making this trek on rubber legs.

"I'm a trifle woozy." Adam's apple bobbed as Shovel Bum swallowed. "Come with me partway?"

Ratliff grunted noncommittally, escorted his guest to the archway, and stayed him with a quick pat on the collarbone. He aimed right index finger like a pistol barrel. "If I'm not mistaken, you're going that-away." He aimed left index finger contrariwise. "I'm going thisaway." He saluted, "Maybe see you down at the dig!" And off he sauntered, squelching rueful vision of shooing Shovel Bum away like a lost mutt.

Every so often he glanced behind to confirm hangdog nebbish wasn't following. He wasn't, of course, and whether weighing down flagstones by the arch or shambling homeward, he wasn't Ratliff's problem. But as the tide of pub-crawlers and late diners flowed indifferently past him, Ratliff again had a hunch that they, or someone sneakier, had him under damning surveillance. His legs were shaky as with hypoglycemia. Was the nebbish on to Ratliff, slyly faking inebriation in a sting campaign to recover stolen relic?

For safety's sake, he slowly surveyed his field of vision in front of the hotel, spotted nobody acting cagey, but would have felt more at ease had he been wearing his glasses. Too bad contacts inflamed his eyeballs! He bypassed the main entrance and ducked into the hotel's sports bar one door down, superficially normal except for catering to quaint British sports: a badminton club and their gear at one table, another table for the horsey set with riding crops and helmets, and cricket on TVs in ceiling brackets.

He ordered an innocuous-sounding cider, and snagged a corner seat with a sidelong view out the window to watch for any skulkers. The cider went down like soda, sowing doubts about alleged alcohol content; what harm then in another pint, an excuse to sit vigilant and exorcise lingering paranoia? He detested how his heart raced at occasional walk-in equestrians, and with glass but half-empty he was fed up with himself, to the unfrugal extreme of breaking camp without finishing his drink, when a gangly dude in bucket hat and plaid loped by before Ratliff could catch his profile.

Nor could Ratliff from his angle discern if the passerby strode into the hotel. And say it was the Yank from Krispy Kreme, why should Ratliff swill his cider and opt for the pub's own Gents rather than traipse through the foyer yet and up to his suite? He hadn't slighted his gawky countryman so seriously as to avoid him, and what were the odds he'd gotten wind of who Ratliff was between yesterday and today?

Pissoirs were in the basement, naturally. Acute urge to go ran roughshod over qualms about descending to that stratum with the pool full of curses. And his nerves were abuzz like a tuning fork in response to the awful racket of ball bearings when he flushed, as if they were bucking the current of wastewater to bust through the urinal. Fuck this Old World plumbing!

The impact of a gin cocktail and two ciders on his bladder was understandable. But for that much liquor to mess with his brain? Preposterous, yet how else to explain why his soapy hands, kneaded together under the cold-water tap, wouldn't budge? Alarm and stupefaction skewed the moment into some more private, arbitrary unit of time, only elongated further by his insistence that this couldn't really be happening. He barely retained the presence to wonder, Would he be less distraught or more if onlookers were present?

Before his hands went numb in suddenly frigid water, he registered they weren't simply immobile, for something both gritty and diaphanous had them, like a sprinkling of black sand for all its vicelike solidity. Ratliff's wishful logic argued the faucet's torrent should have dislodged this invisible film, swirled it down the drain, but it held fast. And as if he weren't unnerved already, the grapeshot clatter from the urinal had migrated to the sink as soon as he'd twisted the tap.

This status quo dragged on a measureless while, till Ratliff dimly fathomed he was lapsing into shock. But at the same unceremonious instant, the tap switched off, the racket cut out, his hands jerked free of the sink, and the door whooshed as someone clumped in. After his unbridled freakout, it turned out he was in one of those high-minded joints with automatic limits on water consumption, freeing him to scoff at his silly overreaction. He couldn't be troubled to eyeball whoever replaced him at the urinal.

Ratliff snatched three paper towels from the dispenser to rub some warmth into his stinging hands. No caveat to the next customer was forthcoming. Good luck to the schnook if he was the hygienic type! Ratliff could say nothing that wouldn't qualify as weird, and anyway, he was done here. Every man for himself and devil take the hindmost: that was basically Darwin's law for both man and beast, right? And as Ratliff tromped up to his suite, a wave of fresh contempt buoyed him along for the sanctimonious have-nots who condemned Ratliff for doing his job, who'd pressured him across the Atlantic.

Who were they if not smaller fish in the same pond of guilt, slipping through the net of justice by and large, lawbreakers one-and-all sometime in their pennyante lives? And these goddamn hypocrites who did drugs, lied to the IRS, falsified price tags at Whole Foods had to persecute some upper-crust scapegoat to compensate for their own ineffectiveness as people, to pretend theirs was the moral high ground, with Ratliff in the slipstream as collateral damage. Yeah, screw that punk in Gents whose hands this very second might be stuck under a spigot!

The incident of the clutching water must have boiled down to liquored-up paralysis, some rare natural phenomenon, in fine, a fluke. But to shy away from washing his hands, showering, wasn't that due caution, as was brushing his teeth out of a hotel glass, no direct contact with faucet output? And whenever he dozed off, overactive bladder sent him dashing to the toilet, a dead giveaway for how perturbed he was under the skin. Worse, when he flushed, buckshot rattle from the building's remote bowels scrabbled up the pipes with otherworldly reverb, spookier than down in Gents, rife with pent-up malice.

Come groggy morning, what more could Ratliff do about the water system than grouse at the management? He abstained from shaving, shitting, showering at this hazy pass, swung into the office and buttonholed the deskman, an owlish chap with bushy eyebrows, the minor tilt of his stance like the lead-in to a complaisant bow, offset by a constant smile that blandly intimated he was in on a joke that Ratliff, for one, wasn't. The term Dickensian, from out of nowhere, popped into Ratliff's skull on shaking the guy's deferential hand.

He'd hardly launched into complaints of clogged-up traps, noisy drainage that threatened disgusting reflux—not the whole truth, but the whole truth often backfired—when someone behind the counter sprang up. Ratliff couldn't believe he'd missed a policeman seated in plain sight. Stealthy devil! He further marked how this half-pint of a peace officer must have had an abnormally small head because his black cap with checkerboard band all but came down over his eyes, sinking them in bandit-mask shadow. "Mr. Ratliff, I take it," the half-pint interrupted.

"Well, I'll leave you to it," the manager announced to neither party per se, raising the hinged section of countertop and ambling out, still smiling.

The lawman introduced himself as Officer Mendip, without explaining how he'd recognized Ratliff, but at least didn't let on if it had been through the media.

"What's this about?" Not exactly debonair of Ratliff, but what the hell?

The manager hadn't lowered the hinged countertop on his way out. Neither Yank nor Brit betrayed an inch of willingness to approach each other through the gap.

"You were in the company last night of a Mr. Boz Whitcombe, were you not?"

Who? Half-pint's officious delivery cradled the weight of accusation. "Oh, you mean the archaeologist?" Huh, so that was his name. Mendip didn't deny it, which Ratliff parsed as default affirmative. "Yes, in the early evening," he admitted as if on the lookout for tripwires. How had Mendip determined his movements, and in such short order? England had the most CCTVs of any country, that was a common factoid, but to be on the receiving end in a surveillance state made him squirm and feel violated, unclean beyond his dereliction of bathing.

Interrogation forged onward to Ratliff's prior acquaintance of Mr. Whitcombe, the nature and duration of their get-together, the amount each had to drink, and Ratliff's subsequent whereabouts. The spectre of big-brother CCTV inhibited him from peddling untruths, though he had to pussyfoot with utmost care through his visit to the excavation, where he'd putatively met Boz, and where he presumed spy cameras weren't rolling. He feigned amazement at the sacrificial mirror, downplayed any interest in curse plaques, maintained Boz was ambulatory when their cocktail klatch adjourned, alluded to numerous personnel at the hotel pub who could testify to Ratliff's pair of nightcaps before retiring.

Mendip wrote nothing down, but a tic at the corner of his mouth connoted he was checking items off a mental list. "Fair to say, then, your chance encounter with Mr. Whitcombe led to drinks and conversation over topics of mutual interest, with no further interactions after you left the Gin Bar."

"Yes," agreed Ratliff, miffed that Mendip's loaded tone, with its subtext of entrapment, inflicted hesitance on a purely candid answer.

"Is Boz all right?" To go from no-name to first-name basis didn't quite sit right, but was probably politick. And if Boz was any kind of pal, wasn't it time Ratliff asked after him?

"He's in hospital." This tiding stood in isolation like a monolith on a plain. No elaboration, nothing of circumstances, clinical status, prognosis emanated from taciturn lips. When Mendip, on whatever arbitrary terms, decided the silent treatment had gone on long enough, he pounced, "You were never in proximity to a body of water? Mr. Whitcombe was never wet, to the best of your recollection?"

Wet? The half-pint obviously wasn't joshing, but Ratliff had to subdue a smirk at the suggestion he'd been oblivious to puddles gathering under Shovel Bum while at arm's length for two hours. He wasn't as blind as all that without corrective lenses! Restraint came much easier after the reference to "body of water" reminded him of the Roman pool, and he had to slam on the oral brakes before blurting, Is everyone else at the dig okay? And then what to say when Mendip retorted, Why wouldn't they be?

"No!" Ratliff shook his head militantly. "Wet? Not when I was with him, and people at the Gin Bar can vouch for that. We separated at the archway down the street the minute we left. That's the last I saw of him."

Mendip stared into him like some unmerciful mythic god weighing a soul in the balance. "You have no witnesses, however, to verify your itinerary from the archway on Queen Street to your lodgings."

"Only what's on the CCTV," Ratliff quipped, discounting the hundred-odd pedestrians along his route, though damned if he could summon up any of their faces.

"Can we reach you at this hotel for the next few days?" Half-pint's attitude had become even harder-assed. Maybe levity about spycams was taboo in this country.

"Yeah, why not?" shrugged Ratliff, loath to cede this pushy little martinet authority over him, yet leery of the fallout if John Law ransacked his suite or simply delved into his CV.

"Nothing further for now," Mendip intoned frostily, as if he couldn't advance past his side of the counter till Ratliff had withdrawn. Ratliff nodded and moseyed, letting his fuck-you demeanor say goodbye for him. Dickensian owl was hanging about cattycorner from the office doorway, affecting the slack posture that too pointedly disclaims eavesdropping. Not that Ratliff gave a damn; for what had to be done, the sooner he hobnobbed with management, the better.

At least the owl didn't fake surprise at being roused from viewless gaze. And he'd happily arrange a reservation for Ratliff at one of Bath's posher restaurants, couldn't go wrong with the White Hart, a personal favorite. Great, Ratliff okayed, make it for 7:30, and on hearing it was scant minutes across the river from the train station, he exclaimed, without elucidating, "Perfect!" As the owl reinstated himself behind the counter, Ratliff noticed Mendip had vacated unbeknownst, or had he dispensed with Ratliff to avoid magically vanishing in front of anyone?

On to breakfast! Gluttony caught him unawares; no exaggeration to accuse him of feral hunger. Plates and bowls piled up on his tray from multiple raids on toast, sausages, yogurt, granola, cheese, salami, a toffee-laced muffin. Overeating offered a coping mechanism, a diversion from heavy-rotation replays of Mendip's scathing incredulity that Whitcombe was intact and dry when he and Ratliff had split up. Guilt, how aggravating, that was it, though Ratliff had committed no felony, been nowhere around when Shovel Bum came to unspecified grief.

Anyone with the knack could push psychic buttons and whip up guilt, it was nothing but a conditioned reflex, no stupendous feat to tar a saint with the self-esteem of a pedophile. A conscience was no brighter than Pavlov's dog; the smart money stamped it out like a crawling hornet as soon as it stirred. Today he couldn't pronounce it dead in its tracks, though, till he'd smeared a final slice of toast with some quaintly foreign spread, Marmite it was, among the mini-capsules of innocent jams.

It resembled a petroleum byproduct, and he savagely spat out the first bite because it tasted no better, like goop ladled from Jersey Meadowlands in soupy July. Had it gone bad? Were the Brits insane enough to crave this flavor? On the upside, one mouthful had cleared his decks of useless soul-searching, and his stupid conscience was fine with writing off that vile mouthful as penance.

He guzzled coffee to cleanse his palate, assembled sandwiches, and discreetly pocketed them along with fruit, a carton of yogurt, cello-wrapped muffins for lunch in his chambers. To lie low, ready for any domestics or detectives with passkeys—how else to keep tabs on ill-gotten souvenir, ensure his eyes alone ever lit on it? Curse plaque indeed, for the supersize headache it was causing. And in his skittish mood, going out by daylight would equal reopening a can of worms, prospects of people inexplicably glaring. No, holing up was the best preventative for strife in general.

How ironic, he brooded, since he was here to evade strife, yet it had tailed him like that OCD Inspector in *Les Miz*. And how exasperating that he hadn't a clue about Shovel Bum's disaster, no details of foul play with which a purloined artifact might connect him. But he'd be a jackass to proceed any differently.

Meanwhile, the weakest trickle of spigots produced a ruckus ear-piercing, nerve-wracking. He hated that half-pint Mendip for butting in before he'd entirely aired his grievance, before the manager could comment, perhaps reassuringly, on the vagaries of local plumbing. In lieu of a shower Ratliff scrubbed his pits with a damp facecloth and slathered on the Ban extra thick. By dusk he was more than eager for dinner. The *defixio* was in suit-jacket pocket.

The restaurant loomed up from a V-shaped intersection like a seawall across a narrow shoal, except much quainter. The façade was white masonry, natch, and on a shelf above the entrance, the white statue of a six-point buck sported golden hooves. It was like a blow-up of a plastic Christmas ornament from when he was a kid, and maybe exerted the power of suggestion behind ordering the venison steak and double-shots of Jäger. And as meat and booze mellowed away his bristly edges, he did warm to the place, nothing opulent, but textbook clean and well-lit.

Contentedly people-watching through Jäger-goggles, he forgot about the leaden shard, the whole impetus for this soirée, till it dragged along his ribcage when he yawned and stretched and tailored jacket tightened. Get on with it, the shard mutely nagged. What's the holdup? Yeah, be just like him to lumber back to the hotel and space out on the one thing he'd gone out to do, he sourly mused, ill-treating himself, as often transpired, like he was his own big bullying brother.

Hold your horses, he chided himself, I have to go to the bathroom. Toilets were to the rear, along the corridor to a fire exit with a square window, beyond which blackness was like an engulfing void, like deadly deep space. Gazing out chilled him, he couldn't help personifying the dark as cunning, vindictive, and he barged with divided mind into the Gents, as if he might have blundered into a trap.

Ah, but the flush of a urinal that greeted him had never rung so wholesome, no clanging, no nuance of danger, just piss down the tubes. A beetle-browed patriarch he'd observed at the head of an extended-family fête shuffled around to the sink, and hallelujah, no percussion accompanied the turning of faucet.

As the patriarch took his stately, palsied leave, Ratliff flushed confidently, recoiled, and nearly shot headlong out the door. The din was as if he'd pulled too hard on a drawer of silverware, which detonated like a shrapnel bomb at his feet. Giving the sink wide berth was a no-brainer, and supreme self-control went into stopping short at the door, inhaling minty calm into his lungs, straightening his lapels, and strutting out as if nothing was awry. Nor was anything visibly awry among the diners. His squeamish glance shunned the fire exit.

He applied directly to the cashier for the bill, darted back in to wedge a lavish tip partway under his plate, still no verdict on whether they tipped in this country, but precious few options were handy to prove he wasn't an asshole, and despite magnanimous gesture, nobody, not cashier nor waitstaff, would glance up, reward him the least eye contact, didn't he deserve that much?

They weren't so balls-in busy, but he tried not to make anything of everyone shunning him the way he'd shunned the fire exit; how to begin decoding what such an equivalence would mean? As he hustled outside he massaged his nose, the rim of his nostrils, nope, no snot, no accounting for the cold shoulders.

Fortune favored him. The restaurant was pretty crowded, but nobody was out on this side of the river for the few moments to the footbridge. Plenty of time for second thoughts, but why squander energy? Unconversant with UK penalties for filching antiquities, to smuggle Exhibit A back onto the site of the crime, dropping it anywhere but the river, was too risky: witnesses always lurked in the woodwork, and his DNA might be sealed indelibly in lead. Too bad about ditching his bizarre curio, but between oneself and it, had he a choice?

And incredibly, his luck was holding. The sole human in the nightscape up ahead went into total eclipse under the half-moon arch of a railroad viaduct, relinquishing to Ratliff the sovereignty of this no-man's land, a provisional realm of freedom with impunity, though he wasn't looking forward to braving that underpass, an ideal habitat for muggers or worse.

On the threshold of the bridge, clumps of birch and willow flanked staggered partitions to encumber any vehicle bulkier than a pram; foliage clattered like bead curtains. The bridge's railings, like girders with big round rivets, were pragmatically industrial, as were the iron lattice sidings, all in aquamarine. On the left, beyond the greenery, flush against the ironwork abutment was a square masonry hut with slate roof and oversized chimney, surely not a sentry box or tollhouse despite appearances.

He threaded the S-curve of the barriers and fingered the curse plaque, keen to put culpability behind him, annoyed that lead crinkle had somehow gashed the lining of his pocket. In the instant his attention strayed from the bridge, a rotund silhouette detached itself from the junction of the hut and the abutment to straddle the path forward. Mystifying that someone of such bulk wouldn't have registered till he was at arm's length, all the more because the figure had had no gap at the junction from which to emerge and definitely hadn't plodded from the hut's padlocked door. Why hadn't Ratliff worn his fucking glasses?

As his eyes labored to fill in the silhouette, its outlines became more crinkly and erratic, like mangled sawteeth or meringue. And the longer it abided stockstill, arms hanging limp, the more Ratliff distrusted his brain's capacity to process information, for he could only believe that a statue, an environmental installation, must have confronted him all along, though he couldn't remember it from his stroll to the restaurant. Its components, on harder squint, bespoke modern art, a mass of metal wafers soldered together, head and neck an unarticulated unit like a bucket, its features shallow dents and furrows, upon the rugged beam of shoulders.

But then like a mechanical toy, the creaky sculpture reached its left paw, palm up, trembling as if impatient, within inches of Ratliff, who took this imitation of life remarkably in stride. In this provisional realm of his, of freedom unbound, let the statuary be interactive, its joints lubricated with deer fat and Jäger, his ego could handle it, however petrifying this development would be anywhere else. If his self-importance surrendered the reins, he'd be done for, of course, he realized that instinctively.

The bulky paw, at point-blank range, showed warped and partial lines of script on each interfolded scrap, excerpts from a thousand Latin curses, and among the thousand inadequate responses to the situation, Ratliff's was singularly off-key, an epiphany that here was how a Golem must have been, not buff and gussied-up à la Hollywood or an episode of *The Simpsons,* but crude, malformed, a travesty. A Golem, though, he could have conveniently neutralized by swabbing Hebrew letters off its brow.

More to the point, Ratliff would have been quicker on the uptake had he been less flustered: what could the brute want besides the contents of suitcoat pocket? He extracted the *defixio* and gingerly plunked it into corrugated mitt, and hurray, he'd been correct, this embodiment of curses pressed AWOL text against its left cheek. Ratliff couldn't see any improvement, though the brute raised a mirror stashed somewhere on its person to its augmented face, tilted the glass at several angles till it lingered over the most flattering. A crease in the buckethead widened into a crescent gash. Nor was it any old mirror; Ratliff recognized the crusty gold pinwheels of the prize find from the pit.

He should have skedaddled, but had to bask a little in the vanity this effigy radiated at its self-perfection, as if Ratliff identified with it, as if his own egoism were reflected back at him in lead. What the hell, he hedged, problem solved anyway, buckethead's happy, not as if he couldn't outsprint it with its smokestacks of legs.

But a smug second later, and shit! No sprinting was in the cards. One lightning grab, with an incongruous rattle as of chains, had him encased, lungs squeaking pitifully, as a visceral knowledge of two millennia's worth of numinosity dug serrations into him right through his clothes. And from the bucket's slimy gash, no longer an upturned crescent, a grating parody of a voice, with resonations of a rake across plate glass, croaked an inch from his face, "Vade mecum!"

Ratliff's glazed and bulging eyes absorbed without amusement the drollery of a "No Diving" sign bolted to the topside of the railing, a heartbeat before lead buttocks swiveled around and crushed it as lead feet sprang airborne with a grinding of striated dross knees. Backward over the railing!

Riverward plunge allowed Ratliff no time to dwell on whether retribution or random spite had caught up with him, or on the roundabout fulfillment of curses, or on which misdeeds he was expiating, and on who precisely had condemned him, and whether his eyes or some divine power were deceiving him, no, he managed only to puzzle, Why the hell would a Golem go plugging toothpaste?

Two corpses were discovered next day on opposite banks of the Avon by a troop of Girl Guides and Council groundskeepers, respectively. The casualties were identified as Americans from different floors of the same hotel, though police couldn't ascertain whether the two were acquainted, had drowned in unrelated mishaps, or had waged a mutually destructive feud.

The constabulary deferred further sleuthing to the US Embassy, which also paid the outstanding hotel balance for one of the Americans, whose lawyers had declared him bankrupt the day after checking in. Forensics and autopsy results were less than revelatory, and Bath's finest were especially frustrated because every CCTV between the hotel and the footbridge had shorted out, as if water had infiltrated their circuits, just as during Whitcombe's misadventure. How could they conduct an investigation virtually blind? How had justice ever triumphed without cameras?

Old Goodman Brown

Faith would outlive him, but to old Goodman Brown she'd been dead for decades. Of this the Archfiend was well aware, for his wiles had driven abiding wedge of alienation between them when they were still but newlyweds. Tonight he wore the grave black of bygone century and a weathered elderhood, belied by how vigorously he rapped with snakeheaded staff upon stout farmhouse door. He swallowed his amusement when Faith answered, pink ribbons of youth still gracing brittle gray braids. She betrayed no recognition of him, if any she retained.

Nor did sympathy warm her haggard features when she ushered hobbling guest into the bedchamber and shook her husband's shoulder to awaken him. Scant sparks escaped hollow sockets to show his eyes were open, and dry wheezing grew louder without filling hollow cheeks. Goodman Brown was sunk deep in feather mattress as if lowered partway into earth already.

"Is it my own grandfather," Goodman Brown murmured, "who rejoins the living younger than myself?" Faith withdrew and quietly shut the bedroom door, no sign of curiosity on downcast face.

"I'm here to render whatever comfort and assistance I may," deferential visitor declared. In the glow of guttering oil lamp, his staff's snakehead seemed to blink under his folded hands.

"You've come to help." Brown vented a rasping laugh. "I'd a lifetime's worth of your help when you lured me, in callow youth, through the woods to that Sabbat of your worshippers. And there you helped me see the truth that we of Salem, and everywhere, drink greedily from sin's chalice, pastors, thieves, matrons, harlots, and my own wife. I am grateful for that truth whether or not you fashioned profane spectacle from fog and moonbeams, for truth is truth by whatever road it travels, is it not? And is not truth to be esteemed above all else?"

"I fear you taunt me," confessed inveterate beguiler.

"No more than do you, in the guise of revered kinsman."

"You wrong me!" Knobbly fingers went defensively to broad linen collar. "This august vessel I deemed most proper to bear the milk of charity, glad tidings of mercy. The sands are soon run from your unhappy hourglass, but say the word and those years are replenished, and your happiness. This I offer in recompense for the misery you suffered at my remiss hands."

"In return for which you ask nothing?" A smile, or more aptly a rictus, spread like a crack in the waxen mask of pending death.

"Have a care not to provoke me! My clemency is finite as the corruptible world." Intimations of an unbecoming leer spoiled the mask of serenity.

"You cannot cow me."

"Do you assume redemption through the crucible of self-torment? Do you fancy your soul purified and invincible against hell's violence? Elevated among the elect, are you?"

"Oh no, quite the opposite," Brown quavered with studied innocence. "I owe the devil his due and mean no flippancy when I give thanks for purging me of trust in Christian virtues, and of doubt in nature's godlessness. Else the scales would have remained on my eyes and I'd never have forsaken received wisdom to loft toward enlightenment, in keeping with others of this age, but surpassing them as the eagle does the wren. I'm indeed in your debt."

Some semblance of pity carved deeper furrows around the guest's grim-set mouth. "Yet here you are. Much good has this enlightenment brought you, and much pleasure." A sadder frown lent patriarch the pout of a gargoyle. "Am I one with whom you should hope to dissemble?"

"I shouldn't wager who or what you are." Color suffused waxen complexion, and passion galvanized frail husk. "You've become of meager import to me, for what are heaven and hell save figments of hoodwinked souls?" The bed quaked at a spasm of coughing. "And what are these purported souls in your ledger," he croaked, "beyond a currency that exists by mutual consent between you and the gullible?" At odds with impiety was the fiery eye of a zealot.

"Why bestir yourself at all for me, who may not exist except in fever vision?"

"You've beheld God's countenance, if anybody has." Goodman Brown became acerbic like a schoolmaster hectoring a dullard. "Tell me, when was your last confab with Him?"

Deceiver wrinkled patrician nose as if the Goodman's hauteur offended it. "You impugned me as Father of Lies an instant ago, and now you goad me for an answer we both know you'd not believe."

"And again you would mislead me into self-doubt, but I'll not backslide. You've done too well at weaning me off the creed so needful to you and your victims alike." Goodman Brown's look latched onto his guest as if with designs to convert the very devil. Guest narrowed uncongenial eyes at prospects of dotty sermonizing, at reservoir of vitality below the still waters of dotage. "The truth shall edify you, though to be edified is nowise to be happier, as if happiness or aught dear to us were dear among the stars."

"You've been among the stars?" Was that a gibe or a question? Goodman Brown's grin was not unlike that of head on serpentine staff. The staff's owner glared at mortal impudence, but before his temper found words the Goodman was underway.

"As my kindred spirit Descartes might have put it, once the x and y axes of sin and saintliness no longer bound me, neither did compunctions toward a spotless repute. I presumed the Ushers, the oldest booksellers in Boston, to have had works by Newton, Hooke, and Halley, names outside your circle I daresay." Goodman Brown gulped a ratchety breath; his guest archly mouthed "I daresay" but held his peace.

"Because of God's absence from these doctors' formulas for fathoming creation, churchmen militant reckoned them ungodly, whereas I hungered after them for just that reason. The clerk, an impish fellow who sniffled and hemmed as though surfeited with snuff, had nothing I sought. But with an air of broaching no new subject, he asked did I know a son of the shop's founder had been jailed for witchcraft? I could only shake my head, and he elaborated how the shackled Hezekiah had escaped through another prisoner's devices, a Goody Mason, who somehow used equations like those of Newton as sorcery.

"The clerk could not specify the manner of this usage, but asserted Goody Mason's grasp of metaphysics would have confounded Kepler himself. What's more, rumor had it she still subsisted in squalid garret out in remote suburbs. If only she were handy, her I should approach for lessons that reduced Newton's calculus to child's play. I thanked him and withdrew hastily lest his sniffles, and his probable derangement, prove infectious, and repaired homeward on purchasing my books elsewhere.

"Some hours past dark I stabled my horse and trudged with weighty satchel to my door. I'd crossed from moonlit path into the shadows below the eaves when a rat scampered where my foot was about to land, near to tripping me, startling me the more because it was the size of a young woodchuck. My hand was fraught with instinct to grab for a pitchfork.

"Cackling burst from the blackness that had harbored giant vermin. 'You'll want worse than a pitchfork to dispatch me and mine!' I was flustered by shrill outcry, and further that I'd unawares been pantomiming my intent, which I surely hadn't voiced. This prowler's cadences of lunacy and menace were moreover alarmingly strange, yet I was convinced she was no absolute stranger.

"Had she, I inquired, been some years ago among Salem's mingled gentry and rabble in the wilderness, where now my acreage was situated, when Great Deceiver contrived joining me and my Faith in a Hallows-Eve travesty of marriage? I'd meanwhile had no luck espying trespasser in pitch-dark shadow, and her pet was gone afield, committing untold mischief.

"She tittered and jeered, 'To indulge such mummery is beneath me. And is it not beneath you too, a would-be disciple of Halley and Copernicus? I'll show entire what they only glimpsed, and much they never dreamed of. Say the word, and all is yours.'

"I had to grant then the verity of my absurd suspicions about this intruder's name, and how curious that both you and Goody Mason besought me with 'Say the word.' But she would never sign your ledger, would she?" The Goodman's diction verged on nettlesome. His audience swatted at an unseen gnat.

"That ledger goes back millennia. Can you recollect every soul with whom you've dealt?" chided the Archfiend.

"Mere millennia," sighed Goodman Brown. "Goody Mason promised I would learn the age and watch the birth pangs of the cosmos, though after consorting with you, how could I not beware of fine enticements? As I strained my sight in vain for the least glimmer of her, I queried, 'At what cost do you propose to school me?'

"'What cost would be too high?' she crowed. 'What of this earth would not pale in value beside my teachings?'

"I prayed she speak more softly, lest she bestir my wife and swaddling boy. 'How tragic that would be!' she mocked in husky whisper. 'Very well, simply nod and we'll adjourn for the nonce.'

"I'd scarce begun to wag my chin when monstrous, insolent rat leapt over my toes and into the blackness, jaws clamped on a mangled rooster's neck. On the heels of my wanton oath was a silence more doleful than in a midnight churchyard. That silence resumed as soon as I'd entreated, 'Goody Mason?' I ventured into black shadow under the eaves and let my eyes habituate. No one squinted back at me, not harridan nor thieving rat, as if I'd been alone all along.

"The next visitation, and each subsequent, disquieted me no less than the first. I was milking cows in the barn at daybreak, as later I'd be shelving turnips in the root cellar or adding fieldstones to a boundary wall, when the scuttle of great rat past my toes and a violet flash, swifter than a blink, heralded my instructress. Stooped and spindly crone curbed my protest at her pet's new depredations that dawn by hissing, 'Whist! You said your wife and baby mustn't hear!'

"While I regathered my wits, she plucked up my lamp and muttered and goggled around till some junction of angles and curves wrought by carpentry and shadows pleased her. She positioned the lamp to preserve this arrangement, whistled like a thrush for her accomplice, and beckoned me to 'tour heavens framed in no Bible story.' With a tittering as human as Goody Mason's, rodent hurtled by me, and then with deceptively snakish speed, crone latched scaly fist about my arm and tugged. I stumbled in tow through that geometry of curves and angles, whose outlines flared up violet.

"Intersections of cow stall and beam and windowsill remained solid as ever, but radiant empurpled edges stood out like a ship's prow, and we penetrated them as though they were cobwebs. We emerged into lustrous firmament, suspended there as if we'd vaulted from ship's prow to lodge in its rigging. I was dumbfounded at this, and at our encasement, or transformation rather, into diversely sized globes and serried rectangles, but likewise was my mind transformed into deeming these alterations meet and natural.

"Some proficiency of Goody Mason's will detached us from the invisible rigging and propelled us into that firmament and toward further gleaming geometries fashioned of nameless constellations and celestial bodies, and she planted in my thoughts some comprehension of the marvels beyond those geometries.

"I therewith became her protégé as she revealed a fabric of reality set forth by no astrolabe or scripture. We contracted through the needle's eye to realms infinitesimal beyond reach of microscopes, where the most elementary particles within all matter madly spun round or bounced off or cleaved to one another, like eternal riot in measureless Bedlam. Else we ascended to divine vantage where our sun was less than a speck of dust in an immense pinwheel of stars, and then we withdrew to such remoteness that our pinwheel was one speck in a countless host dispersing headlong toward ultimate dissipation.

"But within a starless planet's frozen ocean, a lucent portal, contrived from cracks in ice and temple ruins blasphemous to Euclid, led to the most astonishment. For on traversing it, I was apparently home again, except my vision now detected twice what it ever had, a teeming density of grains, formerly clandestine, whose black network and trillion filaments connected and perforated trees, hills, farmhouse, me, and everything material, and made of the air a fluid mosaic, and crowded night sky with whorls like magnified fingertips. It was a world of foreign substance pervading ours, omnipresent, but occluded from earthly faculties."

Goodman Brown broke into raw chuckles that lapsed into feeble coughing. "I'd always pondered how you and Cotton Mather got on," the Goodman informed his guest. "What was he save his day's paradox incarnate? An avid partisan of science, a champion of inoculation against the smallpox, yet he endorsed spectral evidence to root out witchcraft, to condemn the innocent by asserting they trafficked in the Invisible World. And here I was, trafficking with one he'd branded a witch, through whom I was privy to an Invisible World his followers in science may not approach for centuries."

The semblance of Goodman Brown's grandsire pensively kneaded his chin. "Hearsay has it Cotton Mather was among the keenest intellects in the colonies, a claim you'd never arrogate to yourself. Perhaps deferring to his cosmogony would better suit your modesty. Can you prove this Goody Mason was not bedazzling you with phantasms?"

"If Mather's obsolete 'cosmogony,' as you dignify it, were so unerring, then why, among those nineteen whose executions he applauded, were only Goodies Carrier and Corey present at that Hallows' Eve Sabbat of yours? Or were you bedazzling me with phantasms that night?"

Venerable mouth indecorously smirked. "To err is human. A rash decision or two hardly required my whispers in Mather's ear. Your Goody Mason, on the other hand, must have been infallibly rational." Pert as a goat, Grandsire rubbed upraised right boot against left ankle.

"You've had the pleasure of her company, then, to make sport with me thus?" The Goodman's flinty eyes rebuked the Deceiver. "Or need I restate that she and Mather shared their generation's handicap, one foot mired in benighted past, while the other strove toward wisdom? Even as Mather credulously peopled the air with ghosts and witches, she couched ingenious mathematics in the ignorant trappings of magic, mathematics so complex its applications were tantamount to conjury.

"But that was poor excuse for her to affect hocus-pocus posturings, distress at beholding the cross, the fellowship of a beastly familiar, and talk of a 'master' whose book I'd have to sign, especially after she'd professed such scorn for 'mummery.' In fine, I grew skeptical of any genius in her, who taught her transportive geometries solely as rote, with no grounding in their principles. Her 'master,' I surmised, was conversant with those principles, and I was both eager and loath to pay him court. His powers of learning were enough to make him imposing, if not fearsome, unlike Goody Mason, fatuous despite her attainments.

"Between her mentions of his 'book' and calling him 'the Black Man,' I mused he might be another sly embodiment of you, which would have let me dismiss celestial voyages as illusory. I could then have acquitted myself more conscionably as householder, for though my wife and son were none the wiser to my weeks and months of rovings, a premonition of leaving them insecure had come to haunt me. Goody Mason's 'master,' I meanwhile supposed, must have cultivated your likeness to render her more biddable to his hidden purposes."

Archfiend shrugged. "I take many guises. Others may disguise themselves as me. Do not, mind you, underrate me as one who moves in mysterious ways."

"Peculiar how Goody Mason's 'Black Man' said much the same himself." An adversarial smile began to form till some internal anguish quelled it and shortened his breath. "He," the Goodman persisted, "might not outdo you as an opportunist, though his domain was loftier than yours. And whereas you boast of serving no one, the Goody's 'master' answered to a lord whose realm was inordinately grander than your Jehovah's."

"Would you wheedle me into staging a defense of that odious Jehovah? I rejoice in your exertions to take Him down a peg. Why would I not?" Immortal trickster may have tried forging ingratiation on venerable features, but seemed unctuous at best. "And pardon my remarking this concern for family after you ostensibly severed such mawkish ties, at first because sin tainted them, and then with astronomic delvings to preoccupy you. How could the grubbing lot of a farmer compete?"

"Every time the Goody and her pet came to fetch me, I departed feeling as I had that night of hieing to the woods for my rendezvous with you, when Faith and I were blissfully in love. I did not like that feeling." Indignation furrowed ashen forehead.

"Goodman Brown, do not fault me for following a course I never urged on you!" False grandsire's wrinkled brow parodied the Goodman's.

"Nor did I like the feeling, more and more distinct, of others watching over our journeys, whose very act of watching perturbed my equilibrium, and put me in sympathy with the fawn that fears a lurking catamount." To diabolic visitor, bitter grimace was akin to those on myriad clients surrendering to damnation. "In brief, I was near to admitting regret at ever giving Goody Mason the nod."

Unctuous smile once more marred grandfatherly visage. "Regret? Of what use is that? To you fell privileges beyond the ken of angels, the knowledge of worlds barred to them, of mechanisms governing the atoms of Democritus and the tedious doom of this clockwork universe."

"Knowledge, yes, you've always been a great one for promoting knowledge since your antics in Eden," the Goodman interjected.

Deceiver went on as if deaf to irony. "I might envy you the sublime panoramas of suns colliding, of opalescent clouds smothering constellations, of cities and jungles and armadas inaccessible to earthly senses. Are you not enriched by these splendors, haven't wonderment and rapture persuaded you of some magisterial design, is it absolutely certain you've been versed in purely secular mysteries?"

"You overplay your hand." Contempt hardened the Goodman's frown. "You cannot restore me to your clutches by reviving my credence in heaven and hell. For what are beauty, reverence, or love but human valuations, pretty gloss to smooth over chaos and futility, pathetic before omnipotent indifference?"

"You're sadder than I foresaw." Dour assessment smacked uncharitably of reproach.

Goodman Brown shook his head as if disheartened that his pronouncements on the worth of happiness had gone to waste. "No easier for you than me discerning sorrow from wisdom, eh? But we come to the crux." He cleared ratchety throat. "I knew no customary ride impended that night my fellow voyagers emerged from hearthside shadows. Both were exultant as topers, cackling brazenly as if wakening wife and child above us were of no consequence.

"A double shudder of panic afflicted me at vile rat darting from the chamber and toward the stairs, and then at first glance of its abnormal head by inconstant firelight, muzzle too blunt to encompass crooked fangs, irises blue instead of glassy black, ears like a man's, flat against the skull. Goody Mason's imperious whistle retrieved slinking creature to her heels. I undertook no second glance. 'Later for that!' she hissed at it. 'Mustn't violate prescribed order!'

"As if to trivialize that warning she grinned, and bared teeth winsome as her pet's. 'My master may choose you for advancement! Prepare yourself!' she crooned. Her jubilation was of a savory piece with her grin. And had she been more bookishly inclined, she'd have noticed I was preparing, with volume three of Newton's *Principia* by my wainscot chair, as I'd been preparing studiously since that fateful jaunt to Boston.

"She railed, 'You and I are of like humors, are we not? No seasonal rounds of drudgery for us, no fetters of domesticity, no paltry span of threescore years and ten! Of what merit is any ambition bound by human limitations? Hasten, the Black Man finds rich promise in you!' That praise alone reaffirmed for me the Black Man was not you. She warbled how we'd be partners till the end of the world, and when I confessed unease at making her savage pet jealous, she scoffed, 'His perquisites are his own, and they're nothing to you!'

"In the hearth's cavernous maw had formed, by none of Goody Mason's doing, tracery of more royal purple than hers, staunch amid the flickering orange glow, etched from the crane for the kettle, the pair of crescent andirons, the cracks in fireplace back wall, and the blazing logs. 'Go on! Why do you hesitate?' Goody Mason scolded as I charily leaned forward and smelled the hairs on my knuckles singe. From behind, animal chatter added to the scolding, and selfsame gullet, I'd swear, squealed, 'Go!'

"I turned in confusion, and spiteful vermin sprang at my face as from a cannon, a sneer upon blunt snout that no rat could shape. This treachery startled an unmanly shriek from me, and I recoiled tottering into infernal heat and through the violet gateway as my cheeks began to sear.

"My skin still stung, and smoke stank in my nostrils, as I fell to my knees on the yonder side, onto a black floor that was not stone or wood or metal. At the outset, the retention of my fleshly body, instead of mutation into tandem globes, mystified me. Nor had the Goody changed appearance, and her worshipful gaze conveyed she was kneeling deliberately.

"Her creature, meanwhile, scampered between us, and between a plain black altar and plain black lectern with an open tome of black pages atop it, and up shallow black steps onto a black dais, from the center of which rose a rugged black throne. On the throne, the recumbent figure of a man was black and featureless and immobile as everything else, and at his heels frolicked the misshapen rodent, whining in uncouth rhapsody. To survey these outmoded trappings of religiosity, of sheer charlatanism, made me wary and dispirited.

"What's more, this adoration of a statue, as seemed the case, soon paled on me, and I sought for the source of reflected mercurial sheen on every black surface, like the to-and-fro of white minnows in a dark eddy. On observing the stupendous cataclysm that enveloped us I was instantly dizzy and overwhelmed. Our platform sheltered under a pellucid canopy of silence, in the calm eye of infinite storm wherein cyclones and pinwheels and explosions in every hue of the spectrum arbitrarily collided or rebounded or fused.

"And lacking any sense of scale or perspective I couldn't hazard if the turmoil was composed of stars or dust or atoms, and indeed all may have been as one, in this anarchic theatre that made a farce of harmony or any music of the spheres. Nor could I attest whether seconds or eons were ticking by beyond our refuge. Whatever the actuality, wherever we were, the spectacle functioned as billowing stage curtains for the dumb show to which I lowered my daunted sights.

"More discomfiting yet, the greeting 'Welcome!' accosted me in a voice not high nor low, devoid of timbre, accent, or any memorable qualities. Freakish rodent now gamboled about a statue bolt upright and fixing upon me features so regular and nondescript as to give memory nothing to latch onto, like sculpted equivalent of the impersonal voice. This hairless, sexless statue moreover was of no human blackness, but in fact matched that of altar, throne, and lectern, and I was stupefied to recognize it also as that black of secret tendrils and reticulations penetrating all visible substance.

"The Black Man averred that while I lacked instruction to realize who he was, he could see I astutely realized who he was not, by which I gathered he meant you. With an unnervingly artful smile, he registered approval of me. 'The God of your people you condemn as fable,' he intoned as if scanning it on my brow, 'and you would follow erudition's road to its end, there to uncover what underlies all illusion, cant, and religion. Yes, let us depose sham God in favor of the genuine Prime Mover.'

"Both Goody Mason and her alter ego abandoned their piety and harshly dissented, and rodent's ear for English no longer gave me least pause. Despite their muddle of agitation I managed to catch Goody Mason's gist, her disbelief in my readiness, her objection to granting me unearned privilege. Their outburst, as if it were the buzzing of flies, failed to swerve unblinking charcoal focus. We'd defer the formality of my signature in his book, he decreed, for I'd shortly have fewer compunctions about signing.

"Before my escorts could oppose this fresh breach of protocol, the claptrap of black furnishings, and our floor, faded into transparency. I hadn't the presence to note whether the Goody and her pet also swayed off-balance as the swirls like vague white fish at our feet became the churning tempest of the spheres. Concurrently, our canopy cracked open with a thunderclap that shook my marrow, and I had scant chance to cringe at colossal vortices bearing down on us like a host of Olympian boot-heels, when everything in a heartbeat underwent reversal.

"It was, as the song goes, 'The World Turned Upside-Down,' save that we were on no world. We stood firm though not upon ground, my head felt clear and refreshed though falling sky had been about to crush it, and the dazzling tumult had become a lambent black, wherein fleeting white arcs and flecks glimmered on whirling spirals and polyhedrons. And in lieu of that earsplitting collapse of celestial roof, a bass pulsation, more palpable than audible, kept time with none of the black gyrations, and a hoarse piping, sans beat or rhythm or visible pipers or association with aught else, was nonetheless somehow intrinsic to all.

"My grasp of perspective and scale was, if anything, more askew here. Each towering black configuration may have revolved at arm's length or across vast gulfs, and to raise my eyes set me reeling as upon a well-sweep till the zenith became the azimuth. I dared not peer downward. The Goody and her familiar and their master were at different distances whenever I regarded any one of them, feet or yards or furlongs away, yet I never saw them move.

"The single fixity, the one commonality between our prior environs and these, was the black throne, the ever-calm center within rank instability. For this arrant stage dressing to follow us beyond the realm of 'cant and illusion,' I conjectured the strict literality of this vista must have been subject to the Black Man's mediation. Why doubt he had the craft to filter reality through an incisive metaphor, for the benefit of our limited human brains and senses, or to humor Goody Mason's naive preconceptions, writ large in her devout gaze?

"Her adulation of him who replaced the Black Man on the throne was grievously misguided, for who could reasonably ignore the vacant slouch, impulsively flapping hands, aimless, guttural laughter, slack-jawed drooling, and fecal miasma of an idiot? The Black Man, suddenly by my side, commended my clear-sightedness in seeing the Prime Mover for what he was, which the Goody, in her prayerful genuflection, and her pet, with ecstatically switching tail, patently did not. Their mute veneration was doubly pathetic because they failed to acknowledge their deity's milky eyes were blind as any icon's."

"Ah, but prove yours were not the disordered senses. How prideful to assume the inferiority of others!" Archfiend's smug grin only broadened as his deflection of the Goodman's train of verbiage triggered a fit of gulping and snorting for air.

"A pox on you for distracting a poor codger with so few breaths to him," croaked Goodman Brown. "I remind you, the Black Man himself saluted my clarity, allowing for my limited sensorium. No guiding intellect, he confirmed, presided at the core of everything. All was a random production of blind, mindless forces, as personified upon the throne, the divine inanity made manifest as the mechanical pulse, the tuneless piping. How the slobbering creator created himself, or otherwise came to be, abides as sole intractable mystery."

"Yes, unless your sorry shambles of a 'Prime Mover' is no such thing, but one mere creature more of the God you once revered," the Deceiver argued.

"Then who created that God, or how came He to be?" With a wave both feeble and disdainful, the Goodman dismissed further dispute. "Of the idiot god's features, like the Black Man's, I could retain nothing, as if the Black Man were some finer-hewn avatar or emanation of the Prime Mover. The Black Man must have read these intimations in me, for he proposed, 'Are we not each of us more or less felicitous rearrangements of primal disorder? The victims or darlings of almighty imbecility? You're correct to appreciate my ways and substance are too complex for human rationality. But your schooling's done for now.'

"In a topsy-turvy blink, the Black Man was restored to the throne, our sheltering canopy was overhead, and the prodigious black upheavals were dazzling and prismatic again. Goody Mason was at my elbow, and her pet had importunate forepaws on my shin. The Goody held open in outstretched hands the black book from the lectern, and unwholesome glint in her eyes made me dread her master's next words. 'And like any schoolteacher,' he continued, 'or ferryman if you prefer, payment's due me, nothing too exorbitant in light of what you've learned.'

"With a peremptory flourish he drew my attention to a bowl I'd not observed earlier on the altar, of a somber burnish like an alloy of silver and the black material of our surroundings and the 'master' himself. I then descried beside the bowl a round-hafted dagger forged from that same alloy, and I was also positive it wasn't there an instant ago.

"The Black Man was on his feet as precipitously as before, and between him and the altar hovered a purple contour that testified to his adeptness, for it was woven of no more than the arrested drafts and stirrings of the air. I was at once contemptuous of the added flummery with knife and bowl, this pandering to the Goody's taste for heathenish props, yet was I also chagrined at these dire harbingers, and at the total opacity of inhuman aims and pleasures.

"As if in essence to decoy me, Goody Mason thrust the book a hairsbreadth from my waistcoat and demanded, 'Sign it! Sign in blood!' Her rodent, meanwhile, was up on hindquarters, scrabbling at my leg.

"A childish whimper redirected my attention to the Black Man stepping from the purple contour, and cupped in his untender grip was my swaddling boy, lolling as in drugged torpor. I was aghast at apprehending the odious bargain I should have foreseen when the Goody's accomplice tried scurrying to my bedchamber. The Black Man's mirthless smile rendered me more deathly dumbfounded. 'You who've so aptly learned the value of earthly life,' he declaimed, 'and of family and posterity and all other sacrosanct follies, how could you scruple to dispatch your firstborn, what worth can he possess in your elevated view?'

"The dagger, cool and smooth and weightless as talc, was inexplicably in my hand. The Black Man shook my boy's muslin blanket free from his bare chest, and pushed him toward me with the gravity of Yahweh offering Abraham a glorious covenant. My wayfaring comrades were meanwhile pressing closer till my breath mingled with the putrescence of theirs, and the Goody exhorted, 'Sign it in his blood! That should temper your precocious swagger!' Her rat, whose face I still shrank from scrutinizing, chided stridently, and I'd warrant I could sometimes discriminate syllables in some mewling language.

"I was mortified at how the brute rhythms of this clamor had come to throb within my veins, eroding my will. My fingers tightened their clench upon the haft, and my arm involuntarily began to rise. As I struggled against despair and base capitulation, against knuckles that refused to loosen around the knife, I could not say then, and cannot now, whether I acted out of love and loyalty and resurgent Christian

virtue, or out of cold repugnance at this bloodshed as waste and fool-
ery, an insult to august science, a sop to foul superstition, for what authentic purpose could such sacrifice serve?

"In their passion to humiliate me, drag me down to their murderous level and confute I was their better, Goody Mason and her pet
could no longer contain themselves. Supporting the black book in one
hand, she wedged it against me to keep it open, while her other hand
seized my forearm; I bridled at the effrontery of her touch. She fairly
crushed what control I had of my arm to wrench it with dagger in fist
toward my fretful baby. Each second, despite my utmost resolve, the
blade inched closer, and the Black Man complacently nodded as his
underlings labored to fulfill his inscrutable ends.

"The rodent, with gouging claws, raced up my breeches and vest
too swiftly to cuff away, and pounced on my left arm as I flailed haplessly. Sawtooth fangs chomped on my wrist, and foul beast clung to
my sleeve, and hindered my efforts to lift my arm and flap it loose, and
twisted to jeer at me. The face from which I'd diligently shied now met
mine full-on, and shock and outrage staggered me at cognizance of
blasphemously mannish blue eyes, hooked snout, and scraggy beard,
like unto Goody Mason as a son or brother.

"And at this insufferable travesty of nature, I flung the arm in
Goody Mason's grip up at an angle she was unprepared to parry, and
jabbed the dagger into her obscene familiar. I struck hastily but well
enough. Baneful vermin propelled itself away with an agonized squeal.
The Goody weakened and wailed at this harm to her boon companion,
and no sooner had I, with wrath unabated, broken her clasp than I
stabbed her and rejoiced as she screeched and crumpled.

"The book had tumbled thudding to the floor. I hearkened from it
to the rill of blood still dribbling from my wrist, troubled at my fate
should any gouts have spilled onto the pages. My eyes hove to the
Black Man, for he was venting raspy laughter, not at me but at his
writhing disciples. My son he carried unmindfully, as if forgotten and
liable to be tossed aside on rediscovering him.

"Around this kidnapper softly shone the purple nimbus from the
creel of light behind him. I sprinted forth, with fatherly heart goading
me at frenzied pitch, planted dagger in the Black Man's surprisingly ge-
latinous throat, grabbed my child from his unresisting arms, and

shoved against this malefactor's chest, which was in contrast like smooth black granite, and like a statue he toppled backward. I leapt into the purple, but like Lot's wife couldn't help one last glimpse and was confounded by statue already upright, neck bereft of knife, arms outstretched, and the Goody and her creature crawling toward him on their bellies.

"Momentum hurled me from out the fireplace, with nary a spark attaching to me or the swaddling cloth. I was afeard as much of lurching over and crushing my offspring as of anything else this night, and gratefully collapsed into that same wainscot chair from which I'd embarked. The fire still crackled briskly, begging the question of how long I'd been away. Purple configuration also hung steady amid the flames, and I bounced up and strained my ears for more perhaps than the pop and hiss of logs ablaze.

"So engrossed was I in listening that I was near to entranced when animal gibbering and witchy imprecations emerged distinct from the sputtering combustion, indicating the master had repaired his puppets to chase after me. Bracing restive tot upon my shoulder, I snatched a poker and thrashed vengefully at the firewood, the andirons, the kettle crane, wrecking the geometry on which the portal depended.

"And as purple contours receded like incinerating straws, I shuddered at both my narrow escape and at ghastlier shrieks than the dagger had wrought, as if limbs were sheared from torsos, or torsos sheared in twain. I heard as well that inhumane laugh of black larynx as I backed bone-weary into my chair, where Faith almost gave me up for dead in the morning, save I was hugging our languid boy to me as for dear life.

"I never saw more of the Goody and her cohort, but pondered then, and ever after, the import if my blood had stained the black book. Did that account in part for the Black Man's glee? And had rescuing my son amounted to a useless gesture? He grew to independence and resettled beyond the Berkshires, and broken all ties with me; he's been no comfort, and it's as if I'd never fathered him."

The archfiend's patrician mask acquired a more contemplative veneer. "At the root of it, though, homely virtues were victorious over cultish brutality, what matter if those virtues were instilled instead of heartfelt? Does that not suggest something?"

"Yes, that you're deaf as an anvil," the Goodman carped, but fainter of breath, vitality ebbing now his story was told. "Fortune's whim, or mayhap the blind idiot god's, brought me home unscathed. My life or my son's could as easily have been forfeit, or I could have blandly acceded to his slaughter. My survival to this moment signifies nothing."

"Bah!" The Deceiver banged his staff against the floor with the disgust of Moses vilifying a Golden Calf. "I can do naught with you! I leave you on your own!"

"Wait!" the Goodman hoarsely bid as his guest gathered up woolen cloak to turn away. "You fancy yourself so guileful, yet likelihood of imperfect candor in others never dawns on you?" Archfiend bared the vicious snarl of a cutthroat betrayed by a cutthroat. "Mightn't deathbed confession have been a lie? Might I not have patched up differences with fellow acolytes and consorted with them evermore? Shame on you, to be hoodwinked like a silly lackwit imp!" The "lackwit imp" brandished his staff as if to smash a defenseless skull, and he, if not the head of his staff, hissed like a viper. "But here," the Goodman wheezed, "is a trick I've saved for you!"

Without more ado, a tangled cage of purple bars lit up atop the mattress, enmeshing Goodman Brown. And in a trice, both man and glowing shape were gone, apart from gloating laughter and the tangy whiff that lingers after lightning strikes.

Wide-eyed Archfiend had no opportunity to poke at blankets with his staff or curse unsportingly, for in the darkness at his feet, incisors as of monstrous rodent punched through tough boot leather, or at least the illusion of leather, to puncture devilish ankle. In thorough disarray, the corrupter expelled an astounded, disgraceful shout and fled the bedchamber, clouting its door wide open without a backward glance.

Faith, throughout the colloquy, had eavesdropped at the door, nursing hopes she dared not articulate. These had gone to ashes, though, during the course of harrowing narrative. She cowered away as visitor burst forth and bolted from the house, and she hurried to the Goodman's bedside and let slip one forlorn moan at discovering him expired, eyes toward the ceiling and mouth agape, as if he'd never departed.

Sorrow's burden immediately bowed her neck and shoulders and she lamented inconsolably for herself and him, fathoming their doom was worse than damnation, each of them now irrevocably alone without the solace of hell as well as heaven, of any eternal order's surety. Nothing but inchoate void awaited, and she on the brink. And thus upon her tombstone, as on his, no hopeful verse was carved, for her dying hour had been gloomier than his.

Barn

The farmer and his wife never go inside there now,
Not since the day that rust took possession of their plow.
That quaint old barn they built from lofty cupola to floor
Doesn't really feel like it's theirs anymore.

Sentimental treasures fill the attic and the stalls
From bygone generations that they never knew at all.
The things have taken over that they never threw away,
Along with rags and Mason jars they still may use someday.

That barn stored up more memories than they themselves could hold.
The past took on a life in there unwholesome to behold,
Things that should have been forgotten in the ground so cold,
That barn is just unhealthy now for any living soul.

The farmer and his wife will sometimes try to venture in,
But then they hear the sound of feet and turn away again.
It should be possum, cat, or skunk, but very late at night
Something skulks around in there, holding up a light.

Restless spirits climbing from the pictures in gold frames,
Or rising from old furniture, might be the ones to blame,
And then one morning 'round the barn, a mess of bones was spread
Of what looked like it could have been a man long dead.

Purging Mom

Had a typical nightmare on dozing off after two of Holly's Ambiens, no sooner did the red-eye to London clear the runway out of JFK. In my dream I was home, that is, the home whose mortgage Holly and I had paid off with the inheritance from Mom, but all our furnishings had been usurped by those of the maternal homestead where I'd grown up. I rode a wooden rocking horse that hadn't supported my weight since kindergarten. I was slapping its polka-dotted rump, urging it toward the edge of second-floor landing.

How I'd proceed from there was moot because the curio cabinet that had tottered in ruthless pursuit down the hall planted its stubby walnut clawfeet squarely behind me and swung one of its vitrine doors wide open. To the tune of smashing glass it smacked me and my painted pony down the stairs. I woke up gasping, mostly in chagrin that Mom's furniture had tracked me 200-plus miles from her address.

Had I jinxed myself with positive thinking? Shouldn't I have crossed psychic borderlands already, miles safer each second from oneiric outlash? I did have to hand it to myself, arranging to be an ocean away for the grand purge. Leaving Holly in charge sat fine with my conscience, as she'd suffered no nightmares, no pushback whatsoever, while helping dispose of Mom's effects. I was the bad son for busting up the place, whereas during and after Mom's life Holly was a cipher, a negligible bystander at best. This may have come of reciting our courthouse vows amidst the onset of Mom's dementia. She was never necessarily aware Holly existed.

Or maybe Holly was immune to paranormality by virtue of a wholesomely secular upbringing, exempt from church, superstition, folklore. She had no credulity whereon occult influence could gain a toehold. I, meanwhile, was more broadminded, receptive, giving bogies from poltergeists to yeti my principled benefit of the doubt, a sitting duck for the occult. Fortunately for me, Holly and I constitute a case of opposites attracting. She keeps me grounded more often than not.

That said, I gather she encouraged me to skip the country, sticking her with the heavy lifting at Mom's, in preference to humoring my delusions, as she presumably dismissed them, of defunct mother haunting my dreams. Still, what's my alternative, going animist, alleging the souls of grungy furniture were ganging up on me for quashing their decades of domestic stability, consigning them to junkmen and the landfill? A desperate ghost sounded relatively plausible.

What's more, I'd crossed my fingers spirit residue wouldn't cling stubbornly to the earthly plane. But under the most schematic definition of a ghost as a "force of attachment," Mom's unquiet afterlife had been predictable in light of her aversion to change, her truculence about keeping every blessed household article in its assigned place forever. She'd eschewed renovations, redecorating, in an unconscious bid, perhaps, at stopping time, erecting barricades of outdated calendars and soy-sauce packets between herself and death, hiding bulwarks of catalogs and chipped dishware in cellar or attic to avoid accusations of hoarding. And as infirmity advanced, change only became more hateful: upholding selfhood meant killing talk of downsizing or assisted living.

Nonetheless, at age ninety-four, a pelvic fracture triggered tailspin to the grave, whereupon I wagered mere extinction wasn't about to evict headstrong psyche from the environs on which its integrity depended more than ever. But once her monumental inventory began dispersing, theoretically so would she, and damned if she'd submit to that with good graces.

Before a certain tipping point in that dispersal, I reckoned Mom was the invisible helper who deposited missing keys, stock certificates, pearl necklaces on the kitchen table. But thereafter, she became the spiteful gremlin that popped a valve off the furnace to flood the cellar, among other fluke mishaps. Then again, from Holly's healthier perspective, "shit happens." I owe her big time for keeping it together, unlike myself.

Even as I peered out the porthole into starless void, Holly was, if I knew her, sound asleep, well en route to racking up eight dreamless hours as usual. A pettier husband might chafe envious. Instead, thanks to Ambien, I just floated through wine service, midnight dinner, postprandial decaf, all of it good at least for inhibiting my relapse into dreamland.

And thumbing through the balky small-screen "entertainment system," I hit upon a docudrama semi-relevant to this trip, not that the lowdown on Stonehenge was of practical value to me as location scout enlisted to earmark the ideal terrain for the heroic fantasy *Dolmen Wizards: Blades of Bronze*. Stonehenge, right off the bat, was too obvious, too recognizable, and getting permits was next to impossible.

Tinny screaming and minor chords steered my unsteady attention to a writhing, fur-clad reenactor squashed from midriff down by a mock twenty-ton slab in a Neolithic construction accident. Or was I dreaming this, a scene right at home in *Dolmen Wizards?* Was this the stuff of reputable historiography, or my groggy mash-up of infotainment with barbarian-epic hogwash? Whatever, it beat visions of vindictive dining-room sets. When next I realized, the lights came up for breakfast, and I sighed, strung out but grateful at eluding phantom apron strings at last.

The wife and I observe an unmodish rule that might have saved many a less rock-solid marriage. In this age of Skype and iPhones, when I'm away, I'm away, we're on break from each other's little peeves and tribulations, we solve our problems solo. Hence Holly went about her business blissfully ignorant of trains and buses I caught or missed by minutes, to fetch up toward noon, half-delirious with fatigue, at the charming Aubrey B&B from which I'd recon Wiltshire, first of several promising regions on British soil.

She'd have most appreciated hearing nothing of the looniness I dreamed after belly-flopping into bed for a wee nap and waking up four hours later. For once I was aquiver with anxiety at Mom's house and not mine. My ass was pressing grimly against the edge of her mahogany desk in the upstairs office, and surrounding me were even more green metal filing cabinets than used to congest the floorspace.

As if to give my dread some *raison d'être,* drawers of random cabinets burst open with the erratic timing of popcorn kernels, and their endless contents spumed to the ceiling like gushers from punctured arteries. Vintage utility bills, sales receipts, insurance policies, medical records, bank statements spilled out of airborne folders and rained around me. None of them had to pelt me to exert an impact, for here, unmistakably, was Mom's stockpiled past diffusing as her house emptied out, a callous assault upon her ectoplasm.

Still, despite the chaos, this doubtless wasn't her ghostly protest; it too neatly symbolized my own upwelling guilt at expunging her remnant identity one wastebasket at a time, at recruiting Holly to do my dirty work, as I gallivanted with impunity 3500 miles away. Dozens of drawers had yet to erupt when my *Tubular Bells* ringtone jarred me awake, and my arm lunged toward the cell on my nightstand as if doing the breaststroke toward a rescue boat.

I first feared Holly was suspending our code of silence due to some grisly emergency, but no, it was my Brit contact Stephanie, an intern in effect who worked for food, and I was late for the afternoon feeding. Luckily, to join her at the Waggon and Horses, I had only to comb my bedhead hair and cross the road, which, she reminded me, was busy, "so take extra care you look to your right, yeah?"

We'd met across opposite sides of the cordon during a shoot in the carny bazaar labyrinth of Camden Markets, London, where she stood out among the rubbernecks by tapping my shoulder and lauding my choice of locale for its fidelity to the filmscript's literary source. Further dialogues ensued. Beneath the blue meringue coif and tatty apricot leggings of her punkette image beat the heart of a film savant who professed an incorrigible longing to get a foot in the industry's door.

In the years since that initial chat, however, she'd apparently done nothing to advance her career beyond sporadic research for me. Not that she ever spoke of family or relationships or means of support; cinematic art in general and whatever job of mine she was abetting bracketed the range of her conversation. For that matter, I never got around to learning how she knew I was a location scout. Her personal feelings toward me also remain enigmatic and off-limits to broaching aloud.

If she was perturbed at having to nurse a pint in my absence, it didn't impinge on her flirty welcome, her perennial breezy cheer, unless her British social norms were unreadably different from mine. She'd been an angel to arrange our rendezvous here, a literal stone's throw from the Aubrey. And all the better, for as Steph imparted, this pub, replete with thatch roof and sarsen walls, dated to the 1600s, sheltered not one but two celebrated spooks, and had served steak pie and ale to Charles Dickens.

Steph had also assembled a printout of prehistoric monuments, and she must have striven mightily to shortlist the candidates, as antiquities were plentiful here as cowflaps in a pasture. Right out the window above our booth was Silbury Hill, an earthwork on the scale of Egypt's pyramids, built by hundreds of subsistence farmers 4500 years ago using antler picks, shoulder-bone shovels, and bucket brigades of soil and chalkstone. From the vantage of my oaken pew it resembled a colossal green gumdrop, which I declined mentioning, lest it smack of insult to English heritage.

After our palaver about *Dolmen Wizards* played out, she channeled the talk, as always, into moviedom, on the recent spate of Argentine thrillers, on the underrated noir lighting of Nick Musuraca. This saw us through boar burgers and bland stouts, and then Steph had to nip back to London. She didn't explain why, and only muddied our boundaries further with a clingy hug and gratuitously wet kiss on the cheek. Delectable, sure, but what mixed transcultural signals, to keep me up and wondering despite persistent jetlag. On the upside, when I did doze off, my subconscious was too abashed to fabricate bad dreams.

The kid's enthusiastic, absolutely, but she can lose track of basic priorities. I could have avoided miles of wasted motion had I done my own online research. The quest, of course, was for the most camera-ready landscapes, and Ivor my homegrown Uber driver had the air of tussling with his conscience about everywhere I sent us. Must have been a no-brainer to him that "Marden henge," however renowned for its extraordinary breadth and myriad artifacts, retained nothing aboveground, hardly enough gradient to trip over. Nothing to film here!

Likewise, instead of monoliths, a stubby circular arrangement like half-submerged wharf pilings was all that marked the dismantled majesty of Durrington Walls. More dubious yet were the cement nubs that outlined the hilltop Sanctuary. Maybe Steph misapprehended how much CG was in the budget to recreate primitive splendor. I wished that contemplating my cute, effervescent intern didn't prompt the reflection, Well, you get what you pay for.

Ivor, meanwhile, perked up when we headed for Avebury. His indoorsy complexion waxed ruddy through butterball cheeks like a lingering case of the mumps, through five o'clock shadow uniformly stippling his chin and shaven scalp, which with silver ear studs insinuated nostalgia for the heyday of "Oi!" What was it about me that attracted England's unregenerate punks? Yet his formidable husk disguised a mellow temper. Had his bonhomie rebounded because he approved of our destination, or because I was springing for lunch at the Red Lion before surveying stone circles?

Regardless, I was uncommonly comfortable around him on short acquaintance. No sooner was the Sanctuary behind us than sleep deficit kicked in and I nodded off, keeling into another loopy dream. I was still in a speeding vehicle, except it was the Plymouth station wagon of my boyhood. At the wheel was Holly, and it was unnerving only in retrospect that she doubled as Mom. I was in the backseat making out with Steph, while we traversed a patchwork world of my grubby hometown and Bedrock from *The Flintstones* and blasted plains where squalid cavemen skulked about towering menhirs like African termite nests.

But not even the balderdash of stone-age dinosaurs would have pried me off Steph; nor did Holly when she yoohooed, "Everything okay back there?" I wasn't cognizant she'd turned around, though she slammed on the brakes as if trouble ahead had caught her unawares. The frightful jolt that finally extricated me from Steph landed me in the passenger seat of waking reality again, no less alarmed than in the dream. Was this "dream a wish my heart made," to paraphrase some Disney guff or other? Yikes!

"All right, brother? We're here. Red Lion." I nodded, which helped defog me as I blinked around at a parking lot and, across the road, hurray, a smattering of megaliths in a pasture, albeit none half as tall as those I'd glimpsed while smooching. Still, they were big enough to rate a smile, which I shared to reassure Ivor of my well-being as I bumbled from his Ford Fiesta. And incredibly, our bistro, in fact the village, sat amidst the stone alignments.

Harking to Steph's notes, I gathered the seventeenth had been a grand century for pubs, for the Lion was contemporary with the Waggon. Moreover, discounting the rows of picnic tables out front, it agreeably looked its age, half-timbered, whitewashed walls under a beetling roof of black thatch and shaggy splotches of moss. Inside, we nabbed a table next to a masonry well, around which the inn must have been built. The well had a transparent lid bolted on, and the rank, fuzzy flora within amounted to a belowground terrarium; fascinating, but it did tarnish the appeal of my "Avebury Well-Water" ale.

"I like it here," Ivor declared as we tucked into gammon steaks. He flourished his knife toward the window to affirm he meant more than the dining room. He went on about a lot of childhood daytrips to these precincts, how he'd acquired a certain local-color expertise, if he did say so. By way of example, he launched into rumors of hauntings at this very tavern, and it did me no credit, sleep-deprived or not, that my attention drifted to the well, and from there to broodings on how often I'd used my career to skip out on onerous filial duty. Ordinarily I'd have hung on a native storyteller's every gruesome detail.

What was that Yardbirds lyric, "sinking deep into the well of time"? Yeah, thanks to job-related travel, I'd dodged a good decade of eldercare bullets: ER visits for slip-and-fall treatments, flareups of bed-sores and diverticulitis, hospital stints for recurrent pneumonia, tiffs with neighbors and health aides over imaginary pilfering.

But why be guilty today when I, after all, had been scrambling to support Holly and myself, when it felt like Mom would always re-bound and live forever? Not as if she had an expiration date stamped on her person, and let's not forget, some judicious distance was need-ful to safeguard my embattled sanity. Those senior incidents, anyhow, were better handled by professionals.

Something about "the oldest scissors in the world" wrenched my vision from the well and toward Ivor expounding, his eyes earnestly seeking mine, with no evident umbrage when I hemmed, "Come again?"

He patiently recapped, "They're in the museum down the street. They've shifted only a couple hundred yards since the thirteen-hundreds from where they'd been. I ought to show you." He was no doubt inured to the fickle attention of flaky tourists. He came closest to remonstrative when I added a 20% tip to the check. "You don't have to do that here!" he admonished, unlike Steph at the Waggon. But my arbitrary conscience demanded that much appeasement and more.

Ivor had begun lumbering toward the museum; he had to under-stand, though, I had business to conduct before the afternoon sun dimmed. I grabbed my Nikon from his car and in a half-cocked gesture of compromise asked to see where the scissors had lain since the 1300s. Like a caring parent, he barred me with an outstretched arm on the verge between the parking lot and an amazingly active road, led me across the corner of a megalith-dotted field, and repeated the procedure on another verge.

Tromping along, he recounted, "When some fallen stones were being stood up again, during the 'thirties, a medieval skeleton was discovered beneath one, and the theory goes he was an itinerant barber, because of the scissors on him, and that he was helping pious villagers pull down the pagan circle and bury it, till a slab happened to fall on him. They had no way to get him out, so there he stayed, and them too spooked to carry on tempting evil spirits. Or else the people murdered him and tipped the rock on top of his body. Perfect crime, eh? And here we are."

I'd been snapping away as we followed an arc of megaliths, some over twice my height and frankly more imposing than this ten-footer, but ever the completist, I documented the killer slab, its contours like an art-brut apostrophe or incipient bust in profile. After I lowered the camera, Ivor anticlimactically disclosed, "This is called the barber stone." We moseyed on, as he yammered about one megalith almost crushing a cobbler who'd been fixing a shoe in its shade, another that lightning had shattered right after a deacon had sheltered under it from a downpour.

With every word my punchiness mounted as we zigzagged between alleged outer and inner rings inside the henge's thousand-foot diameter. The overall form, so clear in aerial view, was summarily lost on me: none of the circles had survived the millennia halfway intact, and intervening trees and houses further obscured the site's coherence. Efforts to pinpoint our position within the complex set my head swimming, not unlike my recurring vertigo when Mom's had been partly gutted, furniture, books, and tchotchkes in unnatural huddles, and spaces bare where they shouldn't have been.

The terrain and Ivor's narrative flowed along as a commingled blur, while I went through shutterbug motions on autopilot, till Ivor escorted me by the elbow through more traffic and identified a gargantuan, diamond-shaped, symbolically female boulder as the "Swindon stone" because it flanked the road to that town. "Witnesses report these here sixty tons have pirouetted right around at midnight, or skipped across the highway searching for a long-gone consort, an equally enormous phallic sarsen." I dutifully converted "Swindon stone" to digital pixels and followed suit with this fourth quadrant's crescent of monoliths fringing their segment of precipitous ditch around the collective stoneworks.

Aha, and there across this section of lawn, beyond a klatch of blasé sheep, was the Red Lion again. My thirst had grown terrible ever since Ivor's malarkey about menhirs strolling around and dancing. That malarkey rang a bell, may have echoed archetypal folklore, except it resonated ominously, tied in somehow with my broader circumstances, flustered me into neurotic red alert. Imperative that I detune my high-strung nerves, and the balm of alcohol couldn't have been handier.

Ivor, however, bowed out, citing family commitments, and cajoled me into repairing to the Aubrey to "relax and regroup." I could have imbibed on my own at the Lion, which, it developed, was under a mile from the B&B, as Ivor probably knew full well. Was I so visibly overwrought that he wanted me in safe harbor, or anyway in someone else's bailiwick?

Though I couldn't articulate why, I paced my cozy chamber leerier than ever about relaxing, dozing off, re-entering dreamland. At any rate I'd have been too wired to nap without a fistful of Ambiens. Pleasantries I exchanged with my diffident host passed normal, I supposed, en route through the hall to an early-bird repast at the Waggon.

I, sole customer, reoccupied that booth overlooking the colossal gumdrop of Silbury Hill. The strongest ale on tap had an unfortunate aftertaste of burnt rubber, which didn't stop me from downing three and pretending they grew on me. I cushioned it with a savory pie-du-jour, figuring if it's good enough for Dickens . . . The beverages hadn't tasted so insipid in Steph's company, had they? Pairs and more of diners filtered in, and their sidelong glances seemed to question whether I, a loner, was fitter to be pitied or censured. Neither townsman nor proper vacationer fared solo; what was my game exactly?

Not that their opinions were of value, especially as I embarked tomorrow on the next leg of my mission, to Cornwall. I hauled out my phone, speed-dialed Steph, got her voicemail, and encouraged her to join me in Truro, citing my need for a savvy colleague, for her finely honed insights and judgment, and in my heart, none of this just then was a tissue of lies. Sick of evil-eye pinpricks of disapproval, I paid up, skedaddled, and, with the exaggerated prudence of mild intoxication, scurried across the road unscathed.

In my warmish quarters I threw open the window, flinched at how each vehicle thundered by in the nocturnal quietude, and resigned myself, restless with ale and angst, to lying awake indefinitely. Ambiens and alcohol would certainly breed nightmares or worse. I pulled out my phone for companionship. Nothing from Steph, *quelle surprise.* And no stateside news was good news, the maternal haunts presumably stripped to the bones, according to schedule. That should have been a load off my mind, a dose of satisfaction, however little I'd earned it. But no, pronouncing "mission accomplished" sent pangs of remorse through me, like multiple jabs of emotional pitchforks.

What faults in my mental bedrock made me indict myself as hypocritical, traitorous? I had to liquidate Mom's estate, period. Yet a malaise of blame oppressed me, as if simply walking away from the house should have been okay. What easier to do, for the sake of Mom's happiness, than nothing? Off the point that she was defunct, her phantom influence really my imagination, right? I was a heel to the same extent I acted in self-interest.

But if dreams of volatile furniture were pleas from Mom for benign neglect, to spare her dwindling identity, her belongings were, in one sense, of a piece with Neolithic monuments. Did ectoplasmic tribesmen abide on their home turf, like Mom on hers? My overheating thoughts raced on, though their feet were miring in exhaustion. Mightn't those Wiltshire ancestors, like Mom, want nothing more of posterity than to leave their towering "furniture" alone, such that they'd been riled by too much vandalism into tripping a medieval barber into the path of a toppling sarsen? My sprinting thoughts must have hit a patch of quicksand about then, for that's when they went under.

I picked up sprinting, breathless as if this strenuous dream were *in medias res,* along the floor of the formidable ditch around Avebury's rock circles, till the urge possessed me to bound up the steep incline, impetuously, as if catching defenders off-guard. Directly above, the barber stone, poised on the precipice, flipped through midair like a flyswatter, rushed downslope like a toboggan. I hopped aside within inches of being flattened and skittered back to the bottom. Behind me the slab crashed with a din like a tone cluster octaves below middle C.

A brief dash onward and I involuntarily sprang uphill again, to confront the barber stone's twin up top, prefatory to another round of playing chicken with tons of geology, another hairsbreadth escape, another discordant crash. I was philosophical about exercising the volition of a needle on an LP, about prospects of reeling on forever in steady-state fatigue. I worried only on beholding the symbolically female Swindon stone around the bend, balancing on the bottom of the trench, utterly blocking it, like the palm of an upheld hand. My lack of bodily control was now cause for alarm.

As I careened toward the boulder, it rocked minutely like a sea-fan in a gentle current. In those final paces it loomed much grander than laws of optics could explain, and it quaked as in anticipation, and its shadow cast me in darkness as it slammed down like the bar of a mousetrap.

In the microsecond before contact, the sarsen's grating deadfall became the racket of a monstrous truck rocketing by out front, extremely overdue for a tune-up, new muffler, new transmission. I, light-headed with hyperventilation, was staring agog at the ceiling. As the ruckus faded, the chiming of *Tubular Bells* sent me groping around the nightstand; it had to be Steph, better late than never, and if she had a compulsion to return calls at whatever hour she checked her voicemail, fine, we had that in common.

Confusingly, a stranger, and an American at that, was on the line. It's much earlier stateside, I remembered, maybe broad daylight in California, was this my employers at *Dolmen Wizards?* Nope! The caller made officious noises about confirming he had the correct party and then broke stunning news in a monotone, or else American accents registered as flat, affectless, after two scant days of British English. His nasal droning, by design or not, did tamp down any unbridled reaction, aside from basic shock.

A tinge of annoyance was the closest he came to modulation, in remarking his difficulties reaching me. The accident occurred mid-afternoon sometime. My wife had overseen laborers hauling a piano up some cellar stairs and through a bulkhead when the cords slipped or snapped. The piano slid to the foot of the steps and did a "backflip," as witnesses put it, onto Holly. She'd sustained spinal and internal injuries. Efforts to save her were unsuccessful. Sorry for your loss. I hung up then and switched off the phone.

Good Lord, the last thing Holly heard must have been a godawful tone cluster. Bad as I felt, I was unable to cry yet, perhaps because transatlantic distance rendered the tidings less immediate, less vivid. My wife is dead, my wife is dead, I repeated aloud till it made me borderline giddy. And worse, I blanked out to resurface chanting the specious litany of every survivor, It's my fault, I've failed her, if I'd been there this wouldn't have happened; but it also wouldn't if one of umpteen circumstances had differed, say, she'd stood slightly to the left.

Still and all, the room was devolving into claustrophobia, dejection, like the bottom of a well filling with guilt, and damned if I'd lie there and drown. What rank injustice that would be, when my mental processes, without my conscious interference, were feverishly building a case for blaming Mom, constructing a ladder out of this toxic groundwater.

Yes, Mom had been as oblivious to Holly in death as in life. But as we denuded room after room, from attic to cellar, less and less context remained to harness her atomizing selfhood. Reduced to mad smithereens, she'd have lashed out at anyone orchestrating the coup de grâce as if it were me. If I had to be guilty of anything, how about casting Holly in the role of Judas goat?

The way forward was both limpid and murky, or rather I had every idea what to do, and no idea what I was in for. I had to surmise the worst: Mom had killed Holly, and if I returned, would kill me. Her domicile contained nothing to die for. As for the balance of my "adult responsibilities," Holly was no more. The household that was ours was gone with her. And if I did go home, how to refuse driving the ten minutes to Mom's from there?

Let Holly's punctilious kin handle funeral arrangements et cetera. It might even solace them. They're like that. And what, they will cavil, about the marital assets? Binoculars couldn't see that many eventualities ahead. My livelihood, meanwhile, was doable from anywhere. The phone was my office; a fixed address was a virtual albatross. The more I rambled, the better I prospered.

I switched on the phone, sat up against the headboard, and redialed Steph, foreseeing euphoria, then disgrace, every other second, but ready at least with a spiel for voicemail. Don't go to Truro, I'll be in London bright and early, we can take the train together. Much to discuss. Call if you can, please, though my phone won't be on.

Hated to admit, one topic for discussion was her mode of transport. Car, moped, neither? How woefully unacquainted we were. I'd no clue what she'd make of my message, or what I honestly made of it myself. Whatever her response, I decided I was, without libido, as good as dead. But beyond me to hash out if I was leveling with or glamorizing myself.

This non-issue I shelved, and rolled over into a few hours of the serene sleep usually bestowed on problem-solvers. At dawn my eyes popped open, I bounced out of bed, awaited breakfast downstairs, and informed my host and hostess of urgent work-related summons to London. I must have acted impressively frazzled, for my host-cum-cook doffed his apron and drove me to Swindon, where I made the 9:31 to Paddington.

On the train, I played at weighing whether each earthen bump along the hilltops was or wasn't a Bronze Age barrow, but this proved the equivalent of counting sheep. I'd racked up inadequate sleep last night, hadn't I, despite my buoyant start? The on-and-off vibrations of the cool window were soothing against my temple. I conked out.

Then I had the damnedest misperception I was awake, on my feet and oddly anxious about a tunnel toward which the train was hurtling. But I had to be dreaming because I wasn't on a moving locomotive anymore, and never subject to tunnel vision in reality. And if I'd had my druthers, this lowering, ominous black chute would have been a hundredfold longer, such that Mom at the far end would have been infinitesimal.

I had nowhere to look except at her, and as I did, my field of view around her expanded. She was, at rough estimate, the length of a train car away, and I readily discerned her osteoporosis and hunching shoulders, arthritic knuckles and general emaciation. Gray sweatshirt, pink sweatpants, and beige slippers were of major consolation, covering as they did more than bedsores and other dermal insults, since decay had been underway for months, and grisly enough to behold how it had gorged on face and scalp and hands.

Her features were too wormholed for me to decipher her expression as she beckoned, though lidless, fishy eyes smoldered with no inviting warmth. By now the space around her had ballooned to a Cinemascope vista and clarified into a coliseum of the sofas, TVs, porcelain, coffee tables, toiletries, winter coats, vases, rolled-up rugs, meds, bodice-rippers, costume jewelry, washer-drier units, and infinitely more that had been her life. They shuddered like a packed crowd of jostling onlookers, like a projection of her jumbled memory bank, massing for one last stand. Or onslaught?

What the hell was she hoping I'd do? If my behavioral norms weren't altogether lost on her, she'd have realized I'd do nothing, rooted to this dream ground of no specific color or manufacture till the proverbial chickens came to roost. But what was my passive-aggressive defiance against her tenacity, her unholy acumen for sniffing out family blood across the ocean? I didn't know the half of it when I used to say it was orneriness that kept her going.

She let drop her arm, and I grimaced, expecting it to detach. Her jaw, after twitching side to side, dropped too, like a gallows trapdoor, and my queasiness escalated unbearably. Her mushy larynx fought to eke out words and expelled only bubbling, malformed groans. From the oral cavity at that instant also flowed a clammy, acrid miasma of highly distilled death. I jounced awake, bumping my forehead sharply against the window.

I had a leaden misgiving the dream wasn't over, or at best this was an intermission, because the shaky tonnage of Mom's possessions hadn't yet collapsed into an avalanche and pulverized me. Plus, the miasma still infested my nostrils, doubly thick after I tried snorting it out and inhaling fresh oxygen. Was it me, I winced, peeking around for signs I'd incommoded fellow riders. But neither I nor any single offender could have triggered the uproar spreading throughout the carriage.

Passengers were coughing, cussing, squawking in disgust, robustly putting the lie to vaunted British reserve. Some were hustling fore and aft into other cars before I'd drawn my tentative, and even fuggier, next breath. Speculations volleyed to and fro about a toxic spill outside, a ventilation breakdown, a blockage in the lavatory, terrorism. The sole island of calm, the one passenger unperturbed as if her sinuses were incurably clogged, as if she were deaf, sat way up front. From my seat I could just about distinguish the sparse, frowzy white coif straggling from her scalp, and were those multiple port-wine marks showing through?

A fat fly, likewise unperturbed by the bedlam, lazily swooped in and met with no reaction as it lit on the apparently insensate head. With that, the source of the effluvium became as obvious here as in dreamland. The quiescent passenger's hairstyle, albeit from the back and pathetically wispy, had been damnably familiar, and denying I knew to whom it belonged amounted to self-delusion.

Pretending indifference would be especially foolhardy now that she and I were alone in the carriage. Of course, I might yet be dreaming, and if not, well, my first step would be the same, to join the ill-humored exodus. I lurched up and dragged my cumbersome satchel from the overhead rack, frantic to exit quietly, despising myself for every unavoidable bump and scrape. Sneaking off was no solution, but I was thankful for the wherewithal, just barely, to do that, to go with what I knew.

I had to get to Steph, her image wavery like the mirage of a welcoming shore that receded as I swam gasping toward it. My baggage and I had caromed half a dozen rows toward the rear, and my free arm was outstretched to punch the panel that opened the door, when the phone rang. Unbelievable! What the hell had inspired Steph to call now? But the phone was off, wasn't it? I dug it out and checked the number. It was Holly's, not Steph's. I stuffed the phone back into hip pocket.

Lunging forth, I did grasp how unfair I'd be to impose on Steph when two ghosts, in dreams or not, were simultaneously hounding me. But alternatives, I was certain, I had none, not that England equaled safe haven. This was how broadmindedness, receptivity to occult realms had repaid me, though Holly's skepticism had served her even worse.

My sweaty fingertips poked the panel, the door whooshed aside, cleaner air rushed in, and I dared a backward glance. Mom wasn't there, or at least not where I could see her, and on my person, *Tubular Bells* had desisted. My overwound nerves slackened, maybe in purely organic response to breathing easier. And tricky to say, down to semantics perhaps, whether my relief was real or not. I had no means, and might well never again, to verify if I were dreaming or awake.

Before I'd crossed the threshold, three conductors in black jackets and blue ties bustled through the passage and forced a retreat. They were overtly displeased with me, quite understandable if they had instructions to detain me in this car for questioning. "Can you tell us what you're doing in here, when everyone else has fled from this awful pong?" demanded the senior, pockiest guard. "Do you know something the rest of us don't?"

Yes, I did, but wisdom dictated I mutely shake my head.

"Nice opportunity, wasn't it, to go through people's baggage?" piped up the shortest, scrawniest inquisitor in an outwardly chummy tone, as if he envied my pluck.

Tubular Bells emanated from my pocket again. Nobody spoke or moved till my inaction goaded the third conductor, with nigh-albino complexion and pencil mustache, to carp, "Aren't you going to answer that?"

When I shook my head once more, the senior guard archly asserted, "Would you mind passing it to me then?"

I complied, despite my arm's reluctance to cooperate. The conductor dourly squinted from the screen to me. "Someone named Holly. Who might that be?" He pushed the Talk button and raised the device to his clamshell of an ear, which muffled the caller's voice after he barked, "Hello?" He tendered me the phone and gratuitously explained, "For you, right?" I accepted the phone and perfunctorily hit End Call.

I had to say something. The truth was manifestly off limits, so I went with the first words that floated up as in a Magic 8-Ball. "You're right, I set off the chemical agent, and I needn't harp on its success. I also guarantee there's nothing in here you could analyze. I'll go quietly."

They frowned as if it were a shame about my sanity. The senior guard produced handcuffs, and I presented my wrists. Sorry, *Dolmen Wizards*, I guess we're on hold. The Brits, like anyone, seem inclined to deal more harshly with foreign than homegrown terrorists, but my relative innocence will inevitably come to light, with my confession chalked up to gas-induced delirium.

Or else I'm still dreaming, and if I am, let the cuffs chafe, where's the harm? And if not, fine! For all that I'm the "bad son," Mom would never dream of finding her own flesh and blood in jail.

Death and a Locket

Death came for me on a wet April night,
Charcoal suit, yellow teeth, yellow tie.
He smelled of cologne over mildew and dust,
And asked was I ready to die?

Of course I said no, and he offered a deal,
With his skeletal smile cold and sly:
I could name him a loved one to go in my place,
And the thought of you then made me cry.

He lit a cigar, said he'd sweeten the deal,
That I needn't come out and decide,
That if I permitted he'd guess my decision,
And with silence was how I'd comply.

He gave me some seconds that did me no good;
I could not bring myself to reply,
And he took that for answer as I feared he would
And I trembled at thinking you'd die.

He snuffed the cigar and suggested your name
And asked me if you'd qualify,
But I told him no, that I didn't love you,
While I tried looking him in the eye.

He didn't dispute me, just smiled hungrily,
And told me to let my tears dry.
What I'd asked for was done, and he took out a locket,
And commanded me to look inside.

I expected your picture, I was full of self-hate,
But it seemed I had done well to lie,
For the face of a stranger was opened to me,
And your life I'd been able to buy.

But death sat too calmly, asked was I surprised,
Did I wonder whom I'd caused to die?
When I called him a stranger I'd seen once or twice,
His laugh made my throat turn bone-dry.

"In all of the world, this one loved you the best,
Though now you will never know why,
And his life he gave freely, which is something that you
Or your love seem ill-suited to try."

Death left me then, but he's never seemed far,
And at what seemed deep feelings I sigh,
And now I don't know what to do about us,
Or the love whose truth death has defied.

Shed a Tear for Asenath

October 1, 1929: As I mature, I no longer want things so much as I want them back, and not of a banal material nature, but rather youth, time, optimism, spontaneity. I've been going to pot, frankly; Arkham's too stodgy for a poet or artist of any stripe, discounting its campus tyros.

Not to discount them altogether, of course! Where would that leave my Asenath, my embers of *joie de vivre* reviving after epochal dormancy? I don't deserve this spell of happiness she's cast upon me. Conversely, at age thirty-eight, I've waited long enough! And if I hadn't, if I'd bowed to Mother's idea of a "nice girl" in my twenties? My soulmate back then had yet to blow out ten birthday candles, and what a smothered life I'd have led!

October 10, 1929: I'm not getting any younger, despite people's comments about my "boyish" looks, and if only those people were more supportive about my one pass at the brass ring. Do Dad and "my best friend" Dan not realize I caught their dubious glances at Asenath and each other? What must she think? It's not as if I've been oblivious to snide rumors of familial insanity, her father's demise in an asylum, her unclean "Innsmouth blood." Talk about calling the kettle black— Arkham was the Bay Colony's Gomorrah where witches notoriously *weren't* hanged! Anyway, how petty not to give her credit for being her own person!

And no less endearing, I confess, are those enthusiasms we share, all but extinct in me for want of a kindred spirit: the history of magic, its survival in marginal communities, sub-rosa histories of its influence in world-shaping events. How hypocritical of the university to limit its teachings in the occult to "anthropology" and "metaphysics," considering the renown of its esoteric resources.

As for the disapproving jibes and frowns, Asenath laughs them off with a breezy wisdom astronomically beyond her twenty-three years, a wisdom writ plain in her big bright eyes. I adore her the more for it. Time, I trust, will temper the flaming impulsiveness that also shines there.

October 18, 1929: My reprieve from middle age is good as guaranteed! She said yes and, to be honest, had teased me into popping the question, murmuring in my ear, Why was I putting her off, didn't I know it was cruel to keep a girl on tenterhooks?

We were at a movie, *Dangerous Curves* of all things, and a man fat as Taft turned around to shush us. Asenath's hand withdrew from mine and out of sight, and then the man was hacking away as if popcorn were stuck in his throat and he faced front, loosening his collar. Asenath's hand reclaimed mine and she kissed me as if we were already married. I paid no more attention to the man, as I was busy proposing once I had my own breath back.

October 31, 1929: Married on Hallowe'en! I'd entertained hopes our guests would enter into the fun of that, but no such luck. Asenath wore black lace whose daring décolletage suggested lingerie more than wedding dress, and she had me in her late father's Edwardian morning coat with a velvet cravat and striped trousers, because, she sighed, "it was the most tangible way to have him there." How could I object?

She'd cajoled an utterly bemused justice of the peace into performing the ceremony on Arkham Common, under the purported "gallows oak" of Colonial-era infamy. Dad endured the occasion with wooden stoicism, and I worried Dan would indeed speak after that line about anyone knowing "why these two should not be joined in holy matrimony." Even our Bohemian coterie, based on the strained quality of their joshing and congratulations, felt we'd gone too far in some manner that consciously eluded them. Disappointing poseurs!

It's sad, though, that Dan tendered such lukewarm blessings; we'd formerly been so close he named his son "Edward Derby" after me. And too bad Mom couldn't live to see this. But then, the folks had become progressively disposed to keep me the man-child they were used to, the male version of a spinster. Nigh miraculous I ever cut those homebody ties! On to Innsmouth, a novel enough honeymoon destination!

November 16, 1929: Glad we honeymooned in Innsmouth, if only because my curiosity is more than assuaged, and I can authoritatively
separate ugly truth from innuendo. Thank God I've extricated Asenath
and her chattel from that cesspit. She, however, went gadding about
blithely immune to the obvious; perhaps nostalgia blinded her to the
boarded-up, peeling frontages, the rusty, salt-rimed hydrants and early-
American hitching posts, the trash and potholes, the fishy rawness of a
backwater on which, to all appearances, the sun had never shone.

Those appearances also indicate depression beset Innsmouth long
before Black Tuesday. Asenath conceded it didn't help when G-men
arrested much of the population in a raid on some bootlegging ring in
1927, which might explain the dearth of folk out and about and the re-
striction of our social rounds to the senescent gentry. Or else, judging
by physiognomy, the hoi-polloi have intermarried unto infertility, a
misalliance shy of pink-eyed albinos.

And as if testing our vows "for better or worse," Asenath fetched
home three of these characters, the caretakers from her shabby ancestral mansion, pleading they'd been with her since childhood. She must
be deceptively sentimental to want these coarse, taciturn Swampies at
our elbows. I can practically hear Granddad berating them as "scurvy
louts."

November 17, 1929: Rereading yesterday's paragraphs, I regret their
tonic note of snobbery in treating of Asenath's people. My genteel upbringing is scant excuse. If she views them with affection, they must
deserve the benefit of the doubt. My maturity's nothing to brag
about, is it? Shamelessly transparent how I'm framing my judgments
by second-guessing how Dan and Dad would frame theirs, as if whatever I'm marrying into were any of their affair. Most baffling, meanwhile, is my poetic impulse reigniting amidst Innsmouth's squalor and
decay, its first sparks in months. Am I regressing to that decadent
phase when I was Asenath's age?

December 13, 1929: Do I mistrust my happiness because I'm too cyni-
cal to believe it can last, or because of its disconcerting nature? Some
decadent I am, to dither guiltily at pleasure! In bed, when Asenath
takes me in hand, I have the damnedest impression of touching myself,

of being ravished in ways that might occur to any man, but hardly to a woman. These moreover are ways I'd never dare express aloud, casting me in the preposterous role of jealous husband, chafing to ask who before me did dare express how to satisfy him, since this had to lie beyond the pale of "feminine intuition."

Her expertise is, to term it very crudely, unwomanly, but my cravings dissuade me from picking a quarrel that might vex her into withholding that expertise. Besides, I cannot with any candor claim to be well-versed in the female mystique, can I?

Asenath has, on a more quotidian plane, hung up her flapper beads and applied a new sobriety toward running our household. I'm gratified at how she's risen to the challenge, asserting a matronly degree of authority over the domestics, as if "to the manor born." I only wish she'd been a bit less high-handed insisting I shave off my budding mustache. Her father had a silly doormat of a beard; maybe my lackluster results provoked invidious comparisons with him?

April 1, 1930: What the devil is Asenath up to? Whenever I bestir myself to call on Dan or the old Miskatonic gang, she accuses me of neglecting her in order to "go gallivanting," as if I've merely swapped maternal for spousal apron strings. Not that she can ever prevail against headache or enervation or sundry other excuses to accompany me! But right before I give in she always relents and virtually pushes me out the door. I almost suspect she "doth protest too much," snatching defeat from the jaws of victory so she'll have our big, drafty mansion to herself.

And to what end? Is she dissatisfied with me, with my sovereign role as husband? She's actually railed about all she could achieve if only she were a man! For reasons unclear to me, I'm reminded how we used to practice parlor magic, legerdemain, as some couples play Parchesi, and I admit her skills left mine in the dust. Sadly, though, after we began staging mockups of rituals culled from anthropology studies and her heirloom grimoires, her interest seemed to wane.

Or did it? On returning from my hard-won social excursions, I've smelled acrid smoke, sulphur, and less straightforward chemicals wafting from down cellar, where I've also detected haze dispersing at my approach, glistening black stains on the concrete floor, and untidiness around the coalbin as if something's hidden inside. Asenath glibly advises overhauling the furnace and setting rattraps. I'm hurt that she'd go it clandestinely and alone on the occult front, and I repeat, more anxiously, what *is* she up to?

October 4, 1930: Hallelujah, I've proven "who wears the pants" here! Had to redeem some bond coupons down at the bank and bumped into Dad (though he wouldn't be above staging an ambush!), who invited me to dine at his club. Over my first sweetbreads in ages, mostly because the wife hates them, Dad remarked, How time flew, here I was married almost a year, that Georgian pile of mine had plenty of room for a nursery upstairs, didn't it? He was no spring chicken and wouldn't be around forever, if I caught his drift.

Yes, I could plainly see through his homey clichés, and he'd have been as plainly appalled that I weighed his selfish desires to be a grandpa, to perpetuate the family name, against my connubial bliss, which I had no intention of jeopardizing with morning sickness, fetid diapers, lactation, colic, *ad infinitum, ad nauseam*. I choked down my resentment at Dad's bourgeois disregard for my late-blooming garden of earthy [*sic!*] delights, thanked him for lunch, and assured him I'd talk to Asenath.

And I've been as good as my word and had that talk, and high time too, for she's been sounding me out about "our next step together," and what else could that mean? So I wiped the cobwebs off some cognac that predated the Volstead Act and poured us a few snifters and demanded point-blank, Well, what's your view on "blessed events"? Raising her big moony eyes to me from the settee where she lounged, atypically demure by grace perhaps of 80 proof, she replied, "Well, how do you feel?"

Flat out I told her we weren't beholden to anyone's expectations, there was more to us than childrearing, what say we travel, pursue our mutual passions, grow creatively, all of it awfully uphill with kids in tow? She essayed a brittle, resigned smile and sighed, "Yes dear, whatever you decide." Given her accustomed willfulness, that nearly floored me, as when opponents in a game of tug-o'-war simply let go the rope.

Meanwhile a stark realization dawns on me. Though Asenath is hands-down the love of my life, we've never spoken or written the word "love" to each other, as if it's too conventional for our relationship. And me a poet! Not the verb I'd have predicted dropping from my vocabulary a year ago!

October 12, 1930: In my dream I was my soulmate.

> From the blue moons of her eyes I gazed
> Upon myself, and was aghast, amazed,
> At the unloving master, keen to desecrate
> The soul whose charms with shameless guile I'd praised.
>
> Was this my true self that I saw?
> Or had some devil seized my manly shell,
> And was my soulmate's form my endless hell?
> I do not dream; this mad conclusion I must draw
> For I cannot awaken from this spell.

Have I been a bully and a knave? Is that the message from my conscience in these lucid dreams where I am Asenath, timorous and downtrodden?

November 4, 1930: My conscience has stopped needling me since I commenced booking our grand tour, my reward to Asenath for waiving the fulfillment of motherhood. Dad can spend Christmas with his cronies, and by missing Arkham in winter we miss nothing. Asenath has leapt enthusiastically into the planning; any concerns that she bore me a grudge are now moot. But conjointly the empress Asenath is back with a vengeance, dictating rather than collaborating in the itinerary.

I have to ponder again what she does when I go out. Every objective on her list is allegedly essential to research in "metempsychosis and enhanced longevity," but she affords me only the sketchiest details, e.g., a temple to the crocodile god Sobek in Fayum, Egypt; Buddhist monks of the Coromandel Coast whose personal recollections encompass a millennium; subterranean remains in the Australian outback of a primeval race that had mastered projecting consciousness through space and time. Reaching any of these objectives will be grueling and dangerous, but preferable to her contempt if I waver in accommodating her. And why this reticence about her "research"?

November 20, 1930: I'm upset and mystified, when I should be all a-twitter on the eve of our travels. I'd shaved after supper, put the kit back on the shelf to pack in the morning, then had qualms I'd forget and was crossing the bedroom to take care of it. At the open bathroom door I paused, hearing the cup clink into the chrome holder above the sink.

Silence followed; I pictured Asenath inspecting herself in the cabinet mirror, and then she fairly brayed, "I married a man!" A heartbeat later she cackled cynically, as if at the biggest joke of her twenty-four years. I about-faced and sat on the bed. To say my wife was suddenly a stranger qualified as farcical understatement. What could those four little words, delivered so acerbically, signify?

I was on my feet, padding to the doorway as if to verify it was really she inside. I peeked around the doorjamb and spied her stroking her chin, as vain pensioners stroke their capacious beards. She glimpsed me in the mirror and her hand twitched and stayed its course over her silk-robed breast. Immediately reverting to my sweet soulmate, she smiled and lilted, "Out in a sec, honey!"

I'm trying to soft-pedal this incident. But what a stumbling block before we embark tomorrow! My mind's eye volleys obsessively between Asenath's mannish motions and that gilt-framed diptych on her bureau, a snapshot of me beside a daguerreotype of her dad, with bristling whiskers down to his cummerbund. Just as well we're too keyed up for spooning tonight; not optimistic how that would pan out. I wish I'd let that shaving kit go till tomorrow. *Mea culpa*, somehow, as usual!

April 1, 1931: First entry in months, thanks to the first in a rash of memory lapses. Is this what middle age will be about, an ominous preview of senility? I'd have sworn this diary was among some last-minute articles on my nightstand to stuff into a grip, discovered out at sea I'd left it behind, and yesterday relocated it right on the nightstand where I must have forgotten it. Of course, on hectic mornings of departure, it's always hard to see straight.

Not so easy to excuse those major swaths excised from the recall of our "holidays" (Asenath's misnomer for them), a phenomenon I liken to a newspaper with the majority of articles clipped out, and if only I'd had a diary then for filling in the gaps now. To attribute whatever's wrong with me to fatigue, stress, or neurologic disease fails to pacify my nagging intuition. I couldn't even hazard at what point my recollections turned to Swiss cheese—which would serve no material purpose, but might lend the illusion of having a handle of sorts on the problem.

My retention of events normalized once we docked in Boston, preserving an incident I'd sooner have forgotten. A textbook martinet customs officer glowered at us as if we were Bolsheviks, dragged our steamer trunk over, and manhandled its latch, telegraphing his yen to turn everything inside-out. Asenath outright winked at him and performed rapid, spidery gestures. His sourpuss expression smoothed out. He shoved the trunk toward us and torpidly waved us through, along with illicit substances, obscene fetishes, and unwholesome tomes banned in Boston for centuries.

Asenath said nothing, but her canary-eating smirk was damnably eloquent. I was reminded of that evening at the movies when the fat chap choked on his popcorn halfway through shushing us, though her hands hadn't been visible. I should be relieved we're "on the same side," that she hasn't inflicted hoodoo on me, not that I'd be the wiser if she had! Dare I ask, was proposing to her genuinely my idea, and why does it produce an erotic charge to fantasize it wasn't?

July 20, 1931: Am I abnormal? Do I crave being used and pushed around? Dan, with painfully inept stealth, eyes me with a soupçon of pity and reproach as if I were a child. As for the Miskatonic crowd, I'm fed up with their cold shoulders, the ill-disguised condescension, as if I'd backslid from their heights of sophistication! Maybe I put up with wifely predominance because I'm more at home as a dissolute Peter Pan with impiously adult appetites.

Yes or no, isolation seems a common fate of married couples, and for us at least, casual socializing could hardly compete with carnal delights. I've a hunch sex is like a drug she administers to keep me under her thumb, soften me up, *infiltrate* me, a verb I underscore without understanding why. The hell of it is, I'm her willing accomplice, though with every "congress" I feel more like I'm becoming the wife and she the man of the house.

She's furthered her pretense of manhood by stepping out for whole afternoons or evenings without so much as a fare-thee-well. Unlike her, however, I refrain from scolding when she deserts the nest for solo jaunts to parts unknown. Sometimes when she comes and goes I'm prey to an unwonted languor, dozing on the couch—another symptom, I reckon, of middle age; and in another, bizarrely literal elaboration of playing the submissive missus to her imperious husband, I dream more vividly that I am her.

Today brought this oneiric body-swapping to an alarming pass when the rattle of keys in the front door woke me, and there I was, Edward Derby, in the vestibule! I appeared to be startled at myself, awake albeit prostrate and groggy, nauseously dizzy a split-second after, and then blinking away the blear in my vision, sitting up on the couch where I'd definitely been for hours.

To my dismay, I seem to have straddled some hypnogogic line between dreaming and hallucinating, influenced subconsciously, I'd venture, by Asenath's allusions to metempsychosis, souls hopping like fleas between hosts. As if nothing were amiss, she planted a palpably boozy kiss on my forehead, complained she was famished, and rang for the cook to hurry supper.

July 25, 1931: Dan no longer troubles to ask about Asenath when I swing by, to my relief really as it renders small talk less hypocritical for both of us. He's kidding himself, though, to suppose his face doesn't betray a certainty that I'm blind to what's right under my nose. On one level or another he may be correct, and in fairness, no pokerface is a match for my burgeoning skills at skimming the gist of poorly guarded thoughts, one fringe benefit of sharing a bed and a library with Asenath.

Dan's a good listener, but how stodgy he and Mrs. Upton must have been to renounce glorious sensuality for the insipid family way, for bourgeois tedium, unlike Asenath and me. Not to gainsay he may have had a ringside seat for my wife's regrettable outings or fielded gossip from reliable sources. In which case, especially, damned if I'll have a bluenose like him better informed than I am about my own household.

He has some gall, moreover, making out I'm so naïve. Asenath's a woman anatomically, Dan has my personal guarantee on that, and how could she camouflage being otherwise? But I've been savvy to possible deception since our honeymoon, in a respect that surpasseth understanding, mine at any rate. To harbor such suspicions, though, does that imply more about me than her, or am I blind to disgrace right under my nose?

March 15, 1932: Dan hasn't been square with me, nosiree! To be mum about Asenath's indiscretions, that's one thing, but when sovereignty over my God-given body is involved, why the hell wouldn't he enlighten me? He circulates enough to be up on whatever's common knowledge to the "smart set," the least high-falutin' of whom buttonholed me on Church Street with some malarkey about spotting me in defunct Dad's roadster, burning rubber on the Innsmouth road, and this a common sight for months! He commended my pluck; everybody was amazed, on account of my "delicate nerves," to see me behind the wheel.

I nodded and changed the subject. No point correcting him. I haven't learned to drive, but multiple witnesses would testify under oath to the contrary. I'm forced to conclude my dreams and hallucinations of being Asenath are neither. She must sedate or hypnotize me (or whatever she did to the fat moviegoer and the pipsqueak at customs) and then hijack my mortal clay. I'm reduced to the status of a vehicle driving a vehicle.

Before he'd actually met Asenath, Dad ushered me into the library for an over-rehearsed heart-to-heart about the importance of compromise to a solid marriage, surrendering independence, egotism. Hah! Had he any inkling how ironically prescient his words were, he'd have hired a flock of Pinkertons to gather grounds for annulment. But if I want this "tail job" done right, I'll have to do it myself. Who else would know what to make of Asenath's escapades?

Dad had also been a fine one to lecture me on my "independence," considering the short leash they had me on till 1929. Given my druthers, I might have wed a nice, superficial Bohemian and settled down a decade ago, never conceiving of the rapture in which Asenath ensnares me.

May 10, 1932: In Dan I confide dribs and drabs re marital woes that I calculate will pique his sympathy, keep him in my corner, make him more pliable. I've broached how Asenath borrows my body and takes it for joyrides, which shouldn't throw him completely since he's seen me drive while well aware I can't. I've mentioned nothing yet of my impression that she's somehow not a she, because I'm too squeamish about it myself. As for the particulars of Asenath's erotic power over me, Dan wouldn't sit still for any such ribaldry.

That goes double for today's revelations, absolutely not for his prudish ears, now or ever. I can barely tolerate them without succumbing to glossolalia or storming off to have it out with her, restrained solely by my stupefaction over how to fling down that gauntlet.

After lunch I waved away the coffee, not that it was necessarily spiked, but why gamble? Pleading lethargy, I flopped onto the sofa, cracked open and yawned into a doorstop of a Faulkner novel, and pantomimed nodding off. Five minutes later Asenath brushed by as I flipped a page. Out the corner of my eye I discerned her dirty look from the front door, as if clinging to consciousness were tantamount to a broken promise. "Bye!" I yoohooed as she twisted the doorknob. She half swiveled about with a cursory flick of her other hand, the sketchiest of tally-hos, and out she went.

She manifestly hadn't credited me with the moxie to shadow her, for not once did she check behind while promenading through town. Apprehensions quickened and I was glad we were in broad daylight as she traversed River Street with its seedy, derelict-seeming warehouses hemming us in. And then the daylight was insufficient balm for my nerves when she hustled over the Garrison Street bridge and down Water Street. The tenements here were cheap and vulgar when new, and after three decades of riffraff tenants, were already tumbledown sties.

Asenath and a puppy-sized rat crossed paths and ignored each other as matter-of-factly as two stenos en route to respective offices. No slum-dwellers on stoops and balconies accosted me, or I'd have turned tail before Asenath strode onto a rickety porch and through a flimsy door, from which burst music and palaver. No sign above the door or porch proclaimed these premises a restaurant or social club, unless I counted "No Man's Land" incised faintly in worn paint beneath the doorbell. And were this a speakeasy, no lookouts were lurking about, nor doormen demanding passwords. I steeled myself and soldiered in, anticipating a coven, a cult, a secret clan.

The reality was nowhere as straightforward. Was this a saloon or someone's parlor? In the off-putting murk, a hulking bar along one wall flanked a homier complement of couch, armchairs, sideboard, bookcases. While my eyes adjusted, my nostrils flared at a clash of patchouli and lavender and cloves, within a pall of dust and tobacco. Amid the babel of a mob that begrudged me incurious glances at most, isolated snatches from a Victrola in the corner included, if memory serves, a crooner warbling "dingdong, dingdong, fairy bells are gaily ringing."

Comparably telltale details of the décor I shan't describe; suffice to say the drawn curtains were lilac, and I don't even like writing "lilac." I ordered a cognac from the barmaid (a sallow flapper with an unfortunate scar bisecting her cheek), who plunked down a shot glass of purported "brandy," which I gulped at the darker end of the bar while scouting around for Asenath. Mounting trepidation compelled me to beckon for more of the godawful hooch, as I sized up the clientele between scorching sips.

I was seldom, in all honesty, dead sure of what I was ogling. Bevies of glamour girls presented ruggedly virile profiles; and men, based on casual inspection of haircuts and clothes—brawny, stout men at that—were, upon second look, extraordinarily busty, and one of these imposing figures leaned toward me from the adjacent barstool and stage-whispered, "Hey cutie, you a femme under there or just another pretty face?" At my gaping befuddlement, she and her pal cackled ungraciously and resumed their tête-à-tête.

In these cockeyed surroundings, I was hard-pressed to recall what Asenath had been wearing, and had to trust I'd recognize it on sight. My darting vision dodged past ruffles and angora, feathers and paste jewelry, and lit on a sliver of glossy black bobcut, a swatch of jet-black bolero jacket, in a nook between the fireplace mantel and a barrelhouse piano. I uncharitably pictured one of those shiny black wasps that prowl among the honeysuckle.

As my neighbor at the bar had demonstrated, to presume I was attracting no scrutiny would be ingenuous. Asenath posed the glaring exception, oblivious to me as she necked *con brio* with an adolescent waif. The world, for all its bedlam, ceased to impinge on me. I sat stunned, blank, as if kicked by a horse, but what exactly had inflicted the impact: the glimpse per se of my wife's hand up a skirt, her paramour's tender age (with Mary Pickford corkscrew curls!), her indifference to our wedding vows, or her relatively public display of wantonness?

A burly mitt shook my shoulder, no rougher than needful to bestir me. Instead of confirming the assailant was the cackling Amazon, my vision perversely sought Asenath again, homing like a fly toward a pitcher plant. "Hey pretty boy," she cajoled, more mildly than her choice of words would suggest, "you're lookin' kinda pale. You seen a ghost?"

"No," I intoned hollowly, still squinting into space, "my wife."

Amazon mitt rested more gently, almost maternally, on my shoulder. "Go home. You go on home and forget it. Before she sees you and there's trouble. Where's the good in that?"

I nodded foggily. Her argument held as much water for me as for anyone. How could making a scene here work to my advantage? I slid off the stool onto unsteady feet, too spooked to thank the Amazon properly for sound advice, and ducked out, with a few foolhardy backward peeks to verify Asenath hadn't noticed me.

Am I an "invert"? Is that what it means for me to want what I want from Asenath, since she's an open-and-shut invert herself? Or as I've often wondered, do I refer to "her" by the wrong pronoun, who was toying with a girl as a man would have, and again, what does that make me? I uncorked my own brandy to wash away the taste of rotgut, and it took some doing. Whenever Asenath did sashay in, she'd have found me asleep on the couch for real.

May 11, 1932: What a hangover! I blame it for the reckless temper in which, for better or worse, I did have it out with Asenath, marring that pristine breakfast hour I've always consecrated (at frequent cost of biting my tongue) to domestic tranquility. I might well have foundered through coffee, toast, soft-boiled egg in the accustomed fraught silence, had Asenath not absently stroked her chin, in a reprise of tidying invisible beard, at which instant the loutish butler harrumphed and tendered her the morning paper. The mordancy of co-conspirators flashed between them, and I saw red.

Fecklessly perhaps, I sought to deflect accusations of my own duplicity with the locution, "You were observed entering a sordid establishment on Water Street. What about it?"

"Yes, what about it?" she exploded, with both venom and glee. "So you were the little lost lamb who blundered into that dive expecting cognac! I should have guessed when I came home and you were passed out hugging the bottle. If it wasn't so rich, I'd be embarrassed, though nobody associated you with me."

"That's your apology?" I blustered. "That's your explanation?"

"I miss having what I used to have!" she railed. "I miss having a woman! There's your explanation!"

"What you used to have?" I parroted, in over my head. "When would you have had the opportunity for such experiences? You're only twenty-five!"

"Only twenty-five!" she laughed, oozing sarcasm.

The butler hadn't budged, grinning oafishly at our strident melodrama. Doubtless enticed by the ruckus, the frowzy maid had slouched up to goggle beside him. I threatened to sack them both unless they skedaddled, but their inaction, till Asenath's raise of eyebrows bid them go, infuriated me the more, as my exercise of authority had backfired, only underlined my impotence, bearding me in my own den as it were (and ratifying who did flaunt the beard, visible or not).

After they'd slunk out, Asenath, scorning further comment, grabbed the newspaper, and exited too, consigning me to seethe red-faced like a tot who could finish his spinach or sit at the table forever. This "spat," belying received wisdom, failed to clear the air, but did illuminate where I stand, which in one regard has lessened the tension. It's official: the gloves are off!

July 11, 1932: What's there to see in Asenath, now that she no longer cares to bind me with her charms? And if she did, those efforts were likely wasted, for I consistently perceive her, through the lens of neurosis, with a repugnant kinky beard. Our overlaps of selfhood when she "borrows" my body (unless she's drugging me and those are veritable "pipe dreams") expose a metaphorical actuality beneath her girlish surface, or a substrate actuality more literal and abstruse from which my ego detours me.

But those outbursts of hers (audible from cellar to bedroom, as if she can't contain herself) strike me as signposts to that actuality, when she bitterly laments she's "not a man, not fully human!" What am I to make of such self-loathing hysterics? Women have had the vote since 1920; what more can they want?

Whatever her agenda, I speculate she has felt obliged to shanghai me simply because I am a man (and no man handier), to exploit that alleged mystic privilege my maleness confers. Her deceit, her secrecy, even her "joyrides" in my flesh I could live with, were I receiving anything in return, but I'm not any more. She's above bargaining, lacks the erogenous leverage with which to bargain. I will get shut of her somehow.

August 20, 1932: I bet gullible, horrorstruck Dan is still reeling like a punch-drunk after that earful I fed him on the road from Chesuncook. I should be nicer—he did drive halfway across New England to "rescue" me, though I can't work up much more than pity at what a sap he is. I must save a crumb of sympathy for Asenath too, who misgauges how well I shield my thoughts (and the knowledge of this diary's whereabouts!) from her.

In upshot, Dan is convinced I'm itching to kill Asenath over a broken promise not to drag my body to some Mecca for necromancers in the wilds of Maine. As if she deigns to promise anything! What's the difference where I am physically if my mind is under sedation in my own snug parlor? She'd be stupid to endanger her "vehicle" of choice, and I had to rough myself up plunging through burrs and brambles before staggering off to that hick sheriff, begging him to wire my softhearted dupe.

Dan swallowed my hogwash about Asenath terrifying me for no logical reason with the spectacle of "shoggoths," among other lurid figments, in noisome dungeons (under trackless woods, yet!). Shoggoths, rumor has it, are cave-dwelling Antarctic beasts, so what the hell would they be doing down a well in Maine? I'd say I made the most of that stretch when Asenath took a breather, maybe for some shuteye after a strenuous Black Mass or whatever, before reclaiming the wheel, perilously uninformed about my theatrics for Dan's edification.

From behind my thespian's mask, in fact, I blurted more than I was ready to reveal to myself. Asenath's mannish insights into pleasing me, her phantom whiskers, her very hubris had coalesced subconsciously into a raving thesis that Asenath was the mere vessel of her ruthless father Ephraim who'd displaced, eradicated, her spirit months before we'd met. In brief, he'd killed her and inhabited her skin, her identity, the balance of her lifespan with the coldblooded pragmatism of a hermit crab.

And Ephraim, I ranted, was scheming to destroy my psyche next, though he must have been Machiavellian enough to appreciate that two young bodies to possess were better than one. In any event, he won't disembody me as easily as his pitiable daughter. But has Dan cottoned to the supreme grotesquerie here, that I've essentially married my father-in-law? This brainstorm over Ephraim, full-blown from my brow like automatic writing, trumps my earlier incentives, also too blue for Dan, to kill Asenath: her double-life as an "invert," my fixation on her as an abhorrent "bearded lady," and at the crux of it, her uselessness in bed.

September 4, 1932: Asenath, as I still call her—him—it for convenience, must suspect I'm plotting her destruction. Maybe Dan had mistaken whom he was addressing recently and let slip something, and now Asenath is trying to force my hand, give her a pretext of self-defense for murdering me that much sooner. Or else she's resolved to wring what vile enjoyment she can from me, indulge those appetites she curbed while upholding our bourgeois mirage before she lowers the boom.

Either way, I awoke naked this morning, sore in places I couldn't even see in a mirror, chafed red in those I could, black-and-blue from stem to stern, and most baffling, a fleck of carmine shiny on one thumbnail, with the whiff of polish remover on every fingertip, and a knotted lock of wig hair on my pillow. Peculiar muscles ached as if I'd been horseback riding as I hobbled from bed to bathroom, where Asenath in a robe preened in front of the medicine cabinet, raising snide eyes at my reflection. Lurking in wait?

She jostled by me in the doorway, pouting, wrinkling her nose at my proximity. "Brush your teeth!" she carped in passing. "Your breath stinks of Sodom and brimstone!" The hint a titter pulsed under her own none-too-minty breath, and her tone was ominous with warning about the tenor of existence henceforth, down to whims both unintelligible and squalid.

Goad me into a showdown, will she? Fine, but if she's banking on a pushover, she probably shouldn't have sat on her hands so long. Meanwhile, the more she taunts me, the closer I come to lusting after her again, or at least jumping her dainty bones from behind, having my way with her. Sauce for the gander, considering the violations I apparently endured?

October 15, 1932: I haven't been this chipper since Asenath and I became a couple, and yes, it's because we've irrevocably split. I got the drop on her, home free for a minimal investment (a quarter-hour at most) of stealth and patience. Dan, as usual, I must spoon-feed less than the whole truth, but he's instrumental in skewing public opinion of me toward its most benign. The ghastly servants are discharged, he can bruit that about. He'll also faithfully broadcast how I kicked Asenath out, that she's hightailing it to cronies in New York, nevermore to bedevil me.

I'd do neither of us good to retail how a month of her abusive outings drove me to desperate inspiration. They've taken a visible toll, debasing me into a shuffling, dopey roué, and thus after supper yesterday when I muttered I was tuckered out and retiring to the library for some light reading, under no circumstances to be disturbed, what would come more naturally to her than to spy on me scant minutes later asleep at my desk, forehead cradled in forearms? And whatever her plans, they altered upon remarking, on the blotter inches from my elbows, a fountain pen lying across the open pages of my diary.

The bait was irresistible: what did I know of her, what was I up to? If I'd really been snoozing, her furtive approach, the rustle of her sleeve as she plucked up the diary wouldn't have awakened me. The mildest draft through my thinning hair told me she'd whirled around to the pole lamp by the fauteuil. I counted to ten and parted my eyelids by the merest, fluttering slits to confirm she'd turned away, rapt in my lousy penmanship, a corona of lampglow surrounding her like a lunar eclipse.

She always was overly self-possessed, if that's not too loaded a term. She was deaf to the wheels of my well-oiled swivel chair rolling back to let me arise gingerly on stocking feet and hoist a precious heirloom from the desk where my arms had enfolded it, a silver candlestick holder, which I prayed I wouldn't damage upon swinging overhand and embedding in Asenath's startlingly brittle skull. A spasm like high voltage made me unhand my Revere-ware weapon, which stuck in the grisly fissure as she crumpled.

I'd tied a score, restored a balance. I'd become a man. After a campaign both blatant and surreptitious to unman me, take that, Asenath! A man can murder, a child cannot: it's built into our legal structure, our civilized logic. In this my rite of passage, though, I was nowhere near the end of the tunnel, where I could relax, pat myself on the back, not till I'd lugged Asenath's lolling corpse down cellar to dig a hasty grave (I was on a tight schedule, as the servants always slunk home from their "evening out" by 11) and pile a cairn of storage crates on top.

I locked the library, pocketed the key along with every copy I could ferret out, practiced my story of Asenath's exodus on the logy servants ca. 10:30, thrust severance pay upon them along with twelve hours' notice, and sat up in bed all night to listen for any activity beyond their foreseeable imprecations and tipsy efforts at packing. I only regret I hadn't a chance to scrub away the stains on the library carpet, especially as Asenath's "people" seem the type to sniff out blood and burrow swinishly after it.

I'll have to replace the outside locks first thing tomorrow. But this morning, what with stress and exertion and all-night vigil, I had to hit the hay after ejecting the erstwhile staff, and was *hors de combat* till the clock struck five. In doleful dreams I was still squabbling with Asenath, protruding candlestick-holder and all. I'm rid of her otherwise, though, so I can be philosophic about her lingering in dreamland. It's not even twenty-four hours she's been dead; of course I'll have nightmares.

November 20, 1932: Neurologists might have pronounced it an "absence seizure," but I knew better because I was suddenly seated before Asenath's vanity mirror, stroking a fanciful beard. Wise after the fact once more! There was much I should have heeded for weeks, primarily the recurring dreams (products of subconscious guilt, I surmised, or anxiety that murder would out) of slain Asenath railing and rushing at me, rebuffed with inches to spare by the edge of the shaft of darkness encasing her.

I was grossly overdue for the realization of how adept she—he—it is, of the tenacity empowering a spark of sentience to persist in a cold husk, gathering strength to launch itself into me with more impunity, deeper penetration, on each attempt. How even to ascertain when "she" began to succeed? Ironically, since these infestations strike without portent, I have to assume death has amounted to a delay but not a deterrent in Asenath's access to this diary. Circumspection's the word!

December 13, 1932: I won't let a woman beat me! I won't be saddled with a woman's body, let alone a moldering one! I may have been less than a man, or less than a man should be, to wind up like this, but I won't devolve into something less than human! Fuck you, Asenath!

It's beside the point, but I have to admit that, prior to these do-or-die straits, a man-child like me could scarcely have bungled into any other kind of matrimony. If not Asenath, then someone equally overbearing would have gravitated toward my malleability, my stunted development, my Fauntleroy upbringing, and subjugated me. Am I an "invert" posing as a man, and if someone unlike her had married me, would I only have made her, like rainwater filling a pothole, more like Asenath?

And for the crowning indignity, Asenath dead dominates me as easily as Asenath alive. I've had to have my groceries delivered since Thanksgiving. She's ostensibly content to conserve energy and let me be so long as I loaf about the house, but within five minutes of folding shirts and packing them in a Gladstone, noon becomes night, the shirts are balled up and thrown around the room, and I'm almost too tired to breathe.

In the aftermath of these disruptions, Asenath must need to rest, for if the hour's not too onerous, I'm free to limp over to Dan's and play on his sympathies as if I'd never bludgeoned my wife, all the while alert to her psychic fingers seeking, groping, pressing against my skull, like the tentacles of a cuttlefish latching on from behind but slipping off because they're so slimy. By and by, in what seems a social call's normal course, her pull grows vexingly uncomfortable, distracting, and I bow out.

The apron strings of yore have transmuted into tentacles! It would be droll, surreal, laughable if the coils weren't gaining purchase. But none of this *cri de coeur* is news to you, is it, Asenath? Do I amuse you, at least?

January 4, 1933: If I undid everything she's made me do, if she allowed me that much rope, it would only be to make me do it all over again, like Sisyphus with a shovel. She's mainly out to torment me; I'd be crazy to abet her.

Whenever she vacates me nowadays, I've been digging in the cellar, in the dark, so I'm vague on how deep I've gone. Odds are, not very on any one occasion, as Asenath revels in prolonging ordeals. I've restacked the boxes away from the grave, and I've uncovered her lidless eyes, her buffoonish, lipless grin. They greet me when I revive, and the rest of her must be under the flimsiest blanket of soil, for a suffocating wave of putrescence buffets me toward the stairs, though relief is woefully delayed because the rot saturates my sinuses.

That isn't the worst, however. More and more distinctly, I've experienced blurry, muddled episodes of peering up, unblinking, at myself, Edward Derby, standing athwart me and pitching aside shovelfuls of dirt. My face leers down with merry spite. I'm numb, I'm not breathing, I can't move, and I wish I could blame an etiology as benign as sleep paralysis.

These bouts of exhumation I interpret as more than exercises in cruelty. She's proclaiming "checkmate," emphasizing I'm under house arrest: even were I to outdistance her direct influence, she'd snag a passerby on the sidewalk, herd him down the bulkhead to show I'd lied about her exodus to New York. Murder would out, I would hang, and she'd persist within a new host. Asenath—dead for months, but winning! The nerves that moor me to sanity are fraying, snapping one by one. But then, madness may be my sole refuge.

January 25, 1933: Yes, my pissant husband, run crying to your fellow pantywaist Danny. Gild the lily with redundant exhibitions of what a hysterical milksop you are. I give you leave, and make no mistake, you'll never step outside otherwise, nor lose your mind unless I loosen my grip on it. And pardon me rubbing it in, but you're no closer than before to convincing Danny boy you're not deranged. At his most magnanimous, he'll respond to your histrionics by having you committed, and what will that accomplish? You're mine, hubby dearest, whether at home or in Arkham Sanitarium. And I, on an extremely intimate level, will be yours forevermore!

February 14, 1933: Shed a tear for Asenath, the actual Asenath I never met, though she mightn't have given me a second glance. No matter, on reflecting how her own despicable Dad cheated her of falling in love, an education, every adult experience. Instead, she woke up one morning an adolescent girl in the poison-racked, straitjacketed body of a bearded coot in a padded cell in a mental asylum. No wonder "Ephraim Waite" was said to have died raving mad! Consider yourself avenged, Asenath, if that's something you'd have wanted (from inside your former cell, maybe; why not?).

Dan was welcome to declare me insane, which wasn't the same as disbelieving me. As Ephraim learned to his eternal cost, I hadn't the wherewithal to block him usurping my body permanently, transplanting me in Asenath's, but I'm no slouch at leading the unwary down byzantine paths, and who can be 100% wary at every turn? Maneuvering Dan into having me put away was child's play, no occult talents required.

Ah, but maintaining sentience in a broken, festering vessel, restoring its mobility without shivering it to pieces, that takes finesse. I can't overstate the distastefulness of gimping with torturous deliberation across town, leaving a trail of ichor and skin and meat, to ring the bell and rap on Dan's door, foist on him instructions to snuff out that sitting duck Ephraim once and for all, and fall apart in the vestibule (which I alone was in a position to relish as blessed release).

Meanwhile Ephraim, adept or not, stands as much chance of pulling himself together after a bullet through the brain as Asenath after a force-feeding of arsenic. More sauce for the gander! Too bad, as I'd have relished his apoplexy over how I'd outdone him, not merely sustaining a vital spark in a maggoty carcass, but roosting in the lowliest hosts, pillbugs, mice, spiders, while dipping in and out of Dan's oblivious head, carving inroads like a medieval sapper, finally to expel the inborn personality into the withering void and make myself at home. Whenever will that dullard get wise to the lacunae in his daily rounds?

And rationally or not, I do feel more myself after trotting Dan to High Street for my diary and stashing it out of his and Mrs. Upton's household orbits. Any touchstone of unconventionality in this vapid place is invaluable while I ruminate on remaking it more in my image, and speaking of the missus, I've a trick or two, thanks to Asenath, for her grateful delectation. We'll soon see, Dan old pal, who the milquetoast is!

The Demon Thought

What Exile from himself can flee?
To zones, though more and more remote,
Still, still pursues, where-e'er I be,
The blight of life—the demon thought.
—LORD BYRON

Some people make their thinking fit their experiences, and others make their experiences fit their thinking. I wish I knew on which side of this divide I stand. I'd hate to come across as xenophobic. I also hate how relieved I felt after bearing mute witness to someone's execution in my place.

When the train crossed the frontier, nobody in old-school gaudy uniforms checked passports. I could have sworn we were leaving the EU. I must have been behind on who was in and who wasn't, and should have been better informed, but by whom? I can't reliably say who my employers are, just that they wanted me to test the waters, informally like, for some transnational corporate expansions.

To dignify the passing terrain as "countryside" would have been charitable. Woodlots of bare trees with dense brown undergrowth, foundations of factories and warehouses in the thick of rubble, coastal stretches where idle cranes towered over rusty drydocked hulls challenged me to reserve negative judgments till I'd reconnoitered the capital.

A rank copse gave way suddenly, like the removal of a blindfold, to a field of grassy patches and rutted paths, roughly the size of a hockey rink. A couple of beat-up sedans had parked on bald ground, facing a painfully bright orange blaze midfield, overambitious for a campfire, too compact for a bonfire. Several guys in dark sweaters and jackets were milling around as if anxious to dissociate themselves from the fire, but obligated to stay till its fuel was ashes.

And then a windbreak of poplars flickered by and I beheld three duffers trudging with club bags in tow across a golf course. They appeared oblivious to the smoke and fire beyond the windbreak, could have been on a different planet. Whoever the firebugs had been, I couldn't have described their features or their cars, and they couldn't possibly have spotted me, but malaise at seeing something best not seen lingered as the train pulled into the city.

My train had seemed ordinary, like any other on the Continent, a bit shopworn if anything, but came across as excessively streamlined, futuristic, misplaced amidst the time warp out the window. I may have visited such a wrought-iron cavern of a depot as a child, though its grubby antiquation kindled no nostalgia, instead posing a stark reminder that the past is dead, that to embrace it too intimately is to wallow in decay, to court death. The fin-de-siècle authenticity into which I disembarked was a product of inertia and not restoration.

I had to proceed with caution, certainly, or risk reading too much into shabby surfaces. Rash of me to equate them with apathy, enervation; this may have been a vibrant society investing in priorities unapparent to outsiders. Nobody was paying me to regurgitate personal bias.

Based on location alone, this country should have been an economic powerhouse, regardless of governing ideology. At its crossroads of Europe north, east, west, and central, it had no mountainous borders to hinder shipping, and half its seaboard was a penannular harbor. Expansionist powers used to overrun such easy-access hubs routinely, and Russian onion domes, German stairstep gables, art-deco balconies, classic '50s Volvos bespoke centuries of foreign influence. Those unstable days were over, yet I observed no high-rise Fortune 500 HQs, no conspicuous consumption, no well-oiled infrastructure.

Instead, signs of hardscrabble subsistence abounded. The length of one avenue, grandmothers in black shawls hawked amber trinkets on folding tables. In cobblestone squares were mazes of booths where hucksters boasted to passersby of their honey or game meat or ironmongery. This must have been the "old town," which begged the question, Where the hell was the new town? I set off in a straight line till underdeveloped waterfront stopped me, presided over by a giant bronze of Lenin, untouched by any groundswell of post-Soviet nationalism. I steadfastly deny my preconceptions about standards of living unduly colored my critical acumen.

Into the warren of historic streets I backtracked, on the brink of peckish: fair warning to start scouting for restaurants, always a labor of ages in a strange town. Weeding out tourist hokum, underworld fronts, fine dining where an appetizer would exceed my per diem generally devolves into making do with the best bad option. Menus in windows are commonly in English as well as the native language, but local specialties tend to defy translation, and today's recon turned up no familiar fast-food chains where I'd at least know what I was in for.

My deciding factor in choice of bistro was skulking within the portcullis gateway of a vestigial medieval wall. Four bruisers in gruff conference and deep shadow wore black sweaters and jackets like those of the firebugs. And though the odds were microscopic these were the dark outfits of the same guys, my earlier, irrational angst rebounded, and to quiet it I sought the nearest shelter, across the brick plaza, before the bruisers could return my nervous glances. A doorman in Renaissance-Fair foppery doffed his cavalier chapeau and bowed in welcome. Yep, I'd bolted straight into textbook tourist ambush.

The only other customers cemented this impression, a busload of beauty-pageant contestants sipping soft drinks at a banquet table outlandishly long in the cramped dining room. Hard not to stare at this bevy in diaphanous, floor-length pastels and over-the-shoulder sashes, a vision bordering on surreal at this pre-noon hour. From the doorway I had no luck reading the florid text on the sashes, wouldn't even have bet it was in Roman letters. And while complexions ranged from Norse to Sub-Saharan, everyone was chatting lively as sparrows in some lingua franca I couldn't catch. Were they vying for the title of Miss Esperanto?

A certain dynamic in the staff's behavior established this even more damningly as a tourist trap. The Fourth Musketeer of a doorman, the maître d' in leather jerkin and puffy-sleeved doublet, the serving wench in mobcap and brocade bodice couldn't fawn and scrape enough en route to planting me in a square-backed oaken chair, equally ponderous and ornate. But after a one-sheet menu, with the heft of Masonite and promises to "present proudly best of traditional folk cuisine," landed on my burlap placemat, the house tone switched with lightning ruthlessness to neglect with grace notes of contempt.

Flagging down the waitress during one of her rare beelines through the premises, I tried to learn what "our prize-winning ale from abbey recipe" was like. She blew a stray blond lock away from her eye and rested a fist on accordion-pleated hip. "Is normal beer."

Multiple dishes surreptitiously materialized in front of the pageant hopefuls, as if the staff swooped in with trays solely when my look was elsewhere. On next regaining my server's grudging attention, I toyed with noting she hadn't done spicy, rich beverage justice, but chickened out and instead entreated her for more detailed description of the menu's intriguing "Ploughman's Autumn Joy."

"Potatoes and meat!" she practically spat. Her scowl accused me of feigning stupidity just to antagonize her. I hadn't the chutzpah to quiz her further about the menu; my "potatoes and meat" were decent, but then I'm fond of dill and gooseberries. And while this was patently no haunt for townies, or any other customers for the duration of my meal, the glamor girls, like me, were enjoying their feast, or anyhow smiling through it, such that I retracted my snap judgment: if the food was fit to eat, I hadn't blundered into an absolute tourist trap. What's more, for this Podunk republic to host multinational propositions like the putative Miss Esperanto, or to support any credible tourist industry, it couldn't have been off everyone's radar.

I declined to take the waitstaff's sullen dispositions to heart. The perennial tide of loutish foreigners must have eroded their better natures raw, and how could they not be dismally sick of workplace hogwash, of bogus period costumes, Flemish tapestries from Taiwan, gloomy diamond-pane windows, drippy candles in black iron chandeliers? Maybe a follow-up "normal beer" was exerting undue effect, but I was suddenly prone to give this country the benefit of the doubt, to rein in my thinking before it ran roughshod over a few inconclusive experiences.

I paid for lunch with some native cash my employers had fronted me. A busboy with a shock of blond hair like a tumbledown sheaf, a shrewish nose, and a blue footman's weskit with gold frogs, like Sergeant Pepper knockoff apparel, brought my change. I politely requested a receipt, for humoring company bean-counters down the road.

"Why?" he demanded, at once woebegone and caustic, and

tromped away. So much for my empathy, my liberality, my initially generous tip. Well, he'd been the one to diss me, to make it personal. Exiting without my receipt was simultaneously no big deal and a stark matter of honor. I was in the middle of framing a diatribe plainspoken enough for the maître d's English-as-a-second-language, when lo and behold, another customer lumbered in, and my resolve buckled, and I almost slid under the table trying to slump invisibly low.

Brawny newcomer had a black cable sweater and short black bangs and pocky, blunt features. As he surveyed the dining area I couldn't swear he was one of the party in the gateway or in the scruffy field, and he didn't single me out for scrutiny. But the instant the waitress, all servile smiles again, led him to a seat with his back to me, I high-tailed it at the best clip weak knees could muster.

The gathering under the portcullis had dispersed, and the GPS on my company mobile guided me several blocks to company-sponsored lodgings in those inexhaustible Old Town warrens. Where else? It also came as no surprise that an august façade concealed a slipshod, thick-skinned operation. I admit to mild paranoia, gratuitous fussing as I hustled over to the reception counter, anxious to put a locked door between myself and suspicious black-clad characters, only for the whippersnapper crew to ignore me till their phone calls and tête-à-têtes wrapped up.

Worse, when their jaundiced attention got around to me, they regretted my room wasn't ready, and would I come back later? "I'll wait," I huffed, plopping into the cracked red leather of a lobby armchair. That may not have sped them along, and my groundless jitters only escalated as I homed in on everyone coming in off the street, but at least these slacker personnel were on inescapable notice that I was an unhappy camper. And where to go right then that wouldn't have felt foolhardy?

After my fourth bounce up to the counter for status updates, at ever briefer and testier intervals, the girl with circumflex eyebrows and an entitled pout decided, based apparently on intuition alone, I could toddle upstairs. A wheezy deskman escorted me three flights to a further staircase, more like an airshaft with spiral steps, lethargically waved me toward the crowning heights and coughed my room number.

I worry in part about making my experiences fit my thinking because of a pernicious handicap impairing my judgment in new places. It woke in me while I cooled my heels in the lobby, it stretched as I mounted stairway after stairway, and it glared through my eyes at first glimpse of my quarters. It amalgamated unrelated circumstances like shabby hotel service, ditto lunchtime treatment, firebugs in black, everyone in black ever since, into a nefarious pattern, in effect demonizing the general populace, linking people who couldn't all know one another into a plot against me.

Beyond the bad vibes this attic cell instantly gave off, the forthcoming mini-calamities at every turn convinced me, logic be damned, that I was caught up in an endemic network of malice. I naively believed a shower would refresh me, restore me to higher-functioning reason. Hah! In my glorified closet of a bathroom, a water closet indeed, any move to ready bathing facilities for use involved barking shins against the toilet.

Nor could anything happen till I'd piled the towels outside the bathroom, because they were hanging over the frame for the shower curtain and there were no racks or hooks for them. I couldn't balance them on the corner of the sink, which was already overstuffed with a sopping bathmat, which I'd only discovered on the floor of the tub after testing the showerhead.

Worse and worse, the shower stream, though it cascaded straight down, had somehow sprayed the roll of toilet paper, sodden now, a good foot to one side in its wall dispenser; the adjacent wallpaper was blistery and dripping. Either I was the first to make such a mess or, much likelier, nobody cared about water damage. Hoping for the best, I slid the plastic curtain to encircle the bathtub and washed up, only to emerge agape at puddles surrounding the tub, as if the curtain had been cheesecloth.

Thereafter, jotting preliminary impressions on manila sheets, I had frequent recourse to the bathroom to dispense with "prize-winning ale," and ascertained the toilet never flushed the same way twice, obliging me to jiggle the handle, hold down the handle, release the handle, or flush again in five minutes to stop the leaky valve. How could so much bad design in one bathroom not be premeditated?

A brief lie-down after all these petty stressors sounded appealing, but some imp of perversity was out to spoil that too. King-size mattress in this garret made navigating problematic, made getting past the armchair or the bureau a tight squeeze, yet for all the squeaky expanse to sprawl out on, loose change in my hip pocket couldn't merely spill onto the covers, no, it had to pelt like metal rain down the crevasse between the bed and the wall.

Loath to throw cash away, afraid I'd forget if I put off retrieving it, I lurched up and shoved at the corner of the bed to widen the crevasse. I plucked up a fistful of coins and hit upon the dusty bonus of a previous guest's rubbish that the maids had missed or shirked. A paper bag from Planet Hollywood contained packaging for a souvenir smartphone protector, proving a modern district coexisted with the Old Town, taunting me with its leavings under the bed; yet where the hell was it, why was it my forbidden city?

Were rivals from another firm like mine, representing other corporate interests, bribing citizens to impede me on my rounds? Were they partial to black outerwear? I heaved the bed back to the wall and wrote off relaxing as a lost cause. This room I now associated with my every frustration in these parts, with the surmise I was the target of a mystifying grudge, and anyhow I wasn't on salary to lounge around.

A pint or two to steady the nerves? Why not? I'd bypassed a bunch of alehouses in search of lunch and retraced my route to the most memorable, a sunny frontage of a hundred leaded panes, behind which was a surprisingly dusky interior, black paint and curvaceous art-nouveau brass fixtures, restful, cloistered, flanking that unpeopled cobblestone square where giant Lenin presided. The bartender could have been a plaid-flannel hipster in any Western city, and he recommended a local dark lager. I had the rough-hewn slab of a table and a bench to myself; it was the midafternoon lull.

I contemplated the pan-European draft selection of Carlsberg, Heineken, Beck's, Guinness. This country was, at least for some industries, already a lucrative crossroads, a mainstream marketplace, right down to Planet Hollywood. Or was that the face it presented to visitors, a veneer of cultural integration to hide baser, retrograde norms? Hell, I'd intended to cool my jets in here, silence the brooding. Obviously I needed more beer.

Conspicuous on the black wall was a green and gold poster for a Belgian dubbel unknown to me. The bartender thought he might still have the last of it in the cellar, though he warned it'd be room-temperature. I wasn't so easily discouraged, and he insouciantly forsook his station to exhume my order. Nobody raided the register or even entered the building in his absence. He took five more minutes scaring up a Stella Artois chalice for my last-of-its-kind potation. It had a malty, floral, boozy kick.

I smiled, which emboldened the kid to remark, "You know, we never get Americans in here."

"You don't?" His English, like everybody's, went above and beyond barebones phrasebook.

"When my girlfriend worked at the U.S. Embassy around the corner, then yes, she brought them over, but when the embassy went away two years ago, we stopped seeing them."

"That's too bad." Huh. What with menus, signage, and mercantile banter in both English and native parlance, the alleged rarity of Americans gave me pause, till I regarded the draft pumps again and realized the English wasn't for Americans or Brits, but for all the Europeans with fluent English as second language. My lingo was their lingua franca. I was a wholly unintended beneficiary. A thousand years ago, everything would have been in Latin, though nobody would have expected a clientele of centurions and praetors.

Back at my bench I quaffed contentedly and set my empty chalice on the bar, grateful for the calming, bolstering influence of moderate imbibing. I was champing to explore the city in earnest, convey to my employers their money's worth, maybe hunt down that damn Planet Hollywood via GPS.

The plan altered drastically once the pitiful moaning reached my ears. It issued from the dead-end alley beside the alehouse. A ponytailed youth, eyes swollen shut, slit from chin to philtrum as if he had cruciform lips, was pressing a red hand to his left side while slumped against the pitted bricks of the windowless alehouse wall. Above his head in stinking-fresh purple spray paint was graffiti in Cyrillic. He wore a gashed-up New York Yankees blazer. Safe to say, given the Eastern Bloc alphabet, this savagery wasn't the work of Red Sox Nation. Yikes. I blamed this insensitive jest on the beer, whose mild effects were dissipating like a cloudy breath in March.

I bent toward the casualty, hands fluttering hapless inches from his shoulders. I didn't encourage him not to worry, he'd be okay, when I couldn't in good conscience vouch for that. I didn't speak, in fact, since I had nothing constructive to say, didn't dare touch him out of Hippocratic fear it might well do him harm. He couldn't see me past his livid bruising, from which I inferred he didn't grasp I was there. I straightened up, both relieved and skittish at the echoes of approaching sirens, police or ambulance, didn't matter, the alley had to be their destination, right?

I'd do myself no favors sticking around. My proximity to the victim, a putative foreigner, would automatically mark me, another foreigner, as a "person of interest." I had to consider my employers too, who'd hate for even the most adventitious involvement of mine with a crime scene to rub off on them. The painfully near sirens pressurized me to take off before authorities beheld me vamoose from the alley and really implicate myself. The Yankees fan was no worse off than when I'd found him, if the gurgling vigor of his moaning was any measure.

As for his identity, and the attackers', and the *casus belli*, of course I was curious. And of course rationality maintained that the violence had no bearing on me, had only coincidentally occurred scant feet away, shouldn't enter into the pattern of demonization I'd already overindulged. The most I realistically shared with the victim was the possibility I also could have blundered into the wrong place at the wrong time. How weird, though, for an American to land right there, right after the bartender had declared me a unique specimen. Not that Yankees apparel proved country of origin or that his beating was unprovoked, were he an American.

All the same, slinking to the hotel, I foolishly envisioned his assailants wearing black, which spurred me to my next move. I couldn't afford to discount the worst-case scenario of black-clad goons as hirelings of the competition, diligently galling me, thwarting me. But short of that, I'd endured ugly incidents, bad behavior enough to fatten up a scathing report, without too much fudging. As I stuffed toiletries in my valise and scoured nightstand and bedding for stray possessions, I couldn't deny this headlong exodus was fueled by pure generalization, by extrapolating a meager slice of time and geography into a blanket condemnation.

Yeah, but so what? Intuition always plays as big a role as picayune analysis in shaping my summations, and saves my employers a bundle in billable hours. Down at the front desk I palmed the bell till a blasé blonde drifted over and I checked out. Meeting no bruisers in black all the way to the depot was exhilarating, as if I'd pulled off a feat of counterespionage. Pack light, curb the second-guessing, just grab and go: these were my watchwords for quick getaways from ominous environs. Then again, from some viewpoints I was the agent of "foreign powers," wasn't I? "Sinister" can really be in the eye of the beholder.

Serendipity smiled further upon me. No blackguards infested the depot, and a spanking-new train for the border was departing momentarily. I was still on tenterhooks, couldn't focus anywhere longer than a heartbeat as if I'd guzzled a quart of coffee, till such time as the train started rolling. For diversion I ransacked childhood memories for where and when I'd loitered in a similar depot, as much a relic then as now. But I kept defaulting to the sentiments I'd harbored before, that to wallow in the past was a flirtation with death. How prescient of me, in light of how promptly this fusty town had turned on me, how astute of me to clear out before it could do me worse harm.

These musings scattered like mist as the engine shuddered and shook off inertia, and I observed a gent outside my window cast conflicted squints hither and yon as if stumped over which car to board. He was dressed much like me, in ochre sport jacket, yellow button-down shirt, and khaki trousers.

The next instant, three duffers shouldering golf bags entered my field of vision; they might have been the same golfers who'd flashed by this morning, though honestly all golfers look alike to me. I surmised they were also hustling to hop on, more decisively than my dress-alike, before the train chugged away. But at its first hard lurch, I retained the sheerest snapshot of them crowding the indecisive gent, one whipping an iron from his bag, the others bringing down their clubs upon his head.

The train accelerated past the platform and I was alone with my shock, yards past hearing bystanders scream or shout or intervene. No one around me acted as if anything untoward had happened. Oblivious or something worse? Either way, I was doubly glad to be outward bound, at least till serious shakes about my close call set in. I could be

sure of nothing except for being in the dark about what the hell was going on, whether on the platform or anywhere in this hostile backwater.

Executing someone dressed like me may only have amounted to
one more coincidence, though I couldn't suppress pangs of guilt at
some innocent schnook perhaps dying in my stead. More unconscion-
able yet was my relief at golfer assassins' mistaken belief in their mission accomplished, at my free pass out of danger, as if I myself had
gotten away with murder, albeit vicariously. And on yet another hand,
I'd been making too much all along of roughly similar clothing, hadn't
I? I relaxed a little after a once-over of fellow passengers detected no
black ensembles, but no such contingent was really shadowing me in
the first place, was it?

Then I wondered, gawking around once more, do I make my experiences fit my thinking by taking for granted I'm in danger exclusive-
ly from black-shirt thugs or golfers? No one peers back at me, as if
that proves anything.

The competition's welcome to this treacherous morass of a developing market, and I'm overwhelmed by an urge to safeguard my hide
by saying so. I stand, essay fleeting eye contact with random travelers,
and bellow, "It's all yours! I officially withdraw!" No one acts as if anything more untoward has occurred than when golfers stove in someone's
skull. I sit down, shunning the eyes of my reflection in the window.

It seems my experiences have shaped my thinking. Or not. To
generalize in the face of murder and mayhem is only human, but does
my hyperacute mindfulness of every impinging rustle and fidget indicate due diligence or xenophobia? Or does a strange place simply bring
out the strangeness in a person?

When a grizzled dude in a blue nylon jersey thuds into the aisle
seat beside me two stops later, I discreetly rummage through my left
hip pocket. His blank expression betrays no awareness I exist, but that
means nothing. The Bic in my pocket isn't much but will have to do.
Fingertips worry the cap off and clench the barrel. If my seatmate
makes a false move, go for the eyes! Note to myself: watch him on the
QT or he'll definitely get suspicious. If memory serves, I've never been
a man of action, but this is a desperate interlude, isn't it? My God, I
hope we reach the border soon. His life depends on it.

Barley Night

Break o' day, the sun god sat
On the maidstone like a hat.
A sign, a sign since we were born
That time has come to plant the corn.

Thistle sprouting in the field,
Wintertime at last must yield.
But one thing must still be done
To win the favor of the sun.

Have no fear, you'll be all right
If you live through barley night.
Have no fear, you'll be all right
If you live through barley night.

Priest is casting holy bones
Out in front of every home.
As they fall he reads the will
Of the gods for good or ill.

Heaven only talks to him.
Barley day is always grim.
Would that fate had granted we
Should have a captive enemy.

Have no fear, you'll be all right
If you live through barley night.
Have no fear, you'll be all right
If you live through barley night.

End of day, the sun goes down
On the hagstone like a crown.
Priest appears with grease and dung
To anoint the chosen one.

Grab a stone or grab a stick,
If it must be done, be quick.
God decrees it from on high,
Bread for all, if one will die.

Have no fear, you'll be all right
If you live through barley night.
Have no fear, you'll be all right
If you live through barley night.

To the field we all repair,
Scatter blood and body there.
Quaff enough of holy brew,
You may forget the things you do.

Rising sun will smile to greet
Rising smell of raven meat.
By the grace of barley night,
Sun will bless us with his light.

Have no fear, you'll be all right
If you live through barley night.
Have no fear, you'll be all right
If you live through barley night.

Rat Letters

The tannery closed a dog's age ago, its roofline gone swayback, slate shingles shedding to the blighted ground like faro cards flung down in anger. The fieldstone walls were scheduled for demolition to make way for a lunatic asylum, that other enterprise quarantined to genteel society's margins. The tannery lived on, though, in the doddering person of Ariel Dole, who'd spent his apprenticeship curing leather for the Continental Army. And to reward his half-century's toil were a nest egg that kept him in corn mush and salt pork and a permanent air of the sulfur and urine and worse perfumes of his trade, obliging him to dwell at the same remove from town as the tannery.

To Josiah, attending to Uncle Ariel was a duty to postpone till pangs of conscience rivaled those of his gouty shanks. In extenuation, anyone of his girth, he'd plead, required fortifying leisure after due diligence as port inspector. He'd have doffed his boots in Uncle's mudroom, had experience not foretold mudroom conditions throughout the house, on top of the chronic reek that would soon infiltrate Josiah's duds and oblige him to launder them before it set fast.

Worse yet, while Ariel infinitesimally reduced the household pungency by emptying the chamber pot outside, Josiah was thwarted in taking his ease by the rustling of rats behind the smoldering hearth, the wainscoting, the cellar door. He straightaway broached the issue to Ariel, who readily acceded, "Oh, the rats, aren't they awful? They steal my food, and then my stockings, my nightshirt, a hat, a whole jug of rum, and my tobacco besides."

"And have you deployed traps and poison?"

Ariel cannily tapped the side of his meathook nose. "Better than that. Per your great-grandpa Earl's teachings, I pried off a baseboard and planted a rat letter inside, dipped in bacon grease to win their good graces. I saved the practice copy." He plucked out last year's almanac from the tinderbox by the hearth and thrust it upon Josiah. "What's your opinion? Do you agree it was nice enough?"

Nice enough? Josiah withheld the pithier question of whether Uncle really believed a rat could read and donned his cheaters at the prospect of following scribble that barged at right angles through the back cover's "Table of Distances." His lips moved haplessly as he read:

> To My Uninvited Boarders,
>
> I have been generous to a fault sharing my provender with you, but now you threaten to eat and drink me into famishment and strip me naked too, as I fancy beds of leaves and straw no longer suffice and you must filch my clothing for blankets. Surely you observe I am of humble means, on the depletion of which we will all starve. I am also not insensible of the tannery mephitis around me, which will doubtless never mellow, and which I daresay, with your keen snouts, cannot be pleasant to you.
>
> Therefore I urge on you a change of residence, for our mutual benefit, to those new mansions down the road to town. You can treat yourselves there to the choicest viands and brandy, and repose on Chinese silk and Flemish lace, in digs more commodious and fragrant than mine.
>
> The situation as it stands cannot go on. If you won't think of me, pray think of yourselves and heed a word to the wise. Go now and secure your place as first rodents against all comers! Boundless luxury is scarce a mile off, and if you start at daybreak you can gorge on sweetmeats for lunch. You'll not be sorry if you go; you will be if you stay.

Josiah's eyes rolled heavenward as if for counsel. Wouldn't gentle reason and forbearance comport most becomingly? "Dear Uncle, to judge from the scampering behind the plaster while you were gone, I fear the rats have ignored your advice."

"Oh no, they replied on their own good rag bond." Ariel hobbled off to rummage in the bedroom. "See what they snuck onto my pillow."

This development was befuddling in itself, all the more at Josiah's qualmishness about handling the paper as if rat claws had done likewise. He pushed his cheaters higher on his oily nose and marveled at how much neater than his uncle's was the cursive of rodents:

> To Our Gracious Host,
>
> We were here before you, and thus could argue you owe us a fortune in back rent. But let bygones be bygones and not worry about your smell; we like it. Nor are we blind to your grubbing economy, and promise repayment with interest for everything we've purloined. Any variety in our monotonous regimen, you must understand, is irresistible. We hope to prolong our cordial

relations, but should you employ traps and other drastic measures, we also promise repayment in kind. Now will you heed our word to the wise?

No signature was appended. Of course not, rats didn't have names. And damn his biddable eyes, they didn't write letters either. Ariel must have counterfeited another's hand, florid rather than tortuously crabbed. Such attainment seemed beyond him, but who else could have been responsible? Who, besides Josiah, ever abided in that pesthole? "Uncle, did you compose this drollery for sport and forge a different penmanship?" demanded Josiah, aiming for gravity, masking nascent chagrin.

"For sport?" Ariel gaped in puzzlement and the stirrings of hurt. "For sport I'd so mercilessly belabor my rheumatic knuckles?" He shook his aggrieved head. "How I miss the tannery. We were all well-met there, but never since have I belonged anywhere, and even my own kin impugn my candor."

Ariel's melancholia chafed a spark of sympathy in Josiah, and pity vied with guilt to shape his words. "Let's not despair, Uncle, your outlook's not pitch black. I descry must and mildew, rot in plaster and wood. Remedy those and I'll hazard you receive guests aplenty." Or more strictly, Josiah mightn't be quite as loath to visit. "You draft your rats another missive, warn 'em they'll be happier decamping than weathering the noise and disturbance when I restore the walls and floors and ceilings."

Some sheepishness infused Ariel's grin at long-overdue beneficence in the offing. "But should I risk incensing my cohabitants?"

Good heavens, had Uncle grown so dotty he shied from offending plaguey varmints? "You include a proviso in that letter you're to write," Josiah urged, "stipulating that I brooked no dissent, that any complaints at being inconvenienced they must refer to me."

This seemed to quell Ariel's worries, but Josiah's mounted as he sauntered townward reflecting on the labor and expense for which he'd rashly volunteered. True, lodging Uncle in the carriage house or attic would have been cheaper and easier, and he'd save his shins this tribulation of a hike; but for all he knew, Ariel would have shrunk from subjecting polite society to his tannery funk. Such a proposition might only have upset him.

The vagaries of Josiah's office forestalled, as usual, consideration of familial commitments for a week, then a fortnight, his resolve and compunctions waning like the moon till, like the moon, they waxed again as of their own accord. He hastily struck handshake contracts with longshoremen acquaintances and on the outbound road rehearsed a white lie of doggedness in lining up topnotch craftsmen, whom he would personally supervise for as many Sundays as required.

He remarked a new foundation pit and timber frame within a mile of Ariel's, and wondered would Uncle live to be squeezed out of his home by the relentless hegira of suburban gentry, to end up in Josiah's attic yet. Moreover, Constable Hiram was interrogating workers at the site, while a dandy with silk top-hat and corseted waist, the presumptive landowner, glowered as if everyone must be a thief or a fool. Josiah and the lawman were on friendly terms, but no good ever came of buttonholing a fellow whose hands were full with a hornets' nest.

As Josiah struck silver-knobbed cane against Uncle's shabby door, he pardoned as only human his yearning for some way around the task ahead. On pressing the latch and entering, though, he reeled at a tableau far more daunting than months of overhaul would have been: even the mudroom floor gleamed with varnished teakwood, and the odors of drying paint and linseed oil nigh overcame that of Ariel, who beamed from his groaning rocker amid the accustomed rickety furnishings, as if he and all had been levitated during improvements and then plunked down in their perennial spots.

"My clever, clever nephew!" chirped Ariel. "That letter you had me write did the trick! The rats took your point about avoiding domestic upheaval and spared you a passel of bother by fixing up the premises themselves. And weren't they nice not to go overboard and realize a fogey like me prefers the furniture and bric-a-brac he's used to?"

"Did they avow in writing it was their handiwork?" asked Josiah, sinking into a ramshackle Windsor chair before his knees gave out. A foolish question, yes, but better than rank speechlessness.

Uncle's opinion of that question plainly dovetailed with his. "And waste good rag bond? As my learnèd master Captain Drummond oft said, *res ipsa loquitur!* Who besides the rats?"

Josiah was never one to posit devilish influence in mundane events, was in fact no churchgoer, but couldn't help casting his mind's eye toward the otherworldly as he puzzled, What the hell had Uncle gotten mixed up in?

A bolt of inspiration jounced Ariel off his rocker and into the pantry. "As extra proof they were sorry for pilfering, they brought back my rum, hardly touched! Sit tight, we'll raise a cup to their generosity!"

As with the rats' epistle, Josiah balked at fleshly contact with anything the rats had allegedly touched first, and the rational objection that they couldn't drag off and guzzle from a stoppered jug only led to the more harrowing question of who, then, could? Josiah lurched to his feet and after Ariel, to beg off while yet to hear cork pop from jug, citing dockside business he'd carelessly forgotten.

Behind crestfallen Ariel, already reshelving the rum, the cellar door was ajar, squeaking on new brass hinges in an updraft, disgorging wan daylight filtered through sunnyside cellar windows. A faint shadow elongated toward Ariel from something that partially eclipsed the light; not so faint, though, that Josiah couldn't observe it didn't belong to a rat. And intimating acumen beyond a rat's, the shadow sank mercurially from sight, as if feeling his scrutiny. A heartbeat later, two, rather than four, Lilliputian feet clopped with a resonance of tiny hobnails down the stairs.

To charge down cellar in pursuit, espy whatever had thrown the shadow, perhaps penetrate the mystery of the miracle renovations, would comprise the nobler course. But no, he'd claimed urgent business in town. Delay under any pretext might undermine his probity. Likely as not, anyway, dashing down stairs on gouty knees would earn him a broken neck. He congratulated Ariel on his more decorous surroundings and bowed out.

To emphasize the silver lining, Uncle was fine, Uncle was happy. If the occult were at work, remodeling cottages wasn't the most convincing demonstration of skullduggery. Nonetheless, he and his cane put Ariel's behind him as smartly as affliction allowed, to approach the constable squatting alone over the cellar pit, indifferent to his tails trailing in the clay. He was so rapt in a mystery of his own, Josiah could have impudently pushed him in and almost achieved that by commenting, "A relief, I warrant, to have seen the back of that waspish Brummel."

"Yes, had he not been an in-law . . ." He cut that line of thought adrift and mumbled, "How'd they get it all? How'd they do it? No wagon tracks, no sign of men and horses stomping about."

"Get what?" Josiah made bold to ask. And why would Hiram mention wagons and then gape into the pit, where certainly no wagon had been?

"Oh, just building material, a good many hundredweight of it, gone like a dandelion's blowball." His cheeks inflated and he spat tobacco into the pit. "No trace of it except down there, some nails, laths, shingles where the dirt's all churned, as if the earth gobbled it up or someone tipped everything in and buried it. But nobody's that stupid."

"Well, the floor does seem a trifle concave," opined Josiah, though intuition hissed at him to hold his tongue.

"Mayhap that's 'cos the in-law insisted those poor drudges hop in and muddy themselves at fruitless digging, which does tell you who didn't think burying a half-ton of mansion was stupid." He blindly rummaged a plug of linty chaw from a sealskin pouch, bit off a chunk, his stymied sights still trained below, and proffered the rest at Josiah, who bluffly declined.

The makings of a house, Josiah mused, inexplicably go missing, and Ariel's house is inexplicably beautified. Both these events happening at once beggared coincidence, but connecting them meant rats en masse had reconnoitered a building site, transported a relative mountain of resources, and exploited them masterfully and, as the "scene of the crime" connoted, overnight. Or to recall the skulking shadow at the cellar door, if not rats, then what?

"Hiram, I best be going, it looks like rain," announced Josiah, anxious to retreat from the thoughts he'd been hatching and wishing to divert the constable's thoughts before they grew comparably fantastic. "Will you walk with me back to town?" Hiram shook his head and waved Josiah away without even a squint skyward. Josiah, despite the drizzle, was instantly at ease on setting sore foot within the humdrum suburbs.

After his custom, he let avuncular cares slide, what with waterfront duties and a buxom widow to court, keeping faith with his salad-days judgment that connubial bliss were better sought late, if ever. Uncle's industrious rats and their impossible craftsmanship had faded to the vagueness of Jupiter on a hazy night; and then the grocer, with overweening solicitude, had to muster guilt front and center, remarking how Ariel last month had instructed the errand boy to suspend deliveries, that he was "otherwise taken care of." The grocer, whose pear-shaped head would have benefited had periwigs remained in style, simpered hopes the "venerable gent" was well.

Of this development, naturally, Josiah was in ignorance, and though grocers aplenty could have poached Ariel's trade, Josiah savvied better than most how Ariel, diehard creature of habit, would as readily sport a mobcap as switch provisioners.

On the outbound road that afternoon, Josiah grimaced at the rat-despoiled construction site within new palings, a virtual stockade except for an open portal through which laborers had to skip nimbly or be mauled by the pair of straining mastiffs chained to either gate post. He stopped on the homestretch to lean on his cane and mop his brow with a handkerchief as visions of predictable upshots harried him, of Uncle skeletal on his deathbed, or mummifying beside the well-sweep he was too weak to lever.

He did check out back for the pathetic worst before confronting the mudroom and the keener shock of hale Ariel bracing him, "Ah, clever nephew, they entreat me to join them, which they might never have without your intervention!"

Josiah smiled feebly and dropped into the fortuitously nearby Windsor chair. Ye gods, how mortal a sin against Uncle's sanity had his "intervention" constituted? Implausibly, meanwhile, Ariel was positively plumper, but unless Josiah's cheaters deceived him, a few inches shorter, as if malnourishment could reduce height and not weight. So these were magic rats, no less, empowered to transform Uncle into one of their own, though they were obviously magic, to stage overnight refurbishments. "Dear Uncle, am I to infer by your tone that their proposal appeals to you?"

"Why, I'd live forever or thereabouts, they've promised as much, and just as good, I'd enjoy the fellowship I've lacked since the tannery shut down. Lonely nevermore! How many of my seniority even in the thick of town can say that? And to think, I'd contemplated feeding them arsenic!" Ariel clucked remorsefully.

"Uncle!" Josiah exclaimed, profoundly grateful for the change of topic Ariel had unwittingly suggested. "Speaking of feed, the grocer reports you canceled your deliveries. How have you escaped starvation?"

"Starvation! They bring me all my meals now. No more crinkly nose from the errand boy at my miasma! Down in their catacombs, the chef whips up puddings and casseroles and spicy punch just for me." Ariel briskly patted his belly with both hands. "And my new diet agrees with me, does it not?"

Did it? What manner of ingredients went into cuisine from the bowels of the earth, what effects had they already exerted on this trusting fool, did those effects encompass Uncle's altered odor, earthier, yeastier? And to read as much into such capricious piffle as a man's scent, did that not warn of Josiah lending dangerous credence to demented Ariel's gibberish? Why no, delicacy dictated Josiah play along, far preferable to accepting the onus of transferring Uncle to attic or asylum, strife and headache marring the future either way.

Josiah steeled himself with a deep breath. "Uncle, did the rats tell you in plain English you'd live forever? As a rat?"

"A rat?" In quite the turnabout, now Ariel sniffed in distaste. "I had another letter from them and, deferring to their wishes, burnt it after reading, because they misgave it would engender untoward behavior on your part. They're convinced you're not above trying extermination. What's more, they're averse to being called 'rats,' as any of us would be."

Josiah had opened his mouth to inquire what to call a rat if not a rat, but before his tactless logic found voice, a flicker of movement at his feet brought him short. Yes, he reconsidered through a glaze of confoundment, what do you call a rat if it's not a rat? As if sundown had sped up, with shadows lengthening apace, a manikin silhouette stretched forth from beneath Josiah's spindly chair. He bore transfixed witness as it outgrew the shadows of his chair and feet, pantomiming its owner arising from a squat, flexing knotty limbs, projecting a peremptory stance.

Worse, in terms of bolting toward relative safety, a glint as of sparks in the inky-dark fireplace snared his unwilling attention and resolved into two shiny eyes, at the level of a rat on hindquarters, but of manifestly human configuration. Of the body behind the eyes he discerned nothing, nor had to in order to feel entrapped, petrified. "No, Uncle, I don't guess anyone fancies being called a rat," he eked out in a hoarse whisper. Desperate to best his paralysis, he gaped over at Ariel, whose placid regard was unruffled by anything extraordinary.

"Well, nephew, thanks for exercising yourself on my behalf," averred Ariel, rocking on his heels with incongruously youthful aplomb. "But if you'll pardon me, it's getting on toward suppertime, and my helpmeets are sticklers for punctuality." Hurrah, Uncle was offering him an out, and he seized upon it without brooking the least indignation that Uncle was ousting him to suit the whims of rats, or whatever they were. He eschewed glancing back at his chair or into the hearth, wincing from the gouty pains that only propelled him out the more vigorously, like jabs of petite tridents.

Next day, Josiah was still endeavoring to compose himself, resorting to a taproom by the Custom House where he sometimes fraternized with colleagues, though today he withdrew to a dusky nook at the rear, studying the cracks in the hind wall. He didn't begin to relax till he'd lost count of the glassfuls from his carafe of Marsala. And not till then did he credit the evidence of his admittedly imperfect vision: Uncle was harboring *homunculi* under his roof. Hah! For that Latinism to re-emerge, decades after university, was nigh incredible as the *homunculi* per se.

To harp on how such entities were stuff and nonsense ranked as inane understatement, but maybe he should beware parochialism, as acquaintances galore professed otherwise. Those stonemason Indians who'd repointed his chimney—didn't they have myths about wizened little forest sprites? And here in the tavern he'd overheard homesick Irishmen, in town to dig the canal, trading tipsy yarns about their own "wee folk." Why, Josiah's missionary cousin had written him about capricious imps in Hawaii. Maybe he ought only have been surprised had Great-Grandpa Earl with his rat letters not also had some antique lore about Cornish pixies.

But the root of the matter didn't even involve the actuality or not of Ariel's "housemates." Whether he was in diabolic clutches or had simply gone daft, he couldn't stay in that shanty anymore, its renovations notwithstanding. Extricating him against his will was eminently beyond Josiah's beleaguered wits or hamstrung physique. Yet to enlist the constable, in whose bailiwick evictions squarely resided, was tantamount to courting ruination.

Who'd waste more than a roadside sneer at Uncle's cottage and

dream it was palatial with stolen wherewithal indoors? Conversely, anyone stepping inside would be curious, to put it mildly. The constable,
at worst, would recognize floorboards and wainscoting from the in-
law's description, at which juncture Josiah wouldn't have to be directly
implicated to run afoul of scandal, of close kinsman arraigned for felony, loss of reputation and employment resulting. Perish the thought of
removing Ariel via "proper channels"!

But abandoning Uncle to his "helpmeets" would be just as onerous. Something had wrought alterations in him, subtle at present, affecting his height, his smell. Chalk these up to age, to looming
mortality, and since Josiah had beheld no more of these *homunculi* than
their shadows, maybe they consisted of nothing more, their lineaments
a creation of his nerves. Still, leaving Uncle to his dementia, his "rat
letters," his casseroles from the netherworld, was no less an abnegation
of family duty. Josiah resignedly upended the carafe into his glass, tapping the neck with a fingertip to coax out the last recalcitrant drops.

A single course of action was conceivable, on which he fastened
with vinous optimism. He'd trot right over to Uncle's and reason with
him, all night if needful, till Uncle consented at a minimum to a trial
sojourn in the carriage house, where he'd surely apprehend the superi-
ority of flesh-and-blood companionship to that of impish mirages. Josiah had no auxiliary plan should Uncle boot him out, couldn't see
through tippler's fumes to the possibility of failure; more happily,
those fumes benumbed his achy legs as he trod the outbound road.

Optimism hit its first snag in the mudroom, where abiding freshness reminded him not everything about Uncle's "helpmeets" was re-
ducible to illusion. And monstrously more sobering was the magnitude
of Uncle's transmutation since yesterday. Josiah now gawked down
upon bald crown that had been level with his own, and Uncle wasn't
merely shorter: his visage, his anatomy, appeared compressed, as if a
giant thumb were grinding away atop his head. His brow beetled like a
balcony, the mouth was a wry crevasse from ear to jug-handle ear, his
ribcage distended like a keg, gaunt midriff had swollen into a potbelly,
his stance was bow-legged, arms swung scant inches from the floor.

Accordingly, his shirt buttons had popped, the sleeves ended just
above his elbows, and his trousers had ripped at the knees to bunch up
around his feet, covering all but the toes of his slippers. A wonder he

didn't trip over the dragging cuffs when he waddled from the pantry, his gait betraying agitation, but nowhere near the amount his condition warranted. Likewise, Josiah wondered at his own composure and power of speech, especially as his Dutch courage had proved evanescent.

Ariel planted his splayfeet like a gatekeeper, to obstruct Josiah's view into the pantry. His poise was minutely off as if Josiah had interrupted him at some privy business, and his welcome shaded toward novel brusqueness. "Nephew, what possesses you to barrel in at this darkling hour?" A heartbeat later, Josiah was positive a utensil bounced clinking off the pantry floor, though Uncle's stoniness implied stray noises must have originated in Josiah's head.

"Uncle, have you company?" essayed Josiah.

For another heartbeat, no more, Ariel cocked his ear at the silence, then challenged Josiah, "Why not learn for yourself?" He sidled from the pantry threshold with a flourish toward the candlelit interior.

Josiah, with a circumspect glance at gnomish Ariel as at a changeling, called his bluff, and rejected as graceless any comment on the fork upon the floor, in the shadow of a side table. He was more sorely tempted to remark the stubby taper in its pewter porringer, for the flame was whipping like an angry cat's tail, and how to explain this in a windowless, unoccupied space?

He couldn't help shuddering when Ariel was suddenly at his elbow, huffing breaths redolent of dank loam, expounding, "So tell me, where can you point at company, save in a mirror?"

Josiah discounted the question as rhetorical, concentrating instead upon a salver on the counter, in the dark recess below a cupboard. He ambled over circuitously, feigning aimlessness, to swerve about and compass both the dish and Ariel, except Uncle had withdrawn, with utmost stealth despite the ungainly, shortwinded figure he cut. Thankful to ferret with impunity, not scrupling to ponder the wherefore of Uncle's exit, he beelined to the salver and beheld a glutinous dab on its egg-and-dart lip. Uncle's earthy aura, he deduced, lingered too potent for the morsel's own aroma to disseminate.

Obeying an impulse beyond rational control, Josiah dipped a fingertip into the tepid remnant and licked it off. Did it taste of mushrooms or mold, groundnuts or weed roots, was it more resinous or chalky, sublime or rotten? Judicious after the fact, he inferred his piddling dose couldn't have been too virulent, since weeks of the *homuncu-lus* diet hadn't killed Ariel. It was also, come to mention it, of the same savor as Uncle's breath.

A faint scraping from the other room galvanized him, brought to mind a whetstone, which in his skittishness he associated with name-less perils to Uncle or himself that he scrambled to circumvent. Josiah planted his cane upon the hooked rug to steady himself as he observed Uncle squatting in front of the hearth, a pose that lent him an unfortu-nate similarity to a toad by dint of his uncommonly limber bow-legs. He'd shoved the snakeheaded andirons apart, and the iron hatch be-tween them to the ash pit was propped up.

He was evidently in hushed consultation with himself, casting whispers down the chute and pausing for inaudible, Delphic replies. Josiah bucked a tide of malaise, be it from the circumstances or the bite of "casserole," to josh hollowly, "Dumping ashes, Uncle?" He fathomed at that instant how the stick holding the hatch open was ac-tually a gnarly, miniature arm, and before he'd finished uttering his quip the arm was gone, the flap clanked shut.

Ariel spun round and arose with unnaturally youthful agility, though grave sentiments weighted his features. "Nephew, I won't dis-pute you mean well, yet if I foresee what brings you at such a righteous gallop and impetuous hour, pray contain yourself and mark me. Are your designs founded on familial tenderness and well-informed sympa-thy? I wager you'd foist on me the portion anyone would deem proper for anyone of my senescence, as if I were one of a manufactured host. Of this my friends have persuaded me."

He grinned abruptly as if after all in jest, which creased his visage into corrugations like rows of crumbling brickwork, goading Josiah to implore, "Dear Uncle, please believe your welfare's uppermost in my heart. I worry for your sake in case of sickness or mishap, despite your friends' best ministrations. At least indulge my hospitality a few days and then decide whether you're happier, and if you're not, I'll fetch you back here, I swear." Josiah artfully pouted as if wounded that Un-cle would asperse the integrity of his affections.

"Goodness, Nephew, were I to become your tenant, strictly on a trial basis, I couldn't join you this very moment," he protested through the grin that had set like mortar. "I must choose carefully how to fill my haversack. Might I sway you to come back tomorrow?"

For Josiah's money, this mimicked capitulation well enough; what profit in dissecting each syllable for ambivalence? Besides, Uncle wanted him to tarry no more than he, on tenterhooks amidst the eeriness, wanted to tarry. And though the Marsala's bracing influence was depleted, its intestinal onus still called the shots. "Till tomorrow then, dear Uncle; but before I go, discomfort compels me, if you'll forgive my liberty." Josiah's stride had him across the parlor and unbuttoning his trousers above the chamber pot in the corner, perplexed at Ariel's distraught outcry. How would today's and not a hundred previous pisses overstep propriety?

During Josiah's approach through the gloom, the chamber pot's handles in dim silhouette had borne a striking resemblance to Ariel's ears, and a lumpish knob within its craterous mouth had grown more distinct, and by a trick of perspective was poking higher with Josiah's every footfall. At the last second, with manhood in hand, he gaped aghast to discover the protrusion was neither turd nor otherwise inanimate, but rather a doll-sized head breaking ill-advised cover, askance at Josiah exposing himself, patently in pouncing distance.

He couldn't blame naked manikin for glowering at its immediate prospects; but to meet those pop-eyes aswim in abysmal sockets, like scoops of suet in black basins, was to teeter on a void of indifference profounder than contempt, a moral vacuity from which good and evil, remorse and deliberation, had been cast eons ago. Implacable whims governed the will encased in the overripe puffball of a skull, deemed Uncle among the blessed, but what of Josiah?

The ebony clawfoot clock on the mantel ticked once, and he blinked with the insight that all his brooding at the manikin had occurred since the preceding tick. And badly as he had to piss, it wasn't in the cards while he played the unwitting exhibitionist, though if looks could mutilate, he'd be unmanned already, and yes, the baleful devil had started showing snaggleteeth. Panic jolted his free hand into snatching his cane from the crook of his arm and swinging it frantically at the loveless face. The chamber pot exploded into smithereens, concurrent with Ariel's renewed outcry.

Josiah shuddered as if a spell had broken along with the crockery, and before he'd commenced inspecting the wreckage in the soupy twilight, he mumbled, "I'm abjectly sorry, Uncle, I'll replace your pot when I come back tomorrow, whatever you decide."

Surveying the shards was preferable to the ensuing mortification should he dare scan Uncle's expression. But was he solaced or confounded to locate no trace of miniature corpse? There was only the split china bust of George III, a popular feature inside pisspots of Ariel's generation.

Josiah sheepishly rebuttoned his trousers, ruing the relentless pressure on his midsection, and withal the impossibility of relieving himself till he was miles away. Stammering farewell, he chanced the briefest obligatory glimpse of Uncle's countenance, which vented, despite its freakish alterations, the dejection of scenting Vandal blood in the family.

That accusatory frown stamped itself on Josiah's conscience, ushered him out the door and into the suburbs, and he was practically home before it wore thin enough for him to appreciate how seldom he was using his cane, his vagrant urge to toss it aside. His smarting spirit had distracted him from feeling his reprieve from corporeal pains. True, his bladder kept spurring him to a clip he'd not sustained for years, but not a twinge of gout aggravated that ill-ease. When he finally let fly into the hedge behind his flagstone terrace, it dawned on him how nothing save the dollop of Uncle's "pudding" could have been his anodyne.

The novelty of tripping lightly, of pleasure as the absence of pain, instilled a euphoria that persisted through a supper of cured ham, bread, and compote, then on to bedtime, when his candle's flame picked up gleams of rancid bacon grease smearing a sheet of foolscap on his pillow. The florid script of the scrivener "rat" delivered a stiff kick of recognition, knocked the gladsome wind out of him. Donning his cheaters failed to dispel a film of stupefaction that formed on his eyes at his first attempts to read:

> Dear Meddler,
>
> Not to begrudge credit where it's due, we're beholden to you for wising us to that neglected trove of building materials. The house is nicer for our friend the while he's in it, until he joins us permanently. And when he does, we'll have made it nicer for him down among us too, with all the fixings we had left over. Don't friends do one another the most good they can?
>
> But beyond your one good turn, today's apish misconduct confirms

we're your uncle's only friends. We offer him fellowship and a surfeit of longevity; what is your counteroffer? To be cooped up in an attic or loft, bereft of society, loath to venture out and be scorned for skin-deep flaws he cannot rectify? We doubt the honesty of your concern for his happiness, whereas we respect that what's best for him is what he wishes for himself, and we can provide it.

You'll be foolish to incense us more. Refrain especially from browbeating others into submitting to your version of their best interests, and beware. Forgiveness is for the deserving.

The "rat," after its usage, appended no signature. The stationery had, however, bled bacon grease onto the pillowcase, an identifying touch in its own right; Josiah was contrarily amenable about changing that much linen. It lent a prosaic complexion to his nightmarish evening, as did his day's-end ablutions. And once in bed, he lapsed into an irresistible detachment, exhausted by the past six hours of drink, travails, distress. The flow of reverie conduced him to acknowledge a tender vein in the *homunculi,* for all their hostile posturing. They'd bestowed on his closest kinsman their altruism and charity. Didn't that make them *amici familiae?*

On that account in particular, he was sorry about getting on their bad side, but might he not effect reconciliation, contritely restore their good graces? They had some innate kindness to which he could appeal, and adventitiously or not, had cured his gout. Well, to be candid, he'd been harder and harder pressed to ignore a gnawing dread of that palliative mouthful wearing off. Could Ariel intercede on his behalf?

He was, in fine, coming around to Uncle's outlook. If alleviation of an ailment in portions of his anatomy felt so grand, how rapturous the freedom from every mortal ill, from aging, from the allotted threescore-and-ten must be! As the manikin argued, what in Josiah's purview could compete with that? Whatever major adjustments were in the offing for Josiah's appearance, his milieu, what were the long-term enticements of an inspector's post, a buxom widow's hand, an unstylish home in an unprepossessing town? Dotage, death, and less foreseeable reversals would rob them soon enough of any joy they contained. Whose disapproval troubled him? God's? Why should an inveterate backslider start fussing about God now?

Come the morn, his drowsy resolutions were, if anything, more adamantine. Toddling off to the bureau, if only to give notice, never occurred to him; it was a routine he'd left behind with the gout. Out of habit he carried his cane to Ariel's, and as an earnest of good intentions, leaned it against wormholed doorway pilaster before going in. "Uncle?" he warbled and shut the door behind him.

*   *   *

No human utterance lanced out to alarm the songbirds and squirrels, whether because none befell or because the stout walls smothered it, in the days before Constable Hiram yielded to Josiah's nagging cofunctionaries who read foul play or incapacitation into his truancy. Hiram had never sought Josiah's company more than that of any other pompous bore, and was mystified but not heartbroken to find Josiah's townhouse unlocked and neither its owner nor signs of villainy within. When the inspiration of inquiring at unsavory Uncle Ariel's assailed him, he resigned himself to going those several irksome miles over and above.

Like a prize for his dedication, the ebony cane hadn't budged, its silver head wedged against the fluting of Ariel's doorway pilaster. Disappointment soon galled him, though, at hallooing in vain again. He was furthermore nonplussed at the prim interior compared with the seediness outside. No spark of insight ever connected these fresh improvements with the looted house lot down the road, and what logic would have ignited that spark?

The odor wasn't in keeping with his experience, either. The pissy, sulfurous reek of yore had been supplanted not by the balm of new paint and varnish and sawdust, but by an earthen musk as if cellar updraft had been infiltrating for years. It overpowered the aroma from some scraps of mincemeat on a platter on a Windsor chair, and to plumb this one relic of recent household activity for information, he stuck in a fingertip: aha, room temperature, unpalatably congealed, gritty as well as greasy.

He sniffed at the residue under his fingernail and, miffed at its point-blank lack of bouquet, licked it off, which only amplified his uncertainty. Was this minimal taste wholesome or rancid, bitter or delicate, disgusting or sublime? It packed an unholy deal of sensation for such a puny smidgen. And not till now did the risk of poisoning dawn on him; perhaps the funky atmosphere was addling his judgment. A pitter-patter from the fireplace, the pantry, the landing behind half-open cellar door impinged rudely on his brown study. Rats! He hated rats, and his presence wasn't fazing this insolent horde.

The platter merited a sharper squint, to seek for tiny clawprints of those who may have sampled the meal earlier. "Don't eat that!" shrilled a tinny voice at once proximate and awesomely remote, re-tuned to the piercing falsetto of a rodent, except the final consonant convulsed into the screech of a rat springing a trap. Jumping to the conclusion the house was haunted, rather than overrun by talking rats, struck Hiram as more conservative, more reputable; and as for uncle's and nephew's whereabouts, well, he prided himself on diligent crime-solving, but where was evidence of criminal mischief?

And without it, why not obey his impulse to decamp pronto? Whenever Josiah's colleagues badgered him thereafter, he'd deputize them ad hoc to go search Ariel's cellar, if they dared; they never did. Months later, the buxom widow buttonholed him about her missing beau. Shrewd Hiram was ready with a rumor he'd fabricated, that Josiah had dropped everything to escort frail Ariel to a spa someplace beyond the pale, the Florida Territory maybe.

No telltales of felony emerged to contradict him when the derelict cottage was flattened for a more manorial successor. Nor did workmen ponder the cracked pair of cheaters and shards of chamber pot, along with myriad laths and nails, in the palpably softer soil of a filled-in pit in the cellar floor. Why would they, when reddish-black, child-sized fingerprints on dented pewter and a rum jug in the pantry had raised no eyebrows? The insurgent reek of piss and brimstone from the loamy pit did make the senior foreman wonder whether a tannery had ever stood there.

The Sarsen in the Ditch

While walking the Rutway I met with a man. That day, in fact, I met no others, and none ever since. You're the first, aren't you?

More social animals than I would have condemned these West Country downs as wasteland, and our sunken, chalky track has led nowhere of historic import since the Norman Conquest. Glowing acres of yellow rapeseed, flocks of sheep with blue ID numbers on their flanks, brown fields of stubble bespeak absentee human activity that starkly underscores how alone with the elements we are, how helpless in case of mishap. Paradoxically I'd never felt safer, more at ease, at one with the world than as an uncharted speck in this forsaken backcountry. And then I met that man with his deranged proposition.

I'd taken a breather where a trailside signpost put me at a mile from the hazy ochre roofs of Regis Riscombe, half-swallowed by surrounding treetops, silent as a painting. That glimpse of medieval village and gorgeous pastoral vista out to the horizon were actually upstaged, dwarfed, by mere vapor and air, by majestic cloudscape with its billowing flux of shadows and brilliance, an epic, wind-propelled geography. Funny how the ethereal can come across as more vivid, more real, than the bluntly tangible, isn't it?

I spaced out, to blink at another sign on the post with its Trails Bureau mushroom in red stencil. A hundred yards to the right, bearing directly away from the village, was Grim's Camp, the remnant earthen ring and outer ditch of an Iron Age fort.

Like any tourist, I wanted memories of more solid wonders than clouds, hands-on acquaintance with places I'd bookmarked in Wikipedia. A deer-path ran through an archway of boughs in a windbreak of ash trees, and then like a silkworm filament, white against green lawn, it shot straight upslope to the crest of a causeway between embankments. Partway along, I gawked at the ditch left and right that doubled the height of the bank, and whose cliff-edge from head-on seemed to merge with the incline beyond, as it may have done to deadly effect when invading chariots and cavalry had tried charging uphill.

From the summit of the ramp I climbed the extra feet to surmount the embankment, which I voted on impulse to circumnavigate. Why not? I had time, plenty to spare before check-in at tonight's off-trail B&B. Amidst the birdsong and sunshine and wildflower fragrance it was hard to picture stockades bristling with archers and spearmen, centuries of feuding and atrocities, everyman's incessant, stoppered anxieties about repelling the next siege, staging the next reprisal. And after untold generations as the bitterly contested center of a tribal universe, Grim's Camp ended up involved in no struggle more heroic than resisting the plow, victorious only recently thanks to Protected Monument status.

Striding widdershins, watching shadows of clouds race like skittish ghosts across the fort's windblown grassy interior, I pondered, Was it always so gusty up here? Did it drive the ancient Britons nuts, mussing and upending everything, mocking their simple desire for a tidy bivouac, such that nobody could light a fire without half the tinder blowing away? These reflections blinkered me till I was inches away from tripping over the man squatting within a dip in the ridgetop. At first I feared he was defecating; but no, his belt was around his waist, and his sights were avid upon a boulder in the ditch as if it owed him auspices.

A sarsen, and not just any rock, commanded bug-eyed attention. A pitted and pockmarked but uncommonly tough sort of sandstone, it figured in Stonehenge and suchlike archaic constructions, and this specimen, about the girth of a Mini Cooper, was an apparent vestige of breastwork around the base of vanished stockade. Whenever it had toppled, it must have gouged the earth pretty grievously on the rebound, for it overhung a hole too elongated and ragged for a rabbit burrow. Or was that only the sarsen's own shadow?

A flush of heat, as from a spotlight, overspread my forehead and cheeks. I left off studying the sarsen, and so had the squatter. His wild eyes were now upon me. He exchanged his firebrand glare for a welcoming smile and beckoned me closer, closer, till I was a hairsbreadth out of reach unless he sprang at me. Well, that was a chance I had to take, or this freighted situation would all the sooner and more certainly have escalated. You can understand how I felt.

Not that I normally minded an excuse to shrug off thirty-pound rucksack. And if I, three days into this jaunt, was quite the footsore, sunburnt, raw-shouldered prize, he was a prize-and-a-half. Grizzled chin, frizzy reddish hair like an explosion in progress, weren't as arresting as his heady bouquet of leaf mold, the film of trail dust inseparable from his jeans and grey smock and skin, and the impaction of that dust to accent fine wrinkles fanning from chapped lips and smoldery eyes, telltales of age or chronic roughing it at least, though the webwork was preternaturally faint, as if weather or time itself had no firm grip on him, could coax out stubble but no heavier beard.

How to reply when he hailed me as "fellow pilgrim"? I lamely passed him a granola bar from a sidepocket in my pack while fumbling for the inanity, "Been on the trail long?"

He laughed hoarsely, pored over the wrapper as if he'd never seen the like, and punctured it with a gross fringe of thumbnail. "So what's your vocation?" he countered.

I shook my head. Hanging up the laser pointer had occasioned this cathartic walkabout, I explained. The fifth-grade kids I used to teach were at an ideal age really, on the cusp of grownup cognition but still untouched by teen hormone shitstorm. Career-wise, I'd reckoned myself in it for the long haul, till some insidious species of performance anxiety, of stage fright, convinced me I was losing crucial rapport with my audience. And what in my trail-tramp audience was prompting this unbashful confession, discounting his ostensible lack of interest in me while he savored granola bar inch by inch?

The kids and I resided in ever more incompatible worlds, I prattled on, theirs immersed in gadgets, electronically mediated interactions, prefab corporate culture. Or perhaps I lacked the flexibility, the ingenuity, to persevere through the doldrums inherent in every job. In any case, I had to pull the ripcord before my mood disorder, or whatever it was, became too obvious, too humiliating. No matter; it's all academic now!

I was taken aback to find my listener had polished off his snack, its packaging nowhere in evidence, probably windborne, and on his face the qualms I must have shown on first sight of him. Second-guessing what I'd said to jar him would have gained me nothing, and luckily he reasserted who the oddball was by pronouncing, "Thank you for the confection. I don't have to eat, but it's nice once in a while." He reapplied the ingratiating smile that had lured me in. *"Gorau arf, arf dysg,* pardon my Welsh. 'Learning is the best weapon.' Did you arrive fore-armed about our Old Rutted Way?"

I shrugged modestly. "The ruts in the path I can vouch for, but they're nothing to do with the name. That may derive from a Saxon called Rota or a Norseman called Hrut, though of course the Rutway predates them by millennia. Or it may derive from the Old English 'hrythr' for cattle because drovers were using this route since the Bronze Age."

The ingratiating smile persisted intact as my audience chided, "Leave it to a Yank to lecture the natives about their own history. Still, fair enough, far as you go." His vision flicked toward the sarsen in the ditch, then again to me.

"I refer more to spiritual preparations, in hopes you're readier than I to accommodate whatever the trail brings forth from within you. As did I, you've the aura of an initiate on a pilgrimage to god or gods un-known. This walk's an unwitting gesture of worship, and this terrain elicits a reflex of piety, though in hindsight you'd presumably have revered nature or venerability or somesuch shallow abstraction. To what purpose I couldn't venture, but this ground's invested with a much more primal sanctity, and to travel it is to trace forgotten divine contours."

He rocked on his heels in a sudden transport till momentum sat him upon the grass, exposing in mid-calf glory leather boots no hiker of my generation would wear on a bet. They did nothing to allay my giddiness induced by his mystic palaver, and I knew I had to speak or sink. "I'm really not here to worship nature or pagan monuments. Don't get me wrong: I'm eager to learn, grateful for everything I bring away. In that sense I am a humble pilgrim," I practically babbled. "But there's no dishonor in wanting a high-water mark in my life, an epic achievement to compare with everything afterward."

Was condescension tempering the fever in loopy eyes? I soldiered on regardless. Quitting a spiel in midstream would amply prove I was a flake. "To go the distance on the Rutway, to seize opportunity by the horns for once—now that's worth enshrining. I expect I'll romanticize this slog someday, I'll mythologize it, people do that with their adven-tures, consciously or not, and isn't that among the less selfish ways of being good to oneself?"

My interlocutor's eyebrows were arching as if he'd scored a point, or as if I'd blundered into scoring one for him. "To mythologize your past, yes, it's only human. I chose to mythologize my daily reality, and I've never looked back!" Yep, his was the one-upping school of repartee, a type too familiar from the faculty lounge, except they'd been sane, and easier to deflect by pretending fascination with a newspaper. Getting away from present company unscathed would come down, I conjectured, to whetting his combative edge no further.

"You win," I blithely admitted. "I can't match that."

"You could, though." He beamed magnanimously. Porcelain-white teeth dazzled his competitive vibe into remission. The eyes, however, smoldered on. He indicated the turf at my feet as if it were a chaise-longue. "Make yourself at home. I'll elucidate." In for a penny, in for a pound: was that the appropriate chestnut as I warily hunkered down, hugging my backpack beside me, the better to beat a hasty, if doomed, retreat? He, meanwhile, cast a glance into the ditch, warily perhaps, but doubtless not, as I ineptly fancied, worried the sarsen might leap up at him, even as I worried he'd leap at me.

Instead, that transfixing gaze startled me again, lancing through petty flesh into my painfully banal soul. "I, like you, sought fresh perspective, new direction via this trail." For him to pigeonhole me so glibly was off-putting, which wasn't to say he was wrong. At least I qualified as a sympathetic character. "Or maybe foremost was disowning my past, with scant concern for the future. My erstwhile profession isn't relevant and may no longer exist. But as you've gathered, it's not ours to decree where the way of the gods leads: it may well bypass them, and lead to other parties of their choosing."

And me it had to lead to him. If that was divine intervention, the gods could keep it. Even worse, this whacko had me on the back foot from the outset, framing our exchange in terms of lost gods and fuzzier cosmic debris, distracting me with claptrap when my life very possibly hinged on preserving a respectful pokerface, concentrating on tact. Keen to humor him, I doled out a simpatico "Hmph!" at random as he forged on.

"As you've also probably gathered, the trail's a nonlinear affair on both an earthly and occult basis. Sidetracks every mile can disorient careless hikers who miss the signs, and sometimes an obvious offshoot is the true way. You have to watch for those red mushrooms etched

into guideposts and stiles and trees, and I suspected no malfeasance
when the arrow above one sent me down a literal primrose path,
hemmed in with privet. Back then the Trails Bureau was understaffed,
and lonesome stretches might go untended for years." The shadow of
a cloud skirted his toes, and he shrank away as from a rat, but the
monologue resumed a heartbeat later.

"Once I'd ducked into the narrow lane, stiff breezes kicked up,
much stiffer than those here and now, rattling the foliage so hard it
seemed the only noise in the world. I swore at scratches on my hands,
snags in my sleeves, from fending off branches thrashing at my face.
And when I burst into the open, the wind fell as if its function had
been to mask the bustle of the campsite before me. Immediately I realized the red mushroom was counterfeit, for my path ended in a glade,
bound by thorny brushwood. A barren ring of chalk separated the
thicket from the clearing, wherein camp chores ticked sedately along.

"Who, if not these campers, would have misrouted me? But had
they intended robbery or murder, they couldn't have been more indo-
lent about it. All twenty-odd of them, despite my bullish charge into
their midst, kept right on banking cookfires, shining shoes, patching
sweaters, grooming wolfhounds, and anyone, including the dogs, who
could be bothered, allotted me the briefest once-over and then blandly
carried on. Their lack of excitement was at once reassuring and weird,
and the spokesman who left off tuning his mandolin to approach me
didn't differ from the rest in age, manliness, or apparel.

"I was hoping, before anything else, to size these people up at a
probing glance; my optimism was ill-founded. More like Travelers than
weekenders, they were equipped for a long haul, except they wore,
flouting gaudy stereotype, nondescript denim, flannel, woolen garments in muted tones. They also shared a familial resemblance, sleek
black hair over their ears and in bangs, cattily arching eyebrows, and
complexions 'dusky,' not after the facile usage of bigots, but as if their
skins had severed relations with light, casting them in perpetual shadow.

"So was this a family reunion? It lacked the typical, if hypocritical,
bonhomie, and no kids or elders were in attendance. For my money,
nobody was close to pushing thirty, though to layer on further paradox, the austere deliberations of 'old souls' imbued their every motion.
My faltering composure foundered altogether when the spokesman

halted, he just within the chalk circle, I just outside it, and addressed me, 'Welcome, Jason!'

"I fought to rebalance my wits. Yes, Jason was my name, but none back then was more popular and it could have been a lucky stab. Or was he alluding to me as a wanderer, specifically one who'd wandered into his enclave? 'Yes, we're aware of who you are,' he disabused me. 'Now will you admit to yourself you're aware of who we are?'

"With that question he jammed the spokes of my wheeling thoughts, which may have counted as a favor, shock to the system or not. Helplessly I scanned the campers again as if someone might chime in with the answer. Each new impression of these people only put me at a worse loss, drew a more desperate blank. They plugged away aloof at their tasks, among their several tents, which were eccentrically grand, old-fashioned, exotic, like some blurring of yurts and medieval pavilions. More puzzling, how had tents and materiel arrived? No vehicles were parked inside the clearing; nor could carts or vans or even motorbikes have negotiated the occluded access.

"Meanwhile I, like you a minute ago, was chafing under an obligation to say something, anything, and me without so much as your prop of a candy bar or whatever it was. I jabbered, 'Forgive me if we've met before and I've forgotten.'

"The dusky man shook his head resignedly. 'No, we've never met, nothing to forgive there, but yes, you have indeed forgotten us. Might another look around jog your memory?'

"I complied, as briskly as you sat down at my bidding, and I was rather more outnumbered by them than you by me."

A prickly guy, and an incorrigible one-upping bastard, I concluded, and abstained from retorting that one maniac at a time is generally considered a handful. He plowed ahead as if from a script in which it was common knowledge I had no speaking role. "The men were, externally anyway, poured from the same mold, difficult to tell apart, so I tried homing in on the women for traits more distinctive from which to build toward defining the group. And saints forgive me, I found something.

"Singling out the women was a trick in itself. They, like the men, had noses to sundry grindstones, and were dressed the same, as if aiming for androgyny. They categorically weren't preening for my delectation. I had to settle on identifying them by the delicacy of busy hands threading needles, snipping knots from canine fur, peeling garlic. But on steadier observance, drab, baggy outfits became a tease to frustrate and inflame the imagination, an essential part of the enticement, such that I lusted for the sensation of loose fabric covering irresistibly uncharted flesh.

"Replacing my first object of desire with another and then another did no good, always led to unbearable titillation. Was I seriously out of touch with my depraved id, or was some *je ne sais quoi* about these women distorting my workaday libido? I was dangerously lightheaded, as if baser impulses were shorting out my self-control, exempting me from civilized responsibility, urging me toward both libertine abandon and out-of-body buoyancy.

"From miles below, the grappling hook of the spokesman's voice grabbed on and pulled me down to earth. He put it to me, without recrimination, 'Do my sisters tempt you?' I blinked and shuddered like a rudely awakened sleepwalker, and gawked at my feet. How mortifying to have ogled his sisters right in front of him! I studied my footwear more tenaciously as his undertone of invitation, of pandering, sank in. The faintest insinuation of these 'sisters' as finery on generous offer jolted me into recognizing who these campers were or purported to be.

"As if salvation were at stake, I resolutely met the spokesman's cool stare and with kneejerk skepticism took it for the façade of a joker or a fraud, of a mere human in any case. To entertain for an instant his farcical pretense, or what I presumed was his pretense, was shameful; it made me a willing partner in his deception, and he yet to pronounce a lying syllable. Still, wisdom dictated I staunchly refuse whatever he or his clan would ply me with; I'd no more wish to be indebted to scoundrels than to the 'Hidden Folk.'

"He congratulated me, 'I can read on your brow that you do remember, and with scarce any prompting! A precious rarity today for so little rubbish to clog the doorway of understanding!'

"Again I, like you, was chary of igniting ill-will in the middle of nowhere, and I hedged, 'Well, if I've guessed what you think I've guessed, I'm sure you can appreciate it's a lot to digest at the drop of a hat.' Was my phrasing so roundabout because scrabbling after the polite term for these entities almost had me tongue-tied?

"He heaved a disappointed sigh. 'Despite the clarity of your insights, you remain a man of your era, grounded in unbelief. I bow to your scruples, but were I, for example, your God, I'd never stoop to prove my bona fides.' He idly scratched his marble-smooth chin. 'You're not in attire for heavy weather, unfortunately.' His associates stayed their handiwork and cocked their heads toward us, as if at mildly diverting horseplay. His stolid features barely altered except in a shift of focus to somewhere beyond me.

"I'd become oblivious to the alternating bleaker and brighter daylight as the ponderous clouds blocked and released the sun. But now I had to goggle skyward as the gloom of a full eclipse descended in seconds, and looming above us alarmingly low, its scraggy tendrils drooping almost within reach, was a harrowing black thunderhead. In its shadow, the spokesman's complexion darkened to match that of the nimbus, and then cloudburst drenched him and me and the camp, with a violence to persuade me the glade within the chalk circle was about to fill like a saucer, awash with buckets and bottles and cordwood.

"I shivered in a whiplash gale while rivulets trickled down the spokesman's dispassionate face. He blinked, and from the same black nimbus pebbles of hail pelted us. He acted insensible of their hundred maddening stings, and as if stoic honor depended on it, I did likewise. Nonetheless I couldn't contain a snarl of frustration, a shame short-lived because another gale snatched it away, and blizzard piled snow upon my head, blinded me to everything around but the spokesman, reduced to a dull-edged silhouette behind teeming flakes.

"My brain was intermittently blanking out in the punishing cold, my scalp and fingers were numb already, and I was damning the spokesman for overplaying a hand he'd won long before. I resurfaced from a vacant spell into balmy sunshine that none too soon was warming my soggy clothes. The spokesman's, though, were dry, flaunting bright highlights in their coarse weave, and I wondered did he use some secret waterproofing agent, to which the answer had to be no, for the campfires blazed on as if nothing had happened.

"What's more, foul conditions hadn't fazed anyone into seeking shelter or taking their blasé eyes off me, intimating that these folk, my perceptions to the contrary, hadn't spent their past minute in the same reality as me. The grass at my feet, I should mention, sparkled with frozen droplets. This discrepancy rendered me speechless, powerless to inform the spokesman he'd made his point, but he spared me stammering humiliation by entreating, 'Now may we simply enjoy each other's company? From afar you impressed us as the breed of man whose qualities we miss most: broad-minded, well-read, unacquisitive.'

"Any gratification at the spokesman's praise was offset by his overly exacting enunciation of 'man,' suggesting disrepute, inferiority, comicality at best. And during my little interval of dwelling on his nuances, the coterie, whether through lightning stealth or more arcane craft, quit their tasks to form a semicircle behind him, at no safer remove than you are from me. While agape at this, I wrested my beleaguered vision from one intoxicating woman only to replace her with another, reeling inside as if amorously slaphappy.

"Interest in me had quickened on every face, and though no malevolence showed, I couldn't help recoiling intimidated, more wretchedly dumbstruck. The spokesman pressed on, anticipating what I'd have asked had I been more *compos mentis,* 'Yes, I daresay we are drab compared with the naive pipedreams of medievalists and romantics. But our guise must ever evolve to fool the unschooled and unsympathetic, who nowadays dismiss us at first glance as lowlifes or drifters and, unlike you, never question how we set up camp or restock provisions without vehicles or pack animals.'"

Yes, I too questioned that, whoever or whatever Jason's mob actually represented. This unresolved glitch in logic, however, failed to concern my febrile storyteller, who dauntless plowed ahead.

"The spokesman then imparted a curious proverb, which I quote, 'Only the observant person is ever surprised.' He went on to explain, 'Contradictory as that seems, consider that the unobservant cannot be surprised as long as they are unobservant, for they perceive nothing to surprise them. Only if and when they become observant can anything impinge on their senses and evoke surprise. Surprise is a property of observation. That is the logic of my folk, founded upon centuries of experience with yours.'

"He flashed a puckish smile that put me further from my ease. 'You won't deny,' he wheedled, 'your own surprise on observing who we were.' I mumbled some concession, and he shrugged, 'Maybe our own inborn illogic is to blame, but we cannot help interacting on occa-

sion with your race. Mayhap the unstable brevity of your mortal per-
spectives is tonic for us, given the perpetual sameness of ours.'

"I had no more reply to his fantastic outpourings than you've had
to mine, which in nowise discouraged him. He continued, 'But to dis-
port ourselves among mortals has never been more difficult, for the
quiet zones, the green frontiers between our realms, are at their most
compromised and impassable. Your motorways slice up the hinter-
lands, suburban tracts crowd out the crofter and his acreage, even the
remotest country dwellers have unclean electric lights and cars and tel-
ephones and sundry cosmopolitan trappings. These profane environs
are anathema to us!'"

"Aha!" I interjected, if only to demonstrate I had a reply or two up
my sleeve, "Habitat loss! It's the bane of many a species!"

He grinned at me as he had when I'd audaciously lectured him on
etymology, and in what I read as another bid at domination, he leaned
toward me and murmured so softly I had to lean closer, "The spokesman lowered his head like this, as if in confidence, yet confided at a
volume all could hear, 'Nor, I trust, do you feel differently from us, on
your retreat from the crass existence they've fobbed off on you, from
drudgery and family obligations. You miss none of it, do you, here on
the road of simplicity and freedom that you and we alike cherish?' He
was uncannily correct, but in nodding I had a presentiment of stepping
onto treacherous ground."

A songbird in the ditch startled us by warbling stridently. The
acoustics below, I theorized, must have simulated an echo chamber.
My nervous raconteur weathered a bout of trembling after pinpointing
the bird, of a kind new to me, on the sarsen. When the bird fluttered
up to the embankment above our shallow cleft and puffed out its
fluffy red breast and sang no less shrilly, my fellow birdwatcher cocked
a supplicating ear as if grasping at the gist of a foreign radio broadcast.

The bird flew off, and its would-be interpreter spent a minute with
eyes riveted on where it had perched. His chest heaved as if he were performing breathing exercises to calm down, and with a more repressed air
he turned to me and recounted, "The crescent of gray faces, for the seconds I dared survey them, were of a uniformly inviting expression,
which put me the more anxiously on my guard. I reflexively adjusted
my stance to better withstand the narcotic effect of their proximity.

"The spokesman, wryly pouting, tilted back on solicitous heels and proclaimed, 'Please set worries aside! We wouldn't suppose you ignorant of the universal lore, that to accept our delicacies or any material gift, down to the humblest lump of suet, would render you mad. Where's the honor to us in despising your scholarship? Instead we offer intangible blessings, or more aptly, allow you to partake of ours, with no more danger of insanity to you than to us.' If I'd halfway sussed him out, then heaven help me, I was foremost amenable to going along with him so I could ogle his 'sisters' without forfeiting self-control.

"And as I had precedent to fear my baser urges were writ plain on me, my cheeks flushed hot as the spokesman elaborated, 'In fine, we can empower you to do what you want, even as we do, outlasting mortal limitations.' Would he once more imply his 'sisters' were available to me? No, not in so many words anyway, for with sincerest largesse he proposed, 'You'd live forever and roam these sacred trails, without hindrance from hunger, thirst, or fatigue, and repose at night among us. Those commitments foisted on you by the peopled world need never vex you again. But we shall not cajole you; that is for your heart to do.'

"I cracked a smile at that. My heart, eh? Between my equally embattled brain and libido, my heart had yet to get a word in. Meanwhile my brain, at prospects of yielding the floor to punch-drunk emotions, rallied and made me object, 'I won't second-guess why you'd do this for me, but to hike the Rutway back and forth for eternity, how could that not become deadly monotonous, maddening?'

"The spokesman took this sorry cavil in stride and countered, 'You construe me too literally! Our dispensation by no means restricts you to the Rutway, from which branch numerous other paths that branch in turn into manifold more, with you free to follow them all, thereby laying before you the length and breadth of Britain. Hardly a short tether!'

"Yes, I granted, no disputing that, but wasn't he sidestepping the cardinal issue, of locking me into a single unrelenting activity forever? With the verve of a carny barker he remonstrated, 'Begad you're obstinate, forswearing what we see in your heart as if enshrined in glass! This footloose life's your profoundest desire, and though you, like us, would come to shun town and homestead, wherever people congregate, loneliness and isolation need have no hold on you, for anywhere you go, we'd welcome you come sunset.'

"Such candlelit hospitality, to be approached via cavern or the underside of a rock, and redolent of damp earth and roots, kindled no enthusiasm, till I mused again that the magic divorcing me from mankind might also immunize me from the repercussions of gazing on the 'sisters.' Only then did I clearly realize how right he was, how I craved, above all else, endless fresh horizons to conquer. Who wouldn't? Impossible to describe who wouldn't!

"The spokesman had advised I heed my heart, but could a heart set a course so cold-blooded? Some more objective, or maybe callous, part of me plumbed memories of prior travels for homesick moments, and scared up none. Nor had I thought about, let alone pined for, wife and offspring since arriving in the West Country. Yes, I'd have no compunction turning my back on them, on my career. I'd hit the trail in the first place seeking happiness; if it had thrived on the home front, I'd have stayed there.

"To be happy, if that was a worthy goal, I had to choose selfishness. I unerringly foresaw I'd harbor no regrets, and my conscience has sided with me in favoring self-fulfillment over responsibilities." Methought this "pilgrim" protested too much. His bloodshot eyes seemed a far cry from pools of contentment. "Had I genuinely thought this decision through, you may ask," he expounded, "as if I retained the option of rational decision-making? My franker self was flexing away decades of smothering falsehood and hypocrisy, like bedrock shedding eons of sediment. I was champing to blurt out my assent.

"It wasn't like I'd forgotten that receiving anything, of a material nature or otherwise, from these folk was tantamount to entering into contract with them. The mental disorder that commonly resulted, in my opinion, came of the metaphysical implications in those contracts, too sweeping for average minds to encompass. Hence our terms could not be agreed in haste or distraction, but I was in no state to discern whether I was under pressure or not."

A piercing whistle made us both peer skyward. Circling on an updraft, its forked tail twisting in a crosswind, a red kite had no cause to bother with us, though my fellow traveler cringed as if he qualified as prey. The raptor wheeled very gradually away, toward the sun, till its cagey observer flinched from solar brilliance and picked up perfectly on track, "I clutched at those meager straws of misgivings that occurred to me. I entreated the spokesman, Was he dealing with me in good faith, intent on no malice or deceit?

"The spokesman raised his palms and parried, 'Harm you? But why? You're well-versed in the lore, in our renowned benevolence to men who greet us with respect and cordiality.'

"That same lore also cited how capricious these 'Good People' could be, but brooking that might push too hard against vaunted 'cordiality.' Instead, I posed more tepid reservations that our bargain worked unfairly to my advantage.

"He scoffed, 'What do we get out of it, you mean? A gift looks for a return, does it? That was an adage of your Dark Ages, and we are no more medieval than you. Our clothing and possessions should make obvious how our refinements have kept up with yours. As for recompense, your thanks will do, and I warrant your future sojourns among us will be mutually refreshing. And in coming over to us, yet more will accrue to you.' Only then did I behold the spokesman's hand outstretched across the chalk for me to shake."

Jason's nattering onrush was exerting a narcotic impact, similar, I inferred, to that of the "Good People's" proximity on him. The narrative faded into dreamy, muffled nonsense, and when I snapped out of it, after an amorphous while, he was saying, "Reconciled, I shook his hand, a seal lawfully binding since prehistory. I've trod the Rutway ever after, unfettered by appetite, fatigue, or sickness, no threadbare elbows or worn-down bootheels, and never a yearning to quit this trail for human society, or even switch onto a path diverging from this one."

His bulging eyes darted toward the ditch as if in dread the sarsen was eavesdropping. They squinted below as he related, "In making me a fraction more like them, they threw in the wherewithal, whether at a whim or for clandestine reasons, to grant the heart's desire of one convivial pilgrim." He exhorted, as if we were suddenly in cahoots, but with gaze still downcast, "Go on, try me!"

How artfully he'd put me on the spot! At least his "Hidden Folk" or whoever they were hadn't been shy about telling him his heart's desire. What the hell, off the top of my head, was mine? Wasn't I in part upon the Rutway to find out? To weigh his proposition seriously amounted to some degree of surrender, to professing I believed him, as opposed to transparently humoring him by wishing for a million bucks or some equivalent triteness. On the other hand, his grimaces and fidgets warned he wouldn't emulate the gray people's show of patience toward him.

And okay, I'll own up to a superstitious qualm or two. In fables from the Monkey's Paw to Midas, wishes magically actualized have had a way of backfiring; I absolutely lacked the competence to frame a failsafe wish, exempt from unforeseen consequences and ambiguous wording. A workaround dawned on me, but I hated it because it presupposed I set more store by lunatic narrative than I wanted to admit. Yes, I'd make a wish all right, except he'd be the beneficiary, and I'd leave myself out of it.

Jason, meanwhile, scratched his grizzled chin and palavered, as if coerced to spoil the silence or my reverie, "The truth is, I'm most drawn to this section of trail, and the farther I roam, the more emphatically I'm pulled back. At the junction with the path to this earthen ring, I linger on the view of my native Regis Riscombe, on its venerable thatched roofs, a thousand years of tradition, give or take."

I had to clench my teeth to stop my jaw dropping. All along I'd had to buck the current of his story eating away at my incredulity, at my clarity, and now at the sure reality of my senses. I hadn't "lingered" on village roofs as he allegedly had, but could tell at a glance they were red tile and not thatch. Had he absentmindedly misspoken, or had memories of the village in his youth blinkered him to how it looked today?

When had tile replaced thatch anyhow, which begged the more loaded question, just how old was Jason, really? Had he altogether lied about the circumstances of falling in with the "Good People" because it had been preternaturally long ago, or had he made broadly veracious events more current with updated details? Either way, damn him, I'd implicitly bought into his fairytale gibberings.

In hindsight I regret squandering this opportunity to learn what nights were like among the "Hidden Folk," how he'd managed to locate their lairs, and whether he'd finally mastered himself when dealing with their women. But I was too fixated on concocting a wish to humor him, to deny him any more excuse for detaining me.

Did Jason even have a coherent body of convictions, or picture of his past, beneath the guile and delusions? For all I knew, he was positive that granting someone's wish would release him from contractual bondage, pass that bondage on to the recipient, a fine-print clause he'd accidentally on purpose let slip. Fine, let's go with that, I brainstormed, humor him and get him off the imaginary hook. I met his twitchy eyes, smiled, and intoned, "I wish you had free choice in whether you stayed on the trail or not!"

To be honest, I was feeling smugly humanitarian, for nomadic Jason, no mistaking it, was stultified, tormented, by his internment, self-imposed or not, on the Rutway, despite claims of rambling bliss, and I was less admirably curious to see how he'd react to liberation dangling within reach. I'd have been naive to forecast jubilation. The despair, though, the anguish, without the slightest glimmer of relief or redemption on petrified visage, was shocking.

He leapt up, shuddered with head-to-toe spasm, and went stockstill, apart from impudent gusts whiffling his reddish frizz back and forth. The passage of puffy clouds across the sun cast a shadow play of alternating dark and bright upon him, as if his psychic tug-of-war between freedom and immortality were readable in his complexion. Had he been completely aboveboard with me, I decided, he'd have laughed off my Trojan horse of a wish, found nothing in it of appeal to him. Instead, paralyzing turmoil consumed him, and I felt thoroughly sorry for him, striving with puny human faculties to balance everything he stood to gain or lose, whichever way he voted.

An ostensibly myopic rabbit loped onto the turf between us and nosed the air, and as if scent alone had alerted him to us, shot off downhill toward the sarsen. Jason's eyes flicked after him, and in them was the crowning panic of quarry in the crosshairs, and this, I intuited, was on top of tortured forebodings at the Hidden Folk's displeasure should he even envision desertion, ingratitude. But all he said, in a sepulchrally softspoken monotone, was, "They're not going to like this."

The levee of his self-possession burst, and headlong as a cork upon a torrent he dashed to and fro, in figure-eights, in howling gyrations along the ridgetop, as if hornets had swarmed out of his ears to attack, and him tethered inescapably to the sod. I, perchance unscathed by his first blind zigzag charge, scrambled over the inner lip of the embankment, onto the minor slope that converged with the fortress floor.

I had no short-range plans beyond letting my adrenalin ebb away, taking care Jason wasn't about to plow into me, and reflecting that the outcome he'd labored to avoid, the madness attendant on receiving supernatural gifts, had caught up with him after all, though indirectly, and after lengthy delay, and not without unwitting mortal collusion. Or was this outcome predestined, satisfying a malefic, covert agenda of fey "caprice"?

No, don't make bold to answer. Jason, I suspected, had me pegged as a middlebrow at best, at least till I'd inflicted Hobson's choice on him. I don't judge you so rashly, and I won't press you to solve my little rhetorical riddle. Wouldn't be fair, would it, since I've no idea how to begin solving it myself?

Anyhow, these ruminations about Jason's derangement were good for a touch of respite, bedimming his palpable derangement in progress, till a flapping shadow pulsed by and I quailed from boots stampeding an inch from my chin. The invisible hornets hadn't relented in driving him berserk, and I'd reset my sights on him just in time to witness his frenzied sprint to the edge of the ditch and, with his most excruciating screech yet, off into space. It seemed all the more a leap into the void because I heard nothing, not him nor breeze nor birdsong, once he'd plunged from view.

The silence goaded me up and across the ridge on hands and knees to glut my eyes on a gruesomeness I'd have changed TV channels to avoid. But the universe, or some reclusive corner thereof, had inscrutably seen fit to change channels for me. Nobody sprawled with limbs or neck or spine at sickening angles on the floor of the ditch or decking the sarsen like a sacrifice. I blinked vigorously but distinguished nothing below save the sarsen and its shadow that may have been the rim of an underlying hole. I was in no mood to investigate what it really was, or to clamber down and clear up any other mysteries.

And those mysteries extended well beyond the whereabouts of Jason's corpse. For starters, was the marker, official mushroom and all, rerouting me to Grim's Camp a counterfeit too, like that which had lured Jason to his numinous encounter? I had the ominous notion I'd been delivered too expediently to him, even as he'd been delivered to them. But trailbound Jason couldn't have been responsible for signage, had no woodshop at his disposal, so who if not the "Good People" could have produced it? Why would they, though? Bear in mind also, these "Good People" are pure figments, are they not?

But let's for argument's sake make believe, like half the adults over in Iceland, that the "Hidden Folk" do exist, then I've stumbled on a telling insight into their psychology during my own endless ramblings. To put the kindliest light on it, they must deem it plausible, perhaps normal, to be happy forever upon the fulfillment of one desire only. Or else they hold us in such low esteem as to conceive we're inanely simplistic, rather than each of us a bundle of contradictory, jostling desires. Sorry if I'm being pedantic; must be the teacher in me.

Ah, but I'm guilty of digressing—that's what's in your expression, isn't it? How could Jason, flesh and blood enough to snack on a granola bar, utterly disappear? A ghost can disappear, yes, but he can't eat, can he? Besides, ghosts are as mythical as "Good People," aren't they? Or was there ever a deranged redhead, apart from myself, that is? Where's my backpack, is that your next quibble? It's elsewhere. Nothing in it for me anymore, and not your problem, is it?

You do trust I'm on the Rutway solely because it's my heart's desire, and that I checked into my B&B that bygone evening, and into suchlike places nightly ever after. Or was it against fey protocol to divest myself from any wish I made involving Jason? Oh no, don't get all tongue-tied on me, no worries, don't commit yourself out loud, pilgrim.

First I'd like to show you Grim's Camp, quite the vista from the rampart, and you'd be doing me a favor, allowing me to prove I'm not fibbing, there really is a sarsen in the ditch. The sidetrack's just around this bend. It's steep, but you're fit, and I've been up and down countless times and look at me. And while we stroll, tell me about yourself, why don't you? What brings you here? To which gods do you belong?

Deacon Mercer

A backwoods ballad of Appalachian Icelanders

Deacon Mercer did allow
Having almost all he should,
Little missing from his life
Except a wife and fatherhood.

Mercer rode from his estate,
Spurred his horse across the stream,
Till he came to the farm on which
Dwelt the beauty of his dreams.

He called her from the fireside
To stand upon the frozen ground,
He wanted Sara to agree
To spend that Christmas in the town.

He offered her a life of ease,
No more a lowly hired hand.
They whiled the time away with talk
Till dusk lay heavy on the land.

He promised to return on Christmas,
Rode away with heart ablaze,
And when he came to the water's edge
He never saw the icy glaze.

Horse and rider took a headlong
Dive into the riverbed.
Numbing current pulled them under,
Soon the deacon would be dead.

Far too sweet had life become
For him to go beneath the sod,
So Deacon Mercer prayed a prayer
Improper to the ears of God.

He crossed the water as a corpse,
They found him by the riverside,
Current now too hard and cold
For news to pass that he had died.

Snow came down on Christmas day,
Clouds hung thick on Christmas night.
Sara heard one knock on the door,
The deacon stood beyond the light.

He had the one horse for them both
And not a single word to say,
Even at the edge of town
When they rode off the other way.

They sped to the river and across,
On ice that should have been too thin.
She saw the graveyard up ahead;
His hat went flying in the wind.

Moonlight burst between the clouds,
And on the back of Mercer's head,
Sara saw the white of his skull
In the gash from which his life had bled.

A grave lay open in the graveyard.
"Here's a house for the two of us,"
So he said as he caught her sleeve
And grinned at her with a sickening lust.

The deacon pulled, got Sara's coat,
And stumbled back into the pit.
She ran over to the chapel,
Rang the bell till her ears would split.

With every ring the specter weakened,
Powerless inside the ground,
Till the people who were nearest
Came to see about the sound.

Mercer's grave they filled again,
And soon they set a boulder there.
Sara kept on moving West
But she never married anywhere.

Cups of Memory

Do adverts for TV, household soap and brands of tea,
Labels all around tin cans, who would be a painter man?
—THE CREATION, "Painter Man"

What's in every hole? Air, certainly. And what else that eludes the eye, and must be detected by other faculties? Strictly speaking, an empty hole amounts to an oxymoron, a misfire of careless thinking. This doubtless smacks of rank sophistry, and I wish I didn't know better. To beware the invisible where common sense sees nothing, such wisdom came of this fool's persistence in his folly, to mangle Blake's aphorism. Or should I savor recurring symptoms of arrested development as the diehard dregs of my youth?

Obviously, behaviors don't arise in a vacuum. Returning someplace after decades away, for instance, can trigger conduct roundly disavowed in the meantime. Otherwise, how "unlike me" to navigate the Newcastle arrivals terminal based on fleeting, serial infatuations with those manifold "types" attractive to me, tailing nobody long enough to arouse suspicions of stalking (Harpo Marx as older letch?). How unlike me, at least, for most of the interval between my twenties, when I was last here, and now.

Both overseas junkets also preceded, in totally disparate ways, reversals in my glibly shipshape world. On the heels of that first trip, I was still in the throes of homecoming jetlag when the position I'd invested years cementing in Manhattan went belly-up. I'd justified month-long splurge abroad, in fact, by snowing my editor and accountant alike with its bearing on work-related research and inspiration. But even the cathartic role of martyr to inequity was denied me: the whole industry imploded, not just *Phantasmaria* and Warlock Comics' other titles. I was suddenly pounding the same pavement as scores of colleagues.

These days, without money-grubbing ulteriority, I hanker to recapture sparks of youthful spirit, minus the youthful foibles. Pooling resources I've socked away and inherited, I can afford frugal sojourns wherever nostalgia beckons, while pre-dotage vitality remains to make the most of them. And why not start in the place I unfairly associated with ensuing economic disaster? Redeem it with fresh memories that wouldn't, knock wood, be sullied retroactively? Too bad my capacity for foibles hasn't atrophied with age.

Hopes for rejuvenation were initially promising. My ebullience, my functionality held up through transatlantic all-nighter, the Metro to Newcastle's colossal hall-of-echoes depot, the bus from there up the Great North Road to Alnwick, and thence to the National Trail across several desolate miles to my inn. Maybe the luck of the delirious was with me.

Truth be told, my urge to hike the moors dated back, perversely, to *American Werewolf in London.* Its opening scenes in Northumbrian hinterland entranced me; understandable, given my stock in artistic trade. A decent facsimile of Transylvania's wild terrain was, aeronautically speaking, right on my doorstep, sans the language and cultural barriers. So in laudable testimony to my disbelief in werewolves, I packed sketchpads and camera to fanatically record English landscapes and townscapes, cruelly fated by Warlock downsizing never to pass for Carpathian in the pages of *Phantasmaria.*

Despite trepidations year-in, year-out for naught, I'm always pleasantly agog at how an overseas phone call months in advance can book a room, sealed with a casual "You're all set," and on arrival, the reservation is cheerfully honored. The Trusty Musket was no exception, now or in my salad days, though outwardly it could have subbed for *American Werewolf*'s godforsaken pile. The staff, many presumptive regime changes later, was no less courteous, and at the bar, three-hour friendships between natives and tourists sprang up easy as weeds, no matter that people invariably went their separate ways as strangers ever after.

Brass-rail geniality was a British folkway I cherished, though the beer was more insipid than before, maybe as well since I'd been up thirty-six hours and due to crash in short order. Meanwhile, I basked in how imperceptibly, to me at least, the decor had changed, as if successive landlords had valued the old-school trappings, mangy elk heads mounted on smudgy white walls with trompe-l'oeil festoons of hopvines, square load-bearing beams in misaligned rows obscured by framed photos of maypole dancers, mummers, and more esoteric cele-brants. The façade of familiarity, of camaraderie, lulled me into a fanta-sy of belonging.

This fantasy ripened, in the friable soil of my logy condition, into the feeling I'd been reinstated into my more freewheeling twenty-something persona. But as in the airport, was this rejuvenation or re-version? The heady sensation of decades annulled unsteadied my vi-sion, and where it came to rest, at the end of the bar, sat Phantasmaria, draining a pint. Which is to say, some inscrutable quality about her brought my bygone bread-and-butter to mind, for they shared no physical resemblance whatsoever. The more mystifying, Phantasmaria hadn't entered my thoughts since Ed Koch was mayor. And yikes, she was reciprocating with the once-over!

Luckily, blokes at the bar kept shifting in and out of our mutual sightline, lending me scope to clarify my impressions without staring continuously. Straight black hair hung in low-cut bangs and over her flannel collar. Big, wide-set eyes posed me an inexplicit challenge, and tight denim and riding boots encased an outdoorsy figure, but nothing pneumatic: one of my "types," all right. She could laugh into the rear-view mirror at crowfeet years away from overtaking her, but she was no kid either. Whatever our intermittent staring contest portended, I wouldn't exactly be robbing the cradle, she wouldn't exactly be rob-bing the grave. In the Brit parlance, fair do's!

The "real" Phantasmaria, on the other hand, had reinforced the '70s groundswell of softcore macabre in black-and-white comics. A bodacious ghoul in a skimpy shroud, sporting mothwings for no clear reason, she starred in her own serial Guignols and otherwise doled out jokey intros and outros to "filler thrillers." The publisher hyped her, blatant fanboy bait though she was, as a feminist icon; moreover, she foiled evil like a superhero when she wasn't eating corpses. In retro-spect, hitching the wagon of my fortunes to Phantasmaria had been myopic. She was in tune with her times, but times changed.

And amidst my woolgathering, the sham Phantasmaria, quiet as a moth, had stolen over to occupy the stool beside mine. Quite the

Phantasmaria move! Of course, the "real" ghoul wouldn't have given me the time of day, so this dose of attention was more gratifying than troublesome. "Your name's not Maria, is it? In whole or in part?"

She shook her unfazed, exquisite head. "Annabelle. Do I look like a Maria to you?"

"That's the thing, no." Wow, jetlag was in charge of this repartee. "There was somebody in a former life," I hinted delphically.

"You believe in channeling then? Reincarnation?" She'd perked up, but I was too loopy to tell if she were teasing or not. Her winsome smile, either way, reminded me of my manners, and I ordered her another pint, and a half for myself.

"I've had no professional involvement with the supernatural since my misspent youth," I hedged. Not a lie, for a ghoul and her ilk had underpinned my livelihood.

"No worries, glad you've shed your adolescence, not saying you're old, but you're at a stage where I can trust you're a gentleman, can't I? And not stay on my toes to block passes, as you Yanks would put it." Would we? I'd yet to establish the first biographic fact about her, but safe to say she had the shrewdness to preempt any touchy-feely ideas on my part.

Nonetheless, she was the one to initiate bodily contact with a handshake. "I'd wager you're not a Maria either." She raised her full glass. "And thanks."

Considering the headway fatigue had made, just as well she was pushing conversational cues a dunce alone would miss. "Donny Coté," I didn't altogether fib, though I'd only ever signed that nom de plume in the funnybooks. If I'd harbored vain hopes it would ring a bell, her deadpan expression dashed them.

"Hmm. Kind of a name that sounds like another name, know what I mean?"

"Yes, I do." I let awkward silence drag on from there, crossing my fingers she'd drop the subject because I wasn't up to unpacking it. The awkwardness got to me first, however, and I babbled I was an illustrator. This lent undeserved dignity to my post-Warlock career of corporate logos, industrial graphs, annual-report prettifications, worse hackwork. But staving off eviction in the short run sent me (and hundreds of other laid-off cartoonists) scrambling to ad agencies, PR firms, corporations for odd jobs; amazingly, Phantasmaria fans in high places rescued me more than once. And though Manhattan grew ever more nerve-racking, inertia taunted, Where to go from there that wouldn't reek of failure?

For Annabelle I boiled a disappointing adulthood down to that one face-saving word "illustrator." Travel, according to received wisdom, broadens a person, but isn't it even better at imparting the distance from which to assess a lifetime's big picture with painful clarity? I took a hefty swig from my half-pint, plunked down the glass a little too hard, and the crash hit me, my every muscle fiber quivering into exhaustion.

"You okay, Donny? You look knackered. Call it a night, maybe?"

I nodded, mumbled something about sleep deprivation, dimly regretted how our brief exchange had been all about me. Self-centered twerp, wasn't I? No harm done, though, considering that whatever possessed her to approach me, I was in over my head. She was young, gorgeous, woefully out of my league. Perhaps I likened her to Phantasmaria insomuch as she was no less an exotic fantasy from my perspective. Delighted as I was with a fantasy deigning to chat, I stammered excuses and shambled off before proving myself an outright moron. But my God, her smile was mesmerizing—like Phantasmaria's.

At cockcrow I awoke as buoyant as I'd gone to bed leaden. Oh boy, first morning on holiday! I was crestfallen Annabelle wasn't breakfasting in the bar, but rash of me to assume she was a lodger as opposed to a local. The landlord, rings dark as kohl under his eyes, was vacuuming the hall as I sidled by to brave the elements in mere trainers, polyester jacket, and Mets cap. He remarked my luck of sunny forecast for the week as if I'd cheated fate. Out front I winced at a panel van tearing meteorically down the narrow road to Bamburgh, and stole round back to continue up the trail from yesterday.

When I about-faced to survey the ground I'd covered, the rolling barrens had swallowed up the Musket, sole edifice of civilization in these parts. I was immersed 360° in the "blasted heath" where I felt at ease on some primeval level, where patches of lichen and moss garnished expanses of eroded stone, where spreads of green scrub and red heather abutted outcrops of bare rock like torsos defleshed to the bone. In two hours I'd no occasion to observe the trail etiquette of nodding in simultaneous hail and farewell at fellow hikers, not that anyone trekked here to be gregarious.

Civilization and this land had manifestly forsaken each other, which didn't rule out human activity anyplace that caught my eye. Manmade and natural features had had millennia to become indistinct from one another, as some married couples are said to do. Was that a knoll or a Bronze Age barrow, had a glacier dumped those slabs in a zigzag or had entropy toppled a megalithic structure? I'd need an archaeologist to translate each bump and boulder.

The trail had also grown ambiguous, save for shadowy ruts every hundred yards that faded, as I trod near, into one of a good dozen equally faint and tenable pathways. I'd have been leerier of getting lost, had those intermittent straight tracks not reappeared when I squinted back. I was also convinced I couldn't go badly astray in such a piddly-sounding nature reserve as Hernehowe Crags (if indeed I had that right), versus, say, Death Valley.

More vexing was the constant wind that lurked beyond the Musket's purview to tug at my sleeve, buffet my cheeks, snatch away my breath, generally gall me. I was too self-conscious to wear my cap backwards, and had to keep clamping it onto my skull lest a stiff gust cuff it aloft. I'd never dealt with the like; if it had been this blustery my previous sojourn, how could I have forgotten? Every vista had that vague overlay of matching a memory, almost like déjà vu.

As I second-guessed the wavering route up a hillside, the wind shot a speck into my eye. I rubbed at it while I stumbled to the summit. Subjectively, the wind casts nothing smaller than a BB, but as usual, the projectile on my fingertip was practically microscopic. I shook the blear from my vision and peered downslope at the topography I, as a callow Yank, had termed "prairie." And on its eventual upsweep toward a sheer sandstone bluff nestled a lonesome specimen of prehistoric art, and beside it was Annabelle waving at me as if I were showing up for a date.

I should have been surprised, but wasn't. Meeting an affable fantasy in remote wilderness the day after meeting her in a remote pub wasn't that much more outlandish. Chalk it up to atrophy eating into a vacationer's brain sooner than his other muscles, and mine really must have indexed her as a fantasy, or I'd have been too uptight for casual banter.

The steep gully downhill led to no Stonehenge or Lascaux, but I was fonder of this nameless carven boulder than I could be of grandiose, famous antiquities. Out in the middle of nowhere, unsung and vulnerable, it figured in my personal mythology as a beloved discovery toward which I felt protective, despite forgetting about it half my life. The wave of relief and affection that broke over me at finding it intact, or anyway as I remembered it, was paramount, distracting me from Annabelle if only for a moment.

The bracken, on the other hand, which hadn't crowded it back then, was lapping like a choppy floodtide against it. And I had to believe the gorse had propagated like mad too, looming behind my Stone Age treasure and threatening to claw at it, like a mob of triffids with spiky, yellow-flowered branches. A moot point, in retrospect, whether I'd have managed to pinpoint my object of adoration had Annabelle not been up to her knees in ferns beside it.

It had been a hub of sanctity, of cryptic ritual, for numberless centuries, incalculably long ago, although it was the unprepossessing size of a beanbag chair and reminiscent of a clay ocarina. Its tabular surface was riddled with holes encircled and enmeshed by a network of grooves that loosely echoed a family tree. I still, to my credit, retained "cupules" as academe's jargon for these features, as if coining terminology compensated for want of insight into their meaning or purpose.

I'd descended to the brushland floor where Annabelle and I could see eye to eye, and the whites of hers were coming into range, but I hadn't noticed that bottle of red wine she held by the neck, and which was, moreover, uncorked. By way of greeting she exclaimed, "I knew at a glance you couldn't stay away!" She indicated the cupules with a flourish of her free hand, like a gameshow model touting the grand prize. "Fascinating, aren't they?" Was my blithe fantasy becoming less guarded, but no more plainspoken?

"Hello yourself," I ventured, "and sorry I was such a lightweight last night. You were extremely gracious."

"I know jetlag when I see it, and I value it as part of the sacrifice you made to join me here." That settled it. Best I resign myself now to being on the back foot with her, whatever my baseline consciousness.

Simply because she represented some kind of wish fulfillment, I wasn't ipso facto in control of how it played out, was I?

"What are you celebrating?" I nodded toward the open bottle.

"Meeting a kindred spirit, for starters?" Her words weren't flirtatious, but her eye contact was. "Even without trying, you reveal an interest in past lives, in piercing the veil between you and your ancestors."

"Is that what we're doing here?" I stifled a smile that strove to be whimsical but read, I feared, as patronizing. She was spouting malarkey all right, but I was instinctively wary of underestimating her.

"Oh, no worries, I'm a crown priestess of the Lithic Awakening. Don't let my girlish exterior fool you. I'm impeccably qualified." It was no problem keeping a straight face at this notion of reassurance. In fact, I was dumbstruck.

She proceeded unabashed as if I were a vacuum to fill verbally. "Those smug university dullards habitually whinge how the cupules surpass our understanding. We Who Awake could enlighten them, but why cast pearls at swine? You're not like them, though, are you? You're a pilgrim, you deserve to learn what the cupules are for, what's in them, in common with thousands of such receptacles around the world." Her eyes, whose chestnut brown had firmly imprinted on me after twelve hours' acquaintance, shone enchanting, irresistible, as if mine were the agency of a crow enthralled by a bright trinket.

During her giddy spiel, while she fixed my eyes on hers, she'd waded through the bracken, unbeknownst to me, and within boardinghouse reach. So much for maintaining a safety margin. What's more, I "thrilled at her proximity," as comic-strip Wimpy used to say. "Your baseball cap has it you're from New England, yeah?"

Ordinarily, associating the Mets with New England would rate a double-take at least. But what had the ordinary done for me lately? "From the Northeast, anyhow."

Her brow furrowed in fleeting effort to parse where the distinction lay. "Coming from the Northeast then, you had the equivalent of these cupules in relatively recent history." I wanted to ask how, yet shrank from antagonizing her with a skeptical tone. No matter; she construed my speechlessness as encouragement. "A colonist from Plymouth in 1621 described the 'memory holes,' as he translated it, of Native

Americans along footpaths between villages. Each hole marked the site of some noteworthy deed, which passersby would recount to one another. Personages and events thus remained common knowledge for generations, till we brought plague and ethnic cleansing."

"And you theorize these 'cupules' served the same function? To prolong tribal memories?" Her lips pursed as if I were acting pedantic. *Moi,* pedantic? Actually, I've gotten that a lot with girls.

"Oh, they did much more, and we're miles beyond the realm of theory." She waggled the bottle just out of arm's length, as if teasing me to grab at it. Remarkably, not a drop had sloshed down the side yet. "The proof is in the tasting."

With a coy pirouette, she swung the bottle away from me, and swishing back through the bracken, bent at coquettish hips and poured wine to the precise rim of one cupule, righting the bottle without, predictably, wasting a drop. She crooked an index finger at me to come hither.

Loath to provoke her, I complied, but to spin this as less of a capitulation, and risking further charges of pedantry, I quipped, "Is that it? The cupules were a more efficient libation delivery system?"

In oblique reply she pulled a transparent plastic straw, of a gauge suited to bubble tea, from up her denim sleeve. She set the bottle into another cupule as if it were an archaic cup-holder, snagged my right wrist and pressed the straw into my palm, and waltzed back, exhorting, "Don't worry, drink it down. I'm an old pro at this, and I'll be right here for you."

Any fussbudget issues over trust, toxicity, or basic sanitary standards were plainly resolved to her satisfaction. Hence, to balk as tactfully as possible, I quibbled, "But should I be slurping up a libation? Isn't that against the rules? Liable to piss off the gods?"

"I appreciate your scruples." Her nose crinkled adorably. "As you might put it, though, the liquor has served its function as a libation. It's more of a sacrament now. Chug away! No harm, no foul. Trust me."

I'd never gone wrong distrusting people who insisted I trust them. Still, why poison me? Granting she was crazy didn't presume her reckless enough to attempt murder even in the boonies of a nation awash with CCTV and Nosy Parkers. In a last-ditch bid at aborting my stoop toward the putative wine, straw to my lips, I pleaded, "You're not concerned we're begging for trouble, contaminating a scheduled monument?"

She shook her head as if perfectly aware I was clean out of evasions. "Nobody about for acres and acres. You could scream and nobody would hear. We're fine!" Worse, with telepathic acumen, she'd refuted my premise of Big Brotherly eye on every trespass. Just like a cop, Big Brother's never around when you want him. And "fine," really? I had the most vivid sensation yet of Phantasmaria superimposed onto Annabelle: mistress of every contingency, with poise to spare, as she drafted me into her ranks with a numinous brew.

Or was I already a recruit, caving to a power of suggestion that mightn't have been catering to my best interests? In evidence, there I knelt, one end of the straw between my jaws, the other in the libation, and when she nodded assertively, fetching as a pixie with a shaving-cream pie behind her back, I gulped at a syrupy retsina (perhaps), redolent of mushrooms, yeast, chalky dregs, a dubious eye-opener before noon. Annabelle peeked to ensure the straw had hoovered all it could. Creaky knees hoisted me to my feet, and I passed her the straw, noting the bottle was two-thirds full. "And now you?"

"Uh-uh." Her lifting eyebrows criticized my rookie mistake. "I have to stand guard after you doze off. In case of varmints or downpour. Or if you start thrashing around, so you don't bang into anything sharp. Your wakeful self can't possibly bond with the ancestor you've ingested. He'll only get somewhere in a host whose neurons aren't firing like mad with twenty-first-century bedlam. How robustly will you be exerting yourself when you're five thousand years old?"

I was a bit woozy, a routine occurrence nowadays when I stand up too quickly. She'd unpocketed a cork and was bending to stopper the bottle in its cupule holder. But her focus still centered on me. With supernatural alacrity she was by my side, her lovely arm around my waist to brace me as I wobbled. Then all too soon, once she had me sitting with my spine against the boulder, she let go of me. "Why so tense?" she chided. "You're doing great!"

Leave it to my body language to broadcast suspicions my conscious mind wouldn't acknowledge. "This meeting my ancestors," I mumbled torpidly, "that's not a euphemism, is it?" Annabelle had become bleary, like a newly inked Bristol board in the rain.

"I'll be here when you're yourself again." This promise was studded with red flags, but they too were unreadably bleary. I simultaneously sank like an anvil and levitated like a feather on an updraft. My burden of personhood molted away.

*   *   *

Prehistory was in Cinemascope, in saturated, trippy colors as if the visible spectrum must have bleached out in the millennia since. Furthermore, in filmic terms, antiquity kept slipping sprockets in the projector, was rife with clumsy jump-cuts and missing frames, and it blared and flanged, badly overdue for restoration overall. And most off-putting, thoughts made decent sense till spoken aloud, when they became bleating, abrasive gobbledygook.

Oh, but everything to the horizon is beautiful, is of the People! From this hilltop the Forebears watch over all the Holding. It is rich down there, woods in the four directions, oak, beech, hazel that feed the pigs and deer that feed the People. On the east edge of this hilltop everyone is gathered, except the bowmen guarding the narrow gaps. The People do not starve, do not shiver, they have the flax, the grass, the leather to be warm, and come snowtime the furs, they wear their best today in fresh green, blue, yellow. The Forebears flocking to the eastward-facing doorway can see how their children prosper.

The Forebears are generous to the People, and the People to them, sharing the pork, the venison, the millet pottage. To bring everyone closer together, the helper has gone into the Forebears' house for the skulls. He must learn not to carry them by the eyeholes! He will feel bruises for this unmindful disrespect, but better for a living fist to dispense punishment before ancestors do.

People, behold! Here is the father of all your fathers, the mother of all your mothers! Hallow them, pass them among you with love! This is the message to be voiced, though croaking gibberish flaps through the air.

To cross the several paces from the holy quarter to the People's quarter, forsaking the oaken staff because of the skull in each hand, sorely pains the leg with the short thigh. Reveal nothing! To bargain with the Forebears, to lead the rituals, to counsel the axeholder, to visit the Shadow Holding, to heal, these nobody can do who is not born with unhealable flaws. How unjust that those least able to fight are most prone to challenge or ambush by rivals.

The axeholder receives the skulls first, cradles them with the briefest veneration. His nod bids me heed his sickly manchild, who receives the skulls next and almost drops them. The axeholder has been friend and protector, but grows impatient that meat offerings and smoke journeys have not prevailed on the Forebears to deliver a cure. They seldom favor those who cough blood, as if that blood already makes of them a sacrifice that has been unconditionally accepted. One other onlooker, whose spine is twisty like a snake's, knows this too. His grin unsheathes an ugly wish.

The earth bucks underfoot, as when lightning barely misses, and sounds are all chased into hiding. Below, out of the crags, into the Holding wends the narrow gap, and outlanders hurry upon it, seeking concealment in the forest. Behind boulders above the gap, cousins and nephews are ready with arrows nocked. The shortness of one leg makes balance hard up here, beyond the throw of spears, where my jinxing song, spinning bullroarer, birdwing commotions torment raiders. A bludgeon across the back knocks me off the peak. Feathers are of no help now in flying!

*   *   *

I gasped and pressed my palms flat on the pebbly ground to curb ebbing vertigo. As far as my stiff neck could rotate, I scanned the wilderness in vain for company, and smoldered with all the indignation my sluggish brain could muster. Annabelle had promised to stick around, but in lieu of her, a Post-it was safety-pinned to my jacket: "Had to go. You were okay. Weather was fine. Let's compare notes. Meet me at the Musket!" Yes, at the Musket, where decorum forbade I take a swing at her or even have it out too stridently.

I hove myself out of the boulder's shelter, into the windchill. My hat was MIA, a trophy for the gale, I reckoned. The while I regained my bearings and retraced the trail, I bitterly rehashed how broken promises had been the dealbreaker with girlfriends since college. Nothing else stung me into rocking the boat, losing my cool, airing grievances, splitsville resulting. Really though, given the ever hazier border between human and animal traits, keeping one's word is among the last uniquely human virtues. But no blame accrues to womankind for my bachelorhood: I simply had no knack for picking 'em. No misogynist I!

Like strafing gadflies, flashbacks from my freaky naptime impinged on my love-life autopsy. They were more graphic than dream snippets, more like implanted memories, like another existence integrating itself haphazardly with my own. I'd have recorded these as I went along, but had no pen and only Annabelle's Post-it, which referred ironically to "comparing notes" I couldn't write. Drugging me (for educational purposes, right?) I could forgive, but breaking her word, going AWOL instead of transcribing my REM outcries then, my recap now? Did she merit any benefit of the doubt? Maybe she'd been skimping on her Ritalin?

From trail to en-suite shower to the pub, I honed my pithiest brickbats for cavalier Annabelle. For openers, a rabid fox could have gnawed at my ankle, I could have upchucked doctored wine and choked like Jimi Hendrix. But when she slid into my secluded booth, I was working on my second ESB, and Christ almighty, was she bewitching! Diaphanous blouse over tangerine spandex, turquoise nails and matching lipstick, a stunning bait-and-switch from camper to glam! My prepared digs went into the dustbin. This bombshell makeover had me flustered, disarmed, groping for apropos reaction.

"Donny, so glad to see you!" She squeezed my hand for a good three-Mississippi. How easily she seized the advantage, and had me liking it. "I hated to go, but work stuff came up, yeah?" Work stuff? Then she wasn't on holiday, despite the London usage of "yeah" placing her 300 miles from home? And frankly, was "work stuff" a universal solvent for tedious promises? Why antagonize her, though, with a rhetorical question whose answer we both knew?

"I thought something urgent might have come up with your Lithic Wakening cronies."

"Oh?" She spent an off-base second dredging up whom I meant. That was her cult, wasn't it? "No, nothing to do with them. I'm starving, incidentally. Can we order dinner?"

I'd have been churlish to oppose this change of subject. And when I returned from the bar with menus, she batted ingratiating eyelashes. But for a hungry girl, she stared blankly at the menu while ever so ingenuously bringing up today's dream. Dosing and deserting me were implicitly unworthy of discussion. Her eyes met mine as I complied with a halting play-by-play, desisting amidships to ascertain whether she planned to peruse the bill-of-fare or not. "Don't worry, I know what I want," she warbled. She told me, I told the barman and relinquished our menus; he repeated our orders to a slump-shouldered waitress who'd heretofore been invisible.

Annabelle patted the bench beside her as I approached. "Be near me. Let me soak up the emanations of the soul you've welcomed." Sure, why not? Her thigh was in tangential but tonic contact with mine. "Continue, please. You were saying you'd have to beat your apprentice for improper handling of skulls."

I'd have had a hell of a crick were I to look her in the eye too often; plus, I was self-conscious about offending with sour beer fumes. Of course, I was acutely tuned in to her proximity. She, flouting her more limber youth, had her back resolutely torqued and her head cocked toward me, stockstill with fascination. I'd just reached the cliffhanger end when the apparently disgruntled waitress set down both our plates at once with an alarming impact.

We rebounded, tucked in like born trenchermen, I anyway happy for some respite from the taxing frisson of Annabelle's gaze. It couldn't last, not long enough for my bangers to distract me from her persistent thigh. From her third bite of steak pie onward, breathless with ardor, she edified me for each duration of cutting another morsel and dunking it in gravy. "Bet you any money, he was a shaman. He fits the job description to a T. You could drop him in some remote spots today and he could get right to work."

Well yes, apart from details like language, no knowledge of metals, a homicide-friendly social code, but why nitpick and prolong Annabelle's spiel? She further elaborated how "logical" it was for his animus to reside in a cupule, as shaman spirits are wont to inhabit animals and objects and mystic worlds while their bodies vegetate by the fire. "But thanks to you, Donny, he's not mute anymore, or stuck in a hole, he's someplace warm."

We both qualified with photo-finish élan for the Clean Plate Club, and I reluctantly sidled away from her to use the loo and, deeming it the gentlemanly thing, order another round from the bar directly, as the waitress had gone to ground again. I also needed momentary space to mull (in vain) how the shaman's transfer to "someplace warm" could involve me.

Pints were waiting where the plates had been, and was I pushy to scoot in beside her without explicit go-ahead? My glass, after all, was beside hers. She agreeably eliminated the inch betwixt us, and straightaway murmured, "Donny dear, would you be a lamb and pay for us both? They're cash-only here, and I just have plastic."

She toasted my liberality, and exercised an uncanny talent for locating and flagging our goldbrick of a waitress. Check, please! She cryptically remarked we were in the "home stretch," let's sort the bill sooner than later, and bottoms up! I indulged a notion she was concerned about her early morning or somesuch "work stuff."

Three swigs along, that fresh pint was taking its toll, and okay, I did realize what was what because a lousy few hours ago I'd experienced the same groggy symptoms. But instead of copping to the reality of my plight, I gathered the wherewithal to ask, even as Annabelle fondly but firmly maneuvered me out the booth and into a leadfoot shuffle, "Hey, about that poor lonely witchdoctor out in the middle of nowhere, you want to find out any more, maybe go there and chug some of that wine yourself?"

"You have your key? Thanks. That's on the second floor, isn't it? Careful on the stairs now, upsidaisy, there we go. Good heavens, Donny, that wine would do nothing for me. Nor would schlepping back onto those nasty moors. You drank the shaman, Donny. He's in you. What'd you think I meant by 'someplace warm'? Never mind, a little farther, that's it, time for a liedown, I'll get those shoes off you."

I had the capacity for one more dumbass quip. "I was beginning to wonder what you saw in me. Now I know it's someone else." Then I went under, with a cockeyed optimism that Annabelle could intend me no more harm than did the fictitious Phantasmaria.

*　　*　　*

These People are mine, all are familiar, their doings, their past, what they are to me, but their names are not, are nothing but bleatings in my head, like everything everybody says. It makes no difference, for no words will halt this trial, nobody is talking, not the axeholder, nor he who hungers for failure, death, overthrow in order to seize the feathered mantle. He has sown too many cunning words already, bending the People's thoughts as a few crafty handclaps and flips of a blanket stampede a herd off a cliff.

To cure the axeholder's son, one chance remains. The axeholder was persuaded to demand it, and its outcome will decide who wears the feathers. In this circle where drumming and dancing and feasting give thanks for the generosities of sun, soil, rain, the boy lies face-down on a woven grass mat, and may the bowl of sleeping drink not let him wake till tomorrow! What is worse, all are aware that one swallow overmuch from the bowl can also kill.

Good that the axeholder is watching from behind, out of sight, though his shadow looms across the boy's legs. Step back, everyone step back, or anxious feet may heap dust upon the shaven head! Give the powers above and below the room to guide the knife that in one swoop cuts three lines into the scalp, the burin that peels away the flap of scalp to be stitched down later, the hammerstone that must drive the chisel into the skull just deep enough. Pry with the wooden tongue and lift bone away little by little, slowly, carefully, again not too deep!

Had he been younger, before the seams in his skull had knitted fast, the removal of bone would have been less daunting. But maybe that allotment of luck was put toward the release of sickness through the hole, once the bone let go with a pop at which everyone gasped, especially the axeholder, even the challenger for the mantle.

The skull marrow in the hole does not bleed, has not been nicked, quivers like an eggshell when a chick begins to hatch. Nothing more happens, and shoulders among the People begin to relax, the sickness may have fled, that will show as the boy recovers. But then his body shakes and arches as though the soul would take the body with it as it flies skyward. His back is like a bow as the bowstring is drawn, and when the bowstring slackens, the boy is dead.

None will look upon the axeholder in his wildness, except the would-be robber of the mantle, who hides a smile behind his hand, which the People are too distraught to notice. To throw himself in howling grief upon the mutilated corpse, the axeholder shoves me aside as a hamstrung boar is shoved by sacrificial pole into a flint pit whose veins become ungenerous.

The ground gives way like a pit covered with boughs, but on the bottom are no sharp stakes, only more ground as if nothing had happened, yet it is different ground, the chalk holloway, four-sided like the hole in the skull, marking off the defleshing platform. The platform stands high on scaffolding halfway up the hill with outlook on the sunset crags. Skill and reverence are necessary to tread properly, to solace the dead, to cast propitiating herbs. The helper earned another beating for bungling the most common-sense task of routing vultures that vomit on bodies, dismember limbs and strew them onto the chalk, so that crows will not come and neatly strip the bones.

Because of him, more trustworthy hands are compelled to lave the body. No duty, despite the hardiness of experience, is nastier, more galling, between the vomit and the rotting. Much linen is befouled that can never be reused. Does the would-be usurper have the learning to perform this and a flock of other disagreeable chores? The smell is murderous, and heartbreaking are the innards poking through scavengers' gashes, the blue shreds of skin instead of a face.

Where the outlander was born, where he brags of mastering the spirit arts before marrying among the People, were those outsiders' ways the same as the People's? If his claims of wisdom are not idle, would he not have been too important to let dwell elsewhere? The axeholder nods at these doubts, but the outlander has his ear, all the more after the blood illness chose to kill rather than depart from the manchild.

Here comes the axeholder up the hill, dictating a pause in the laving, and the homage of clambering down before hailing him. How much kinder with mismatched legs if speaking from above were allowed! Fleas hatch and hop inside at suspicions over his purpose, but to mourn at the platform is customary, and who does not carry his spear in the borderlands? His words are gibberish, yet their meaning burgeons clearly in my head.

He says nothing ominous in itself. Sad how the helper blundered again and this laving had to occur! Futile to press him on whether the boastful outsider has his own helper, or would employ the perpetrator of today's desecration. Besides, the axeholder has more dire concerns. Watchmen have detected raiders climbing the slopes to the narrow gap into the Holding. The axeholder has sent bowmen to ambush them. The jinxing dance and cursing song are crucial to lend the bowmen extra advantage. He will post cousins here to stave off vultures till the intruders are purged.

The axeholder demands nothing out of the ordinary. And complete the laving first, for it is meet, he pronounces perhaps archly, that he who presided at the outset of his boy's journey to the Forebears' doorway should see it through. He turns to go downhill before his face can show anything his words have not. The platform to be remounted in painful haste mocks and taunts. Up goes the foot of the shorter leg onto the lowest crossbar, and pain's arrow shoots up my spine, into my head, and fells me.

Dust clogs my throat, my stinging eyes. My face is on the ground. Coughing out the dust, staggering up, straining eyes into gloom, it is plain straight off, this is the Shadow Holding. Where the Holding has hollows, here there are hills; where the Holding has crags, here there are crevices; and nothing grows. This land is well-known to anyone fit to wear the feathered mantle, but they who do not ride the smoke to travel here must be summoned by its denizens.

There is the manchild, dim as the country around him, no less dim as he drifts nearer, which is merciful on account of his riven scalp. His language is as garbled as his father's, but its import likewise fills my mind. He forgives, he does not blame me for his death, his father heeded false counsel from the scheming outlander, nothing could have saved him from the sickness, he knows that now. How worthy an axeholder the son, felled on the verge of manhood, would have been!

But beware! He grows flickery, fainter, as urgency excites him. Just as no one hesitates to beat a cloddish helper, bereaved father has no forgiveness for a failed healer. The son flutters in and out of sight like a tentflap in a gale that buffets him alone. He ekes out snatches of warning about the treacherous outsider, whose prowess trespasses on the Shadow Holding, conjuring this dry storm to muffle and disperse benign ghost. Upon his own folk's Forebears he imposed such influence and harm that everyone was glad to marry him off and be rid of him, and he will keep his powers secret among the People till the feathered mantle is his.

My fists, meanwhile, have been slyly ensnared, and my arms stretched apart, pinioned before I was the wiser. I tug to free them, but the bonds tighten. Has the enemy entrapped me in the Shadow Holding? Panic blinds me to everything but the nightmare that my body is already destroyed, and I am forever among the Forebears.

*   *   *

My eyes snapped open in desperation for an escape from desert afterworld, and this juncture was doubly disorienting as I'd have sworn my eyes were open all along. Annabelle's solicitous visage was inches from mine, jolting me into the twenty-first century, and as she withdrew a tad and her seated weight shifted slightly on my bed, I inwardly applauded her for sticking by me. Maybe she was back on her Ritalin. The lights were on and the curtains drawn, affording me no insight into the passage of time or the hour of day or night.

Then I went to shift my own weight, relieve the pins and needles in my rump, which set off cramping in my shoulders, irremediable because my arms were maximally splayed, wrists bound to bedposts. "I had to err on the side of caution," Annabelle leapt in. "You might have thrashed about and been hurt. How are you?"

"I'd be happier if I could scratch my nose."

She leaned in and gingerly raked a turquoise fingernail up and down my nasal bridge. "Better?" Given her manifest IQ, she must have been willfully oblivious to my subtext, whereas I was still clueless regarding her gameplan, stonewalled behind that perpetual winsome smile. Blowing up at her would get me nowhere. "Please, before you can forget, describe every detail about being a shaman as it recurs to you. Don't bother putting events in order; I'll sort that later." She had a spiral-binder notepad with ballpoint hovering a centimeter above blank page, like a secretary poised for dictation.

So I reeled off oneiric contents with intent to get this over with ASAP, promising she'd afterward be out of excuses for my constraints. I could always scream blue murder if she balked at untying me. Again, my recap had more the substantiality of memories than of dreams, or at least of movie scenes that sometimes interleaf with one's own recall. She jotted feverishly. Writer's cramp presumably beset her: she smacked her notepad against my stomach for an impromptu countertop. If she were interested in a more stable surface, the ploy backfired because the pen tickled.

And wouldn't she have predicted that? On she soldiered nonetheless, as if determined to ignore whatever effects she exerted, as if she'd
never roped me to the bed. Of what profit to her was this chronic un-
dercurrent of titillation? She emanated an equally definite air of re-
warding any physical advances (whenever that option was back on the
table) with evasive maneuvers or a shiner at worst. Her expression
grew probing as longer intervals separated my recollections.

I wrung my gray matter dry with an isolated bit about hawking
chalk dust into a shallow gully while on lopsided all-fours, then hinted
bluntly she'd forfeit no data by unbinding me instead of drilling her
inquisitional focus any deeper. She yanked the notepad off like a mustard plaster and stroked my wrinkly shirtfront smooth with lingering
fingertips. Her eyebrows rose toward severity as if I'd deliberately
omitted vital info. "No dealings with the cupules? Not a glimpse?" she
finally coaxed.

I shook my head as neutrally as semi-crucifixion allowed, losing
myself briefly in her chestnut irises despite my discomfort.

The mattress creaked as she fidgeted back a smidgen and sighed,
as if resigned to my disappointing narrative. "Listen, you've come out
of prehistory, but you've partially brought it with you. You did ingest a
Neolithic tribesman. Flashbacks have been reported."

Was she going to free me or not? That question must have glowed
like neon on my features.

"I'll loosen one hand and then I have to run. But I implore you,
don't act rashly, be sure you're all right before taking normality for
granted." Artfully she bent forward, practically brushing my left knuckles with hers, reconsidered, pivoted to plant a quick smooch on my
lips, and at last undid the knots restraining my left wrist, shy of un-
looping the rope. She flounced out of grabbing range with the whiplash speed of a gorgeous tubeworm, and was out the door, jiggling the
outside knob to ensure it would lock, without a farewell glance.

Well, I may have fallen for a regrettable lot already, but not for that
flimsy ruse to accrue some distance between us. Shaking off the coils
around my left hand, I liberated my right, and had to admit Annabelle's
kiss out of the blue was an ingenious stroke for throwing me off my
stride, breeding abashment with a soupcon of euphoria. I could almost
credit she'd applied lipstick for the distraction its taste would inflict.

I bolted out without trifling to slam the door behind me, harassed by an impression that unwinding the cords and cramming feet into boots had consumed ages. The corridor was of the same brightness as the room, and sepulchrally hushed; the window at the top of the stairs gave onto dead of night. Astonishing that I'd been in cahoots with Annabelle less than twenty-four hours, back and forth to prehistory twice. No less astonishing was my klutzy momentum, and heaven forbid it conked out now!

On the theory she wasn't a guest, intercepting her in the parking area was a damn fool proposition. She should have been miles down the road, but I'd never forgive myself if some fluke had detained her while I twiddled my thumbs. I could picture gawking out my window, idly catching my breath, as she impudently peeled off, doubtless in a Lamborghini. That's what Phantasmaria drove (with mothwings magically retracted). Past the reception, lit solely by red PC power button, and out the front I scrambled, where the glacial cold pounced with a bear hug that knocked the breath out of me.

Shuddersome to empathize with my shamanic alter-ego braving every winter in the piecemeal coverage of vegetable fibers and pelts! The frosty air, in my underdressed, rickety condition, made for heavy wading as I lurched toward the side lot, hearing no screech of tires en route, nor a Lamborghini or anything else revving up. On the deathly quiet tarmac, pausing to let the fire in my lungs die down, I mused, How had this terrain looked to him? What, if any, constellations did he extract from these teeming stars?

At a loss for Plan B in the hunt for Annabelle, I lapsed further into putting myself in Neolithic shoes, and yes, I had a distinct recall of those shoes, of deerskin with rawhide laces up one ankle, as if traipsing barefoot in British snow was ever a tenable option! Hokey as it sounded, some "fellow feeling" had germinated, some manner of identification with him. We were both artists to the extent our respective societies enabled us. We both built our reputations on negotiating, on elucidating fantastic, alternate worlds for a mundane audience.

He, however, had to operate as a generalist, as his precursors had for dozens of millennia, and would do for centuries more: music, dance, verse, theatre, pictorial arts were interwoven into rituals at once religious and pragmatic. To win divine favor, to minimize ill-chance, these life-and-death priorities mandated an "interdisciplinary" approach. I didn't envy ancient priesthoods the creative spectrum they had to command. And who can prove that none of these practices ever transcended mumbo-jumbo to interact with spiritual realities?

This prospect upped my shivering a notch. I'd compounded exposure to the cold with exposure to a more penetrating danger. Empathy with my prehistoric magus had blurred into a balmy wish that he could see through my eyes as I'd seen through his. Not the first time a penchant for fair play has bitten me on the ass! I'd yet to infer skips in my footage of this murky tundra, as was par for the Technicolor dreamscapes. But I steeled myself every second for a jarring lacuna as I scurried back to the Musket, loath to blank out where hypothermia was minutes away.

I had, on the other hand, been eager to confront Annabelle, and when the front hall's warmish air flash-thawed my brain, I cottoned that my cause might not be lost. If she were registered here, and I hadn't established she wasn't, her name and room number would be on record at reception, not ten feet away. An aura of criminality weighed on me as I tiptoed behind the wood-composite desk, ogling around for those discreet CCTVs alleged to monitor every square yard of the UK. Nope, short of disguised cameras à la James Bond, I could rifle with impunity.

In upshot, though, accessing the computer, embedded amidst paper like the aftermath of an overturned wastebasket, would never become a problem. A spark of triumph, like that which must have warmed Inspector Dupin's heart on finding the Purloined Letter, warmed mine at recognizing the open guestbook half-buried by a fantail of past-due bills from a plumber and an ébéniste, whatever that was. I swiped these irrelevant documents aside, figuring they wouldn't be in worse disarray for it, but wincing at my caveman deportment anyhow.

My eyes followed my index finger down the roster of several signatures on the most recent page, then to the chock-full page preceding, and on back to a fortnight ago. No Annabelles! I grunted in frustration, a bit too brutishly for my taste, and salvaged my morale, and temper, by cross-examining the assumption she was legally Annabelle. The Trusty Musket was cash-and-carry, wouldn't have consulted a credit card to confirm her identity.

Why, only yesterday she mooched a meal off me by lamenting her plastic was no good here! Speculating she was still in the house was, of course, an astronomic remove from nailing her room number. I clenched my teeth in futile rage, visualizing the chaos were I to indulge my Hail-Mary resort of tromping door-to-door, pounding and railing till I'd flushed her out or wound up in the Alnwick hoosegow. Even this much affirmation of my inner caveman was, I instinctively grasped, a grievous mistake, at which I bit my lower lip.

And it was the flavor of Annabelle's lipstick that provoked another's grip to wrench from mine the wheel of my consciousness. In that last sliver of a second before self-possession went into a nosedive, I apprehended the squeak of springs and rise of a shapely silhouette from an armchair in a dark corner.

* * *

Nothing here makes sense, I cannot tell what anything is. I stand on a floor with walls around me, yet cannot conceive of what they are built. This is not the Shadow Holding or my sunlit world. Have I not given the outlander his due? Has he hit upon, or created, a new world? Fury boils up in me, like broth in a cooking-skin that receives a red-hot stone, at the bewilderment, the cringing, that every least object kindles in me.

Nothing is of the good flint. On the impossibly flat slab in front of me are very many white, four-sided things, thin and rustly like flayings of birch bark, and thick with black markings like countless tiny tattoos. More stupefying and distressing are those numerous other things of a size to be gripped in one hand but that I shrink from touching, with surfaces smoother and better rounded or more sharply angled than the best-polished stone, but looking no less hard and weighty.

Most unsettling and maddening of all is the smooth, four-sided thing, black as a deep pool, unnaturally upright on too slim a black stem: some sort of fire-pouch, I decide, because a dot of red glow slowly pulses in one corner. Its freakishness is mortifying.

Everything in this world must have been produced by, and overladen with, magic. For me to have been so utterly outmatched by such unfamiliar magic inflames me to both flee terror-struck and lash out in frenzy. But I dare do neither, and may as well be hanging by one foot in a snare. And how is it I have flesh, and am not simply spirit, in this otherworld?

Nor am I alone! She who suddenly watches from the opposite side of the cluttered slab startles me, though I may have been distracted more than she was stealthy. She is a stranger, but arouses both mistrust and longing as if someone else's experience of her is woven into my remembrance. Is she spirit or flesh? Since she wears colors and substances whose like I've never seen, then whatever else she is, she is surely a sorceress.

"Please, come with me. You're angry, I understand that, but you can't do anything here except hurt yourself." Her speech is some chirpy, singsong gibberish, and I am yet more mystified by how perfectly plain her meaning is. "Everything will be as it was, once you lie down and get a bit of rest. I've been through all this before, haven't I?"

If I am to lie down with her, then yes, I am keen to go. My outrage with this place is like a drawn bowstring, though, and I cannot go while it is like that. I growl and, despite the untouchability of everything, backhand a rasping swath of the white birch-bark flayings off the slab. What I would do next is a riddle nobody will ever solve. Swift as a bat, she has come around the slab, encircles my arm with fingers too sleek to have pounded millet or scrubbed linen. To allow the touch of a sorceress is unwise, every child knows that, but I have no wish to pull away, whether or not I am bewitched, as she leads me forth.

I have second thoughts, however, when we have crossed a floor covered in some perplexing thing that is like both moss and wool, to pause at the bottom of handiwork as much like a ramp as a group of one narrow ledge after another after another. She urges me, with a trace of unease as if I may have alerted whatever lives here, "Let's go!" She starts up and almost drags me along. I put both feet on one ledge before climbing to the next, and the sorceress, who would have skipped all the way up by now were she on her own, pouts as if at a grandfather, impatient, but with kindness.

We arrive at a broader ledge, though my relief is dashed when we turn to one side and there is another ramp of ledges to surmount. To my amazement, only now do I comprehend my leg and spine do not torment me. I no longer limp, and have no use for a staff. My body in this world has healed, or is it spirit and not body after all?

At last we have no more narrow ledges, and ahead stretches a passage, like that which ends in the chambers of bones in the house of Forebears. It is fantastically longer, though, and all its doorways save one are sealed, and it is of the same otherworldly, smooth white as the walls below.

Through the single open doorway she conducts me, and into a room where the biggest thing is yet another slab, flat and white, and as she pulls me along to sit on it beside her, I am dumbfounded that it is soft. Whatever it is made of, I am dismayed, for like so much else here, it is white, and white is seldom auspicious, is mostly a color of death. This whole world is built of magic and death.

The sorceress instructs me to lie back, and her fingers release my wrist to pat the yielding slab invitingly. Has this been a ploy to lull me into a position where she can slay me for an offering? The slab is plainly suitable for that. But she beseeches, "I promise, you'll be yourself again, you'll be fine, you just have to calm down."

I do not budge, I resist abetting her in killing me, in spite of which I begin lapsing into sleep while stubbornly sitting up. I am like a fisherman's sinker stone tossed into a pond, and can do as much for myself. I am so heavy and sink into rippling darkness, to the bottom, into the black mud on the bottom.

*　　*　　*

She lied. I was better off with her, the soft white slab, the perplexing world. Once more I blink in the dazzling brightness of the Holding, but am more like a fishing stone than ever, without arms or legs to stay the sinking that has not abated from that world to this, that feels in my belly like I am plunging, but in my shoulders like I am a stone being pressed into cold, stiff clay. And worse, my lumpish stone of a body spins slowly, unstoppably.

I realize then my spirit and not my flesh has become ponderous, for as near to me as if in my lap, my earthly body circles past, its neck and backbone and limbs snapped at shocking angles, blue face gaping into the blue. As my vision reels on, it grants me a glimpse of my bier, the hallowed boulder, where holes are chiseled to commemorate the heroic Forebears, to remind the People of their deeds. The Forebears are said to reside in these holes and proclaim their stories to those with a gift for listening, a gift I had yet to master.

Then my glimpse of the boulder passes away, and into view looms the hateful outlander in my feathered mantle, gleeful, gloating, performing some strange, wicked ritual. His arms claw downward over and over, as if casting a net or forcing someone to sit, and with each full pronouncement of his uncouth chant, I descend one full turn of a spiral. Soon the rim of the new-chiseled hole is in my sightline, and then nothing but the inside of the hole into which my spirit is being driven, to be trapped beneath an everlasting plug of magic.

Whose fury is more impotent than a corpse's? And when that burns out, and there is no measure of how long that takes, I can do nothing but brood on bygone life, and come to perceive how I go missing, I cease, I am nowhere between broodings. Snow, rain, warmth, cold, sunshine, moonlight impart the season, whether it is day or night, but not the count of years, when thought requickens on its inconstant own. I can hark back to earlier broodings just enough to sense they become ever vaguer, more remote as if my life were another's, and mine a presence apart, a captive onlooker who blames and hates him for how he died, barring me from the Shadow Holding.

*   *   *

I was not dead, which was confounding, hard to reconcile with being dead for literal ages. Restoration to life was actually a discomfiting miracle for my inner shaman, so long accustomed to oblivion punctuated by fractured retrospection. I, "Donny Coté," had to thrash breathlessly up from those depths of yearning for death, pummel through that veneer of Neolithic otherness, but it handily melted away at my fortifying, belated awareness that I wasn't tied to the bedposts. Not that Annabelle wouldn't have been more justified restraining me this go-around, considering my antics downstairs. Yes, I retained that manic episode all too clearly.

She'd ditched me with my feet flat on the floor, arms outstretched, a crick in my neck from collapsing backward onto the mattress with no pillow to support my head. Milky sunup slanted through a gap in the grommet curtains. As far as I was concerned, I was already dressed for breakfast, premising that unwashed hikers were the norm here.

Of course I performed bathroom ablutions first, if only as a test of locomotive ability, shambling at best till I splashed cold tapwater into my kisser. This kick-started my cerebrum into intuiting, Well, if Annabelle's not in here, she must have gotten what she wanted of me, has no reason to linger. Or had she come down with cold feet after I ran amok at the front desk? Money, credit card, passport were intact in my pants; I'd never taken her for a thief, but had she been a professional, who would?

Proof of her absence from the place was still pending. Her absence from my bedside, though, argued for the worst. She'd previously hovered about to save me from self-harm, even emerging from the gloom to intercept me mid-rampage. She'd also been anxious to transcribe all my prehistoric minutiae while at their peak freshness.

Clumping down to breakfast, I had to clutch the rail, bracing against a mini-attack of dizziness before each footfall, as if some recessive fraction of me hadn't reacquired the hang of stairs. And the usual unbidden flashbacks to shaman-channeling unsteadied me further. Too bad Annabelle had abandoned her post as recording secretary, though I never had supplied her with coherent, high-resolution material, had I? A fount of someone else's resentment gushed up in me at that farewell spin past his mangled corpse on the hallowed boulder, at the foregone conclusion that enemy claimant to the feathered mantle would hardly ordain reverential excarnation and entombment.

I found myself seated in the public room, with a view of the doorway into the reception hall. My dream glimpse of the ocarina-shaped bier was troubling: its contours didn't jibe with those of today. The ancient surface had eroded, and its cupules along with them, which I deemed one contributing factor to jerky and disjointed witch-doctor saga. Personhood had eroded along with the rock in which it was ingrained, to be rendered impaired and fragmentary, like a damaged CD across which the laser skips erratically, when it functions at all.

Poor demolished man! To dwell on those who might languish in adjacent cupules, or in cupules everywhere, wearing away through the millennia, evoked a pang, or was that just a stitch from poor positioning on the bed, or even stomach acid from nervous hunger?

The same waitress who'd made herself scarce at dinner was lolly-gagging at tableside, demurely coughing for my attention. She brought

Phantasmaria, or anyway Annabelle, to mind, and speak of the devil, there she went, transiting the doorway, and in a red vinyl slicker yet, en route to the desk. I bounced up, wincing at resultant shooting pain from the crick in my neck, and reflexively barking at the girl, "Full English!" She ought to be well-pleased to meet no uglier Americans this month.

Was Annabelle really pretending my hot breath down her collar was imperceptible? She was jawing breezily with the kohl-eyed landlord and tendering hundred-pound notes that must have slipped her mind when pleading she was cashless to mooch dinner off me. "Bailing, are we?" I finally interjected at the back of her head, aiming for her degree of breeziness.

She betrayed no cognizance of sarcasm, no defensiveness, no admission I'd gotten the drop on her. She twisted around enough to see me out the corner of one eye and lilted, "Donny! I only reserved through last night. I have to check out now." She turned to the landlord, took her change and receipt in one hand, picked up a blue canvas Gladstone with the other.

Okay, forget that fib about cash deficit. Her dereliction of duty was a damn sight more onerous. "But Annabelle, you can't go yet! I have a lot more for you to write down." She was sashaying out the door and closeting any irritation that I was keeping pace with her. "Won't your Lithic Awakening be disappointed if you come up short with your research? After all the hassle you and I have been through together? I've got a handle now on how your shaman ended up, and how the cupules were used!"

My persistence did elicit a put-upon sigh from her, halfway across the parking apron. She drew up without setting down the valise. "Listen, Donny, there's no Lithic Wakening. I made that up. I'm disappointed you've made me spell that out for you."

"What are you talking about?" On the wavelength where linear thinking happened, this was no revelation. But I refused to let her off the hook till she'd worked for it. "If there's no Lithic Awakening, who's going to archive that trove of information about the shaman, his environment, the rituals, day-to-day details about shoes and food and such?"

"The wine in the cupule had a hallucinogen in it. So did your last beer at dinner." She let that sink in a second. "Nothing too heavy-duty," she added by way of extenuation. She derived no externalized pleasure from bamboozling me. Her demeanor was more of peevishness at having to explain herself. Must I be a nuisance? She wasn't a turn-on at all anymore. "Power of suggestion did the rest. The drug ought to be clear of your system in a day or two."

Confession notwithstanding, to brand her a hoaxer rather than a loony, a cultist, was heart-wrenching. For that gloss of exotica, of glamor (of Phantasmaria?) to tarnish into mere fraudulence was impermissible. "But why? Why drug me and interrogate me and put us both through the wringer for nothing?"

She reprised that winsome smile. "It was just a bit of fun. You should appreciate the attention at your age." She began to shuffle one foot restlessly, kicked at a pebble. All righty then, you want to hit below the belt, fine, that won't get you off the hook any sooner, quite the reverse!

"Annabelle isn't even your real name, is it? You're not in the guestbook unless you've been here over a month."

"As if your real name is Don Quixote or whatever. I certainly didn't read that in the register." Funny, but I had weighed her potential as a mean girl on first sight at the bar. She exploited my seconds of discombobulation to set off again. This increasingly scornful act of hers, though, didn't absolutely add up either.

"Those papers with all your dictation, where are they? A lot of effort went into them on both our parts. They're mine too, and if they're a joke to you, I might want to do something with them."

Whatever model of car it was whose driver-side door she was unlocking, it wasn't a Lamborghini. She chucked her Gladstone onto the passenger seat. World-weary she frowned and pointed toward the rear of the inn, as if conceding to play fetch once more because I wouldn't stop whining. "Go scrounge in the skip if you like, or the dumpster as you damn Americans call it."

While I craned my sore neck in the direction indicated, she ducked into her somewhat unprepossessing car and slammed its door. I jogged thataway; what good in dawdling to watch her accelerate out of my life? The dumpster was indeed where she'd pointed. I hoisted its floppy plastic lid. Nope, nothing inside. And the grind, rumble, squeals, and thuds of a dumptruck emptying a bin hadn't impinged on me earlier. What the hell?

A nigh subliminal drizzle burst into deluge. Annabelle, slinking off in her red slicker, had exhibited a modicum of psychic talent in distrusting the rosy forecast. I dashed indoors. Subjectively we'd been having it out for hours, well past hopes for breakfast, but there at my table was the "full English," almost warm in places. It was like the morning was mine to live over again! Nor would I squander it on the repulsive canned mushrooms and tomatoes, depressingly cold already, that threatened to mar by association the sausage, beans, home fries, bacon.

I probably chose less wisely in dwelling on Annabelle's behavioral glitches, as if consistency was ever high on her list. This shaman-channeling trip was fantastic from the get-go, but its hallucinatory dreams were so vivid and painstakingly etched, down to the purpose-built chisel for trepanning. Would I resolve more of Annabelle's quirks into a unified framework by theorizing a grander experiment wherein I was one of various guinea pigs to imbibe the elixir-in-liquor, and with whom she'd sever contact before any could marshal data on their own to compromise her independence as an occult investigator? And was that the same as deducing she was sane?

Concurrently, a mystery drug would be active in my bloodstream for another plus-or-minus twenty-four hours. Or else I'd ingested a prehistoric magus till death did us part. The poetic logic that my stint as a comics artist (a fantasist, if I may) had instilled in me proposed an antidote, whether one or both eventualities were fact-based. How to proceed sprang to my forebrain courtesy of a memorable chapter in a home-remedies catalog for which I'd done spot illos during Clinton's first term.

A darting survey assured me the waitstaff had, true to form, gone to ground, and my few fellow breakfasters were engrossed in victuals or newspapers. I slipped the plastic squeeze-jar of Colman's Mustard from the array of tabletop condiments to the concealment of my shirt-tails. My remnant breakfast I forsook to the relentless cooling of entropy and scurried upstairs. I unscrewed the jar's dunce-cap lid, added water from the bathroom spigot, replaced the lid, shook well, and hot-footed to the trail, with jar in jacket pocket. My plan mightn't have issued from an impeccable rationale, but I couldn't buck the conviction that every minute counted. No telling when a "flashback" would knock me for a loop! The rain was letting up; that had to be auspicious.

I peered down upon the cupule stone from the hillcrest to its east, musing on the alter ego from which I aspired to be sundered, as if glassy-eyed stare were a fitting protocol for bidding it adieu. His hadn't been an open-and-shut rotten life, had it? "Nasty, brutish, and short" as the old saw went, yes, but he'd attained to his highest available echelon, he'd done his folk the greatest possible good by their low-tech standards. And maybe he was survived by the helpmeet and mate of his own for-real Phantasmaria.

No envying how he'd died barbarously and too young. I'd been blessed with the revelation, though, that death was not the end, not for him anyway. I wouldn't volunteer to trade places, but couldn't begrudge credit where it was due. In balance, he'd made more of his time than I of mine. I twisted the cap off the mustard-water, raised the jar in a non-ironic toast. My attitude toward quaffing the stuff was, for me, pretty gung-ho till it came near my lips, and a cloying whiff went up my nose. I thereupon seesawed between dread of a godawful gut bomb and self-scorn because I liked mustard, so how bad could this be? "Here goes nothin'!" I gamely saluted the boulder.

I swigged, gagged, caterwauled, sobbed, spat repeatedly. I was very lucky not to reel herky-jerky over the edge. Fuck almighty, get a grip! That five-alarm blaze in my sinuses, spreading down my bronchial tubes, detonating in my abdomen had to burn out sometime today. The crying need right now was to career downhill and reach ground zero before it was too late.

I lurched up to the boulder despite my zigzag course as if a prodigious gyroscope were off-balance in my stomach. I keeled forward, scraping my fingers in grabbing onto the rock to stabilize myself, and frantically pegged the correct cupule by its muted purple wine stain.

And thar she blows! Undigested "full English" erupted with such seismic convulsions that my direct hit inside the cupule rated amazement. Between ejections, I was dourly ambivalent about the merits of purging narcotic dregs, since I should have metabolized any drug hours ago. But a personality couldn't be absorbed via the same mechanisms as a drug: maybe his was a discrete if incorporeal quantity that could be expelled by the same route through which it had entered.

My heavings had become destitute of overt foodstuffs, yet perse-vered mercilessly, scouring my intestines of foamy yellow bile dis-gorged in ragged streamers, heavy on the mustard. With the depletion of tangible jetsam, wracking tremors delved into a profounder terra in-cognita within me. I'd long since overloaded the cupule, and the spill-over of ghastly morsels of meat, pasty nuggets of toast, intact beans (graphic reminders to chew more patiently!) threatened to blanket the rock, befouled the catchment of other cupules, compelled me to plant my bleeding hands farther apart to avoid disgrace.

The rain was pelting down again in a hapless stab at cleansing the boulder, measly pockmark by pockmark in the voluminous puke. One climactic gut-punch of nausea, and a portion of me split off, an inti-mate portion but of no erstwhile acquaintance. Its irrevocable ousting stirred feelings of both liberation and loss, and not the rush of relief I'd have expected at casting the shaman adrift. In the same rancid breath, I re-experienced that synchronous levitation and sinking from my first gulps of doctored beverage here. I didn't pass out so much as my selfhood went into suspension.

I awoke in yellow muck still undiluted by torrential downpour, and weathered a bout of panic at the prospect of drowning in my own vomit. Where I was, and how I'd gotten here, should have been obvi-ous enough after the out-of-body adversities I'd shared. Righto then, I had no problem fitting in here for the same reason I didn't suffocate: I wasn't breathing anymore, though the eyes of my soul, as it were, en-joyed 20-20 vision. Annabelle's concoction must have contained one hell of an active ingredient to make me vomit myself out of me. "Nothing too heavy-duty" my ass!

And what of my "alter ego," my dawn-era hijacker? Within a sound brain in a sound body, as opposed to a timeworn hole, was his coherence, his mental wholeness, restored? Or did he not get very far in my magical world with his irreparably abridged wits? To worry about him, or about me, for that matter, in my snug cavity, would be shamelessly gratuitous, as I'm beyond all except geologic harm. I do chafe at the amount of eternity that might expire before anyone else drinks from my container, in addition to the span (of which I'm sudden-ly cognizant) when nobody went near it till my "full English" matrix was dispelled by precip, by less fussy species of wildlife, by microbes.

And nary a blink of my very own Phantasmaria. She's moved on to other cupules, evidently. It's also evident I subscribe to the thesis of Annabelle as bona fide occultist protecting self-interests by throwing me off the scent of metaphysical verities. If I'm not in a petite stone pit, where am I? I should hate her for double-crossing me, for failing to warn of consequences if I tried evicting my tenant primeval with an emetic, but I don't, seeing as she's made me virtually immortal. Besides, my discarnation did serve to "get her out of my system."

If anyone should hate her, well, the shaman drew the short straw, entrenched in my aging mortal husk, perhaps pushing up daisies already, whereas I'm still ticking. Meanwhile, it hasn't been an unexamined life, if that's the kind not worth living, and by that criterion, given his millennia of retrospection, the shaman's was the most worthwhile life imaginable.

Who's really to say how long I've been here, how often I've entertained these musings between lapses into enervated oblivion? Maybe it was prescience, and not nostalgia, that had me contemplating these windswept moors as homey, lo these many months or generations ago. At least I can answer the perennial riddle of what's in a hole: in this instance, me. Or, if history's capricious enough to repeat itself, you.

Mummify Me

When my time comes, mummify me,
Just as good a way as any,
Save about me what was best,
Go ahead and lose the rest.

Keep my heart inside my ribs,
Guess it gave what it could give.
For all that I was good or kind,
Let it function as a shrine.

Like they did in Rameses' day,
Throw my foolish brain away.
Often it was not my friend,
And couldn't help me in the end.

Decked in sacred amulets,
Let me have my bygone pets.
They were best at bringing out
What being human was about.

Put my innards, lungs, and liver
In white jars of alabaster.
Don't know why, but it was done
Along the Nile for everyone.

And then lest I give offense,
Take honey, salt, and frankincense.
Immerse me in them seven weeks
While my spirit heaven seeks.

When at last I'm wrapped in gauze
To hide forever any flaws,
For my choice of mausoleum,
Show me off in a museum.

Acknowledgments

"Barley Night," first published in *Spectral Realms #3* (Summer 2015).

"Barn," first published in *Spectral Realms #2* (Winter 2015).

"Cups of Memory," original to this volume.

"The Dark at the Top of the Stairs," original to this volume.

"Deacon Mercer," first published in *Spectral Realms #4* (Winter 2016).

"Death and a Locket," first published in *Spectral Realms #5* (Summer 2016).

"The Demon Thought," original to this volume.

"Gone to Doggerland," first published in *Innsmouth Nightmares*, edited by Lois H. Gresh (PS Publishing, 2014).

"Mummify Me," first published in *Spectral Realms #2* (Winter 2015).

"Naked Revenants," original to this volume.

"Old Goodman Brown," first published in *Gothic Lovecraft*, edited by Lynne Jamneck and S. T. Joshi (Cycatrix Press, 2016).

"Old Graveyard in the Woods," first published in *Spectral Realms #1* (Summer 2014).

"Plenty of Irem," first published in *Black Wings V*, edited by S. T. Joshi (PS Publishing, 2015).

"The Poor in Spirit," first published in *Weird Fiction Review #6* (Winter 2015).

"Purging Mom," first published in *Nightmare's Realm,* edited by S. T. Joshi (Dark Regions Press, 2017).

"Rat Letters," first published in *Weird Fiction Review* #7 (Winter 2016).

"Ritual Damage," original to this volume.

"Sand Bar," first published in *Spectral Realms #3* (Summer 2015).

"The Sarsen in the Ditch," original to this volume.

"Shed a Tear for Asenath," original to this volume.

"Vade Mecum," original to this volume.

In addition, "Old Graveyard in the Woods," "Sand Bar," and "Barn" were the beneficiaries of musical settings by Angel Dean and Sue Garner on their CD *Pot Liquor* (Diesel Only; available through iTunes and Amazon). "Old Graveyard in the Woods" has also received the compliment of a spooky interpretation by Dave Myers on YouTube.

Note of special pleading: "The Demon Thought" occurs in neither Old nor New England, obviously; however, it is based on observations from a train between London and Reading.

www.ingramcontent.com/pod-product-compliance
Lightning Source LLC
Chambersburg PA
CBHW050339030726
47503CB00008B/2522